Murder is a Tricky Business

Phillip Strang

Copyright Page

Dedication

For Elli and Tais who both had the perseverance to make me sit
down and write.

Chapter 1

'Murder is a tricky business when you don't have a body, a suspect or a motive,' Detective Chief Inspector Isaac Cook mulled out loud in the confines of the office. He may as well have called it home – he had spent so many hours there of late.

'What do you mean, "no motive"? The woman was a bitch,' Detective Inspector Farhan Ahmed replied. He was a dedicated cop, destined as was his senior officer, Isaac Cook, for great success in the police force: London's Metropolitan Police, politically correct and aiming to fast-track anyone of superior ability with a non-Anglo-Saxon background, a display of embracing all cultures, all religions, and all colours.

It was the ideal place for two ambitious men. Cook, the first generation English-born child of Jamaican parents and Ahmed, ten years in the United Kingdom, initially for training, and with no intention of going back to Pakistan. It irked some of the older police officers – Anglo-Saxon and white – now being overlooked for the late arrivals. The occasional disparaging comment in the corridors of Challis Street Police Station, discreetly aimed in their direction, was shrugged off, although it sometimes upset the young Pakistan-born DI.

'Who told us she was a bitch?' DCI Cook asked as he looked out of the window.

'Admittedly, those she worked with.'

'Being a bitch is not much of a motive. And we're still assuming she's been murdered,' DCI Cook said.

'We'll find the body. You know that. It's just a case of knowing where to look.'

'Do you?'

'Not yet, but we haven't rummaged in the dirt yet. If we dig enough, we'll find her, or what's left of her.'

'So where do we start?' Isaac asked.

'Her fellow actors on that damn-awful soap opera.' It was an unexpected outburst by the detective inspector.

'I've not heard you speak in that manner before.' Isaac felt the need to comment.

'It's my wife. She's obsessed with the programme.'

***

The death of Billy Blythe did not come as a surprise, forecast as it had been for several weeks. The final week before his death the magazines were awash with front page speculation. Eight million, five hundred and sixty thousand viewers, a new record the night he was bashed to death in the local playground by three youths.

The executives at the television station were delighted: record advertising revenue, premium rates. The only one assumed not to be delighted was the actor who played his fictional sister: she had gone missing. They had spliced in some earlier footage of her for the episode to conceal the truth from the viewing public.

The programme was pure fiction, but for millions across the country, compulsory viewing. Whether they recognised the soap opera for what it was, or whether it was an escape from their mundane lives, was for psychologists to analyse, advertising executives to take advantage of, and television stations to profit from.

The melodrama had been on the air for twelve years. The lives of an apparently benign group of individuals in a small provincial town had kept a nation enthralled. There had been murders, rapes, thuggish behaviour, even incest, but the characters still played out their parts in the innocence of a community where nothing ever changed. One week, it was a murder, the next, a wedding, and Billy Blythe, the local villain, had had his fair share of weddings: at least one every eighteen months to two years and none had lasted.

The country, or, at least, the less discerning – according to Charles Sutherland, the actor who had portrayed the erstwhile Billy Blythe – had been enthralled by his nuptials, but he had become fat and unpleasant, due to a more than adequate salary and an inappropriate fondness for alcohol and junk food.

Marjorie Frobisher portrayed his elder sister, Edith Blythe, in the series – her character matronly and demure, ashamed of her brother, hoping he would reform.

Isaac Cook considered the situation. He was a smart man, not given to extravagance and not inclined to speak without some forethought.

'So why does everyone assume it's murder? She's only been missing for three weeks. She could have just gone incognito, decided it was time for a break.'

Farhan saw the situation differently. 'The newspapers continue to put forward the idea that she's probably dead, even if it's not murder.'

'And we base our evidence on what the papers say?' Isaac Cook had not achieved the rank of detective chief inspector on the basis of 'someone said something' or 'what the newspapers are reporting'. He needed evidence, and so far there was none, only innuendo.

'Of course not,' Farhan replied.

'We deal in facts, not what the press and the gossip magazines print.'

Farhan continued. 'Marjorie Frobisher is at the height of her profession. She had just been given another three-year contract, at a monthly salary five times what you and I receive in a year, and there is her record of service.'

'What do you mean by record of service?'

'In the twelve years since the programme first went on air, she has only missed five episodes, and that was because she had no part to play.'

'Where do you get this information?' Isaac had asked the production company for some updates when they had first been pulled in to investigate, and he knew less than his colleague.

'From my wife, where else?'

Isaac sarcastically asked, 'Does your wife know what happened to the body?'

'According to my wife, there was a similar situation in another series about six years ago. One of the characters went missing for no apparent reason. Ted Entwhistle, the local butcher on the programme, just disappeared. You must remember, headline news for a couple of weeks.'

'So what happened to him?'

'They dragged it out, milked it for all it was worth. They thought they were dealing with a fictional disappearance, not a real-life murder. It appears that the actor portraying Ted Entwhistle had been messing around with an actress in the series, on-screen and off. Her off-screen husband got wind of it, strung him up on a meat hook in an old derelict barn. Poetic justice, the husband said when they caught him. Anyway, that's what my wife is saying.'

'A copy-cat killing inspired by a soap opera. Are you suggesting we seriously consider it?'

'Why not? Marjorie Frobisher's missing, and according to Detective Superintendent Goddard, she's probably been murdered.'

'Is that what's happened here?' Isaac had heard it all in his time as a policeman. The idea that a murder could be committed based on what a scriptwriter at the lower skill end of his craft could make up seemed implausible.

'Ted Entwhistle was real enough. Fiction often overlaps with reality on the television these days.'

'But you said you don't watch it.'

'That's true, but it's always on at my house.'

'If your Ted Entwhistle could be found strung up on a meat hook, what would Marjorie Frobisher's fate have been?'

'According to my wife…'

'Facts, please.'

'What I was going to say was that Marjorie Frobisher's character, Edith Blythe, had been the headmistress at the local school. In retirement, she took over from the church organist,' Farhan said, a little annoyed by Isaac's oblique criticism of his wife.

'Let's go out on a limb. What's does your wife believe happened?' Isaac felt there was no need for an apology.

'I know it sounds crazy, but she believes she's in a church.'

***

Charles Sutherland, a classically trained actor, or he felt he was, was not classical enough or not trained well enough, or the casting agents were defective in their recognition of genuine talent. He believed it was the latter. Early in his career had been a few walk-ons at some of the best theatres in the country in some of the most prestigious dramas. But they did not last long. It soon became apparent that he was deficient in two critical areas: his ability with accents and his attitude to fellow cast members.

Isolated and penniless, he had over the years been relegated to soap operas: the one area where he had achieved success. Billy Blythe had been his latest reincarnation after other long-running shows of a similar vein. He had been an undertaker, a shopkeeper, a philanderer, even a man of the cloth, but Billy Blythe had been his pièce de résistance.

They had killed his character; it was as if they had killed him. He knew it was the pinnacle of a disappointing career, and that he would neither forget nor forgive.

It had been assumed that his fictional sister would take on the mantle of bereavement, with the small, tight-knit community rushing to her side. The only problem was that she wasn't there.

The executive producer was the first to react to his leading actress's disappearance with alarm.

'What are we going to do?' he had screamed at a meeting of his production staff two weeks earlier. The programme was always recorded one week in advance, so there was time to work round an integral character. 'Marjorie's gone and done a disappearing act on us. Has anyone any idea where she is?' Richard Williams had been in the business almost for ever. He had reluctantly entered the world of soap operas as a script writer on a now defunct episodic programme. A plausible plot about an inner-city school full of delinquents and idealistic teachers in the north of England, it had somehow failed to capture the viewing public's approval.

He had left the University of Sussex over forty years earlier with a BA in Journalism, and a desire to be a war correspondent, travelling the world, helmet and bulletproof vest, ducking the bullets and bombs, 'bringing you the news from the front line'. The farthest he got was a protest outside the Iranian Embassy in South Kensington, when the police had come in with tear gas, and he had received a severe dose and a rock to the head for his troubles.

He was soft-spoken yet authoritative. He had guided this soap opera through its early years to where it stood now, predominant in the United Kingdom and sold to twenty more countries around the world. Nowadays, he mostly left it to others to deal with the daily episodes. It was rare for him to leave his elegant office with its sweeping views of London and to venture to the production facilities, a prefabricated town of frontages, held up by plywood and paint, located in what had once been an old industrial wasteland. He had reached his sixty-third year. He was not an attractive man, a little short, yet slim. His hair, once black and thick, now came courtesy of a bottle and an expensive hair.

'Marjorie is nowhere to be seen, hasn't been seen for a few days.' The script producer, Ray Saddler, had been with the soap opera for the last six years, and he had moulded a formidable team of script writers.

'Has anyone looked for her?' Williams asked.

'Of course, we have,' the series producer, Jessica O'Neill, said. She had joined the production team six months earlier. There had been dissension in the ranks on her appointment. Her demanding manner and excessive attempts at perfection, resulting in numerous retakes, sometimes late into the night, irritated some of the older hands in the business.

'Milady,' an antiquated term of respect for a female member of the British aristocracy, was often used in derision behind her back. Charles Sutherland had said it to her face once, but he had been drunk.

The meeting had not been going long before Richard Williams made a pronouncement, as he was apt to do when presented with an imponderable. 'Write her out, and if the woman turns up, we'll deal with it then.'

***

Isaac Cook had one uncertainty which concerned him greatly. Why, as a senior investigating officer, had he been pulled out of the homicide incident room to search for a missing woman? He needed to ask his superior officer. Detective Superintendent Goddard was a decent man, a man that DCI Cook respected enormously – their relationship based on mutual respect and friendship.

Challis Street Police Station, an impressive building, at least on the third floor where the detective superintendent had an office with a good view. Goddard sat behind an impressive wooden table with a laptop and a monitor to the right-hand side. In the centre, there was a notepad. A bookcase stood against one wall, full of legal books. A hat stand stood in one corner, where the detective superintendent's jacket and cap hung.

It was the office of an efficient man: a man who had an admirable habit of not going home at night to his wife unless the desk was clear and all the work for the day had been concluded and filed away. Some days that meant staying late into the night, but that was how he worked, and no amount of cajoling from his wife or his colleagues would change the habit of a lifetime.

He rose and walked around the table as Isaac entered. A firm handshake and both men sat down on comfortable black leather chairs placed to one side in the office.

'Sir, why are we chasing after a missing person?' Isaac asked.

'Do you know who she is?'

'She's just an actor in a mundane television drama.' The detective chief inspector, the only child of Jamaican immigrants, had been a diligent student at school, in part due to his parent's decision not to have a television in the house. His appreciation of the missing woman and her fame was limited.

'Marjorie Frobisher is hardly just an actor in a mundane drama; she's one of the major celebrities in this country.' Detective Superintendent Goddard understood the reluctance of his best detective to become involved.

'So why are we looking? There's no body, no motive and certainly no reason for us to be involved. It should be registered with missing persons.'

'Agreed, but you don't understand the situation.'

'What don't I understand?'

'Influential friends...'

'Is that a reason?' Isaac asked, although he had heard it before. Someone with influence using it to get preferential treatment.

The detective superintendent had hoped to avoid this conversation, and that Isaac would have continued with the case and got on with it. He realised now that it would have been best to have told him upfront. 'What do you know about Marjorie Frobisher? Apart from the fact that she's an actor of little note in your estimation.'

'I've no idea whether she is good enough for an Oscar or a bit part in the local drama society's production of *The Importance of Being Earnest*.'

'Are you telling me to keep looking for this woman?' The respect between the two men separated by nearly twenty years and rank allowed a little impertinence.

'This is highly confidential. It must never come into your discussions with anyone. Don't tell anyone in your office.'

'Okay, give it to me straight.'

'There is a very senior member of the government applying pressure to find this woman.'

'Any names?'

None that I've been told, but it's clear that this woman either knows something about someone, or she's important to someone influential for reasons unknown.'

'Is that the best I'm going to get?' Isaac asked.

'That's all I've got.'

'I'll ask no more questions,' Isaac said.

'It could be that she doesn't want to be found,' Richard Goddard said. Isaac thought his senior's statement a little obscure.

Chapter 2

Isaac's next visit was to the reclaimed plot of land that housed the fictional town of Bletherington. There were questions to be asked, the mood on the streets of the plywood town to be evaluated. He had been told that the series producer was the best person to talk to.

'Edith Blythe, what can I say? Brilliant characterisation, excellent delivery, great timing – undoubtedly the star of the show.' A well-dressed, prim and proper woman in her mid-thirties, Jessica O'Neill had come to the position of series producer through a torturous route. She had started some years earlier as a continuity editor on a period drama set in seventeenth century England. It had not been well-received in that the script writing lacked tension, and the intensity of the novel from which it had been adapted had been lost. It lasted one season before the production company pulled the plug.

Jessica, attractive, slim, and articulate, had found herself very quickly out of work after such a promising start. The one highlight of the programme according to Alexander Lewis, one of the directors of the production company, had been the quality of the continuity.

Jeremy Lewis, Alexander's eldest son, was only two years older than her. They had dated for a while, became lovers, moved in together only for her to move out two months later. No reason other than they both felt they were too young, and they still wanted to play the field. The one result of the coupling was that she acquired a close friend, and he had guided her career since then.

He ensured that her career progressed in a succession of increasingly important jobs, including a stint working with a news unit covering an outbreak of insurrection in the Middle East. She had been enamoured of the job when it was first offered – soon became disillusioned after she had become separated from her team during a demonstration.

She had found herself surrounded by a group of men who forgot what they were protesting about and turned their attention to her. It took a few soldiers and a lot of shots to get her away from them and to the nearest hospital. She decided after the wounds had healed and the trauma had subsided that she was better off back in England.

The series producer's job had come about as a result of the previous incumbent having a blazing row with one of the directors over editorial content, and storming off the set.

She had been brought in at short notice on the recommendation of her ex-lover, and most, at least the senior production team, agreed that the end result was good, but her dictatorial style was hard to take. She had taken control of the Billy Blythe episode where he met his fate and had done it well – even dealt with Charles Sutherland when he called her an arrogant little bitch. It was clear to her and senior management that she was going to stay, and a two-week stand-in had extended to six months and looked to be continuing for the foreseeable future.

Isaac Cook's previous question had generated a glowing reference. His next question would be more telling. 'Miss O'Neill, the actor who portrays Edith Blythe?' he asked.

'Call me Jess.'

'Jess, of course. Marjorie Frobisher, the person, not the actor.'

'Unless she's confirmed dead, I have to be careful what I say.' Her manner had changed. Isaac noticed that she had subtly pulled back from him. Before his earlier question, she had been close, personable. Now, she was professional and distant. The change interested him. He determined to persevere.

'Jess, you're right, of course. At the present moment, we're not dealing with a murder, only a missing person.'

'But you're here from the Serious Crime Division. I can't see why they would send a detective chief inspector purely to find a missing person. It seems incongruous to send someone as smart as you to look for her unless there's something you're not telling me.'

'Orders from on high or I wouldn't be here. I've got enough bodies out there looking for a culprit. Here is the last place I want to be at the present moment.'

'DCI, I'll give it to you straight, in confidence.'

'Sure, in confidence. This is not an official enquiry yet, so what you tell me doesn't have to be reported. Of course, if it does become official, then what you say may become relevant and on the record.'

'Marjorie Frobisher was not a nice person. In fact, she was not popular at all with anybody here. Always pushing her weight around, causing trouble, debating her lines, the camera angle, her profile. She saw herself as a prima donna, an A-List movie star, but what was she? Just an actor.'

'But you said she was brilliant.'

'Brilliant, of course, but this is hardly *Gone with the Wind* or *Casablanca*.'

'What do you mean?'

'She was at the pinnacle of her career. I know she believed she was destined for greatness in a major movie in America, but that was never going to happen.'

'Why do you say that?' Isaac struggled with the answer. Jess had once again relaxed and moved closer to him, disarmingly close. It was always an occupational hazard. Start interviewing a female witness and they were invariably charmed by his good manners and his black complexion.

He was not a vain man who regarded himself as automatically attractive to the opposite sex, but he was not impervious to reality. He remained single, not out of any great desire for bachelorhood but because a succession of attractive women was constantly heading in his direction and his bed. He did not want Jess O'Neill to be one of them, especially if a body was found and the missing person's case became a murder investigation.

Conflict of interest would have been an issue if one of the witnesses, possibly one of the suspects, possibly the murderer, was sharing his bed as well.

Jess continued. 'She was ideal for a television drama. For a woman in her fifties she was certainly attractive, but not attractive enough for a major movie, or, at least, not as one of the leading ladies.'

'That's a broad statement.'

'I worked on a major movie here in England. Just one of the script writers, but I interfaced with some big names in the business, Oscar winners.'

'And?'

'There's something about them. They had a presence, magnetism, a "je ne sais quoi". Marjorie Frobisher didn't have it.'

'Is that because they are major movie stars?'

'In part I would agree, but that definable quality is, I believe, with the person regardless of their star status.'

'Are you saying that Marjorie Frobisher was at the peak of her career, and it was downhill from here?'

'Yes, that is what I am saying.'

'Does she know this?'

'In the strictest confidence, yes. Please don't use it and certainly don't let the gossip magazines hear of it.'

'I'll agree, but if it becomes a murder enquiry.'

'She's becoming older, maybe too old for the programme. There's a decision to reinvigorate the programme. Bring in some younger characters; get rid of some of the older ones.'

'I thought you had record ratings.'

'Record ratings, but they drop and very quickly if you don't give them something new.'

'Older characters. Is Edith Blythe one of them?'

'She's out in three to six months at the most. They'll honour her contract, but she's going. We killed off Billy Blythe, her brother, now it's time for her. Mind you, Billy Blythe's death generated record ratings and substantial revenue. What do you think will happen when we kill her off?'

'This is your game. You tell me.'

'We had over eight million viewers in England alone for his death. She should generate somewhere close to nine if it's promoted correctly.'

'No doubt it will be.' It was odd that he had barely heard of the programme. He had watched a recent episode on the internet, three hours earlier. It did not impress him.

'Don't worry, they'll get the numbers. The increased revenue will cover the cost of paying out her contract.'

Isaac prepared to leave. The conversation had ranged from stand-offish to amenable, then to professional, and eventually back to very amenable. He was feeling a little uncomfortable with the situation, and a little concerned that he found Jess O' Neill an attractive woman. Any other time, he would not have hesitated to make a play.

He stood up to leave, sooner than he would have preferred. 'Just one question.'

'Yes, what is it?' She had made a point of shaking his hand and moved forward as if she was going to give him a hug.

'Did Marjorie Frobisher know that she was going to be written out of the series?'

'I told her in confidence.'

'How did she take it?'

'She hit the roof, gave me a diatribe about how she was the programme, and that once she left the ratings would plummet through the floor, and we'd all be out on the street looking for a job.'

'How did you react?'

'I stood my ground and told her the facts.'

'So when did she go missing?'

'She never came in the next day.'

'Do you believe it was you telling her that prompted her to leave?'

'I'm not sure. She may have been angry, but for all her faults, she was a professional. I can't see that it was the reason, although it may have been.'

'Just one more question, maybe two: was it your responsibility to tell her and whose idea was it to write her out of the script?'

'I told her on a directive from the executive producer. My timing was not great; I should have waited until we finished shooting Billy Blythe's death, but she had asked me a direct question about script development. Not really for me to answer, but it was a question, and I told her the truth. It seemed the only professional approach that I could take.'

'And the second question. Whose idea was it to write Marjorie Frobisher out?'

'I had put forward the idea some weeks earlier at a production meeting, and there was unanimous support. It was only a suggestion during a brain-storming session, but it appeared to hit a nerve, and from then on it was accepted. The date when she leaves is not clear. There may still be a change, even at this late date.'

'Does she know the suggestion came from you?'

'After she stormed out of here, she drove out to Richard Williams' office, the executive producer, and confronted him. Apparently, he acknowledged the fact that I had been the catalyst, and she left soon after.'

'Any idea what was said?'

'You'll need to ask him. I only know what I was told. I'm told the conversation was acrimonious, lots of shouting, some bad language.'

'Who told you this?'

'The fact that she had confronted him? The executive producer's personal assistant. She'll corroborate my statement, but don't let on that I told you.'

'Marjorie Frobisher would see you as being responsible for her removal.'

'Clearly, and I don't think she's a person who forgives easily,' Jess O'Neill said.

***

Isaac Cook's dependable colleague Farhan Ahmed focussed on trying to find the missing woman: the standard approach, visit the nearest relative. Robert Avers, Marjorie Frobisher's husband, was an avuncular man who warmed to the young policeman immediately.

'Come in, please.' The house, in one of the better part of Belgravia, was obviously expensive and exquisitely decorated. Farhan was ushered into the main reception room. A maid went off to make tea: no milk for the policeman, milk and two sugars for his host.

'We've been asked to assist in finding your wife.' Farhan wasn't sure if his questioning would be appreciated. Typically, it would be the nearest relative who opened a missing file case, not somebody of 'influence'.

The reply allayed his fears. 'Detective Inspector, I don't know what the fuss is about. She's become a pain in the arse recently with her celebrity status. She sees herself as better than the likes of me.'

'Does that indicate any marital issues? Would that explain her disappearance?'

'Not at all. I just ignore her. She gets over it soon enough. Give her a few weeks, and she'll reappear.'

The maid entered, poured the tea and left some chocolate biscuits on a plate. The conversation temporarily halted while she was present. Farhan took one of the biscuits.

'Has she done this before?'

'When we've had a blazing row, she puts on this "you never appreciated me. I'm going to find someone who will" attitude, and then two days later she's back.'

'The marriage was strained?'

Robert Avers laughed out loud, a raucous bellow. 'Not at all, although this is longer than usual. Mind you, it's not aimed at me, is it?'

'I wouldn't know.'

'They're going to dump her from that soap opera she holds up as a beacon of art.'

'Does she hold it up?'

'In public, but she doesn't believe it, though. It's an inane insult to the intelligence.'

Farhan, increasingly comfortable with the man, said, 'My wife is addicted to it.'

Robert Avers adopted a serious tone. 'Apologies if I offended.'

'Apologies not needed.'

'Mind you, it paid for all this.' Robert Avers waved his arms around the room, indicating the house in general.

'Then it seems that you've both done well out of it.'

'Sure have. Let's be honest, Marjorie can be a bitch, especially with the people she works with, and then if we walk out the door, it's the photographers and the drooling fans. It's bound to make anyone a bit difficult.'

'Difficult for you?'

'Not really. I just let her have her tantrums, and then it's fine.'

'So where is she now?'

'She sends me the occasional SMS.'

'We're anxious to talk to her, check she's okay.'

'I don't follow up on her, although I suppose you could check the location from her phone.'

'It may not be so easy: rules and regulations, protection of privacy, that sort of thing.'

'I'll leave it up to you. Just let me know Marjorie is okay, but I don't need to know where she is or when she's coming back.'

'Why's that?'

'She's an affectionate woman. There'll be plenty of making up when she gets back.' Marjorie Frobisher's husband let out another raucous bellow. 'You know what I mean.'

***

Isaac and Farhan met later that day to compare notes, plan strategy. Detective Superintendent Goddard stuck his head briefly around the door for an update. He was off, apparently to another of the conferences which seemed to occupy a lot of his time. He was a man destined for greatness – or that was how he saw it. Any opportunity to press the flesh with the shakers and the movers, government or otherwise, and he was bound to be there.

'It's irritating, sir,' Isaac said when asked for an update. He had just made himself a coffee and was seated at his desk, Farhan on the other side, a cup of tea in hand.

'What's irritating?' The detective superintendent realised where the conversation was heading.

'We've got a murder of a ten-year girl, a grisly death down by the docks, and here we are traipsing around the countryside to try and find a corpse, or if she's not dead, a vain and silly woman with air and graces.'

'Understood, but this woman is important. I don't know why, but I'm bound to be grilled by a couple of people tonight, and some of them are very influential. And besides, we have a Murder Investigation Team dealing with those cases.'

'I'm the senior investigating officer. I should be leading them.'

'That's fully understood, but for now, you and DI Ahmed are to focus on the missing woman.'

Isaac, realising that any further debate was pointless, focussed back on the woman. 'Names, do you have any of these so-called influential names?' Isaac persisted, mildly irritating his boss, who was in a hurry to get any information he could pass on, in case he was waylaid by pertinent questions later. Apparently, the prime minister was to make the keynote speech.

'Official Secrets Act at the present moment. If it becomes necessary, then I may be able to get you a special dispensation. We've deputised your position on the Murder Investigation Team. You stick with what you've got. I don't know much more than you do. Just keep digging. Any updates, make sure to let me know.'

Farhan was the first to reply. 'The husband believes she's got the huff and taken off for a while.'

'Huff, not a police term that I am familiar with.'

Farhan realised that he had overstepped boundary of familiarity with the senior officer.

'Sorry, sir. Occasionally, when they've had an argument, she takes off for a few days – maintains contact by SMS. He's a little worried, but he assumes the news from the soap opera she stars in is giving her concern, and she's taken off until she cools down.'

'What news is this?'

'She's being dropped from the series,' Isaac said. 'Took it badly by all accounts. If that gets out, it may make my best contact hostile.'

'Don't worry, Isaac. I'll keep it under wraps. If they ask me tonight, I'll say that she has had an argument with the husband and is hiding out for a few days. She's done it before, and until we receive further updates to the contrary, that's our official comment.'

'Thank you, sir.' One significant doubt remained in Isaac's mind after the detective superintendent had left the room. *Why is she so damn important to someone in a position of influence?* he thought.

With the detective superintendent dealt with, Isaac and Farhan sat down to evaluate the situation. The office they occupied was not large, but it was freshly painted, with a good desk for Isaac, a smaller one for Farhan, as befitted his lower rank. To the right on entering the office were three comfortable chairs and a coffee table. More private conversations could be held down the corridor in a sound-proofed room. Isaac had all his accreditations framed, and up on the wall. Farhan was not so concerned and had none, just a calendar and a picture of his children.

'Farhan, getting back to the situation before our unexpected visitor poked his head around the door,' Isaac said, 'what did you find out from the husband?'

'Made me very welcome.'

'But what did you find out?'

'Her husband believes she's just annoyed and has taken off to cool down. She's done it in the past when they've had an argument. I suspect they have arguments quite frequently. Not my idea of an ideal marriage, but he seems devoted to her. Whether it's reciprocated, I don't know.'

Isaac attempted an evaluation of the facts so far. 'What do we have? Firstly, there is an assumption by persons unknown and influential that her disappearance is suspicious. Do these persons, whoever they are, concern themselves with her safety, or is that a minor consideration?'

'Why is she so important?' Farhan asked.

'You can focus on that,' Isaac said. 'Secondly, what was the blazing row between Marjorie Frobisher and the executive producer? What was said in anger? Was it just her sounding off at him for dumping her, or was there more to it?'

'Everyone has skeletons in the cupboard. We just need to find theirs.'

Isaac appreciated his colleague's style of thinking. Farhan had been born in Pakistan and had, like many thousands of others, made the trip to England and its cold and damp climate. A Muslim, his faith was private and pragmatic, and he blended into the department and society well. He was not averse to a half pint of beer on a Friday night – team building he would say – but his mother would have been shocked and his wife disappointed. There had been a murder six months previously in a pig abattoir, and he had even conducted the investigation. Pork was 'Haram', forbidden, but he was a serving police officer, and he carried out his duty without complaint. He never told Isaac about the three showers with a scrubbing brush when he arrived home that night, trying to remove the stench from his body.

'Thirdly,' Isaac continued, 'Does someone know something that we don't?'

He laid out a plan. In the absence of a body, it was just the two of them. Confidentiality required that no one else could be brought on board. 'Farhan, this is what we do. We'll follow your suggestion and try and find out what Marjorie Frobisher's importance is, and why someone influential is interested. I'll head back out to the production site and keep quizzing the people there. I'll also speak to the executive producer. See if he'll tell me all that happened between him and his star, or soon-to-be-ex star.'

'You'll need corroboration from his personal assistant,' Farhan said.

'You're right. I'll ask her confidentially, see if it aligns with what he says. I've also got another source that may or may not give me some further insights.'

'Jessica O'Neill?' Farhan quizzed. Isaac had already told him that she was giving the right signals, and he knew his superior's reputation.

'Don't look at me like that. If it turns out there's been a murder, she could well be a suspect.'

'I realise that. Until the mysterious lady deems to make a grand entrance, then we treat everyone with suspicion.'

It had been a long day. There was a slight drizzle as they left the office, and both knew that they were in for a slow drive to their respective homes. Farhan had managed to buy a small terraced house in Wimbledon, not far from the railway station. Isaac had secured a loan on a two-bedroom apartment in Willesden. It cost him more than his salary could bear, but he was an ambitious man. He felt he could stand the financial strain until his next promotion.

Chapter 3

The next day Farhan met up with Robert Avers at the Churchill Arms in Kensington. Farhan felt a neutral location may be preferable. It was evident that Avers appreciated good food. The Thai restaurant at the back of the public house served a good meal, and with a couple of pints down him, Farhan thought the man would be even more open than at their previous meeting.

His estimation proved to be correct. They had managed to secure a table inside, and there was no fear of being overheard. It was crowded as usual, and the noise from the increasingly inebriated patrons would ensure that no one could hear what they said.

'I'll be straight with you,' Avers said. He had just consumed his meal voraciously, almost shoved it down. His approach to a pint of beer was similar, down in two gulps. 'We had what is quaintly called an "open marriage". Hope I don't shock you there.'

Farhan, a conservative Muslim in an arranged marriage understood what he meant, not sure if he approved. 'Shocked? Not at all. It seems incongruous in today's permissive society,' he said.

'You're right of course. The young people of today certainly would not understand the concept. They no longer see the need for marriage, and having multiple partners without the sanctification of a priest is accepted nowadays. Marjorie and I come from a different generation, and we both came to the marriage bed, if not entirely chaste, at least relatively naïve. We've been married a long time, and for the first ten we were faithful, but then her career blossomed, and my business took me away from home for lengthy periods at a time.'

'So it was a mutual agreement?' It was not a subject Farhan felt entirely comfortable discussing, but he felt a direct answer from Avers could well prove to be significant. The well-fed and well-drunk husband continued to down the pints. Farhan stayed a distant second with two half pints of beer.

'I suppose so,' Avers replied. 'I don't know who was first to stray, and initially there were some incredible rows at home and over the phone, but then we came to an agreement. It's held us firmly together for the last fifteen years. I've shocked you, haven't I?' He repeated his previous statement.

Farhan was indeed shocked by the frankness of the man, but it did not seem wise to offer his opinion. 'I've heard worse.'

'Just one thing. When she takes off, there's never been another man.'

'Are you certain?'

'Totally. We're open if there is any dalliance by either party.'

'So, where is she?'

His fifth pint consumed, Avers willingly conceded, 'I haven't a clue, and honestly, this is much longer than the previous occasions. In the past, it's been a few days, a week at most, but now we're looking at over two and a half weeks.'

'It's imperative we find her as soon as possible,' Farhan said.

'You have access to her phone number. Did you trace the messages she sent me?' Avers asked.

'Inconclusive. Mainly from the north of the country.'

'Not like her to be secretive.'

'We're aware that her disappearance has raised concerns in influential circles. Anyone you can think of?' Farhan broached the question that concerned him the most, the primary reason for being in a noisy pub; the reason he had downed another half pint. The reason he was feeling decidedly unwell.

'Not really. Her history before our marriage is vague. Since then, no one I can think of.'

'You don't know any names?'

'She'd tell me if I asked, but I'm not sure I want to know. The openness of the marriage is more on her side than mine, and we've always been discreet. At least, I hope we have.'

With no more questions and thankfully no more beers for Farhan, they left the public house. Avers took a cab; Farhan walked unsteadily to his car and vomited in the gutter, stale beer and the Thai meal. He then took fifteen minutes to drink some water and compose himself. He felt ashamed that he had sinned; he would offer additional prayers by way of compensation. Before arriving back at his house, he sucked on some mints to remove the smell from his breath. His God may well forgive him, his wife would not.

***

Richard Williams, the executive producer of the soap opera, proved to be an elusive man. Isaac had come out early to his office in the city, not on the draughty and wet production lot. Williams' personal assistant, Sally Jenkins, a vivacious woman in her mid-twenties with a tight top, her cleavage showing, and wearing a skirt that could only be described as no more than a bandage, was most agreeable. She was steadily plying the detective chief inspector with cups of coffee and biscuits. He knew what she was, a prick-teaser. He had come across her type before, making out they were available, taking every opportunity to show the goods on offer, and then when a man got up close and cosy, they would go coy and tell him they were not that kind of girl. Of course, if the man came with a Ferrari or a Porsche, they would be available. She did not interest him.

After Isaac had waited forty minutes, Richard Williams came out of his office, apologising effusively. 'Busy day, production schedules delayed, temperamental actors, and the weather is not helping with the outdoor scenes. What can I do for you? My apologies, by the way, unavoidable.' His statement by way of an introduction, Isaac felt, was disingenuous, hurried.

He chose not to comment and responded in a cordial manner. 'That's fine. Sally's kept me occupied, looked after me well.'

'Sally, I don't know what I would do without her.' The executive producer looked over at her as he spoke. She acted embarrassed, yet smiled a knowing smile back at him. Isaac had seen the look before. He knew something was going on between the two. It seemed unlikely that she would give him much assistance about the fracas between her boss and Marjorie Frobisher.

In his office, Williams beckoned Isaac to sit on a comfy chair to one side of the room. Isaac declined, and sat instead on a chair on the far side of the large desk at the end of the room. A window, the entire rear wall, gave a panoramic view over the city. Richard Williams, unable to maintain the upper hand in the meeting, acquiesced and sat facing Isaac in a high-backed leather chair on his side of the desk.

'Detective Chief Inspector, what can I do for you?'

'Marjorie Frobisher.'

'It's not the first time she's disappeared,' the executive producer said. Isaac noticed the slower pace of his speech. Before, it had appeared rehearsed, now it seemed measured. He realised that the man was used to manipulating conversations.

'We're aware this is not the first time.'

'Why the interest of the police? It seems melodramatic to me. The sort of thing we may well put in a script, but hardly real life.'

'I thought that is what you are producing, a representation of reality.' Isaac realised he was baiting the man to see how he would react.

'Have you ever watched the programme?' Williams asked. He had taken a defensive posture, his arms folded, leaning back in his chair.

'Once,' Isaac admitted.

'And what did you think?'

'It's not my kind of programme.'

Richard Williams weighed up the situation. He realised he was not dealing with a member of the viewing public, but a seasoned and astute policeman. His answer was honest. 'Fodder for the masses, but it draws the viewers in, makes everyone plenty of money.'

'Don't you feel some guilt that you are spoon-feeding it to millions of people?' Isaac needed to break Williams' guard.

'Are you one of those do-gooders, those holier-than-thou types who feel that we should be uplifting the people, educating them?'

Isaac knew that he had annoyed the man, his intention. 'Not totally.'

'This is a commercial world, dedicated to the pursuit of money. If a few million wish to watch the programme and pay us plenty of money, then so be it.'

'A few million? I'm told it's between seven and eight million.'

'Okay, okay, you've made your point,' Williams said angrily. 'I'm a busy man. If you haven't any more to discuss, we should end here. Any more questions or can I get on with what I do best?'

'There are some more questions. What did you and Marjorie Frobisher argue about the day before her disappearance, and what is your relationship with her?'

'There was no argument, just a heated discussion. Who told you this?'

'I am aware that there was an argument.' Isaac was circumspect. He did not want to reveal what Jess O'Neill had told him.

'You're right. She was going to be dumped. Good for ratings and the future of the programme, not so good for her. I can't blame her for being angry.'

'Were you angry as well?'

'In the end, I was. Marjorie's a professional, been in the business for many years. She knows how it works, and it's not as if we're putting her out on the street. There was every intention of paying out her contract.'

'But her career was coming to an end?'

'She's not immortal. It was going to happen at some time, and then there are all the chat shows and the newspaper interviews to keep her occupied. Maybe do a few adverts. She'd be fine.'

'Is that enough for someone like her?' Isaac asked.

'For Marjorie, never. She wanted the continuing adulation. She's welcome to it, but I'm no longer going to supply it.'

'How long have you known her?'

Isaac noticed a change in Williams' manner. He leant forward, rested his arms on the desk and said, 'I've known her for over forty years, ever since she had a one-line walk-on in a dreary period piece. We've always been friends.'

Isaac could see no more to be gained by prolonging the meeting.

He would talk to Sally Jenkins about the argument at a later date.

***

Charles Sutherland had accepted the death of Billy Blythe graciously. At least, that was how it had been publicly portrayed. The appearances on the chat shows kept him occupied for a few weeks, the bottle for a few weeks more. His agent had put out the feelers for some more work, but he was typical of many who had enjoyed the comfort of a long-running soap opera – he was type-cast. The only parts were for villains, for another 'Billy Blythe', and he had had enough of him. He saw himself as a Shakespearean actor, a classicist involved in a major production at one of the major theatres in the country, not playing an overweight, aged hooligan. The tough-talking, the bad language if they could get it past the censors, the pointless fistfights – they always used a stand-in when his back was to the camera – failed to impress him. He saw himself on stage reciting Hamlet's soliloquy to an enraptured audience. *To be, or not to be: that is the question*…Maybe even, *Hamlet* Act 5 Scene 1: *Alas, poor Yorick!*

He had earned good money, and if it had been invested wisely, he would have had sufficient not to work again. However, an extravagant lifestyle meant that he continued to rent, although, in Mayfair, it was hardly a slum. Not like the place where he had grown up in the west of the country. His parents, good people, had struggled all their life. A son that always complained had not helped. The only motorised transport was a tractor that rarely started and an old Land Rover that did start but rattled atrociously. The food was wholesome. The animals: never more than twenty or thirty cows and a bull to keep them serviced, several dozen sheep, a few pigs and chickens. The 4 a.m. starts in winter to look after the animals and collect the eggs, before he walked the three miles to school over frozen fields, still brought back unpleasant memories. He had been an inherently lazy child, a trait that continued to adulthood, but laziness was not allowed by a stern father who was capable of removing the leather belt from his work trousers and giving the young Sutherland a good thrashing across his bare backside.

Charles Sutherland never considered that the principal acting parts eluded him because of his inability to resolve his West Country accent. He had made significant improvements, and for Billy Blythe, a country accent was just right, but the classics required an eloquent tone. To reach the heights he desired needed more than he could give. It needed discipline and perseverance, and he possessed neither. He was a sloppy man, both in his hygiene and his movements. His car, an ageing Volvo, was full of discarded crisp packets and sweet wrappers, the ashtray full of ash from unpleasant smelling cigarettes. He presented poorly, but he did not blame himself – he blamed others, and the person he blamed most was Marjorie Frobisher. He knew it was her who had him killed off, Jess O'Neill had told him, and he didn't have much time for her either. If he was to suffer, then others would as well. That was how he saw it.

***

Sam Avers, the son of Marjorie Frobisher and Robert Avers, was a major disappointment to his parents. Their income had given him the best of opportunities, the best of schooling, but he had a weakness for alcohol and an ever-increasing dependence on recreational drugs. His father was a heavy drinker, but he came from a generation where people drank heavily, got drunk and stopped. The son came from a generation where people drank until silliness and then started hitting the shots of tequila or vodka: his favourite, Slippery Nipple, a mix of Bacardi rum and Wild Turkey bourbon. He had grown up in the better parts of London, Chelsea mainly, and the clubs and the pubs were awash with binge drinkers. He had been flush with money; his father was successfully running an import/export business, his mother was an increasingly affluent and famous celebrity.

He had little time for either, and by the age of seventeen, his relationship with them was irreparably severed. The family home was big enough for him to enter and leave it without having to do more than briefly acknowledge them. The only time he granted them a conversation, short even then, was when he needed money or to top up his credit card. They gave in with little resistance. Their lives were full and busy. A delinquent child who had neither the innate charm nor the good looks of his parents left them with a feeling of apathy towards him. Marjorie Frobisher and Robert Avers could not love him as parents should, and the son realised this. The more alcohol in his system, the more he disliked them, the more vengeful he became.

There had been a period in his early twenties when a good and decent girl had attempted to love and change him. They had moved in together, enjoyed a loving relationship, mainly sober for three years before he had fallen off the waggon and hit the booze again. The relationship passed the honeymoon stage, although they had never officially married, and domesticity caused him some troubles. She moved out, and the intervening years had been of casual relationships, mainly one-night stands, and days spent in a drunken and drug-filled haze. He had attempted a career while sober, managed to find a job as a junior auctioneer at one of the most prestigious auction houses in the city. He wasn't sure how it had come about, but he figured maybe his mother was screwing one of the directors. Yes, he knew about her shenanigans and his father's. That was what men did, but his mother? He could never forgive her, them, for their lifestyle, their affairs, their wealth, when he had been forced to play second fiddle, even third, in their affections.

He hated them both with a passion – his mother, the most. *If they were only dead*, he increasingly thought. *Then I'd only need to share their money with that bitch sister of mine. There would be plenty enough then, enough for me at least.*

Chapter 4

Detective Superintendent Goddard continued to be reticent as to who was pushing the search for Marjorie Frobisher. So far, all the probing from Isaac had failed to elicit a clue.

It was now close to four weeks since Marjorie Frobisher had been seen. Her credit cards occasionally used in one location; the next time, a hundred miles away. Her mobile phone, switched on long enough for an SMS to her husband, – 'Home soon, love you' – and then turned off, barely gave time to triangulate its position.

'Sir, this is going nowhere.' Isaac Cook tried one final time to get an answer from his superior at a hastily scheduled meeting at Isaac's insistence. They met in the detective superintendent's office, an office that Isaac aspired to within the next two to three years. He regarded policing as a vocation; the detective superintendent's office the next major goal to aim for. A goal now being hampered by the forlorn search for a missing person.

He was determined to hammer out the situation with his boss. 'I'm suggesting we pull out until the woman is found, alive or dead. This is just a waste of time.'

Richard Goddard understood the frustration of the man sitting in front of him, but there was nothing he could do. The investigation had to continue. 'Isaac, you've got to stay with it. It's either the woman or the body. The pressure on me for a result is intense. I can't take you and DI Ahmed off the case.'

'But we're wasting our time. The woman was not popular with the people she worked with, but she's not short of money. And she messages her husband every few days. What's the point of all this?'

'Are you sure about the SMSs? Is she sending them and using the credit cards? Is there a signature?'

'The credit cards only need a pin number. We can't be sure about that either, but why? People go missing all the time.

31

Normally, there's a cursory investigation, and then life goes on. Sometimes they turn up somewhere down the track, or they don't. It doesn't mean they've all been bumped off, weighted down and thrown to the fishes or fed to the pigs.'

'Isaac, I understand your frustration, but it's out of my hands.'

Isaac admitted defeat and left. He did not like leaving on such a sour note. His boss was still answerable to others and forced to follow orders, no matter how illogical.

Frustrated with the conversation, Isaac met up with Farhan, and they went out for a meal at an Indian restaurant not far from the office. It had been a long day, and neither had achieved much. Isaac had managed to speak to the executive producer's personal assistant, Sally Jenkins, but that had revealed nothing. He had even met up with Jess O'Neill, and she was still giving him hints that some further investigation, outside of office hours, was acceptable. He was tempted, but the timing was wrong. If Marjorie Frobisher did turn up alive, the first thing he was going to do was to ask the series producer out, even conduct some serious probing of a personal and intimate nature, which looked a strong possibility after his last meeting with her.

'Sally Jenkins, what did you expect?' Jess O'Neill had said. 'Did you pick up on the signals?'

'Her and Richard Williams,' Isaac proffered an answer.

'Yes, of course. He must be nearly forty years older than her, but he's a pants' man. Sorry for my crudity, but he hits on everyone if they're female and attractive.'

'Has he hit on you?' Isaac asked.

'Sure has, but I told him to shove it. I don't need a sugar daddy, no matter how much money he's got or what car he drives.'

'Out of interest, what sort of car?'

'Ferrari. Why?'

'I recognised the signals in the office with Sally Jenkins, surmised it was either a Ferrari or a Porsche.'

'I don't need a man with a fancy car. I'm more than capable of getting my own if I want one.'

'I've got a blue one, flashing light with a siren as an optional extra.' Isaac regretted the comment immediately.

'Blue car, flashing light, sounds fine to me.' Isaac no longer regretted his previous comment, but had felt embarrassed that he had transgressed from professional to personal.

Farhan continued to enjoy his meal while Isaac updated him. He omitted the intimate exchange with the series producer.

Farhan was more interested in finding out who the influential person was. Both were frustrated about where this was heading, or what more they could do. Isaac would continue to interview Marjorie Frobisher's fellow actors, the production staff, the script writers, but he couldn't see anything new happening there. It was evident she was full of her own importance, but he had spent time perusing the magazines in his local newsagent and it was obvious she was immensely popular with the public – the indiscriminating public, as he saw it.

The plan for the following day: the same as the current day, and those previously – keep probing, maybe turn up a needle in a haystack.

Chapter 5

Angus MacTavish of the Clan MacTavish was a proud Scotsman who spent most of his time across the border in England. This stance sometimes put him out of kilter with his clan brethren, advocating for separation from the United Kingdom. Elected ten years earlier to the British Parliament in Westminster, he saw no reason to moderate his views on independence or any other subject. A safe seat in the Scottish Highlands ensured him the opportunity to further his political and personal aims.

A man used to command, the position of Government Chief Whip suited him admirably. His primary function, to organise his party's contribution to the business of Parliament. If that meant twisting arms to ensure the maximum number of party members' votes at divisions in Parliament, so be it.

He was also expected to know of all the party members' peccadilloes and indiscretions. Sometimes to help them; sometimes to ensure they fell on their swords.

Detective Superintendent Goddard arrived early for his meeting with MacTavish. He presented himself at the security gates that closed off Downing Street to the general public. The necessary accreditation and his police identification, coupled with his name on the typed list of scheduled visitors, ensured entry. The office where they met, first floor, Number 9, was one house down from the prime minister's.

MacTavish wielded substantial unseen power, and when he spoke it was with the full authority of the Prime Ministerial Cabinet. The detective superintendent knew this; he also knew him to be a taciturn man who said little but implied a lot.

The man barely raised himself from his chair when Richard Goddard entered, other than to grab the policeman by the hand and shake it vigorously. A firm handshake – an indication of power.

'Detective Superintendent, my instructions were clear in this matter.' A gruff manner, deep-voiced, with a strong Scottish brogue, MacTavish intimidated many, scared most. Tall, with red hair, his forefathers had fought against the British at Culloden – killed more than their fair share. Even today at Highland gatherings over a few drams of whisky, Scotland's finest gift to the world in Angus MacTavish's view, those who had fought and died were remembered.

MacTavish was a pragmatist. Time had moved on. Nearly three hundred years separated the past from the future, and it was the future that he saw as important. He professed no great allegiance to the British Monarchy, but he kept his views guarded, and besides, he would not be averse to a seat in the House of Lords at the appropriate time.

'Sir, I realise that I was meant to keep my people from asking too many questions about why they were looking for this woman.'

'And you phone up asking me for this information.'

'My apologies, but this investigation is going nowhere. My people are charging up blind alleys, hitting dead-ends, and just wasting time. We know she was subject to bitchiness, and there seem to be some unusual arrangements around the marital bed, but they hardly seem sufficient to believe she is dead.'

'Detective Superintendent, you don't understand. Dead is not the problem. It's if she is alive that causes concern.'

Taken aback by the statement, Richard Goddard had to ponder the situation. His people were looking the woman, and indications were that she may still be alive. Why was she so important? He had the ear of the Chief Whip, now was the time to pressure for more.

'In confidence, I'll give it to you straight,' MacTavish said. 'I know about the so-called open marriage, her promiscuity when she was younger, and the banal programme on the television. What is of concern is who the woman has slept with. What dirt she has on them. What scandal she could cause if she spoke out of turn.'

'Is she likely to do that?'

'Yes. She's a vengeful woman, even threatened to commit such an act.'

The senior policeman saw it all too clearly. It was an election year; the government was likely to hold on, but only by the slimmest of margins. The last thing they wanted was a scandal, especially if the scandal was related to a senior member of the government aiming to hold on to his seat in a marginal electorate. 'But would she?' he asked.

'Detective Superintendent, she's soon to be out of this programme, and will be paid to dish the dirt on one or another chat show, and then there will be a biography of a life well led, or in her case well laid.'

'Can't you put a restraining order on its publication, Official Secrets Act?'

'If it's published in this country, yes, but if it's scurrilous enough, the publisher's lawyers will call our bluff, ask us for a reason for halting its release. Once the gutter press gets involved, well, you know the consequences.'

'Yes, of course.'

MacTavish relieved that he had given his reasons, phoned for some tea. Five minutes later, a pleasant middle-aged woman entered and placed the pot and two cups on the desk, with some small cakes on a plate to one side.

'Mrs Gregory makes them for me. Wouldn't know what I would do without her fussing over me.'

'Please sir, you'll make me blush.' With that, she left the office unobtrusively.

Cups of tea in hand, and cake consumed by both men, the conversation continued. 'Detective Superintendent, here's the deal. We know she will talk, and there's every sign that she is becoming irrational. We've had some experts assess her behaviour, and there are the early signs of premature senility. She may well say something inadvisable, even when she intends not to. We can't take the risk. If she's dead, then that's fine. Harsh to say, of course, but there it is. If she's alive, we've got to stop any publications and her talking out of turn.'

'But how can you do that?'

'That's the hard part. We're a democratic country, with free speech, so we can't restrict her or the media. I wouldn't agree to that anyway. It's a dilemma, and I'm pleased to say that's not my responsibility.'

'What does she know?' The detective superintendent wasn't sure he would get a response.

'You're putting me on the spot. It's privileged information, on a need-to-know basis, and frankly you don't need to know.'

'Sir, I can understand the dilemma, but is it that serious?'

'Political dynamite! Hits at the highest levels of the government. It could cause a major electoral defeat.'

'Who she's been screwing recently, or in the past, that sort of thing?'

'In the past, and yes, there's plenty of what you just intimated, plus some more.'

'We'll keep looking. I'll tell my people that it's important. They'll just have to trust me on this one.'

'Will they?' MacTavish asked.

'If I give my word, they'll accept it. It won't stop them fishing around.'

'If they get too close, let me know.'

***

On the face of it, Fiona Avers had all the right ingredients: celebrity mother, acting ability. There were, however, two elements apparently vital in the acting profession that the daughter of Marjorie Frobisher did not have, the most obvious being that she was not attractive. In fact, the less generous would have said she was plain, verging on ugly. The less obvious of her two main failings was a violent temper, coupled with an incredibly short fuse. Unattractive women have reached the pinnacle of acting success, but invariably they came with a winning personality, a willingness to understand their shortcomings – in fact, to embrace them.

Fiona Avers was a tall woman with what could only be described as masculine features. Her arms were bulbous and appeared a little short for her height: substantially taller than her mother, a good head and shoulders above her father. Her legs were also on the fat side, her calf muscles tending to bulge. Attempts at rectification through exercises – her parents had paid plenty to help – had come to nought.

Her face, some would say, showed character, but they were generous in their comments, and the only one who said it with any conviction was her friend, literally her only friend, Molly Waters. They had met at school, experimented with lesbianism, even when at their most precocious, most promiscuous, and most willing to screw any male they could lay their hands on. Unfortunately for both, there was a surfeit of young and attractive females, also at their most precocious, most promiscuous, and invariably both Fiona and Molly were left with each other to satisfy their carnal lusts. Molly did not find the experience unpleasant, Fiona did, although she endured and eventually embraced the experience.

Molly was fat at school, although she had a pleasant face and a personality to match. The fatness of youth had carried over into adulthood, and now she was severely in need of a healthy diet and a good makeover. The pleasant personality remained, and it served her well in life. She had tried men for a while, even found a man who treated her well, moved in with him for a few months, but realised from her early intimate encounters that it was women that satisfied her sexually, especially a woman by the name of Fiona Avers.

Fiona Avers, however, felt no such allure for the female body except for hers when a man was labouring on top of her, and that was rare. The world, the society that she moved in, was awash with attractive women, and she was invariably left the wallflower at any social gathering. 'The girl least likely to get laid' had become a catchphrase among those she regarded as friends, although they were fair-weather friends lured by her spending and her tenuous connection with celebrity.

Her face – only Molly Waters saw it as beautiful – was large with a pronounced forehead. Her eyes were sullen with overhanging eyelids. Her ears were small with a distinctive lobe which she concealed by growing her hair long, which did not help as her hair was curly and harsh. Her nose had also given concern. Cosmetic surgery had dealt with that problem, although it had done little to help with her overall appearance.

Her mother had elegantly balanced features and could only be described as beautiful; her father had a rugged look about him with strong masculine characteristics. Not handsome, but interesting – women felt comfortable in his presence.

Everyone in her close family, uncles and aunts mainly, always said that she reminded them of Great Granny Maud, but the only photo that Fiona had seen of the family stalwart was old and grainy – she could see no resemblance.

Her father had shown her great love, made her feel special; her mother had ridiculed her, kept her out of the limelight, and had belittled her too often. How often had she seen her mother telling her friends that her daughter's looks came from Robert's side of the family? How many times, when there was a function to attend or an event where the cameras would be clicking, had she been denied the chance to participate? She remembered her brother Sam attending, but then her mother had always said, 'He's much older than you. You're too young to attend such events. People get drunk, make fools of themselves. At your impressionable age, I want to protect you from such influences until you're older.'

Fiona remembered well enough. As the years rolled by through her childhood and formative teenage years, the non-attendance continued, although the reasons given varied.

Her father ensured that her mother's rejection was countered by his love and generosity. As a child, she looked for a mother's love. As a teenager experiencing her first period and then her first playground crush on a boy, rejected with scathing insults, she looked for a mother's support, a shoulder to cry on.

As an adult, she no longer needed her mother, only her hatred for her.

Her father she adored. She knew full well her mother's promiscuous behaviour caused him great concern, although he never admitted it, at least to her. He always said that was the way she was, and they should accept her for her flaws. She could see the hurt in her father's eyes, and the look on his face when he thought no one was looking.

Her temper had been an inconvenience as a child, just a tantrum, but as an adult it had become an embarrassment, even to her. A failure to obtain an acting part, an inattentive shop assistant, a hairdresser who had failed to achieve a satisfactory result – not difficult given the substandard material that he had to work with – and she would see red, and blow off steam in an uncontrolled manner.

There had been a production at a theatre in the centre of London, and she had managed to obtain a decent part. Mainly because it required a name to pull in the paying public, and the daughter of Marjorie Frobisher was better than no name, but only just. Secondly, and less important, was that the part of an embittered unattractive woman matched Fiona Avers. The casting agent saw that little makeup would be required.

There had been a lesser reason, although to Fiona it had been significant. The director of the play, one of the Russian classics, had a perversion for unattractive women, which he made clear the first night of rehearsals, in his office at the back of the theatre. Everyone had gone home; she had stayed for some additional coaching at his insistence and encouragement. He had plied her with alcohol, vodka mainly, which had little effect, as she had a substantial capacity for drink, having regularly drunk too much since her teens. There, sitting close in his office, the touching, the compliments, and it was not long before they were both naked on the floor. The carpet was old and dirty, although both were beyond caring and it was her that was underneath, her breasts feeling the heaviness of his body and the scratching of his chest hair. It was soon over. Once he had expended his lust, she had quickly been hustled out of the office.

The next day he was cool, maybe from guilt, perhaps to show a neutral approach to the cast in his praise and criticism of them all. At least, she wanted to believe that, until she saw him approaching Mary O'Donnell, the lead actress, and his request for her to stay back for some extra coaching. Fiona knew that yet again a man had used her for his base needs and had left her high and dry, emotionally and sexually.

The weeks passed by, she kept her emotions in check, until he had criticised her once too often, and the cow Mary O'Donnell had offered some choice comment about Fiona's acting, and that she was an easy lay. It was clear that the director had told Mary about his night-time encounter with her and the office floor.

Unrestrained, Fiona slapped the woman hard across the face with such force that she fell back and banged her head against a box in the corner of the stage. They took her off to hospital and evicted Fiona from the theatre.

Since then the parts had been few, and she saw her career was at an end. She blamed her mother for her life, but the few times they had met in the last few years her mother had been unapologetic. 'It was my career, darling. I had to do what was right, what was necessary to look after the family, and you always had the best.'

Fiona knew she had had the best that money could buy, but not what she longed for, the love of a mother for a daughter. She hated her mother, the one emotion that was not subject to scathing comments from talentless actresses, critical seducing directors, and playground arbiters on her lack of good looks. That one emotion, hatred for a person that she should love, could only hate, remained constant.

Chapter 6

With Isaac out looking for Marjorie Frobisher, Farhan had taken on the responsibility of finding out why she was so important. So far, he had only come up with blanks, but he and Isaac had decided it was integral to the case to know, although they had been told to focus on finding her.

Their boss, Detective Superintendent Goddard, should have known better than to ask a detective to look in one place, avoid another. A good detective looks everywhere, no matter how insignificant and supposedly irrelevant. A jigsaw puzzle is meaningless without all the pieces, even if it's the smallest piece in the blandest area of white cloud or blue sky. A criminal investigation follows the same principle. Set out all the facts on a whiteboard, put all the names and the faces and the motives and the reasons there. Just one question mark and it's impossible to bring the investigation to a conclusion.

It had been Isaac who had suggested Rosemary Fairweather, Marjorie Frobisher's agent, the previous night. They had been going through the case. The fact that it was a disappearance, not a murder, annoyed them. The best they could do was to get on with it, find the damn woman and then get back to some serious policing.

Farhan noticed framed photos of some recognisable faces on the wall in Rosemary Fairweather's reception area as he waited to be invited into the inner sanctum – Barbara Reid's words, not his.

Barbara Reid, Rosemary Fairweather's personal assistant, was a talkative woman, smartly dressed, designer clothes. She was in her late forties, tending to middle-aged plumpness, but her face maintained the look of youth, or, at least, expensive cosmetics.

'I've been Rosemary's right-hand person for the last eighteen years,' she said.

'Good boss, then,' Farhan replied. He found her remarkably agreeable, with a mellow, soothing voice. His wife was a decent woman, but she was always covered as befitted a conservative Muslim woman. He could feel loyalty to her as his faith and his family required, but certainly not love, and rarely lust. She had given him two healthy children, a boy and a girl, with another on the way. His attraction to other women was not unknown to him, but his religion and his beliefs were important, and he would not stray from the marital bed. Farhan hoped that Rosemary Fairweather would not summon him into the inner sanctum too soon.

'The best,' Barbara Reid continued. 'When I came here there was only one client, Marjorie Frobisher, but now—'

'The photos on the wall.' Farhan interrupted the personal assistant mid-sentence.

'Yes, they've all been in here, plus there are more that Rosemary rejected, some big names even.'

'She's very selective?' He was enjoying his conversation. It was not often that he chatted with an attractive woman in a pleasant environment. It was certainly more agreeable than where he and Isaac worked. There it was clean and functional with everything in its place. Here it was bright, the walls in the reception area painted pale blue. The chairs where he sat were leather and comfortable. The coffee table was glass-topped, obviously expensive, and on the top rested some magazines, recent and related to the acting profession. Barbara Reid sat at a functional table, not overly large, with a laptop in the centre. A computer mouse was to the right, an additional monitor at the far right of the table. Apart from that, her desk was totally clear. From the outside the building, no more than two hundred yards from the Strand in Central London, was Victorian in construction and style, although inside the interior had been gutted and rebuilt in the very best modern style. It was a large building. Rosemary Fairweather's office occupied the third floor.

Farhan was on his second cup of coffee. The PA had been insistent that he try the freshly brewed coffee, and unable to resist such a pleasant invitation, he had agreed. To him, it was too strong, but he could only say, 'It's great, thanks very much.'

43

The inner sanctum summoned him, all too soon for Farhan. He carried the coffee in with him.

'What can I do for you?' Rosemary Fairweather asked. The reception area was tastefully decorated, the office more so. The carpet on the floor, fitted and plush, the walls adorned with original artworks. The desk, unlike the PA's, was cluttered with files and photos.

'Apologies for the mess. There's a major film going into production in three months' time. I'm trying to get some of my people onto the set.'

'You have many?'

'Too many. The photos on the walls are the primary clients. I suppose you recognised some of them.'

'Most, especially Marjorie Frobisher.'

'Marjorie, dear Marjorie.' Farhan could not be sure if Rosemary Fairweather's response was a sign of affection or sarcasm.

'I'm told that she was your first client.'

Expensively dressed, hair immaculate, and with an absolute assuredness of her own importance, Rosemary Fairweather sat in a leather chair behind a glass-topped table, her knees and legs clearly visible. In her fifties, but with few lines on her face, she sought to lower her age by a combination of clothes that were too tight and too short, and makeup which would have suited a younger person.

'My first client, my best client financially,' she replied.

'I saw some more famous faces out there. Some major movie stars.' Farhan had particularly noticed one face, an actor successful in America.

'Marjorie has been around longer than most, always employed in one programme or another. My commission adds up. The big star you saw outside; he's only come onto the scene in the last year or so. He's bringing in plenty of money now, but for how long, who knows?'

'Tough business?' Farhan said, realising that he needed to bring the interview back to the questions he wanted to ask.

'It's tough for the actors, harder for the agents, the poor suckers who have to keep them occupied, deal with their neuroses, their doubts, and then still try to find work for them.'

'Marjorie Frobisher?'

'She's fine. She can be a bitch, but I've not had any trouble with her. Mind you, I am as well. You have to be in this business.'

'Any idea where she's gone?'

'You know about her lifestyle?'

'Her sleeping arrangements?' It seemed the subtlest way for Farhan to mention the subject without giving too much detail.

'Discreetly put,' she replied.

'Is it relevant to her current disappearance?'

'Unlikely, and I don't know of anyone recently.'

'Has there been someone in particular in the past?'

'It's none of my business, but sometimes she feels like talking.'

'Anyone she could be with now?'

'She's taken off in the past, but there's never been a man. I don't believe she would be with anyone. She was always open with her husband when something was going on, poor man.'

'Why do you say poor man?'

'Robert, he's a good person. He went along with the agreement, but I don't believe he often strayed; no more than any normal heterosexual male, but Marjorie...'

'She was more likely to stray?'

'She was rampant in her younger years, but now...'

'Now?'

'She's in her fifties, menopausal. The fire doesn't burn as strong. It's part of the ageing process, unfortunately.'

'Are you saying she doesn't stray anymore?'

'Not too often, but there are tales I could tell you, who and where.'

'Such as?'

'I've said too much. Client confidentiality.'

'It's important that we know,' Farhan insisted, a little more forcefully than maybe he should have.

'I'm not at liberty to say more. She's only gone missing. It's not the first time, you know.' Her reply was curt.

'That may be the case, but we're treating it as suspicious.'

'Until it becomes an official investigation, I don't believe I can help you anymore.' With those closing words, he was quickly hustled out of the room with a flimsy excuse. He regarded her change in attitude as suspicious. Not about her, but the people that Marjorie Frobisher knew: her paramours, past and present.

***

Isaac had been out at the production lot. He had decided to keep clear of Jess O'Neill, not because the situation was becoming complicated, but because there were other people he needed to talk to. The production office, set at the rear of the car park, consisted of some portable offices arranged into a compound. They were functional and warm, which was as well as the rain was spasmodic and a gusting wind was blowing through the area.

Ian Stanley, the producer of the series, was not hard to find, a small man with a big voice. That wasn't how the person outside the office constructing a plywood-fronted house to add to the fictitious town referred to him: 'Loud-mouthed prick,' was his estimation, 'always pushing us around.' There were a few expletives which Isaac chose to ignore.

It was evident to Isaac on entering the first office building that he had indeed found Ian Stanley. A little gnome-like man, with accentuated features, pointy ears, an ungainly gait, and the top of his head barely reaching the shoulders of those around him, was holding court. *Napoleon complex,* Isaac thought.

'Yes, what do you want?' His initial response to Isaac as he stood patiently at the door, waiting for him to be free, was indicative of the man.

'Detective Chief Inspector Isaac Cook. I'd like to ask you a few questions.'

'Apologies,' Stanley's manner changed. 'I assumed you were here to sell me something.'

He may have had a Napoleon complex, but his office did not reflect his self-perceived *Big Man* status. It was relatively small, cluttered with papers, and had a distinct smell of cheap cigars. Isaac found out later that Ian Stanley was the least politically correct person at the production lot. He was not averse to insulting his actors, production team, scriptwriters – in fact, anyone who was subservient to him. He also found out that he was a sycophant who sucked up to those who would keep him in his position.

'Apology accepted,' Isaac magnanimously replied. He instinctively did not like the man. *Racist, crude, and a bore*, he thought.

'What can I do for you, although I suppose it's related to Marjorie?'

'We're trying to find her.' Isaac took a seat.

'I don't know why.'

'Her disappearance is regarded as serious.'

'It's playing havoc with the series, but apart from that, she's not been missed much, especially by me.'

'Why do you say that?' Isaac asked. Ian Stanley seemed to be a person who had no problem speaking his mind.

'Look, she's a pain in the arse, but for me…'

'Would you care to elaborate?'

'Yes, why not? It's a bloody hard job bringing this together on a day-to-day basis. We're here six days a week, most days fifteen hours at least, and that only gives us five days' worth of thirty minute daily episodes. It has to be run with military precision. We've no time for prima donnas past their prime.'

'Is she a prima donna?' Isaac had heard it before. In fact, it seemed to be the general view of Marjorie Frobisher.

'She's the only one I can't control out there, and the only one who holds up the production, apart from that stuck-up bitch Jess O'Neill. She's only here because she's screwing Richard Williams.'

Isaac was perturbed to hear the reference to Jess. He decided to continue with the interview and to come back later to that particularly disturbing piece of news.

'I was told she is brilliant,' Isaac said.

'Of course she is. Made the others look as if they were straight out of a school production of Macbeth. She knew how to act, I'll grant her that.'

'So why the pain in the arse reference?'

'As I told you, we need to run this with military precision. This is not the Royal Shakespeare Company. This is just entertainment for the masses.'

'Are you saying she was too good for the production?'

'That's what I mean. She could have achieved something in the theatre.'

'Any idea why she didn't?'

'Fame and glory.'

'I don't understand,' Isaac replied.

'It's a simple equation. Here, she is paid a handsome salary, King's ransom, or in her case a Queen's ransom. Out there in theatreland, she'd have her name up in lights being paid a regular actor's wages. She wanted the fame, the adoring fans, and the money. She couldn't have it all.'

'Was she bitter as a result?'

'Maybe, probably explains why she screwed around so much.'

'Did she?' Isaac asked.

'Not as much lately.'

'How would you know that?'

'She'd tell me.'

'Why would she do that?'

'You don't get it, do you? I'm a bastard, she's a bitch. With me, she could be honest. I wouldn't repeat what she told me in confidence, would I?'

'I don't know. You said she was a bitch, screwed around.'

'Everyone knows about her screwing around. And as for the "bitch", she'd admit to that.'

'Her current disappearance, what do you reckon?'

'Unusual. She's done a vanishing trick before but still managed to show up for her scenes. This time, it's out of character. Look, I've got a show to run here. If there are no more questions, I need to get out there and start shouting at people.'

'Just one more question Jess O'Neill and Richard Williams?'

'Richard, I've known him for years. He can't keep his hands off the women, including Marjorie in the distant past. As soon as Jess turned up, he was on to her.'

'And she succumbed to the charm and the Ferrari?'

'They all do, but most wise up soon enough. He screwed Jess O'Neill a couple of times, that's all I know. The personal assistant, you've met her?'

'Sally Jenkins.'

'She's the standby. Just a bit of fluff, not very competent. A screw at the end of the day, that's how Richard sees it.' With that, the series producer rushed out of the door shouting at whoever. Isaac also noticed that his language had changed, and a great deal of bad language spewed from his mouth.

Chapter 7

With little more to achieve that day, Isaac and Farhan met back at Challis Street. Neither was in a good mood: Isaac, because of the revelation about Jess O'Neill; Farhan, because spending time with Barbara Reid and then Rosemary Fairweather had made him realise how dull his home life and his wife were.

'Farhan, what are we doing here? We used to spend our time on worthwhile murders, and here we are, just messing around, making nuisances of ourselves, asking dumb questions.'

'And the woman is likely to walk in the door at any time soon.'

'Is that likely?' Isaac asked.

'What do you mean?'

Isaac was sitting on his side of the office, the window behind him. Both men had loosened their ties. Unless the situation changed, they would leave early, which in their cases meant before 8 p.m.

Neither was anxious to leave, mainly because where they were heading was less agreeable than where they were now. Farhan had a dreary house in a dreary street with a dreary wife and a dreary television blasting out all day and virtually all night. The children gave him comfort, but they would be in bed, fast asleep by the time he arrived home. His wife, heavily pregnant, would not be receptive to his amorous advances, and after spending time with two not young but very attractive women, he was in need of an outlet. There was no outlet, he knew that. The best he could do was to keep working until exhausted and then go home to sleep.

'I believe Marjorie Frobisher to be dead,' Isaac said.

'Why do you come up with that conclusion?' Farhan could see them remaining in the office for a few more hours. He recognised he had the traits of a workaholic, but he could never be sure if his diagnosis was correct, or whether it was a result of an unsatisfactory home life. It caused him great conflict. He had

50

attempted a discussion with the Imam at the local Mosque that he tried to visit every Friday for Jummah, the most significant prayer time in the Muslim calendar. He rarely made it, and would on most occasions make his prayers in a quiet part of the office, or out at a crime scene.

The Imam, although excessively conservative, could offer no tangible advice other than 'Allah will guide you. It is for you to trust in his wisdom.'

'Let's look at the facts,' Isaac said. He was on his third cup of coffee, and hunger had set in. A potential world-class runner in his day, sub-ten seconds for the one hundred metre dash, but he was not as dedicated as he should have been, and academia had been where his parents wanted him to focus. He reflected on that fact as he ordered the pizza, the third that week, and noticed his slight paunch, a clear indication of too much fast food and lack of exercise.

'I realise we don't have a corpse,' Isaac said as he consumed the last slice of pizza.'

'You may well be right. Detail your analysis,' Farhan said.

'One, she's disappeared before, but never for so long, two, she's never missed her work obligations, and three, there's the interest of the so-called influential persons.'

'There are a lot of uncertainties in there. It wouldn't hold up in a court of law.'

'Farhan, we're not a court of law. We are just speculating.'

'Okay, then let's analyse what we know.'

Isaac stood up, moved over to the whiteboard and started to write. The whiteboard marker was dry. He chose another. It worked. 'Firstly, it is now over four weeks,' he said, 'almost five since she was last sighted. The most she has disappeared before has been a week to ten days.'

'What about the SMSs?'

'If it's not her, then someone else is sending them.'

'But why?'

'What if someone doesn't want us to know she's dead?'

'Is that possible?' Farhan asked.

'What else can it be?'

'Can we prove this?'

'I don't see how we can. We know the general location of the SMSs, but they are only triangulated off the nearest communication towers. They will be accurate to within ten, twenty yards at most, maybe more if it's a remote area.'

Farhan moved to the whiteboard. 'If one of the SMSs came from a remote location in the countryside it might be possible to pinpoint it. If the area is sparsely populated, then maybe it's possible.'

'And then one of us goes there and starts sniffing around.'

'It's a long shot, but what have we got to lose?'

'Okay, let's do that.' Isaac continued his analysis; Farhan resumed his seat after idly drawing a circle on the whiteboard and then rubbing it off.

'Secondly, she has never missed a work commitment before. That validates my opinion that she is dead. From what we know of the woman, she would not have missed her opportunity to play the grieving sister when her on-screen brother died. It would have been irresistible for her.'

Farhan could only agree. He didn't mention that his wife had put forward that conclusion. *A housewife and she comes up with a better result,* Farhan thought.

'These so-called influential persons, any luck there?' Isaac asked. He had resumed his seat. A cursory glance at the clock revealed that it was after ten. Outside, it was dark, and the rain had started. He sent a text message. He did not want to conclude the day with a hot drink and a cold bed.

'Not really. The most I've found out is that there have been a few previous lovers of significance, but they're not recent.'

'Her agent, what did she have to say?'

'She had plenty to say, but then she started clamming up.'

'Why?'

'She was very agreeable, as was her PA, but once I started to dig deeper, she hurried me out of the room. She knows the dirt, or at least some of it.'

'And she was not going to dish it out to you?' Isaac said, aware that Farhan's easy and pleasant manner of drawing out information, especially from women, was exceptional.

'If we have a body, she will give names.'

'That doesn't help us much, does it?'

'We're at a dead end,' Farhan said.

Isaac, before he could respond, was momentarily distracted by an SMS on his phone, *'see you in one hour'*. At least his bed would be warm tonight. 'Farhan, let's wrap it for this evening, meet tomorrow early and discuss our strategy. Interviewing people will not get us anywhere. We need to go and find this woman, or what remains of her.'

Farhan agreed. He had heard the beep on Isaac's phone, seen his smirking smile. He wished that it had been him going home to a willing and liberated woman. He had little to look forward to except the sullen expression on his wife's face, and a complaint about the late hour.

Chapter 8

Sophie White was a decent person. Isaac knew that well enough. They had met three years earlier, during an investigation he had conducted into the murder of a hooligan in an alley in Brixton. It had appeared to be a case of rival gangs indulging in a tit-for-tat: 'you kill one of ours, we'll kill one of yours'.

That was how they wanted to record it down at the police station. It was just too much paperwork, and one less hooligan only served society well. The police realised that catching the guilty gang members was the ideal, but invariably there were extenuating circumstances: still a minor, self-defence, deprived childhood, mentally unstable. There were just too many opportunities for the guilty party to get off: slap on the back of the hand, community service, or time in an air-conditioned reform home.

That was how Isaac's boss saw it. A gnarled, old-school policeman, he remembered a time when a kick up the arse and a good beating were perfectly acceptable forms of crime deterrent. He didn't hold with the modern style of policing: too politically correct, too cosmetic, too soft on the criminals. He believed that a villain respects authority and strength and that the police handbook did little to help.

Isaac, then a detective sergeant, fresh out of uniform, understood his plight, but he had been university educated, his boss had not. Thirty years previously, a different style of policing was suitable. Those were the days before heavy drugs, Islamic terrorism, and a population explosion. Isaac had studied the period. His boss had been prepared to write off the hooligan's death as death by misadventure, person or persons unknown.

Sophie White had changed all that. She lived in Twickenham, worked in Brixton as a social worker. As Isaac was wrapping up the case at his boss's insistence, she had come forward with new information. She had seen a person running away from the alley, his arm covered in blood.

The inevitable questions had come up when she walked into the police station: Why had she waited so long to come forward? Why did she believe it was not gang-related? Did she recognise the person?

She had answered them all with aplomb. One, she had just finished work and was heading to the airport. Her sister in Canada was getting married, she was the maid of honour – it was checked out, found to be true. Two, the person she saw did not dress like a gang member. There was no hooded jacket, no trainers, no surly look about the individual – in fact, he was dressed well in a suit. Three, no, she did not recognise the person, although it was not an area where you saw men wearing suits too often.

With the case reopened and his boss none too happy, it was left to Isaac to do the legwork, to further interview Sophie White and to wrap up the case, *tout de suite*. His boss had just bought a renovator's delight in France as a retirement project and was continually trying out his basic French. Isaac, who had studied French at school and spoke with a reasonable fluency, ended up the recipient of some very crude French with a pronounced cockney undertone. It grated on Isaac's nerves, but he said little, only offered encouragement.

Sophie White proved to be a good witness with a remarkable skill. She had a photographic memory and was able to give an accurate description of what she had seen. She was able to remember the detail in the clothes of the assailant, the scuff mark on his shoes, his hair, which side it was parted, what colour and so on. It had been half-light, dusk when the attack had taken place. She had not seen the attack although she had seen the blood. As she explained, it happened all too often in the neighbourhood. Normally, she would not have stopped at the shop across the road from the alley, but she was feeling at ease, and her sister had asked for some favourite chocolates, not the sort they sold out at the airport.

The hooligan's name was Michael O'Leary. He had been born in the area, ran with a gang of ne'er-do-wells down by the water's edge. Nineteen and barely literate, apart from a few run-ins with the police he had not been in much trouble. He was of a lost generation with no hope of redemption. He had been cocky in his early teenage years, bragging about why he didn't need an education and how he had wagged school. 'What do those cock-sucking teachers know? It's out on the street that matters,' he would say.

Those he bragged to had ended up on the street as he had, indulging in gang-related warfare, partaking in petty theft when they could, and major theft if they had the brain power for such an activity, which most did not.

It transpired that he had got a casual job as a runner for an illegal gambling syndicate. They would organise the dogs for fighting in an old warehouse close to the docks. He would collect the money, transport it as required, and receive a commission for his efforts. He thought he was smart in creaming off another one per cent. It was an easy scam, virtually undetectable. An intelligent person could have made an easy one hundred pounds every few days, but O'Leary was not smart; he had got the percentages wrong. He had taken ten percent, due to his inability to listen to the 'cock-sucking teachers' that he had been so critical of.

The syndicate knew immediately. They sent in one of their people to teach him a lesson: a severe beating, a few broken bones and don't do it again. The story once they had picked up the killer – a standover merchant from up north – was that he had been brought down by the syndicate. And that O'Leary was not willing to take his punishment and had drawn a knife. The killer stated it was self-defence; he received ten years for manslaughter.

Sophie and Isaac became an item, and she had moved in with him for a while. A brutal childhood, a violent marriage in the past – domesticity did not suit her. She felt love for Isaac, he felt a fondness for her, but she could not commit and had decided that she needed a man and sex, but on her terms.

She and Isaac had formed a deep bond, and a phone call from either would often result in a coupling of bodies, no commitment. It suited Isaac, although he found sex without love intimidating. For Sophie, it proved an ideal arrangement.

She had sent the *'see you in one hour'* SMS.

***

The next day Farhan met Robert Avers, the now apparently long-suffering husband of the missing woman. This time, Avers had agreed to meet at his house in Belgravia. The detective inspector was more relaxed than in his previous encounters with the husband, and certainly more sober than their time at the Churchill Arms in Kensington. He did not want to repeat that experience.

Avers, accommodating as usual, welcomed him into the house. 'Detective Inspector Ahmed. Pleased to see you.' Still polite, still friendly, but the previous bon vivant was missing. The man, dressed in a suit, had a dejected appearance.

'Detective Inspector,' he confided, 'I'm worried. It's just been too long.'

'But you said she has done this in the past.'

'Not for this length of time,' Avers replied. Farhan could see the man was visibly distressed.

'There have been more than a few men over the years,' Farhan said.

'That's right…'

'And ideally, you would have preferred none?'

'It's how she's wired. She needed the men, the thrill, the sexual encounters.'

'You didn't approve?'

'I always assumed the need would pass eventually and then all would be fine.'

'Has that time arrived?'

'I believe so, but why this disappearance? I just don't understand it.'

'Sorry, I need to ask.'

'There had been some lovers in the past; some before we met who are now influential men in this country.' Avers wanted to talk; Farhan willing to let him continue. Avers was tense, sitting upright on a hard chair in the sitting room; Farhan sat back on the comfortable sofa. His posture looked relaxed; he was not. He switched off his phone. The worst distraction was it ringing at the moment of confession or revelation.

Chapter 9

'What did you gain from Robert Avers?' Isaac asked Farhan in the office, their end of day meeting. He was still in a good mood, a leftover from the night before and Sophie.

Farhan had had no such romantic encounter, only a lecture from his wife on why he did not spend more time with the children, how he loved his work more than her, and what time of the night did he think that was to come home?

'Robert Avers is a broken man, seriously worried,' Farhan said, although he was distracted. He realised his welcome home of the previous night would only be repeated, once he left the office. He sighed to himself. It was true, he did love his work more than his wife, but then work was exciting, whereas she was not, and as for his children, he did have some regrets, although he tried to keep Sundays free for them. Not always successfully, though.

'Let's state that the woman is dead,' Isaac said.

'I thought we agreed on that yesterday.'

'You're right, but we still maintained a glimmer of hope. Let's throw that out of the window and go for broke. No longer do we regard this as a missing person investigation. Now, we classify it as a murder enquiry.'

'Can we do that?'

'Officially, it may be difficult. Unofficially, I don't see a problem.'

'I still think we need to bring the Super in on this. Maybe grill him some more as to what he knows.' Farhan made the suggestion, realising that Isaac and their boss had an easier relationship, and Isaac would be the better of the two to do it.

'I'll phone him now,' Isaac said. Before he could call, his phone rang. He excused himself from the room. Farhan could hear a muffled conversation. Isaac returned sheepishly five minutes later.

'Important?' Farhan asked.

'Jess O'Neill.'

'Some new evidence?'

'Maybe, maybe not. It's more likely a ruse to meet up.'

'She's a good-looking woman.' Farhan had seen a photo.

'Good-looking she may be, but we've just upgraded this to a murder investigation. It wouldn't look right if I were playing around with a potential suspect, would it?'

'And if she wasn't a potential suspect?'

'You know the answer to that already.' Isaac smiled.

Isaac, no longer making excuses for a possible future romantic encounter, phoned their boss. It was nine in the evening, but Isaac knew his phone call at such an hour would not cause any problems.

'Sir, we want to upgrade this to a murder investigation.'

'Okay, stay where you are. I'll be in the office within the hour,' Goddard said.

It was closer to ninety minutes when he arrived, pizza box in hand. Isaac, who had promised to look after his diet better, could only thank him for the food.

Farhan could see that it was going to be a later finish than the previous night. *Maybe she'll be asleep when I finally make it home*, he thought, but realised it was just wishful thinking.

Isaac was the first to speak after they had finished with the pizza. 'These so-called influential persons, are they critical to the investigation?' His question was levelled at the detective superintendent.

'You're asking questions I'm not able to answer.'

'But why? If it's a murder investigation, doesn't that change the situation?'

'I don't see how.' The detective superintendent appeared to be stalling. 'There's no deceased, so how can you call it a murder investigation?'

'We're just calling it a murder enquiry. Do you want to make it official?'

Richard Goddard sat upright before he continued. 'I don't know the full story, not much more than you. Dead is okay by them. It's if she is alive that worries them,' Richard Goddard said.

'What do you mean?' Isaac could see them treading where they were not wanted, asking questions certain people did not want to be asked.

'Isaac,' his senior said, 'drop the case. Just declare that she has gone missing.'

'But why? I thought we were meant to find her. Are you suggesting we should walk away from a potential murder?' Isaac sensed the trepidation in his senior officer. It was something he had not seen before.

'We must. I'll tell my contact that we're pulling out. I'll tell him that the leads have gone cold. She's disappeared of her own free will, and will no doubt reappear when she feels inclined.'

'Do you believe what you just said?' Isaac looked the senior officer direct in the eyes.

'If her reappearance frightens some people, then what will happen if you manage to find out why she's disappeared?'

'Is that a reason to pull back?' Isaac asked. He realised what their boss was trying to say, Farhan did not.

'Some people have a reason to wish her dead. Have we considered what they might do to keep it that way?'

'Do you think it's as bad as that?' Isaac asked.

'Official Secrets Act? What do you think?'

'I believe you're probably right.'

'Then we pull out?' Richard Goddard posed a rhetorical question.

Isaac looked at Farhan. 'What do you reckon?'

'We continue.' Farhan was resolute.

'I was told by my contact that if you get close, I was to communicate with him,' Goddard said.

'We'll agree to that.' Isaac looked at Farhan, who nodded in agreement.

The detective superintendent excused himself and left the room. He returned five minutes later. 'I'm meeting with my contact tomorrow at eight in the morning. I will brief you on my return.' It was already two in the morning. Fifteen minutes later, all three left the office: Isaac to an empty bed, Farhan to a complaining wife, and Richard Goddard to a comfortable house in a pleasant suburb. Detective Superintendent Goddard was a worried man. He knew he would not sleep much that night.

***

Angus MacTavish showed none of the affability he had shown the detective superintendent on his previous visit. The man was not in good humour. 'I told you to keep your people out of this, Detective Superintendent Goddard.'

'I was under the impression that the investigation was to continue.' The detective superintendent's hackles raised by the tone of the man in front of him: the man who had deliberately failed to shake his hand.

'I thought I made it clear that they were to focus on finding the woman, not delve into speculation as to her importance.'

'It's a police investigation. How do you think it's conducted? They pry, probe, ask awkward questions, and dive into the dirty laundry that everyone carries around as baggage.'

'Don't get smart with me, Goddard. I know how the police work.'

Richard Goddard assumed the changed attitude came with being the Government Chief Whip: when all was going well – magnanimous and affable; when it wasn't – exactly what he was experiencing now. He saw no reason to let the man ride roughshod over him. He had not become the senior officer of the Homicide and Serious Crime Command at Challis Street by allowing aggressive and bombastic individuals to take control.

'Sir, your attitude is not conducive to this meeting. Last time I was here, you were more agreeable.'

'That was different.' It was clear that Angus MacTavish was used to putting other people on the spot, making them feel uncomfortable. He did not enjoy the policeman's comment.

'What was different? The fact that you fobbed me off by appealing to my good nature?'

'No, of course not; well, maybe. Apologies, this is placing me in an awkward position,' MacTavish said.

'And my people in possible danger?'

'That's possible.'

'I can call them off. Is that what you want?'

'I'm not sure. The problem is that I don't know the full story, just some parts of it.'

'Are you saying there may be some validity in them continuing?'

'We still need to find out the truth. It was one thing to be out looking for a missing woman, but if we find her murdered, then by whom? The answer may have repercussions that none of us can comprehend.'

With both men more relaxed, MacTavish called for some tea. Mrs Gregory, after a short delay, entered the room and served the tea. Both men moved from the formal seating to a couple of more comfortable chairs to continue the discussion.

Mrs Gregory, polite and agreeable, indulged in some banter with her boss. *She must have heard the raised voices*, Richard Goddard thought. *Must be used to it, I suppose.*

With the tea poured, MacTavish spoke again, this time in a more agreeable manner, 'Have your people seen any unfamiliar faces?'

'Should they have?'

'They're being watched, I'm sure of it.'

'By whom? Or is that secret?'

'I would say the security services. MI5, probably.'

'What does this woman know that's so important?'

'Detective Superintendent, I'll level with you. Initially, I thought this was about an affair she had when she was young with a senior member of the government.'

'What's so wrong about that? We live in liberated times. It's hardly a case for murder.'

'That's what I would have thought, but there was a child.'

'What about the child?'

'I don't know. It was a different time, the baby was adopted.'

'There are large swathes of the public that would see that as unacceptable.'

'Which part? Having a child out of wedlock, or the adoption?' MacTavish asked.

'Depends on which public we're talking about.'

'The voting public.'

'A child out of wedlock, thirty plus years ago, would have been seen as sinful. Necessary to cover up at all costs. Even so, would this being revealed affect the outcome of an election?'

'It could make a difference if the parties were running neck and neck, especially if the woman has been murdered.'

'That's how my detectives see it. It's the only conclusion.'

'I don't believe the government would condone murder. Silence the woman, prevent publication of her life story, but murder?'

'Are you saying that if she is found murdered, it has more sinister undertones?'

Angus MacTavish paused for a while. He seemed to the detective superintendent to be doing mental calculations, analysing the pros and cons of the situation. 'If it is found that she has been murdered, it can only mean one thing,' he said.

'Yes?'

'It's not because of an illegitimate birth and an adoption.'

'Then what is it about?'

'I don't know, and I need to know. We all need to know if we are to make rational decisions.'

'And whether it will impact the result of the forthcoming election?'

'I think an electoral result for or against the ruling party may be a minor issue if people are willing to commit murder, and on the face of it an officially condoned murder.'

'An assassination, is that what you are saying?'

'I believe that is what I am saying.' Angus MacTavish's affable manner had changed, not to anger against Richard Goddard, but to worry as to what this all meant.

64

'Detective Superintendent, your two men. Brief them as you see fit, and put them out in the field. Make sure they are carrying weapons. This is possibly going to be nasty.'

'Who will you inform?'

'The prime minister, in the strictest confidence,' MacTavish replied.

'Is he the father?'

'Information on a need-to-know basis. You know that.'

'On a need-to-know basis. That's correct.'

Chapter 10

Isaac and Farhan, not clear about the direction to take, and temporarily out of leads, had taken the morning in a leisurely manner. They saw no reason to continue until their senior returned from meeting with his contact. Isaac never asked the name, although he had a shrewd idea who it was.

Farhan had managed to take the children to school for the first time in a month; Isaac just lay in bed for an extra hour and thought about Jess O'Neill. He could not see her as a murderer. However, he had learnt a long time ago that the least likely person, especially in a murder case, often turns out to be the culprit. Jess O'Neill seemed to have no connection to Marjorie Frobisher, other than they were work colleagues and Jess had told Marjorie that her starring days were drawing to a close. There was still the issue of Jess and Richard Williams. *Could she have screwed Williams just because he drove a Ferrari and was rich?* He resolved to find out.

Just as Isaac intended to roll over for another five-minute nap, the phone rang. 'Two o'clock, your office. Make sure DI Ahmed is there as well.' Richard Goddard had made the call as he exited MacTavish's office.

Isaac and Farhan were in the office well in advance of the nominated time. Richard Goddard, a stickler for punctuality, arrived on the dot. He had not brought a pizza this time; Isaac was thankful.

'If she has been murdered, then the situation has changed,' the detective superintendent commenced hesitantly.

'Let's assume she has,' Isaac said.

'Her death would be advantageous.'

'Are we condoning murder here, sir?' Farhan asked.

'That's a preposterous statement.' Goddard was not amused.

'Your statement was ambiguous. Farhan was right to ask.' Isaac had almost made the same remark.

'Let me clarify.' Goddard said. 'It is evident from my contact that certain people would not be sorry to hear of her demise.'

'And why?' Isaac asked.

'She has, or had, information that would prove both embarrassing politically and personally.'

'Would they be willing to kill her to prevent that information being revealed?'

'My contact assures me they would not.'

'And others?'

'I don't believe they would have given the authority for her assassination.'

'Are you certain?' Farhan asked.

'I can't be sure of anything. I may have been fed a line. Have you seen anyone suspicious?'

Isaac answered first. 'I've not seen anyone.'

'DI Ahmed?'

'Sir, I thought it was suspicious at the time.'

'What was?'

'The time I went to the Churchill Arms with Robert Avers. There was one man. I assumed he was a local propping up the bar. Then today, when I dropped the children at school, I could swear I saw him across the road from the school.'

'Are you certain?' Isaac asked.

'I believe I am. What does this mean?'

'We're treading on toes, and they don't like it. This is where it gets complicated. We're possibly upsetting powerful and dangerous persons.'

'What kind of persons?' Isaac asked.

'The type who carry guns and MI5 identification. They may just be doing surveillance, but who knows?'

'Are you serious?' Isaac asked.

'Deadly serious. There are two options here. The first is we back off.'

'And the second?'

'If you continue, it could get nasty.'

'I'm not one for backing off,' Isaac said.

'Neither am I,' Farhan agreed.

'Very well. You will need to carry guns, just in case.'

***

Barely interrupted by the disappearance of Marjorie Frobisher, production of the soap opera watched by millions continued – skilled scriptwriting had glossed over her disappearance: nervous breakdown due to shock over her brother's death, followed by a heart attack, followed by death.

The show had even managed to ensure that the long unbroken run of record ratings continued. The storyline had gone on for six weeks, long enough according to the market researchers. In the seventh week, five weeks since Isaac and Farhan had become involved, she finally died. The hospital scene: her lying in the hospital, face mask supplying oxygen. A stand-in actress with similar features, or in this case a lie-in, as all she had to do was remain motionless.

The death spread over two weeks; the viewing audience hit over nine million. It was regarded as a great success, celebrated with gusto by those remaining in the production, production staff and actors alike.

The magazines reported her death in detail, interviewed people who Marjorie Frobisher had worked with. None wanted to be the person to spill the beans: to tell the world that she was a promiscuous bitch and good riddance. Not until a dishevelled and by now homeless Charles Sutherland, the former Billy Blythe in the soap opera, was waylaid one morning as he dragged his weary body along to the local charity soup kitchen.

He had hit rock-bottom. In less than two months he had gone from famous to forgotten to destitute. He had milked it for a few weeks after his removal from the show, but despondency had driven him to a binge of expensive alcohol and even more expensive women. The parties he had thrown, the money he had spent, the cocaine he had snorted were legendary. The so-called friends while he was throwing the money around, plentiful. The so-called friends after he was evicted from his upmarket accommodation for non-payment of rent and for trashing the place, non-existent. It was a bleary-eyed morning after his unceremonious eviction, basically a kick in the arse from some thugs employed by the landlord, closely followed by his few meagre belongings. The landlord seized anything of value and dumped the rest on the street with their owner.

Two days later and sober, Charles Sutherland acknowledged the reason for his current situation: Marjorie Frobisher. *She was the bitch*, he thought. *She put me here.* He was still an arrogant man, desperate as he blamed his life on others, not himself.

***

When the gossip magazine journalist found Charles Sutherland sitting on the pavement not far from the soup kitchen, holding a roll in one hand, coffee in a paper cup in the other, he was, at first, reluctant to talk. He thought she had come to do a story on him and his fall from grace. He was correct in his evaluation until he started to talk about why he was out on the street.

Classically trained, destined for great things, Sutherland told her. Boring and mundane, that was what Christy Nichols, a freelance contributor to the scurrilous magazine that catered to the followers of minor celebrities and nonentities, thought. She had found him, thought there may be a story in it, a story that she could get published in the magazine; but the more he talked, the more she realised he offered no great copy. He was an arrogant, overweight, and smelly man, worthy of no more than a photo and a thousand words.

She prepared to leave: her, with the picture and a signed clearance to use it; he, with two hundred pounds to use wisely or otherwise, although she knew which option Charles Sutherland would choose, as did Charles Sutherland.

'You know about Marjorie Frobisher?' he said.

'Her disappearance?' Christy Nichols sat down again on the dirty pavement, her freshly pressed, cream-coloured skirt picking up some dirt marks. She was a good-looking woman, a little overweight, which was how Sutherland liked his women. He had no time for skinny tarts with no breasts and ribs so prominent you could play a tune on them.

'Not that.'

'What then?'

'She was a bitch, you know that?' Sutherland had nothing new. Christy Nichols stood up again. There was no news here, she reasoned. She needed to change, and now there was a dry-cleaning bill to worry about. A glamorous job, others thought, writing copy for a magazine, but she was freelance, paid for the published copy, not for sitting with a man down on his luck. She had no more time, and there was a minor starlet due at the airport within a couple of hours. *Another empty-headed individual with inflated breasts, wafting into England, hoping to resurrect her career,* she thought. The celebrity was better known more for her poor choices in men and her predilection for drugs than her acting ability. She was good copy, and if Christy could score an interview and a few photos, it would pay more than a soap opera cast member, once important, now forgotten.

'There's something else.'

'What do you mean?' The disappearance of Marjorie Frobisher was still newsworthy. Her character, Edith Blythe, had been kept in the public eye for weeks due to the clever scripting on the programme. Some magazines, even the one where Christy hoped to sell the story, were running articles on what type of funeral she would have. Would it be a cremation or burial? What clothes would her friends on the programme wear? How many episodes would be consumed by the funeral and the mourning afterwards? Her death on the programme had been milked for all it was worth, and so would her funeral.

'She screwed around.'

'Hardly newsworthy, is it?'

'Maybe it is if you know who she was screwing.' Sutherland let the conversation hang.

'What do you have?' *To hell with the skirt and the dry cleaner,* the reporter thought. She was aware of the rumours, most people were, especially in the industry, but it was never regarded as good copy. Marjorie Frobisher was revered as a celebrity; her character, Edith Blythe, a pillar of society. One magazine had alluded to her unusual marriage, tested the waters, but the response had not been favourable, so they had desisted.

'I'll talk when I'm paid, only then.'

'No one's going to pay just because you make a statement that you have something of interest.'

'*Something of interest.*' Sutherland emphasised the words the reporter had just said.

'Is it that good?'

'It's dynamite.'

'I can't get anyone interested just on your word. I need facts.'

'Talk to your editor. Tell her what I've got.'

'And what have you got?'

'Unmarried pregnancy, a child adopted. Is that enough to be going on with?'

'Marjorie Frobisher. Do you mean Marjorie Frobisher?'

'Who the hell do you think I mean?' Charles Sutherland said.

***

It looked to Isaac and Farhan as if, finally, they were to get down to some real policing. Both Isaac and Farhan were armed. Isaac had one issue to clear up – Jess O'Neill and Richard Williams. Farhan felt he needed to update Robert Avers.

Robert Avers took it well. Farhan saw no reason not to tell him what they believed. Avers' reaction was of a man expecting such a statement.

Isaac's issue was complicated. His discussions with Jess O'Neill were meant to be strictly professional, yet if she had been sleeping with Richard Williams… It hardly seemed relevant to the case, although he tried to convince himself that it was. He decided to resolve the confusion in his mind once and for all.

It was a good day out at the production lot. For once, it was sunny, and Isaac had to admit the fictional town looked good. As he walked down the main street, past where the Saturday market was held, left at a grocery store on the corner, across the street and down a side alley to where Jess O'Neill's office was situated, he reflected on the task ahead. At least, that was what Isaac tried to think about. He wanted to seem professional when he encountered the woman, not a love-sick puppy, which he thought he was at the present moment.

He saw her soon enough, obviously in conference with a group of production people. She soon concluded the meeting and came over to him: too friendly, too close. He pulled back a little, she came forward. The safest approach was for him to take a seat and then her seat would, at least, maintain a professional distance. It did not as she leant forward and adjusted the position of the chair.

Isaac saw no reason to attempt to move again. He felt embarrassed, hopeful it did not show, although blushing on a black man is not the same as on a white man.

'Jess, there are just a few questions.'

'Yes, Isaac.' *Too pleasantly said*, he thought. He endeavoured to sit back on his chair. It did not help.

'We're concerned about Marjorie Frobisher's disappearance. We need to cast our net wider.'

'What does that mean?'

'I will be moving out of London, travelling for a few days.'

'Does that mean I won't be seeing you?' Too agreeable for Isaac, too tempting.

'That's correct. Before I leave, there are a couple of questions.'

'You've already said that,' she said. Isaac realised that she was on to him. She knew he was embarrassed, and she was clearly enjoying it. 'Just ask me straight. I'm certain I know the question.'

'Richard Williams…'

'You want to know whether I slept with him?'

'It's a loose bit of information that needs clarifying.'

'Not that it's relevant, but I know that Ian Stanley brings it up every chance he gets. He doesn't like it that a woman is his superior.'

'He was fine with me.'

'He's against anyone and anything that's not white and male. I'm surprised he was so pleasant to you.'

'He wasn't until he saw my badge.'

'For the record, and I do not see this as relevant, I did go out with Richard Williams a few times. He was good company and very generous, but I did not sleep with him.'

'Ian Stanley was just making mischief?'

'On one of the occasions, there was an exhibition of production equipment up north. We spent the night there, separate rooms.'

'I assume he tried it on?'

'Yes, of course, but I wasn't buying it.'

'Thank you for clarifying.'

'Now, Detective Chief Inspector Isaac Cook, was that question entirely professional?' She smiled as she made the comment.

'Purely professional.' Isaac tried to maintain a serious face, but couldn't. He smiled as well.

'For the record, I've made my choice.'

'Choice on what?'

'You did not make detective chief inspector by being naïve, did you?'

'Not at all, but we are treating this as a murder investigation.'

'And you can't be seen to be fraternising with a potential suspect?'

'That's about it.'

'I can assure you, I'm not guilty, but she could be a bitch. Not a difficult person to dislike.'

'I'll keep in touch.' He prepared to leave.

'If you want to phone and tell me you fancy me, professionally of course, then that will be okay, won't it?' She came near. She kissed him on the lips. Compromised, Isaac left soon after, but not before he had kissed her back. As he walked back down the main street on the production lot, he only hoped she was not involved.

Chapter 11

Isaac first noticed the car as he left the production lot. At any other time, he would have regarded it as inconsequential, but the situation had changed. As he weaved through the traffic, he noticed that the car kept reappearing. He wasn't sure how, as his car was a lot more powerful and he wasn't a slow driver. The car behind was pushing hard. He phoned Richard Goddard.

'Let it follow. Don't let them know you've seen them.' That was precisely what Isaac had intended in the first place. It was an unwelcome intrusion into the investigation, and a sour conclusion to an otherwise pleasant day. He failed to mention he had just kissed one of the people close to Marjorie Frobisher. He could only imagine his boss's reaction if he told him.

Isaac had planned the remainder of his day carefully. Jess was still off-limits, Sophie wasn't. He had planned to pick her up from her workplace, but decided against it with a car on his tail; better if she found her way to his apartment. She understood when he told her it was the pressure of work that prevented the pickup. As she said to him later: commitment-free and no obligation on either party to look out for the other. Pickups were not part of the deal; however, good company and good sex were.

With the car following, Isaac headed back to the office at Challis Street. Farhan was in the office. 'How's your day been?' Isaac asked.

'I told her husband that we believe his wife is dead.'

'How did he take it?'

'Better than expected. I believe he was prepared for the news.'

Farhan was not looking too well. Isaac asked the reason.

'My wife wants a separation. She believes I'm married more to this job than to her.'

'Is that possible in your religion?'

'It occurs, and besides this is England. She can do what she likes,' Farhan admitted.

'I always imagined she was a conservative woman.'

'She's certainly more pious than me. It's her mother, no doubt, who put her up to this, aiming to force me to make a choice.'

'Choice between what?' Isaac had come over to Farhan's desk, bringing a chair with him.

'Between her daughter and the police, what else?'

'But you need to make a living.'

'They believe I should be running a corner store.'

'You would be working more hours than you do now.'

'They have this idea that the shop will be downstairs and the family up.'

'What are you going to do?'

'It's the children, not my wife. They are my primary consideration.'

'Are you saying if she goes, she'll deny you visiting rights?'

'No, she can't do that. I'm worried they'll be susceptible to being radicalised.'

'Do you need time off to figure this out?' Isaac asked, although he could not see how he could accede to such a request, or how he could refuse.

'No. We've got a murder to solve, and besides, if those guys following us decide to take us out, then it's theoretical.' It was an attempt at lightening the sombre mood in the office. It did not work.

'Let's ignore those following us for the moment. We need to find a body, assuming she's dead.' Isaac was pleased that Farhan was staying on board. He was also glad that so far he had remained single. Sophie White had the right idea, he thought, but one day he could see stability and marriage and children, and in that order.

'Where's the first triangulation off her phone?' Farhan seemed to pick up in spirits after he had offloaded some of his burdens onto Isaac.

'Central Birmingham,' Isaac replied. 'Not much use to us, too many buildings, too much traffic. We need somewhere isolated.'

'We need a rural area, preferably with few buildings. A small village may be best. Even then, it will be like trying to find a needle in a haystack.'

'What else do we have?'

'Malvern, Worcestershire.'

'Too big, too many houses,' Isaac said.

'Not if there is a camera on every other lamppost.'

'That's true. What's the best way to check this out?'

'I'll go there,' Farhan offered.

'No, best if you stay here. See if you can draw a trace on any vehicle following you, and then talk to our boss. His contact may be able to help with identification.'

'You don't need to leave me here just because I've got family problems. My staying here won't change the situation, and besides, I'm not resigning from the police force. This is more than a job, it's a vocation. She doesn't understand. People sleep calmly in their beds at night because of us. What to do about my children? That's another story.'

It was later in the afternoon, after their discussion in the office, that Farhan left early to pick up his children from school. Isaac could see he was concerned, and he was making a special effort. He wondered for how long.

Police work, especially with the Murder Investigation Team, did not come with a nine to five schedule. Hours were flexible, forty a week according to the book, but most weeks more like sixty to seventy, sometimes eighty to ninety, and then there were the weekends. Saturdays, often working, Sunday, more times than he cared to remember. Sophie was flexible, Jess O'Neill may not be, but he'd take her in an instant. He put her out of his mind and left early as well.

Richard Goddard had organised a contact in Worcestershire, about three hours west, or it should be, but there was the London traffic to clear first. Isaac decided to leave early, before seven in the morning.

He wanted to call Sophie, although he didn't want her endangered. Those following him earlier in the day were unknown, possibly dangerous. Just as Isaac was leaving the car park his phone rang, hands-free.

'I'm being tailed,' Farhan said.

'Number plate?'

'I'll SMS it to you. Can you forward it to Detective Superintendent Goddard?'

'That's two to give to him.'

'You've got a tail as well?'

'Yes.'

'We'd better hope these guys are harmless. I'm heading to my home.'

'If they are who we suspect, they'll know your address already.' Isaac realised they would also know where he lived, probably knew about Sophie as well. There seemed no reason to worry. He called her. She would be over later.

***

Charles Sutherland was enjoying his redemption. The magazine had been suitably impressed, continued to be, as he revealed little snippets – enough to keep them dangling.

He was not a stupid man; he knew the value of a legally drawn up contract signed by both parties. He also knew the worth of some cash up front and the remainder when he delivered the dirt. If he gave too much, too quickly, their offer would reduce or evaporate. He was not willing to let that happen.

The mention of an open marriage titillated the magazine's editor, an attractive middle-aged woman constantly on the television offering advice on how to be successful as a female in a man's world, how to power dress, how to be like her. Sutherland found her obnoxious and overbearing, full of the smugness that comes with a portrayed persona and an inner bitchiness. He didn't trust her one bit. Sure, she was pleasant to his face, but he could see the sideways glances, the raised eyebrows when she looked over at her deputy – he had no idea what her function was in the office, didn't care either. They were paying the money and he wasn't going to upset the apple cart with a snide remark.

'You've given us very little.' The editor pressured for more.

'I've given you plenty,' Sutherland replied. The room he sat in, one of the best at one of the best hotels in the town, came with a well-stocked drinks cabinet, and the cost to him was zero. He was already halfway to drunk, and he was not going to let them get between him and the euphoria he was looking forward to. He had already phoned for a couple of high-class whores, and they were on the magazine's expense account.

Sutherland saw himself as Lazarus rising from the dead. He intended to milk it for all it was worth, and to hell with the bitch magazine editor and her girlfriend. The contract, legal and very tight, was well underway; some minor clauses to iron out, some significant money to be handed over, and then he would dish out the dirt. The magazine wanted more than salacious tittle-tattle, although it was such nonsense that drove the sales. They wanted names and events, and the more important, the more titled, and the more likely to fall from grace with a major embarrassment, the better.

'Look here,' Sutherland said. He was slurring his words, making suggestive glances at Christy Nichols, who had rescued him from obscurity. 'This will bring down the government. I guarantee you that.'

Christy Nichols, now on a suitable retainer from the magazine, had been assigned to ensure that Sutherland did not go blabbing his mouth off indiscriminately in a bar or elsewhere. She had been given a room next to his. She did not want to be there, but the retainer, the possible lift up in her career, in an industry that was full of casualties who did not make the grade, kept her firmly rooted.

She had agreed reluctantly, although she found Charles Sutherland to be a crude man with a debatable style of lovemaking. She had walked in on him when he was in full fettle with a couple of whores, all naked on the carpet in the main room. It was an innocent mistake on her part, as it was all quiet and they were hidden by the sofa. Upon seeing her, he had stood up, waved his insignificant wares at her and demanded that as he was her meal ticket, she had better strip off straight away and join in the fun.

The whores thought it was hilarious, but Christy Nichols assumed it was because they were being paid. She realised they were tolerating the nasty and unpleasant man for the same reason as her.

It was another two days before the contract was signed, and Charles Sutherland had to come forward with what he knew. He was a troubled man, not because of what he knew, but because the proof was vague. *What did he really know?* he thought. Certainly, there was plenty of innuendo, some prominent names and some – if it were true – information that would embarrass the government, especially its senior members. That's all he had, and how the editor and her lesbian friend would take it, he wasn't sure.

He decided to deal with the issue when it arose. In the meantime, he intended to enjoy the luxury on offer. He would have preferred Christy Nichols, the prudish prick-teaser as he saw her, but as she'd refused to have anything to do with him – *he should have put her availability in the contract*, he thought – then he would get her to sign for the whores. There was time to while away, and he wasn't going to sit reading a book, drinking a cup of tea, for anybody.

Chapter 12

It had been a miserable trip to Worcestershire for Isaac, rain all the way and his speed had been reduced as a result. It was close to four hours before he pulled into police headquarters in Worcester, the principal city in the county.

Inspector June Brown greeted him warmly after he had waited for ten minutes in reception at the modern, clinical looking building.

'Isaac, it's good to see you.' It was then he remembered her from his police training days. Then she had been a brunette, slim, with a figure that all the young police cadets had lusted after.

'June, long time, no see.' It was clear that he was embarrassed.

'You've forgotten me already,' she said, half-serious, half-teasing.

'No, of course not.' He had not forgotten her. The others cadets may have lusted, but it was only he who had sated the lust. She had latched onto him in the second week of training, only to let him go when the training concluded.

'Isaac, it was a good time, and you helped me through, but that's the past.'

'I never forgot you.'

'Don't talk rubbish,' she joked. 'Two weeks, and I guarantee you were shacked up with another female charmed by your obvious attributes.'

'That's not true,' he protested, not sure if she was serious or not.

'Look at me,' she said. 'I'm married with two kids, and the body not as you remember. I married an accountant, not as charming as you, but you're not the settling-down kind. You weren't then, I suppose you still aren't.'

Isaac had to admit that she had changed. Back then in training, she had a figure that could only have been described as sensational. What he saw now was a very attractive woman, but

81

the weight had gone on, and the face had aged. He assumed he had changed as well, but he thought it could not be as much as her.

'Three,' he said.

'Three what?'

'Three weeks.'

'Okay, I was out by a week, but what woman is going to resist a man like you? You were gorgeous to women back then, still are. Am I correct?'

'I'm not sure about that, but so far I've not settled down. Tried to. A couple have moved in with me, or I've moved in with them, but it's not seemed to last for long.' He wondered if Jess O'Neill might be the one. He discounted the thought. He inwardly smiled, when he thought of the passionate embrace and the kiss when he had left her the last time.

With so much history between them, June and Isaac spent the next hour chatting about their lives. It was June who finally brought them back to the present situation.

'What's important about this woman?' she asked.

'I'm not sure I can tell you. Besides, I don't know too much myself.'

'I suppose it doesn't matter.' She resigned herself to the fact; she knew him well enough not to press for more.

'It's a directive from senior management to find this woman.'

'I know who she is, of course. The sad life of a married woman and mother, when watching the television becomes a nightly highlight.'

'It comes to us all, I suppose,' he said.

'Suburbia and raising a family has its drawbacks. I'm not complaining, though.'

Isaac felt the need to change the subject. She had become melancholy; better to focus on the missing woman. 'We know Marjorie Frobisher's phone was used there.'

'Are you certain she was though?'

'Cameras, surveillance, security may have picked her up.'

'I've already had someone looking at any there, although it's not London. There will not be so many. How long are you staying?'

'Until I get some answers on her whereabouts.'

'Good, then you can come over to the house for a meal one night.'

Isaac replied in the affirmative, but sitting down with the husband of a woman he had known intimately did not sit well with him. He would endeavour to steer away from the subject if it came up again.

The assumption that a camera would have picked up Marjorie Frobisher proved not to be so accurate. There were cameras in the banks, the hotels, even some of the shops, but relatively few of them kept the tapes for more than a couple of weeks. The stores were interested in shoplifters, and if none had been apprehended, then there was no reason to keep the record.

At the end of the first day, Isaac was anxious to get on with the task. So far, he had spent more time at the hotel than at police headquarters. It was not a case of avoidance, but the invitation to dine with the husband of a former lover continued to unsettle him.

'June, this invite to your house,' he tentatively broached the subject at the office the next day. There had been some developments in the case, but before she told him, he wanted to clear the air, state his position.'

'Tonight, at eight, come casual; my husband is looking forward to meeting you.'

'I'm not sure I can come.'

'Why?'

'It's a little embarrassing.'

'Isaac, what do you mean?'

'Our past history.'

'How quaint,' she replied, mocking him with fluttering eyelids and a coy smile.

'I'm not sure your husband would want a past lover in his house.'

'You mean the man who took my virginity.'

'Did I?'

'Of course you did, and as to being embarrassed, do you think I never slept with another man before I married my husband? I lived with his best man for six months before I started going out with him. It was even mentioned in the wedding speeches. Everyone thought it was hilarious.'

'If you're certain it's alright.'

'Of course it's alright. Anyway, you wanted an update.'

'What have you found?'

'Marjorie Frobisher stayed at one of the hotels in Malvern. She had a wig on and her face concealed. The receptionist at the hotel identified her, recognised her even, although she didn't like it and left soon after. She used a false name.'

'Any ideas after that?'

'That's all there is. As to where she went?'

'You don't know?' Isaac asked.

'All the receptionist could tell us was that she took a taxi to Worcester. The driver dropped her off at the railway station. From there she could have gone anywhere.'

Isaac's time in Worcester was at an end. It was not the function of a detective chief inspector to find out where the woman had gone. He realised they needed more help in the office.

He had only one more obligation. June Brown's husband proved to be an excellent host, the meal was perfect, and the wine that Isaac had taken, ideal. His premonition about how awkward the situation would be was ill-founded. He left for London early the next morning.

***

Isaac arrived back before eight in the morning. He had purposely left early to avoid the traffic. Not that it made any difference, as there was early morning fog on the motorway. For half the distance his speed was almost down to a crawl. It was four and a half hours of stop-start driving. Meeting up with a past lover had left him reminiscing. He felt the need of a woman. Sophie would almost certainly come over that night if he gave her a call.

He had barely walked into the office – Farhan was already there – when his phone rang. 'You've heard the news?' It was his detective superintendent on the other end.

It was evident from Richard Goddard's tone that there had been a development. 'What's happened?' Isaac could see that an early get-together with Sophie was looking unlikely.

'We've got a suspicious death.'

'Marjorie Frobisher?' Isaac asked.

'It's her brother. I heard ten seconds before you walked in,' Farhan said.

'I didn't know she had a brother,' Isaac said.

'The fictitious one.' Richard Goddard seemed excited.

'Billy Blythe?'

'That's right. The actor who played him, Charles Sutherland.'

'Do we have any details?' Isaac asked.

'Vague at the present moment. The body was found twenty minutes ago, at his hotel.'

'I need to be over there with DI Ahmed,' Isaac said.

'The local police will be taking control.'

Isaac and Farhan left the office soon after. Isaac mulled over how this impacted on the missing woman but kept it to himself. He was still tired from the drive, and not in the mood to indulge in random conversation with Farhan, who looked excited, but distant.

The trip to the Savoy Hotel took twenty minutes. It was one of the best hotels in town, and Charles Sutherland's suite was one of the best. The media was already setting up on the street outside. He intended to find out how the information regarding a minor celebrity had been leaked. It was regarded as a suspicious death, not a murder, and definitely not a free-for-all.

'Farhan, what's the matter?' Isaac realised that something was troubling his colleague.

'It's my wife. She moved out, took the children.'

'When was that?'

'This morning, when I left the house early.'

'But why?'

'The normal. How I love my job more than her. How the children never see me.'

'Doesn't she realise how important our work is?'

'She's not rational. Mind you, if I had told her who the body is, then maybe she would have changed her mind.'

'It's hardly the basis for marriage, the machinations of a soap opera.'

'Agreed, but she's like so many others.'

'What do you mean?'

'The separation of fact from fiction.'

'I need you here now.' Isaac realised that Farhan should be dealing with personal issues, but now there was a real case. He could not let him take time off.

'I know, and besides, this is where I want to be.'

How many times had he heard it? Isaac thought. *No wonder the marriage breakdown rate is so high when the spouse and the family become the lesser priority.* He knew that Sophie was just a woman to spend time with, but Jess O'Neill may want a different kind of commitment, a commitment he was unable to give.

Downstairs, the hotel looked calm. Guests were checking in, checking out. The cafes and the restaurants were open; the people appeared to be oblivious to the death upstairs. How they could avoid the melee of media outside, he was not so sure, but some were probably used to media intrusion. He recognised a few famous faces as they moved through the foyer.

His train of thought was abruptly interrupted as they exited the lift on the top floor.

Outside the lift door, a well-presented fresh-faced police constable in uniform intercepted them. 'Sirs, this area is closed off.'

'Detective Chief Inspector Cook and Detective Inspector Ahmed,' Isaac said as they both presented their identification badges.

Clearing the first obstacle, they walked to where the constable had directed them.

'Yes, what can I do for you?' A tall, red-faced man, who, at least to Farhan, looked in need of a healthy diet, stood in their way as they entered Charles Sutherland's suite.

'Homicide and Serious Crime,' Isaac said.

'Sergeant Derek Hamilton, Charing Cross Police Station.'

'Good to meet you, Sergeant. I'm DCI Cook. My colleague is DI Ahmed.'

'I'll need to see your IDs, gentlemen.'

'Fine,' the sergeant said, after checking. 'Forensics is already here.'

It was clear that guests on either side of Sutherland's suite were being moved out, their luggage visible in the corridor.

'Inspector Barry Hopkirk. Pleased to meet you.' Isaac instinctively did not like the man on introduction. He appeared to be in his fifties. He wore an ill-fitting suit, crumpled as if he had slept in it, a tie skewed to one side.

Isaac saw no reason for subtlety. 'Is moving the other guests' luggage standard procedure?'

Hopkirk, a man with a short fuse, immediately went on the offensive. 'Is that a criticism?'

'This man's death is regarded as suspicious.'

'That may be, but when we arrived, there was only a dead body.'

'You're moving guests and their luggage off the floor. Have they been interviewed, checked for a possible weapon?'

'We've got their names; they're not exiting the building, only changing rooms. Besides, there's no sign of a weapon being used,' Hopkirk said.

'That may be, but have you considered that they may be involved?' There were clearly set down procedures in the case of a suspicious death, and Hopkirk was not following them.

'There was nothing suspicious when we arrived.'

'The Savoy Hotel, a former television celebrity. You don't think that's suspicious?'

'I'm not aware of his importance.'

'Charles Sutherland. Famous actor. Are you telling me that you have never heard of him?'

'I never made the association. All I saw was a dead body.'

'What do you have here?'

'Forensics will bring you up to speed. They're inside with the body. And make sure you put on footwear protectors,' Hopkirk said.

Isaac and Farhan moved to the room where the body had been found. 'Who is the crime scene examiner in charge here?' Isaac asked.

'Who's asking?' The reply came from a small man, bent over examining the body. He wore a white coverall, his hands gloved.

'Detective Chief Inspector Isaac Cook.'

'Give me a couple of minutes, and I'll be with you.'

The dead man was naked and sprawled on the floor. It was not a pleasant sight, as the victim was clearly overweight, verging on obese. It was clear from the faeces that his bowels had relaxed.

'Nasty business,' the small man said as he came over and shook hands with Isaac and Farhan. He had removed his gloves first, thrown them into a plastic bag. He was short, ridiculously short, and Isaac had to angle his neck down to look into his face, although mainly saw the top of his head. 'Gordon Windsor,' he said.

'I don't see any sign of violence,' Farhan said.

'And you won't.' The crime scene examiner spoke with a Welsh accent. He talked slowly. Isaac thought it might be a way of controlling a stutter.

'Why not?' Farhan asked.

'Poison.'

'How did you know it was murder?'

'I didn't. Hopkirk did.'

'I just blasted him out,' Isaac said.

'That may be, but he came here due to a death at the hotel. Apparently, standard procedure at the Savoy to call the local police when there's a death.'

Isaac realised that he may have been a little harsh on Hopkirk. If that proved to be the case, he would apologise later.

'How did Hopkirk figure it was murder?' Isaac asked.

'The body lying on the floor, the drooling, the defecation. He can tell you better than me, but my understanding is that he came here for a dead body, and then he found out about the wild parties and wondered if it was drug-related, overdose or something similar.'

'What did he find?'

'Cocaine, but not much else – certainly not enough to cause death. That's when he looked around, found clear evidence of poison.'

'Careless to leave the evidence here,' Farhan said.

'Careless or disturbed? I've no idea. That's for you to find out,' Gordon Windsor said as he removed his coveralls and picked up his bag. 'For me, it's to get the body back to the morgue, deal with Forensics and then write a report. It's going to be a long night. Wedding anniversary, I was going to take my wife out for a meal at an excellent restaurant. Curiously, the restaurant downstairs, just off the foyer. Hopefully, she'll understand.'

'Will she?' Farhan asked.

'She's used to it. She'll pretend to be upset, but she'll be fine.' Farhan could only reflect on why his wife was not as sympathetic, but he assumed that Gordon Windsor did not have a mother-in-law constantly in his wife's ear.

Chapter 13

With the crime scene examiner's departure, and Inspector Barry Hopkirk a little friendlier after Isaac had apologised to him, Isaac and Farhan returned to their office. Farhan could clearly see long hours on the case. He knew it would not help with his marriage. He had a job to do, a family to provide for, whether his wife liked it or not, and being miserable and moping around was going to solve little. He decided to snap out of it and get on with the job.

'This changes the situation,' Isaac said.

'The question is whether it's related to Marjorie Frobisher,' Farhan replied as he sipped his coffee. It was a little too hot for him.

'What do we know about Charles Sutherland? Could this be unrelated?'

'Possibly.'

'If it is linked, then you know what this means.'

'What did he know?'

'Or who was he?' Farhan put forward another possibility.

'What do you mean?'

'How did he get to know of anything worth selling? It's not as if Marjorie Frobisher went around the production lot sounding off to anyone in earshot. There's also the animosity between them.'

As expected, DS Goddard was soon in their office. 'Is it clearly murder?' he asked.

'There's a strong possibility,' Isaac replied.

'Not confirmed?'

'The crime scene examiner will let us know when the autopsy has been conducted, as well as keep up updated on the toxicology analysis on the contents of the bottle.'

'The poison was in a bottle?'

'That's what we are led to believe.'

'If it's a confirmed murder, then we'll need to set up a Murder Investigation Team.'

'We've just been discussing this,' Farhan said. 'We could do with the help, sir.'

'Isaac, you'll be the senior investigating officer. Is that okay with you?' the detective superintendent asked.

'Fine, sir.'

'Now, what do I tell my contact? He's bugging me for information.'

'Downing Street?'

'Isaac, it's best if you don't pry too much into my contacts.'

'What do you know?' Isaac asked.

'Not a great deal, other than Marjorie Frobisher would be better off dead, but the murder of Sutherland? That's another situation altogether.'

'There has been no connection made between the disappearance of one and the murder of the other,' Isaac said.

'Then make the connection,' the detective superintendent replied.

'And you, sir?' Farhan asked.

'I'll see what I can find out.'

'You'll talk to your contact?' Isaac asked.

'This afternoon. He wants an update. Give me what you can before then.'

Sophie messaged soon after Goddard had left the office. Isaac replied that it was not possible. She messaged back 'understood', which with her it was.

Farhan had received news that his children were at school and fine.

Isaac decided to travel out to the production lot. It was a murder unless confirmed otherwise, which seemed unlikely. For whatever reason, the people he had interviewed needed to be re-interviewed, including Jess O'Neill.

Farhan headed back to the hotel.

***

If they were aware out at the production lot that one of their former stars had met an untimely death, it was not apparent. The place was a hive of activity. Every time that Isaac had been out there in the past, it had been towards the end of the day or early morning.

The end of the day, they were invariably looking through the day's filming or else finalising the script for the next day's shooting. Early morning, the production people were still in the offices, and the cast were in their dressing rooms. This time, it was just after two in the afternoon. Isaac had been on the go since three in the morning and he was starting to feel a little weary. He knew it would pass once he started interviewing the people again.

He saw Jess O'Neill from a distance. He could see her arguing with someone, but then that was her job, and apparently she was good at putting people in their place, getting what she wanted.

Richard Williams was at the production lot. It seemed unusual to Isaac. He decided to talk to him first. He waylaid him as he walked swiftly towards the central offices. Isaac was well aware that Williams had seen him and had been trying to get out of his way. To Isaac, it was a red rag to a bull. He quickened his pace and caught up with Williams just as he opened the door to the first office.

'Mr Williams.'

'Now is not an ideal time.' Richard Williams said, catching his breath. He was not as young as Isaac, not as fit, although that didn't stop him when it came to chasing the women. Sally Jenkins was nowhere to be seen, but Isaac assumed she was back in the office in the city. *No reason to bring the end of the day bit of fluff out to the production lot*, Isaac thought. Richard Williams was always on the prowl, and the production lot would be a good place to look for a new conquest. There were invariably some extras hired for the day. The pretty, young, and female would be easy prey for someone as suave as Williams. Isaac had noticed the Ferrari when he parked his car.

'It's important.' Isaac replied.

'You're here about Charles Sutherland, I assume?'

'You've heard?'

'It's all over the media. They say he's been murdered.'

'There has been no official confirmation.'

'I'll take your word on that. The media will beat anything up.'

'Officially, the death is regarded as suspicious.'

'Suspicious! That's as good as saying he's been murdered.'

'Not at all,' Isaac replied. 'A well-known person is found dead in a hotel room. There has to be an autopsy and an official investigation. That does not mean murder, or not to the police.'

'It certainly does to the media; you must know that by now.'

'In the short time that I have been involved in the Marjorie Frobisher case, I have formed a greater understanding of how the media works: hyperbole, innuendo, assumption, and clever wording.'

'Yes, you've picked it up. Marjorie Frobisher, is that murder as well? I didn't know you had found her body.'

'I need to be careful what I say. Marjorie Frobisher is still declared as missing and there is not a corpse. Is that clear enough?'

'Clear enough. Unless you have anything more to talk about, I'm busy.'

'Why are you here?' Isaac asked.

'I had to get out of the office; too busy down there with the media. The phone's ringing off the hook. I needed some space and time to work out an appropriate response to his death. Some carefully crafted words on how sorry we are to lose such a great actor in the prime of his life. Those sorts of words.'

'A truthful reflection on the passing of such a great man,' Isaac said sarcastically.

'A pain in the arse, a lousy actor, and no great loss. Is that what you expect me to say?'

'You and I need to talk.'

'Give me fifteen minutes while I draft a statement. I'll give it to the scriptwriters to tidy up the grammar.'

'Thirty minutes. Fine,' Isaac replied. He headed to the coffee machine. Seated next to a window, the sun shining in, his tiredness finally caught up with him.

'Isaac, Isaac.' He woke with a start.

'Jess,' he said, bleary-eyed.

There was no one around; she attempted to kiss him. He pulled away.

'Sorry, Jess. I don't want to be rude, but the situation has changed.'

'Charles Sutherland?'

'You've heard?'

'Who hasn't,' she said. To Isaac, she was a vision of loveliness. The sun was shining in through the window, the blouse she was wearing, delicate and almost transparent. He felt as though he wanted to grab her there and then and seduce her, but knew he could not.

'I'm here in an official capacity now.'

'He was murdered?'

'It's still listed as suspicious, but it looks that way.'

'I'm sorry that he's dead.' She seemed sincere.

'I thought you argued with him?'

'That's what happens when the pressure's on.'

'Richard Williams wasn't much concerned. Does that surprise you?'

'Not really. He's a bastard, anyway. He only cares about number one.'

'Capable of murder?'

'Richard, no way. As long as he gets plenty of frivolous women to lay, then he's harmless. Tough businessman, good at his job, but murder? I don't think so.'

'You seem to care about Sutherland's death.'

'He was actually an excellent actor.'

'That's not the impression I get around here.'

'Professional prejudice, that's all that is.'

'So why do you say he was an excellent actor?'

'Simply because he was. His problem was his attitude. Sure, he wasn't major movie star great, but in the theatre, he would have been.'

'I thought he failed in theatre, and this was his last stop before the rubbish heap.'

'It was. He did have some failings though. I'm afraid Charles Sutherland was his own worst enemy. His decline was inevitable, but...'

'Not his death.' Isaac completed the sentence.

'Why would anyone want to murder him?' she asked. Isaac had completely forgotten about his arranged meeting with Richard Williams.

'I don't know. Do you have any ideas?'

'Not really. He could be a nosey bugger, always sticking his nose in, listening at keyholes.'

'Is he likely to have heard anything?'

'It's possible.'

'That's for me to find out. Anyone else I should talk to?'

'Not really. He certainly had nothing on me.'

'Is there anything I should know?' Isaac realised he had weakened. His reply was perilously close to personal concern.

'Nothing that you need to worry about.' Sensing the moment, she moved closer to him. He failed to move away. She kissed him on the cheek.

Isaac had yet again failed in his attempt to maintain a purely professional relationship with Jess O'Neill. He left soon after.

What is it about her? he thought as he drove away from the production lot and back to the office. *Why do I keep doing this?*

***

'I've been sacked.' These were the first words to emanate from Christy Nichols on Farhan's return to the hotel. Farhan and Isaac had not spoken to her on their first visit – they had left that to Inspector Hopkirk.

'You'd better explain,' Farhan said as he sat down on the chair in her room. Not as good as Charles Sutherland's by far, he noted.

'It's for the hired help when the rich and famous come to stay.' She had observed him looking around the room.'

'And you were the hired help?'

'He thought I was more than that.'

'What do you mean?' He could see she had been crying.

'I found him out on the street. Have they told you that?'

'No one's told me anything.' Farhan had a basic understanding of the situation, in that the tab for the room was being picked up by a magazine, one of the magazines that his wife liked to read.

'I intended to write an article for the magazine. In fact, any magazine that would buy it from me.'

'What sort of article?'

'Lightweight, the type that most people want to read. Anything to do with fallen celebrities is good copy; makes us all feel a little more human, I suppose. If it can happen to them, then maybe the reader's imperfect life is not so bad after all.'

'You mean those that are no longer in the limelight?'

'That's it. Charles Sutherland was a big star, at least in the UK, and then all of a sudden he disappears from sight. After they had kicked him off the programme, he was visible on a few television chat shows, but that didn't last long.'

'What happened to him?'

'It's not what happened to him, more likely what he did to himself.'

'I'm not sure I follow.' Farhan was enjoying his time with Christy Nichols. The setting and the woman were too pleasant. He stood up, moved to the window and looked out over the panorama of London.

'He had been fired. He had plenty of money, so what does he do?'

'Saves it for a rainy day?' Farhan knew the remark was incorrect.

'Not our Charles Sutherland. He's out partying, sometimes at his place, sometimes in the various clubs around town where the drugs are available and the women are costly.'

'He blew all the money?'

'In record time, and then his landlord dumps him on the street. Throws him a couple of bags with clothes that can't be sold second-hand, and there you have it – the fallen celebrity.'

'And you were going to write a story about him?'

'Not only him. There are a few more out there.'

'Did you find the others?'

'I know where a few are supposed to be, but I found Sutherland first, and then he gives me this story about Marjorie Frobisher.'

Farhan, his interest piqued, sat down again close to her. He noticed the smell of her perfume. He got up again and sat in another seat, this time more uncomfortable. 'What story is that?'

'He knew things about her that would rock the nation, bring down the government, and so on.'

'Did you believe him?'

'I wasn't sure what to think. He seemed to know facts not commonly known. He appeared to know a lot about Marjorie Frobisher.'

'What sort of things?'

'Past lovers, some prominent. He also alluded to something more significant.'

'Her personal life is not that well hidden,' Farhan said.

'It is to her fans.'

'The magazine puts him up in the Savoy, supplies him with whatever he wants – purely on the basis that he knows a few names?'

'Yes.'

'It seems very generous. Are these names important?'

'According to him, they are.'

'You don't know the names?'

'The magazine editor may. She's the one who agreed to pay for all this. She even picked up the bills for the prostitutes.'

'Many of them?'

'A couple that I signed for. I suppose they would be called escorts, but they performed the same function as any woman off the street.'

'The women were here?'

'On a couple of occasions. The hotel complained, but I managed to smooth it over. It cost extra money, but Sutherland said for the magazine to pay or he was walking.'

'Walking where?'

'Another magazine. If what he had was dynamite, he could sell it with no trouble. He knew that.'

'Smart man?'

'Foul habits, but he knew how to negotiate. Yes, I would say he was smart.'

'You didn't like him?'

'Not at all. Not that I would kill him, though. He was my meal ticket out of freelancing into a responsible and steady position, but he could make me feel dirty.'

'You alluded to that before.'

'He thought I was paid for as well. I couldn't tell him that I found him morally reproachable and that I wished he was still in the gutter.'

'You could, and then you would be out of a job.'

'That's right.'

'Could one of the women have killed him?'

'Do you see that as likely?' she asked.

'I would have thought not. They typically perform their function, take the money, and leave.'

'I never saw anyone else in the room, but I wasn't watching all the time. It's possible, I suppose. Prostitutes murdering clients seems a little far-fetched.'

'I agree it does,' Farhan said, 'but someone was here, and subject to confirmation, someone administered the poison. We need to find these women and check out their alibis.'

Chapter 14

After leaving Christy Nichols, Farhan headed over to the company that had been supplying the women for Charles Sutherland. Located in a modern office block not far from Tower Bridge, it did not look to be the sort of place to provide prostitutes, but as Marion Robertson explained, 'We supply escorts of the very highest quality, not street-walkers. Our women are educated, beautiful, and articulate.'

'But they are available for sex?' Farhan needed to clarify.

'If that is what the client wants.' Marion Robertson was a stunner. Farhan, with an awkward wife, found solace in her presence. Christy Nichols had not been calming, quite the opposite. Marion Robertson was in her early forties, he assumed. Still slim and exceedingly attractive.

'What else would they want them for?'

'Escorts. I believe the name says it all. Some men need a date, someone to take to a function. Sometimes that is all they want.'

'It seems unusual.'

'Not at all. Rich men sometimes crave the company. They may have passed the age of wanting to screw every woman they can lay their hands on. Their wealth may have come at a cost, especially if they had started with no money.'

'What do you mean?' he asked. He noticed her mobile phone. The case appeared to be gold.

'The phone?' She had seen him glance at it.

'It looks expensive.'

'It is. A grateful client.'

'Exceedingly grateful.'

'Please, don't misunderstand,' she said. 'Not for services rendered by me. One of my girls spent a couple of weeks with him. It was just a way of showing his gratitude.'

'You mentioned before that wealth comes at a cost.' He returned to an earlier question.

'Some men, in the climb to succeed, dispense with relationships, others suffer broken marriages, others take advantage and marry a twenty-something bimbo. At a certain age, they find they need the company of a woman, but not the long-term hassles and not always the sex.'

'And the person who gave you the phone was one of them?'

'Yes. Exceedingly wealthy, obscenely, in fact. To him the cost was negligible. He was in his early seventies, and while still an attractive man, he had no need of a nymphomaniac blonde. The woman I supplied was in her late forties, highly educated, and fluent in several languages. It was her company he wanted, not a quick lay.'

'He didn't sleep with her?'

'He may have; I didn't ask.'

'Charles Sutherland. I don't think he was either rich or attractive.'

'With him, it was pure sex,' she said. 'Perverse, threesomes – that sort of thing.'

'What kind of women did he like?'

'Early to mid-thirties, stunning, not skinny and flat-chested.'

'You're able to supply that type of woman?'

'The two I sent him were exactly what he wanted. One was a housewife making some extra cash on the side. Not sure if her husband knows, probably not. The other one was single and into casual sex. She works in the city somewhere, or maybe she doesn't. I don't ask too much about their private lives. I ensure that I don't become too friendly with them.'

'More like an employment agency than a supplier of women for hire.'

'You seem not to approve of what I am doing here,' she said.

'That is not the issue here, is it? Charles Sutherland is, and the women you procured for him.'

'Procured, such an unpleasant term,' she said. 'It sounds illegal, and there is nothing illegal about what we do here. The women come of their own free will. They are not coerced in any way. The only requirements I have are that they are medically certified with a clean bill of health, and if I set up an appointment for them, they keep that appointment. Also, if they negotiate another meeting with the client, they inform me, and I receive my commission.

'Any problems with difficult clients?'

'Rarely. On the first meeting with a new client, I have a man who takes them to the meeting and brings them back. The woman also has a panic button if there's an issue. It's happened once in the last three years.'

'Charles Sutherland, what else can you tell me about him?'

'Not a lot. I never met the man.'

'I need to contact the women.'

'I can't let you do that. They do their job, go home. Their private lives are sacrosanct.'

'At this present time, we regard Charles Sutherland's death as a possible murder. I could get a court order – even a police car to deliver it to their front door on a Saturday morning, flashing light as well.'

'I understand.' She came forward, touched him on the knee. He felt a tingling sensation go through his body. 'Is there an alternative?' she asked.

'I could meet them at a neutral location, but I'm not sure how I can keep them out of the limelight indefinitely, especially if there is a murder trial.'

'I will set it up. Give me a couple of days. One of the women has a husband and two children. She does it for them. Don't you think they will be harmed if her activities are revealed?'

'I will do all I can to keep her and the other woman out of the courts and the news,' Farhan said.

***

Isaac needed an update on how Charles Sutherland came to be sprawled naked on the floor of a hotel room. Gordon Windsor, the crime scene examiner, had alluded to a suspicious death.

Isaac knew that the suspicious death of a celebrity would require a full autopsy. He also knew that would take time, weeks possibly. An interim evaluation and the entire Murder Investigation Team could be mobilised. Gordon Windsor was his best bet for an update. He phoned him.

'I'll be in your office in an hour,' the man replied.

In one hour, almost to the minute, he walked into the room. He was as Isaac remembered him at the crime scene, only this time he was dressed in a suit, his hair combed over to hide a bald spot.

'Gordon, give us the facts without the jargon,' Isaac said. Farhan was also in the office.

'The poison was administered in a drink,' Windsor said.

'Any sign of drugs?' Farhan asked.

'Cocaine, but it did not kill him. There was more alcohol than drugs in his system.'

'What type of poison?' Isaac asked.

'Arsenic. It's tasteless, odourless, and colourless. It was used to kill rats in the past.'

'Is it a subtle method of killing a person without it being discovered?' Farhan asked.

'Subtle, yes. The risk of it being discovered is minimal.'

'But you found it?'

'The toxicologist did. Mind you, that's only the initial analysis of the bottle found at the scene. How much was in his body, and whether it was the sole cause of death, will not be known until the autopsy report comes in.'

'Then it's a murder investigation?' Farhan asked.

'Unless advised to the contrary, that would be correct,' Gordon Windsor replied. 'They used to call it the inheritor's powder.'

'What do you mean?' Isaac asked.

'Favoured poison of women in the nineteenth century. Sprinkled in small amounts on the husband's food over a period of time and a guaranteed death, totally undetectable.'

'And today?'

'Forensics will pick it up. Only one issue, though.'

'What's that?'

'Normally a person cannot be killed with a single dose.'

'Why?'

'A sufficient dose usually causes the person to vomit.'

'But you consider it murder?'

'Vomiting is not automatic. If he had been drunk and spaced-out, he might have kept it down for long enough.'

'Are you indicating the murderer may not have known this?' Isaac asked.

'It seems possible, but they must have known that a well-known celebrity found dead in a famous hotel and in apparently good health would be subject to an autopsy.'

'Would they?' Isaac put the possibility forward.

Gordon Windsor thought for a moment. 'If it was a professional hit, they would have known.'

'Are you saying this was not a professional assassination?' Farhan asked.

'I'm purely the scientist here. You are the detectives. What I am saying is, that if they were professional, they would have known there would be an autopsy.'

'And they would not have left a bottle in the kitchen with the poison in it,' Isaac said.

'Precisely, unless they were disturbed, but even that appears unlikely. Professionals don't put bottles in kitchen sinks in the first place. Normally, it would be coat pocket to drink and then back to coat pocket.'

Gordon Windsor left the office soon after.

Both Isaac and Farhan left a little later. It was five in the afternoon. Neither would be having an early night. Isaac, so far, had not caught up with Sophie, and he was feeling in need of her.

Farhan also felt the need, but he had no Sophie; in fact, no one except an empty house.

A Chinese restaurant close to the police station provided dinner. Prawn chow mein for Isaac; chicken for Farhan.

'We've assumed his death was related to Marjorie Frobisher,' Isaac said on their return to the office. 'Is that an assumption we can make?'

'What other option do we have?' Farhan replied.

'Which brings up another question. If Charles Sutherland was murdered to prevent him saying something to this magazine, then who else knows something? Is anyone else targeted for elimination?'

'How do we know?' Farhan replied. 'We only have assumptions.'

'Farhan, you're right,' Isaac said. 'I've still to meet up with Richard Williams. It is possible that he knows something.'

They were a good team, able to bounce ideas off each other, reach conclusions, formulate plans of action

'I thought you went to see him the other day.'

'He left the production lot before I had a chance to talk to him.'

'You're playing with fire,' Farhan said.

'I'm keeping my distance,' Isaac replied, a little indignant.

'No one is free of suspicion, you know that.' Farhan realised he had not been as diplomatic as he should have been, but Isaac was not only a colleague, he was a friend. As a friend, he was advising him to keep his distance from Jess O'Neill. He was sure Isaac would take his advice in the manner it was given.

***

Marion Robertson was not in a good mood when Farhan phoned the next day. 'My girls value their secrecy. I still regard this is an intrusion.'

'Marion.' Farhan knew that a degree of familiarity usually defused the tension. 'I understand your concerns, but I'm doing my job, and until told otherwise, your two women were the last persons to see Sutherland alive.'

'I understand, but they're blaming me for fixing them up with him.'

'From what you said, he paid his money, and they came to no harm.'

'That's correct, but the magazine is refusing to pay; probably afraid their reputation will be tarnished if it becomes known that they paid for prostitutes.'

'You've had non-payers before?'

'Of course, but I can hardly take them to court, can I? That will let all the cats out of the bag. Besides, I'll still pay the women.'

'Regardless of payment, I need to meet with these women. I'm trying to help you, but you will have to trust me.' Farhan said.

'I've already set up a meeting with one of the women for you. I'll send a photo. She uses the professional name of Samantha.'

'What's her non-professional name?'

'I'll let her give it to you if she wants.'

'Where will I meet her?'

'Hyde Park, close to Marble Arch. You'll find her at the entrance to the park. She'll be wearing a blue jacket. I'll send you a phone number so you can call her when you are there.'

'Time?'

'Midday, she works nearby. You can pretend to strike up a conversation with her, admire the flowers, whatever.'

'And the other woman?' Farhan asked.

'Tomorrow, but she is married and would prefer to stay that way. Her husband would probably not understand. He thinks she pays the mortgage on the money she earns working in an office somewhere.'

'You have to trust me on this. If they're not involved, then we will refer to them as X and Y,' Farhan said.

Chapter 15

The first thing Isaac noticed when he entered Richard Williams' office was that the lovely – available if you drove a Ferrari – Sally Jenkins was absent. In her seat sat another equally vivacious woman. She introduced herself as Linda. *Another rent-a-lay*, Isaac thought.

'Sally Jenkins, what happened to her?' Isaac asked as the new woman showed him into Williams' office. She hadn't been employed when Marjorie Frobisher had disappeared, and she was clearly another prick-teaser.

'I had to let her go,' Williams replied in an offhand manner. It wasn't a good enough explanation.

'It's important. Where has she gone?'

'I had to sack her.' A curt reply. Still not good enough.

'I need details. She may well be a material witness. I may need to talk to her again.'

'No doubt she will tell you the story. She started talking marriage and settling down, having a few children.'

'And you don't want that?'

'I'm still paying one silly bitch who managed to get me down the aisle. She made sure she was pregnant before we got that far. Still bleeding me for all she can. It takes my lawyers all their time to keep the situation under control. You're a tall, good-looking man, you must have similar issues?'

'True enough, but I only have a policeman's salary.'

'You're young, plenty of stamina. I need a good dose of Viagra to get going. They're with me for the money and the good life. Why can't they leave it like that?'

Isaac thought it was an honest answer. He had never regarded the women he bedded in such a manner, and he would never have spoken about them to other men. 'I need to talk to you about Charles Sutherland,' he said.

'How did he die?'

'Suspected poisoning.'

'Fine, it's a murder investigation now. I can't really avoid you anymore, or you'd have me in the back of a police car and down to the station for an all-night grilling.'

'A little melodramatic, wouldn't you say?' Isaac replied.

'A great storyline. The masses would love it, but as you say, a little melodramatic. But when has our programme been factual? Maybe once this is all over, we'll incorporate it into a storyline.'

'I would advise against it for now,' Isaac said. 'This is an official visit.'

'I know that. What happened to Marjorie? Any updates?'

'I'm not at liberty to discuss it. We are following up on various leads.' Isaac thought it a somewhat dumb response.

'You don't know where she is, correct?'

Isaac chose to ignore Williams' evaluation, unfortunately accurate. He returned to Charles Sutherland.

'Did anyone have a grudge against Charles Sutherland, a reason to want him dead?'

'A few, but murder? That's a whole different issue.'

'What do you mean?'

'A person's death may make certain people more comfortable, but killing that person…'

'Why do you say that?' Isaac realised Williams knew something.

'Murder and it's twenty-five years, hard labour, breaking rocks.'

'There are no rocks these days.'

'Yes, of course.' Williams picked up the phone to the outer office and asked the new PA to bring in some freshly brewed coffee. It gave him some time to think about what to tell the persistent policeman, and how much.

Five minutes later, and the latest plaything, who managed to give a good impression of being competent, entered and placed two mugs on the desk. She gave Isaac a pleasant smile as she left. He gave one in return. Sally Jenkins was clearly a prick-teaser, a wealthy man's entertainment. Isaac revised his earlier thoughts on the latest PA being the same, but then maybe he was biased – he fancied her for himself.

Isaac continued. 'I need you to tell who may have had an issue with Charles Sutherland.'

'I understand that. Where do you want me to start?'

'Just give me the details.' Isaac recognised procrastination. He thought it reasonable. Nobody likes dishing the dirt on someone else, and a murder enquiry always puts everyone on the defensive.

'Marjorie, obviously.'

'Why Marjorie?' Isaac knew there was mutual antagonism, but wanting someone dead indicated something more serious.

'He was always sticking his nose in, attempting to listen in on other people's conversations.'

'Is that a reason to want him dead?'

'For Marjorie, it would have been.'

'It is clear that you are not inclined to give an honest answer.'

'Confidentiality seems more important to me.'

'The seriousness of the situation demands your full compliance.'

'I know, but as the executive producer, I make it a habit to maintain the confidence of all the people that I am responsible for. As long as it's not criminal, then I don't care if they are adulterers, closet gays, incorrigible gamblers, or whether they cheat on their tax.'

'I can understand, but this is a murder enquiry. You know I could take you down the station for questioning.'

'Not without my lawyer, you couldn't. Okay, here's what I know. Sutherland had picked up some dirt on Marjorie, enough for her to be seriously worried, enough for her to come in here and demand his withdrawal from the programme.'

'You agreed?'

'I tried to reason with her, but she was adamant.'

'She threatened to walk out of the production?'

'No.'

'So why did you agree?'

'I ran it past the scriptwriters first to see how we could get rid of him.'

'Once you had a storyline, you let him go.'

'He was going anyway. Marjorie and I go back a long way.'

'I believe that has been mentioned before. Maybe you could elaborate.'

'Nothing sinister. We were both starting out. I saw myself as the great international news correspondent; Marjorie, the next great movie star.'

'Neither of you achieved your aims.'

'That may be the case, but we've both been successful.'

'It's hardly a reason to accede to her demands.'

'We lived together for nine months. The first great love for both of us, and we have helped each other over the years. Shoulder to cry on if needed. I would do anything for her.'

'You don't seem concerned that she is missing.'

'Marjorie, what could happen to her? She's a survivor, same as I am. She'll reappear when the time is right.'

'You seem remarkably confident.'

'I've known her for too long to believe that she has been murdered. And besides, what proof do you have?'

'Apart from a confirmed sighting.'

'Malvern? I knew about that.'

'Have you been withholding information?' Isaac raised his voice. *What else does Richard Williams know?* he thought.

'I'll rephrase. I assumed that was where she had gone. It was her hideout in the past. I have been there a few times in the past to meet with her.'

'Are you still maintaining a relationship with her?'

'You make it sound dirty. When she was upset, she would disappear for a few days. It didn't happen often, but she would always phone me, ask me to join her. She would do the same for me.'

'You slept with her?'

'When?'

'When you went to Malvern.'

'No, not at all. You don't understand. We have a lot of history. She knows about my skeletons, or most of them. I know about hers.'

'Is there something I should be aware of?'

'Charles Sutherland knew something. Believe me, I don't know what it was.'

'Enough to kill him?'

'I don't know. Everyone knew about Marjorie and her open marriage, and she could be a bitch, but murder!'

'Anger, dislike, and hatred gravitate to murder,' Isaac said.

'I've been too long in this business, too many scripts, not to know that administered poison is not a spur of the moment action. It's premeditated and by someone with knowledge of poisons.'

'You should have been a policeman.' Isaac had to admit the man was correct. 'Who else would *not* be sad about Sutherland's death.'

'I don't think you'll find anyone in mourning.'

'Anyone else who would have been pleased?'

'There's only one.'

'Who's that?'

'Jess O'Neill.' Isaac sat up straighter, which caused Richard Williams to offer a comment.

'I see that you know the lovely Jess.' Williams smiled. Yet again, Isaac severely embarrassed that he was allowing personal to interfere with professional.

'I've spoken to her a few times.'

'And found her delightful?'

'She is an attractive woman, I'll grant you that.'

'I tried it on when she first arrived.'

'I assumed you would have, but I'm led to believe it was not successful.'

'I even took her away to an exhibition up north. We went up in the Ferrari, best hotel, few too many drinks, but she wasn't swayed. Looking for love, I suppose.'

'Any hard feelings after that?' Isaac visibly relaxed at Williams' affirmation of what Jess had told him.

'Not at all, but be careful. You've got a murder investigation, and it's clear that you are attracted to her.'

'Why should I be careful?'

'Not in regards to Jess, but you're here on official business. It would not seem proper to show preferential treatment of one witness over another, would it?'

'I can assure you that our relationship is purely professional. Who else believes that we have a friendship?'

'Everyone out at the production lot; it's a great place for gossip.'

'Let's get back to why she would not be sad to see Charles Sutherland dead.'

'She's not told you?'

'I know she told him that his time on the programme was over, and he had responded with some choice words.'

'Stuck-up bitch, that sort of thing?' Williams said.

'That's about all I know.'

'I think you'd better talk to her again. It's more serious than that. Nobody out at the production lot knows – only me and maybe Sally Jenkins.'

'Why only you two?'

'Firstly, Jess came and told me, and secondly, Sally had a tendency to listen in to conversations.'

'What is it that Jess had against Charles Sutherland?'

'It would be best if it came from her.'

'Let me have your version first?'

'I'm afraid I cannot do that. It would not be helpful if I distorted or misinterpreted what she told me.'

'I'll grant you that. I need to see her as soon as possible.'

'Then I would suggest that you bring her in to the police station, sit her down and get her to explain. It may become an integral part of any future trial. Not against Jess, but against Sutherland.'

Chapter 16

The first of the two escorts was not difficult to spot. The entrance to Hyde Park, just across the road from Marble Arch, the designated meeting place. It had been a good choice as it was a bright and sunny day.

Farhan could not help but be struck by the woman's beauty. She was of medium height, full in the figure, not fat, dressed in what looked to him to be expensive clothes, and her shoulder length hair dark and full.

She had a pleasant smile when she came over to him and introduced herself. Farhan thought the smile was a veneer.

'I've taken time off work to come and meet you. Everyone thinks I'm at the dentist.'

'I hope I'm not as painful as all that,' he joked. He warmed to the woman, the embodiment to him of the ideal female. She appeared to have some Indian heritage, although her skin tone was light.

'It's not you. I have an image to maintain, and this man being murdered has put me in an awkward position.'

'Why?' he asked. They moved from the gate and strolled through the park. He was enjoying himself. She was nervous, but not as nervous as she had been when they first met.

'I work for Marion, but it's not the sort of thing you want your friends and family to know about, and certainly not in the office.'

'Where do you work?'

'I work with a legal firm, not five minutes' walk from here. I'm training to be a lawyer.'

'Why the escort work?'

'It pays well. Life is expensive. A junior in a legal office doesn't get paid much.'

'Is it purely money?'

'Not altogether, but it's a large part of it.'

'What's the other part?'

'I like sex.' It was an unexpected admission.

'The men can't always be pleasant,' he said.

'It's a balance. Most of the men are ageing but generous. I make sure they enjoy themselves. You don't know what kind of an aphrodisiac the money is.' It seemed to Farhan the words were spoken as a defence mechanism.

'Charles Sutherland. I am under the impression that he was not a particularly pleasant man.'

'I remember him. He was into threesomes, and he liked some lesbian play before. He liked to sit and watch.'

'You had no problem with his watching?'

'Why should I? Law school is expensive, and I intend to get through with honours at least. Then I'll find myself a good position as a lawyer, corporate law. That's where the money is.'

'And escorting?'

'I'll stop as soon as I finish law school.'

'No regrets?'

'Of course not. You sound prudish. Do you disapprove?'

'As long as no one causes anyone harm, then I maintain a neutral view.' Farhan realised he had made a similar statement to Marion Robertson, the purveyor of women such as Samantha.

'My family would disown me.'

'Then why take the risk?'

'I see nothing wrong with what I do.' She failed to answer his question.

'Can we get back to Charles Sutherland?' Farhan had deviated from his questioning. He, like Isaac, was susceptible to the charms of a woman. With Isaac, they saw him as a stud. With him, they saw someone to mother.

Isaac would take advantage; he never had, at least not yet. He had made a decision. The purity and boredom of a loveless marriage did not compensate. He would protect the children, but as for his wife, he had no further use for her.

'I wouldn't say it was an enjoyable night,' she continued, 'or two nights, as we went back again. We provided the service, spent a few hours there, and left.'

'The night he died. Were you there?'

'Yes, but when we left he had a smile on his face. He was very much alive.'

'The other lady?'

'I only know her as Olivia. We don't talk about our private lives.'

'What time did you leave Sutherland's suite at the Savoy?'

'Just after midnight. I always check the time of departing.'

'Why's that?'

'I need to ensure that my parents are asleep when I get home. I don't want any awkward questions as I walk in the door.'

'You live at home?'

'A good Muslim girl. Yes, I do. I've shocked you again.'

'Too many years as a policeman. I've seen it all. I'm not easily shocked, but a good Muslim girl, a beautiful woman, acting as an escort...'

'My name's Aisha.'

'Your real name?'

'Yes. You will keep my involvement confidential?'

'That's what I promised Marion. I will make the same promise to you, although you must realise this may soon be out of my control.'

Unaware, they had walked some distance, further than expected, and found themselves on the other side of the park. In a flurry, late for an appointment, she hailed a taxi. 'Call me once this is over,' she shouted to him from the open window. 'We can meet as friends, have a meal.'

***

'I'm sorry about this, Jess.' Isaac, acting on information supplied by Richard Williams, had no option but to call her in. If it was, as Williams had suggested, 'important', then he had to follow police procedure; no longer an informal chat and a brief kiss.

'My client will only answer questions pertaining to Charles Sutherland.' She had brought along legal representation.

Isaac had phoned her before her official summons to the police station, advised her that it would be a good idea.

She had been taken aback initially but acquiesced when he had explained the situation. 'Vital evidence, evidence that may be used in court, needs to be given in the correct manner. It's best for you to come in, honestly answer the questions and clear the air.'

'I thought you were protecting me,' she had said.

'I still am. Believe me, this is the best way. We need to clear up a few accusations that have been made.'

'My dislike of Sutherland, is that it?'

'Please say no more. Come to the station in your own vehicle. Park it around the back, and no one will know you've been here.'

It was late in the afternoon when all the concerned people were present. Isaac conducted the formalities.

'This interview is being recorded and is being held in Interview Room 2 at Challis Street Police Station. I am Detective Chief Inspector Isaac Cook. Miss O'Neill, could you please introduce yourself.'

'Jessica O'Neill.'

'Detective Inspector Ahmed,' Isaac said.

'I am Detective Inspector Mohammad Farhan Ahmed.'

'Mr Wrightson.'

'I am Michael Wrightson, Solicitor, of Wrightson, Loftus and Evans.'

'The time, if we can agree, is 4.10 p.m. At the conclusion of the interview, Miss O'Neill, I will give you a notice explaining exactly what will happen to the tapes. Do you understand?'

'Yes.'

'Do you understand the reason for the interview?' Isaac asked.

'Yes,' she replied.

'Thank you. I would remind you that you're not under arrest, you need not remain here, and you are entitled to legal representation.'

Farhan sat alongside Isaac, facing Jess O'Neill's legal representative. Neither Isaac nor Farhan liked the look of him. He was a tall, slender man with pronounced features. The man spoke in a superior manner.

'Miss O'Neill, thank you for coming in.'

'I will answer all questions put forward, subject to my legal representative, Mr Wrightson, agreeing.'

'That is fine, Miss O'Neill,' Isaac responded.

'Please call me Jess.'

'Jess, it is,' Isaac replied.

She looked at Michael Wrightson. He nodded his head in affirmation and spoke to the microphone in the middle of the table. 'That is acceptable.'

'It is known that you argued with Charles Sutherland. Is that correct?' Isaac asked.

'Argued, yes, but it hardly seems relevant.'

'Why?'

She looked over at Wrightson before responding. He nodded his head. 'It's part of my job to maintain momentum, to put everyone in their place. It's a tight schedule on production days.'

'Are you saying that you only argued on production days?'

'I argue with a lot of people on production days, but nobody takes it seriously. Tensions are high, tempers are short, and some of the actors think they're major stars, worthy of preferential treatment, kid gloves.'

'Charles Sutherland. One of those?'

'Charles Sutherland and Marjorie Frobisher were the worst.'

'We will come to Marjorie Frobisher later.' Isaac realised he could not go too easy on her, and besides, Farhan was there as well. He could not be seen to be weak in front of his junior.

'My client is not sure where this is proceeding.' Wrightson felt the need to speak. 'Miss O'Neill has not been formally charged. Why is she here?'

'I am informed that Miss O'Neill had more than a dislike for Charles Sutherland. It has come to my knowledge that she had a hatred of the man.'

'That is not correct,' Jess protested.

'My client does not need to respond to that accusation,' Wrightson said. Isaac had had enough of the man; his input was obstructive.

'I am not asking Miss O'Neill to incriminate herself. I am purely giving her the opportunity to confirm her hatred for this man categorically and why. It is understood that there may have been reluctance before. The previous times that we spoke were unofficial and unrecorded. It is imperative that your client is entirely honest with us.'

Jess turned to Wrightson. 'Michael, what should I do?'

'May we halt this interview for five minutes,' Wrightson asked. 'I need to advise my client as to her legal position.'

'4.25 p.m. Interview with Miss Jessica O'Neill halted.'

'Thank you,' Wrightson said.

'I'll send in some coffee. Take as long as you like. We'll be outside.'

'Make it tea for me.' Jess managed a weak smile.

Isaac and Farhan left the room.

***

'Michael, what am I to do?' Jess turned to face Wrightson.

'You haven't done anything wrong.'

'I know, but it's a clear motive.'

'It will look worse if you don't speak now. DCI Cook, what's the situation with him?'

'I like him. He likes me. No more than that.'

'He seems to be going gentle on you. Did you sense it?'

'He seemed very rough to me.'

'I've been in these places before. He's trying to help. It would be best if you trust him with this information. I'm not only your legal representative, I'm also married to your sister. I'm

117

family. I suggest you state clearly the full story in your own time, make a statement.'

'Why? There was no one else there.'

'It always comes out. One day, when the pressure's on the police to wrap up the case, when they have a suspect in mind, you will let it slip. I just don't think you're a good enough actor not to let it out.'

'Not good enough for the soap I produce?'

'You may be good enough for that.'

'I will follow your advice.'

'Good. If they find out later that you lied here today, they will have a clear motive.'

'It is a motive, you know that,' Jess said.

'People have murdered for less.' Michael Wrightson hoped his sister-in-law had seen sense. He was sure she had.

***

Ninety minutes after exiting the interview room, Isaac and Farhan returned.

'Interview recommenced 5. 55 p.m.' Isaac said.

'My client wishes to make a statement,' Wrightson said. Isaac hoped it was not a confession.

'Miss O'Neill, you are aware of what you are saying?'

'Yes.'

'Then please commence.'

'Charles Sutherland was a thoroughly despicable man.'

'Why do you say that?' Farhan felt the need to speak. He could see why Isaac was drawn to her. Even in a moment of sadness, which was etched on her face, she was still lovely. He wanted to put an arm around her and tell her it wasn't all that bad.

'Please allow my client to make her statement,' Wrightson said.

'Charles Sutherland,' she repeated the statement from the start, 'was a thoroughly despicable man. I can only feel intense hatred towards him. His death did not cause me any sadness. On

118

the contrary, I was relieved and pleased to hear that he had met an unpleasant fate. The question as to why I feel relief, and why I hated him so much, is for me to explain.

'I came from a sexually abusive and violent childhood. It is something that I do not talk about. I do not want to speak about it now. On the advice of my legal representative, Michael Wrightson, who also happens to be my brother-in-law, I am making this statement. I am well aware that what I am about to tell you would form the basis for murder.

'I must state here and now, that I was not involved in the murder of this man, although the person who did kill him has my gratitude.

'As a child with a stepfather who treated the female children as his personal property for his obscene sexual gratification, I am well aware of what constitutes abuse and improper behaviour. My stepfather died when I reached the age of fourteen, early enough for me to forget the horrors of what he inflicted on me and my sister, Michael's wife. Even Michael does not know the full extent of what transpired in that evil house, and never will. My sister still suffers some lasting effects. For me, I have completely adjusted, never forgotten, but it has not caused me anguish since about my sixteenth birthday.

'Since then, there have been several men in my life, good men, who have always treated me with the greatest respect. Let me come to Charles Sutherland.

'Two weeks before his leaving the programme, I went to see him in his dressing room. It was late at night, sometime after 10 p.m. and I don't believe anyone else, apart from the two of us, were out at the production lot. I wanted to discuss his part and the script change for the next day. I would often do that with the other members of the cast, even with Charles Sutherland, so there was no reason for me not to go and see him.

'I found him in his room, drunk, from what I could see. I did not realise that he had been snorting cocaine until he became insistent that I take some with him. He was in an unusual mood, even for him.

'He became more demanding, trying to force me, attempting to grab me and to make me have a drink with him, to lighten up. I tried to leave the room, but he locked the door and put the key down the front of his trousers. He was baiting me to take the key from him. I was in a state, and at that moment, I saw my stepfather there. I kicked at him, attempted to hit him. I shouted at the top of my voice, but no one responded. The more I reacted, the more excited he became. I've seen him before in a similar situation, but now it was extreme, and I was on my own.

'He came at me, grabbed me by my shoulder and threw me on the ground. He ripped off my blouse, started fondling me, and all the time I was screaming. He tried to pull off my skirt, but I managed to take control of the situation and kneed him in the groin with all the force I could muster. He collapsed in agony. I quickly regained the key and left. That's the end of my statement.'

Nobody spoke for some time. Wrightson was the first. 'You must understand that what Miss O'Neill has told you is of great embarrassment to her. It is clear that she is distraught and should be excused from further questioning.'

'Agreed. Interview concluded at 6.20 p.m.' Isaac said.

Jess left in tears with Michael Wrightson supporting her. Isaac wanted to rush up to her, put his arms around her, and kiss her, but he did not.

'It's a good enough motive for murder,' Farhan said after she had left the building. Isaac did not answer.

Chapter 17

Angus MacTavish was not pleased when Richard Goddard phoned to make an appointment. He relented when told that confidentiality in relation to Charles Sutherland's death and Marjorie Frobisher could not be guaranteed. He was also concerned that she had been confirmed alive four weeks after her disappearance.

As usual, they met in MacTavish's office in Downing Street. 'Detective Superintendent, what have we got here?' MacTavish asked. He was not friendly.

'What do you mean?'

'This Frobisher woman still remains hidden from sight, and then we have a failed actor threatening to sound off to a magazine about something earth shattering. What's going on?'

'I think that is a question you could answer.'

'What do you mean? Are you suggesting I'm involved?'

'Not personally, but you know more than I do. You've admitted that much in the past.'

'Certainly, I know more than you. My requirement was to keep her quiet. We would never condone murder.'

'It's important that I receive more information.'

'I don't see that I am at liberty to give you much more.'

'Then I don't see how I can protect you or whoever you're trying to protect.'

Richard Goddard knew he was in treacherous waters. There was a promotion he wanted, and he was aware that getting on the wrong side of MacTavish, who answered to the prime minister, who was good friends with Commissioner Charles Shaw, the senior man in the Metropolitan Police, was not ideal.

'Detective Superintendent, of course you're right. Let's look at it from where I'm sitting. Sutherland's death may be totally unrelated. Correct?'

'Correct.'

'What sort of man was he?'

'Unpleasant, heavily into alcohol, recreational drugs and prostitutes, if he had the money.'

'Gambling?'

'Gambling as well, but that's taken us nowhere so far. We haven't found any evidence of anyone hassling him to pay up.'

'And if he's dead, he won't be paying anyway.'

'He was aiming to make a lot of money by selling his story. A gambling syndicate would wait their time before threatening him.'

'Then who killed him?'

'You mentioned the security services before.'

'I've checked with my contacts. They say it's not feasible. A kill would require paperwork. The official line is that it doesn't exist.'

'Do you trust them?'

'Not entirely.'

'The motive for killing Sutherland is still unclear.'

Angus MacTavish, at a loss on how to move it forward, excused himself from the office. A minute later, Mrs Gregory came through the door with a fresh pot of tea and some more biscuits. Richard Goddard teased her about his attempts to lose weight. She laughed, told him not to worry and left the room. It was thirty-five minutes before MacTavish returned. The detective superintendent had drunk all the tea in that time, looked out the window, and stroked the cat that had wandered in. He sensed the politician had been taking instructions.

'Sorry about that,' MacTavish apologised.

'Not a problem.'

'I told my superiors that I need to take you into our confidence.'

'They agreed?'

'Reluctantly. I've told them that you cannot find Marjorie Frobisher or solve Sutherland's murder without additional facts.'

'That's true.'

'There was a child,' MacTavish said.

'You mentioned this before.'

'The father is important, the child more so.'

'The child, does it know who its parents are?'

'Not yet, but it is trying to find out.'

'How old would this child be?'

'Late thirties, early forties.'

'Do you know who this child is?'

'No.'

'Do you know who the father is?'

'Yes.'

'Then where is the complication? Surely you can stop the child finding out.'

'It cannot be stopped for much longer.'

'What if the father made a public statement, acknowledged the errors of the past, embraced the child as part of his long-lost family?'

'It's more serious than that. I've told you as much as I can,' MacTavish said. 'Any more would place you and your people in a precarious position.'

'How about you?'

'I'm already compromised. I'm a marked man if this gets out.'

'And you don't really know what you are compromising?'

'I am aware that revealing the father will almost certainly bring down the government. Revealing the child is potentially catastrophic.'

'How serious?'

'My life for one, and I don't know the full details.'

'What do you want me to do?' Richard Goddard felt sympathetic towards Angus MacTavish; fear for himself and his team.

'Find out who killed Sutherland and find Marjorie Frobisher, dead or alive.'

'One more question. Does Marjorie Frobisher know who the child is?'

'It's possible.'

'Could it be why Sutherland was killed?'

'Yet again, it's unknown. My contacts think it's unlikely that he was murdered by an official assassin, but then again, who really knows?'

Detective Superintendent Goddard knew that telling Isaac and DI Ahmed was going to prove difficult. They needed to find Marjorie Frobisher, and they needed additional help.

***

Farhan had drawn the short straw. That was how he saw it when he met the editor of the magazine that had been paying Charles Sutherland's bill.

'I paid plenty out for him, including his whores. God knows why *that* Christy Nichols approved them.'

He had barely entered her office before she started with the invective, barely had a chance to introduce himself and explain the reason for his visit. A formal introduction, cut short, about how it was a murder investigation and that he would be recording the conversation.

He had set up the meeting for three in the afternoon. Her personal assistant had made it clear any earlier was not possible. He had reminded her that it was a murder investigation, and his demands had precedence over the magazine's deadline. The personal assistant made it clear that it was non-negotiable, and if he wanted to take it up with her boss, then he could. At the end of their conversation, she had quietly advised him that it was best not mentioned if he didn't want to be on the end of an ear-bashing.

As he sat there, increasingly agitated, listening to the editor, he heeded her personal assistant's words.

'What do you want to know? My time is precious.' Victoria Webster, the editor, as well-known on the television as off, was a tall woman, certainly taller than Farhan.

Close up he could see that the beautiful skin, wrinkle-free whenever she was on the television, was a result of the makeup people.

In the confines of the office, she spoke in an aggressive manner. On the television, a different persona with charm and decorum. Farhan realised that the woman that millions admired was no more than a street fighter, brought up on the street, fighting tooth and nail to be where she was, and she wasn't going back.

Her background was well-known. The illegitimate daughter of an Irish housemaid and a Roman Catholic priest. How she had risen from obscurity and despair in an austere orphanage. How she had put herself through university, worked three jobs to do it, and then at the age of twenty-two had joined the magazine. The first position, in the basement mail room, and after that, year after year, she had worked her way up the corporate ladder, until she occupied the top office, on the top floor, with the best view overlooking London, overlooking her loyal readers.

It was a good story, although not entirely accurate. Victoria Webster never intended the truth to get in the way of her ambition. Irish, she was, but it was middle-class suburbia and parents who were married. The orphanage after they had been killed in a car accident when she was eight years old, but it was not austere. University and the three jobs in part truthful, although the jobs were short-term. She was a brilliant student and many a student, and some lecturers, had succumbed to her charm and assisted in her financial viability, even sometimes with the reports and the papers she had to submit. The basement at the magazine, correct, but it was not all hard work. There was no doubt that she was brilliant at her job – the circulation attested to that fact – and her public persona was flawless, but the rise from the basement was in part due to competence and hard work, and in part due to her seducing whoever she needed to, invariably on the floor above. There were a few who, once seduced, found out that she had taken their job. She made sure that they were evicted from the building quickly, and with minimal fuss, with a generous redundancy package to ensure their silence. A few had tried to inform the owner of the magazine what she was, but he did not care as long as it was not illegal, and as long as she delivered the results.

'Miss Webster.' Farhan attempted to get a word in.

'Mrs Webster.'

'Mrs Webster, it is understood that you were willing to pay Charles Sutherland a substantial amount of money for information that he possessed, information you would print in your magazine. Is that correct?'

'That is correct.'

'I assume you are aware of the nature of this information.'

'Your assumption is incorrect.' She looked at her watch and glanced over at the man sitting next to her. She had not formally introduced him, other than to say that he was her legal adviser.

'Why is that?' Farhan asked.

'Mrs Webster is answering your questions in a spirit of goodwill,' Victoria Webster's legal adviser said.

'And you are?' Farhan had not come to Victoria Webster's office to be intimidated.

'My name is William Montgomery. I am the senior legal adviser for the magazine.'

Montgomery had been sitting on the far side of the editor's desk when Farhan had entered. Farhan thought it strange at the time that he had not risen to shake his hand. He then saw why. Montgomery was in a wheelchair.

'Mr Montgomery, Mrs Webster, I would like to remind you that this is a murder enquiry. It is fully understood that you may both be very busy, but my questions take precedence.'

'We realise that,' Montgomery said.

'Get on with it,' Victoria Webster said. 'I don't have all day for you two to have a social chat.' It was clear that Montgomery was in fear of his boss.

'This information, Mrs Webster?'

'How the hell would I know?'

'You wouldn't pay him until he had given it?'

'Do you think I'm stupid?'

Farhan found her an incredibly rude woman – nothing like her personal assistant who was sitting outside. He wondered how anyone could work for such a woman, but then with egregious abuse probably comes great reward for those who can handle the situation. Montgomery probably could, Farhan thought, even if he appeared to be a mild-mannered man, obviously under the controlling thumb of a difficult woman.

Farhan returned to the conversation. He chose to ignore the 'Do you think I'm stupid' comment. 'He may have been killed for that information. It may place you at risk. Have you considered that possibility?' It seemed to have the desired effect. Farhan hadn't considered it before, but it seemed plausible. Temporarily quietened, Victoria Webster sat down and whispered in the ear of her legal adviser.

'We would request a few minutes to discuss this, before Mrs Webster answers. Will that be acceptable?' Montgomery said in a more agreeable tone.

'Fine, I'll wait outside. Call me when you are ready.'

***

Outside the personal assistant organised coffee for Farhan and a sandwich. He reflected on his wife. *How is it that every woman I meet is exceedingly kind and generous to me, whereas she is hostile and unpleasant; everyone that is, apart from Victoria Webster?* he thought.

He decided to give the editor the benefit of the doubt. She sat supreme in the publishing industry. She had taken a lame-duck of a publication devoted to knitting patterns and handicrafts and transformed it into the premier publication in the country devoted to celebrities and movies and music. Every corner store, every newsagent, every street vendor carried the magazine, prominently displayed. He realised that she had not got to where she was without being tough when she needed to be, gentle when needed. He assumed he was not going to see that side of her today.

Twenty minutes later, his sandwich finished, his chat with the PA not ended, he was invited back into the editor's office. He noticed that this time it was an invitation, not a begrudging opening of the door.

Montgomery had moved to another part of the office, closer to some comfortable chairs.

'Detective Inspector, we will sit here if that is okay with you.' Farhan had been wrong. He was to see the gentle side of Victoria Webster.

'Fine by me,' Farhan responded. Two minutes later, the personal assistant walked in with some more coffee. He had already drunk two cups outside, but it would have seemed impolite to refuse.

Montgomery was the first to speak. 'Do you believe that Sutherland died as a result of the information he was willing to give to us?'

Farhan felt it necessary to clarify. 'It is only a supposition at this time. We have established no clear motive.'

'Are you saying there is nothing for me to worry about?' Victoria Webster asked.

'On the contrary. I will be open with you. Charles Sutherland was not the most pleasant of men. He had a tendency to argue with people and to behave in a manner outside of the acceptable norm, especially when drunk or under the influence of drugs.'

'He was a horrible toad of a man,' Victoria Webster interjected. 'I didn't like him at all.'

'Please let me finish.' Farhan needed her to be concerned, not frightened. He was choosing his words carefully. He did not want to reveal the attempted rape of Jess O'Neill as an example, but it was in the back of his mind. He also did not wish to reveal the attempt to draw Christy Nichols into Sutherland's threesome.

'Victoria, it would be best if we let DI Ahmed continue uninterrupted,' Webster said.

'You're right, William. My apologies.'

'I can understand your apprehension concerning the matter.' Farhan could see the veneer of invulnerability cracking.

She appeared more than a little nervous. 'We are aware of some gambling debts, a predilection for prostitutes, usually high-class and expensive, and the occasional abuse of drugs, cocaine mainly. None of those activities as far as we can ascertain made him a candidate for murder.'

'Do you know why he was killed?' Montgomery asked.

'Am I correct that you were willing to pay him up to half a million pounds for the story?' Farhan asked.

'The final price was dependent on what he gave us,' Victoria Webster said. 'If it were only that she played around, slept with some influential men, then he would not have received the full amount, maybe one hundred thousand.'

'What were you expecting to receive?' Farhan asked.

'An illegitimate child.'

'Is that worth the full amount?'

'He said it was.'

'Did he tell you?'

'Only hints. I was going to give him another week at the Savoy, allow him to drink himself under the table, screw as many whores as he wanted, then I was going to throw him back on the street. Before throwing him out, I would have given him one more chance.'

'Do you know the name of this child?' Farhan asked.

'No idea, that's the truth. Am I at risk?'

'It is uncertain, but it would be best to take extra precautions.'

'I could make a statement in the media.'

'I would not advise that as a course of action,' Farhan said. 'Mr Montgomery can advise you. You are just focussing attention on yourself.'

'DI Ahmed's correct. It's best to keep a low profile on this.'

Farhan left soon after. Victoria Webster thanked him for his consideration. William Montgomery shook his hand.

Chapter 18

Richard Goddard was in a verbose mode when he met Isaac and Farhan. 'What do you have? he asked.

'It's not what we have, it's what you have,' Isaac said. Farhan would not have been as direct.

'I've met with my contact.'

'And?' Isaac said.

'There's a child.'

'We know that. That appears to be the clue to this whole sorry mess.'

'What do you mean?'

'Charles Sutherland was using it as a bargaining chip with Victoria Webster,' Farhan said.

'Did she know who it was?'

'No, but she's scared that she may be a marked woman.'

'Is she?'

'Potentially,' Isaac said. 'If this is dynamite, then anyone even remotely involved is at risk.'

'Including us,' Detective Superintendent Goddard said.

'We've considered it.'

'Any more tails on your cars?'

'Not recently.' Isaac said.

'Detective Superintendent, your contact. What's he got to say for himself?' Isaac asked.

'He's not willing to reveal who the child is. I believe he doesn't know.'

'Did Marjorie Frobisher, and if so, how?'

'My contact did reveal that the child is looking for the mother. They can't hold him off for much longer.'

'Are we looking for a male?' Farhan asked.

'A slip of the tongue. The assumption is male, but there's no reason to believe that it could not be female. Marjorie Frobisher would have known.'

'And the father, presumably.' Isaac said.

'Maybe, maybe not. The birth could have been hushed up, remote location, remote hospital, probably private. Even the adoption records could have been falsified.

'Let's come back to your contact, sir,' Isaac said. He was sure there was something else, something vital.

'You want more information, correct?'

'Correct.' Isaac stood up. He aimed to hover close to his senior until something more definite was revealed.

'I believe my contact is being honest when he said that the person he is reporting to would not condone murder – even if the child could be responsible for the collapse of the government.'

'Are we saying that Charles Sutherland was not a sanctioned murder?'

'Not at all. My contact stated that revealing the existence of the child would have more severe repercussions than a change of government.'

'And he doesn't know who it is?' Isaac persisted.

'I don't believe he does.'

'Someone does.'

'Who then?' Farhan asked.

'The father would be a fair assumption,' Richard Goddard admitted.

'Then why don't we talk to the father?' Isaac suggested.

'I'm not sure who he is.'

'You've a fair idea.'

'I'm pretty certain who it is.'

'Then why don't we make an appointment, and go over and meet with this person.'

'Not so easy.'

'Why not?' Isaac asked.

'He doesn't answer his phone, at least, not to us. It would need to be the Commissioner.'

'Then ask him.' Isaac saw no issue. He had met Commissioner Shaw on a couple of occasions; thought him a reasonable, approachable man.

'If we tread on too many toes, we could find ourselves back on the street directing traffic.'

'If we don't tread a little harder, we may as well let a murderer get away free and easy. Is that what you want?' Isaac asked.

'Okay, I'll talk to the commissioner, ask him to coordinate.' The detective superintendent could see his career plateauing, just as he started on the ladder to the commissioner's office. He wanted the top job in the Met, although it was still ten years away at least. He had no great wish to broach the subject with the commissioner, and he certainly did not relish confronting the father of the illegitimate child.

***

Marion Robertson had been on the phone to Farhan. The other escort was ready to meet him. He scheduled the meeting for the next day at four in the afternoon. Marion said that would be suitable, and that Olivia would meet him out in Richmond, close to the park. He allowed himself forty minutes to get there.

The next day he was late. She was angry. 'I agreed to give you ten minutes of my time, and you arrive late,' she said. Farhan remembered Samantha and how pleasant she had been. He could not say the same about Olivia. She was plainly dressed, her hair pulled back tight. She wore an old raincoat, and clothes that looked neither fashionable nor modern.

'My apologies, traffic.'

'I don't have much time,' she replied brusquely.

'This is a murder investigation. You must appreciate that I may need longer.'

'That may be, but I'm the designated mother. I'm picking up my two children as well as next door's.'

'If we can't conclude today, then maybe another time,' Farhan said.

'Secrecy is paramount. You do understand?'

'Yes,' he said. She gave a weak smile, the first sign of friendship. The smile changed her whole persona, so much so that the dowdy clothes and the severe hairstyle faded into the distance.

'You're not going to ask me why I prostitute myself, are you?'

'I'm not here to offer an opinion. I'm here because a man was murdered. A man you were intimate with.'

'I would hardly call screwing a man for money "intimate".'

'What would you call it?'

'A financial necessity.' She kept looking at her watch.

'How long have you got?'

'Twenty minutes maximum. I've been working all day, explains the clothes.'

'What type of work?'

'I work in a factory, manual work. It's dusty and not very pleasant.'

'Why do that if you can work as an escort and make decent money?'

'There you go, the same as the rest, aiming to reform me. Mind you, most want to tell me to work in an office, find a decent husband. At least you're original.'

'Believe me. I have no intention of reform. I need to find out what I can about the death of Charles Sutherland. Your background is relevant if it removes you from suspicion.'

'Or makes me more likely to be the murderer of that horrible man.'

'I suppose you're right.'

'Of course I'm right.'

'Then maybe you can answer the question why you work in a factory.'

'You'll need to know something about my life story.' They both sat on a bench by the side of the road.

'I led a troubled existence up until I was about eighteen. No abuse, good family environment, but I was wild. Something in my genetic makeup, I suppose. I moved out of the home and into a small apartment with a couple of other girls. We always had men over, more like boys on reflection. Anyway, the two girls moved in with their boyfriends, and I was left with the rent to pay. I was too proud to go home and ask for money, and jobs were hard to come by. I saw an ad in the paper, women wanted. I assumed it was prostitution.'

'Did you have a problem with that?'

'Some, but it wasn't that much of an issue. The woman I met, upmarket part of the city, took one look at me and told me I was a lot better than the usual women that came through the door. She took me under her wing and soon I was working as an escort. Great money and the men were invariably kind and gentle. A few were a little kinky, wanted me to tie them up, that sort of thing. I worked like that for about eight years.

'One day, I'm out walking through a park, idly minding my own business, when a man comes up to me. He just wanted to say hello. He meant nothing by it, and he certainly was not attempting to seduce me. We started meeting on a regular basis. He had no idea what I did to earn a living.

'Anyway, I realised that I loved him, and I wanted a life similar to my parents. We married, and all was fine, two healthy children and a mortgage. A few years ago, the economy tightened, and my husband was unable to make the payments on the house and the schooling. I said I would go out to work, so I took the job at the factory. It was purely a cover.

'Each day I would go off to the factory, bring some money in, but it wasn't much. I saw no problem with going back into escorting. Most men like an older, more experienced woman anyway, and I knew I was still attractive, even if a little rounder. I found Marion Robertson through an ad. She's been a godsend, and she always pays promptly.'

'Your husband doesn't know?'

'He must never know. I do this for him and my children. Not for any other reason.'

'I will give you the promise that I gave Samantha. I will maintain your confidentiality. I cannot guarantee that I will be able to indefinitely, but I will try. What can you tell me about Charles Sutherland?'

134

'There's not much I can tell you. We went there a couple of times, put on a show for him, gave him the threesome he wanted and left.'

'Your husband, wasn't he concerned that you were out at night?'

'Nightshift at the factory.'

'And he accepted it?'

'He's a trusting man, even thought I was a virgin when we first met.'

'Thank you, there's not much more I need for now. Hopefully, we will not need to meet again.'

'I hope we never do,' she said.

***

The Murder Investigation Team was now in full operation: collating, investigating, researching in the hunt for whoever had killed Charles Sutherland. The forensics report had come through: death due to a combination of alcohol, cocaine, and arsenic poisoning.

Coupled with the dead man's obesity and a heart condition, death was recorded as manslaughter, possibly murder. It was ambiguous. Isaac phoned Gordon Windsor. His statement: the arsenic may not have been of sufficient quantity to kill an average healthy male, but Charles Sutherland was obese with a heart condition. This raised the question of whether his death was the objective. Regardless of the reason, it was imperative to find the person responsible.

Before the murder, Isaac's and Farhan's activities had been kept relatively low-key, due to the sensitivity of Marjorie Frobisher's disappearance. With Isaac now juggling two jobs, one as the senior investigating officer of the MIT, the other as part of the team with Farhan looking for the missing woman, it became apparent that another person was required.

Both of them knew Constable Wendy Gladstone: Farhan in passing with a cursory 'Hello', 'How are you?', Isaac better as they had worked on a couple of cases together in the past. If you needed to find someone, then she was the best person for the job.

She came into the office early. When Farhan arrived just after seven and Isaac fifteen minutes later, she had already found herself a desk and put it close to Farhan's.

'If anyone is missing, they won't stay missing for long,' Richard Goddard had said when told that she would be joining the team.

She had given Farhan a firm handshake when he had walked into the office. Isaac received a bear hug and a kiss on both cheeks.

'Who do you want to find?' she asked. She was a smoker and the smell of stale tobacco was anathema to them. If it became a problem, Isaac resolved to talk to her about it, but not today.

'Marjorie Frobisher,' Farhan said.

'My favourite actress, my favourite programme.'

'You like the programme?' Isaac asked.

'Why not? After a day in here dealing with misery and violence, a bit of nonsense does no harm. You don't like it?'

'Neither of us likes it much,' Farhan said. He liked the woman, although he was more sensitive to the smell of tobacco than Isaac.

'Each to their own,' she said. She had brought her own coffee mug and was seated comfortably at her desk.

'Where was she last seen?' Wendy asked.

'A hotel in Malvern, Worcestershire,' Isaac replied.

'Positive identification?'

'The receptionist said it was her, and she was picked up on a street camera.'

'How long ago?'

'Three weeks, in Malvern.'

'That's seven weeks missing. Where has she been?'

'No idea' Isaac replied.

'Probably she rented a remote cottage in a nondescript village and kept a low profile,' Wendy said.

'Why would she do that?' Farhan asked.

'I don't know. Where she is now is what's important.'

'Wendy, we'll bring you up to speed,' Isaac said.

'Fine, let me get another mug of coffee. You want some?' Both Isaac and Farhan declined. Isaac knew that they would need to buy more sugar for the office.

Once she was sitting down again, Isaac commenced. 'Marjorie Frobisher's disappearance has caused some concern.'

'I know. Her fans are distraught,' Wendy said.

'It is not her fans that concern us. Marjorie Frobisher led a colourful life. In her earlier years, before she became a major star, she was involved with people who are now very influential. Those people need to know if she is dead or alive.'

'Don't worry about me. I can keep a secret.'

'We know that.'

'What's the tie-in between Sutherland and Marjorie Frobisher, then?'

'We believe he had some knowledge relating to her.'

'Enough knowledge to get him murdered?'

'It seems likely.'

'I'd better get to Malvern. Is this dangerous, by the way?'

'How are you fixed for security?'

'Pepper spray and a kick in the groin.'

Later that day, with a cash advance, a police-issue credit card, and a car, Constable Wendy Gladstone was heading to Malvern. Isaac and Farhan felt confident that she would find Marjorie Frobisher, dead or alive. Until then they had to carry on probing, asking, and hoping for a breakthrough.

Chapter 19

With Wendy in Malvern dealing with the disappearance of Marjorie Frobisher, both Isaac and Farhan were at a loose end. It had been so quiet the previous night after she had left that Isaac had left early to meet Sophie. Farhan had gone home to an empty house, although his wife was talking about coming back. He was pleased for the children, not for himself, as what she considered to be love was not how he saw it. It was a dilemma for which he had no solution.

He was a proud Muslim, and what he was contemplating was contrary to all he had been brought up to believe. His family would not understand, his children would probably not as they grew older, but he had become a contradiction, a contradiction to his faith. He knew what he must do. He was not sure how it would turn out. He needed to sow his wild oats and then maybe… Maybe then he would go back to the all-encompassing traditional family.

Isaac arrived refreshed the following morning; Farhan, the opposite, as he had not been sleeping well since his wife left. Samantha, or Aisha as she preferred him to call her, had phoned him once or twice, exceedingly friendly, but he had to remind her that as it was an ongoing murder investigation, he was not in a position to meet other than on official business. Aisha understood, or she said she did. Maybe she was like Olivia, looking for a good man. *Could he be that man?* he thought. *Could he forgive her for all the men she had slept with?* He wasn't sure, but it concerned him, kept him awake at nights thinking about her.

'Farhan, coffee?' Isaac asked, bringing him back from his daydreaming.

'Yes, please.'

Both sat at their desks.

'You're satisfied the women that Sutherland had in his room are not involved?' Isaac asked.

'I'm certain they were only there for sex.'

'Then someone must have gone in after and given him the drink.'

'A fair assumption, Isaac.'

'It doesn't help, though. Security cameras. Any at the hotel?'

'Not in the rooms and not on the floor.'

'Then someone could have entered without being spotted.'

'That's correct.'

'And it must have happened after the women left and before the maid found the body.'

'We know that he died around three to four in the morning.'

'Any record of him phoning for another woman?'

'None has been found.'

'What does that suggest?'

'That he knew the person.'

'Precisely,' Farhan agreed. 'And why didn't Christy Nichols hear the knocking and the commotion?'

'Good question, you'd better ask her.'

'What are you going to do?' Farhan asked.

'I intend to meet up with Marjorie Frobisher's children. I need to see how they feel about their mother's disappearance. Whether they are involved.'

'Why would they be involved?'

'I'm not altogether sure. If the woman is alive, then there is no involvement, but if she's dead…'

'They could have killed her.'

'If they had a motive.'

'We are assuming her death would be a sanctioned assassination?'

'It's only an assumption. We know that people in senior places in this country want her dead. That doesn't mean, however, that they committed the murder. Maybe someone else did, and it has proven advantageous to them. Charles Sutherland was a loose end; his death may have been an assassination or someone out for revenge.'

'You know what you just said. I said it on the day of the interview with Jess O'Neill. You chose to ignore me.'

'I heard what you said. I just didn't want to hear it at the time. It is a strong enough motive,' Isaac finally admitted.

Farhan changed the subject. 'I'll go and see Christy Nichols. You can go and see Marjorie Frobisher's children.'

***

Christy Nichols was not hard to find. Her experience at the Savoy had left her downtrodden and downhearted. She had temporarily given up any hope of fame and fortune in the publishing world.

'It's a cut-throat business,' she admitted when she met Farhan. They had agreed on a location in the east of the city, a small coffee shop he had visited in the past, and she knew. He had ordered cappuccino for them both, served by an Italian woman. He had made small talk, assumed she was a member of the family that owned the café, but she had told him she was just a backpacker aiming to make enough to pay her weekly costs. She said that no one in the family would work there for the hourly rate, but it was cash, so she saw no reason to complain. Besides, it was the tips that made it worthwhile. He made sure to give her a good tip.

'What are you doing at the moment?' he asked Christy.

'Licking my wounds.'

'That bad?'

'That bad. You know she refused to pay my expenses?'

'Victoria Webster?'

'You've met her?' she asked.

'On official business.'

'What did you think?'

'It would be inappropriate for me to comment.'

'I understand. Policeman's code, something like that.'

'Yes, something like that.'

'She's a bitch, isn't she? Don't answer that,' she said. Farhan smiled.

'She's right of course. It's a dog-eat-dog business. If you're soft and kind-hearted like me, it's impossible to make it.'

'Christy, did you see anything?'

'The night he was murdered?'

'Yes.'

'I saw the two women enter, but after his behaviour the previous time, I was keeping well away.'

'The women that you saw, can you describe them?' Farhan asked. He had met them both. It seemed a good idea to confirm that she was referring to the same women.

'Both were attractive, heavier build than me, but not fat. One seemed to be Indian, not very dark though, and the other one English, in her late thirties, maybe early forties. They were both well-spoken. I had to pay someone in the hotel to let them in by the back entrance.'

'Your description sounds right.'

'You've met them?'

'They didn't want to, but it's a murder investigation. I could have forced them to come to the police station.'

'You didn't?'

'No, I met them separately in neutral locations.'

'What did you think?' She seemed curious.

'I liked them both. As you say, apart from what they do.'

'It's not for us to judge, is it?'

'Not at all,' Farhan replied. 'Life is tough. People sometimes need to make decisions to survive. Both were desperate to protect their identities.'

'Their alter egos.'

'You make them sound like superheroes or superheroines.' Farhan was not sure where the conversation was heading.

'Not really, but I can admire strong-minded, strong-willed people. I can admire Victoria Webster, not necessarily like her. I can even admire the two prostitutes, although I could never imagine myself doing something like that. What if they were seen by someone they knew? What would they do?'

'I never asked. I will the next time.'

'They won't like it,' she said. Farhan ordered two more drinks. It was evident she was in no hurry to leave, neither was he.

'It's an interesting thought. What if they had seen someone that night, someone who should not have been there? Would they have told me?' Farhan said.

'Probably not. Protecting their lives outside of prostituting themselves would be more important.'

'I suppose so.'

'You know so.'

'I agreed to keep what they told me in confidence. Christy, level with me. Why are you so interested?'

'Don't you ever feel like throwing away people's perception of respectability, just being yourself?'

'Sometimes,' he admitted. *Often*, he thought.

'Sorry, I'm just feeling sorry for myself. I'm not doing a lot at the present moment, just working for a local rag, gossip column.'

'How did you get into that?'

'I've been doing it for some time. I mainly work from home, make up most of the "Dear Marigold's". It pays the bills.'

'You don't look like a Marigold.'

'It's my middle name. A great aunt that my mother was fond of was named Marigold. I think my mother was having a bad day when she gave it to me.'

Farhan realised he was enjoying his time with Christy Nichols, although it was still a murder investigation, and she still remained the closest person to Charles Sutherland. He had discounted the two escorts; he couldn't call them prostitutes anymore. He didn't want to think of Samantha aka Aisha selling herself on a street corner. An escort sounded more refined. He also realised that he needed to meet her again: firstly because there was a valid reason, and secondly because he wanted to.

'Coming back to the night of the murder,' Farhan refocussed. 'The women said they left around midnight.'

'I never saw them leave.'

'Why's that?'

'No reason to. I showed them in, but I certainly did not want to see Sutherland flashing me again. I've led a sheltered life.' She seemed to be joking.

'Sheltered. What do you mean?'

'It's just a silly remark really. I had a very conservative childhood. My parents did all they could to shield me from the seedier side of life. There were no late-night parties or boys over. No alcohol in the house and certainly no bad language. I stayed there until I was in my early twenties, and then the company I worked for transferred me to London. It's left me a little prudish, not sure how to handle some situations.'

'Such as Charles Sutherland when he's high on drugs and women.'

'Yes, Charles Sutherland. I suppose another woman would have slapped his face, kicked him in the groin and screamed for help.'

'Why didn't you?'

'I think I froze.'

'Then what happened?'

'It's too shocking.'

'You need to elaborate, it's important.'

'I'm ashamed.' She was shaking visibly. Her face was red, and tears were welling up in her eyes. Farhan beckoned the Italian waitress to bring another two coffees.

'He made me do something.'

'And the other women?'

'They weren't there. They had left by then. I should have gone out with them, but I was scared.'

She sipped her cappuccino. 'He made me perform fellatio on him.'

'Why did you agree?'

'I was scared of what he would do.'

'And afterwards?'

'He laughed at me, told me I would have been a lousy screw anyway, and that I was only good for a blowjob.'

'Did you report it?'

'To who? Victoria Webster would not have been interested. Charles Sutherland was more important than me. I was only the hired help. She would have assumed I encouraged him.'

'After you left?'

'I went to my room, put my fingers down my throat – he made me swallow it all – until I vomited. I then stood in the shower for hours, so hot it almost burned, until it went cold. After that, I lay on my bed sobbing. I didn't sleep that night.'

'Thank you for telling me.'

'It makes me a murder suspect, doesn't it?'

'It's a strong enough motive. Why didn't you tell me before?'

'I was ashamed. I was concerned that it would be seen that I had encouraged him – that I was a slut.'

'You wished him dead after that?'

'Of course, any woman would, but it does not make me a murderer, does it?'

He didn't answer her question. 'Why did you tell me today?' he asked instead.

'I trust you,' she replied.

Chapter 20

Wendy Gladstone was pleased that her time in Isaac and Farhan's office had been short. She had spent thirty years in the force, pounding the beat initially in uniform with a whistle and a baton; another five, maybe six years before she retired. The concept of retirement did not excite her, but she was getting older, and arthritis was starting to set in. No one knew, not even her husband.

He had retired five years earlier. He was ten years older than her, a strapping man when she had first met him, an embittered man now. He blamed it all on the migrants coming into the country, taking everyone's job, turning the neighbourhoods into ghettoes. 'Bloody Paki,' he would say every time he saw someone Asian in the street. She had no problems with them; the family two doors down had come from India, and they were fine. She knew he would not have liked Detective Inspector Ahmed.

It was minor, and she would not make a scene about it. And the office no longer allowed smoking. In fact, she had to go out on the street, rain or shine.

She didn't hold with these modern ideas where you couldn't smoke, drink, discipline your child, or call a spade a spade in case it offended someone. Her father, a potato farmer, humble and poor, smoked all his life. He downed his five pints every night at the pub, was not averse to disciplining the children if they needed it, and he had been a good man. He had lived to his mid-eighties. Her mother, teetotal, gentle and a housewife, barely made it past sixty before she had a stroke.

Ambition had never been the driving force in Wendy Gladstone's life, although policing had, ever since childhood. Her earliest memories, apart from her doting mother and her firm but fair father, had been the local police constable: uniformed, tall helmet, riding around the area, a rugged and scenic part of the Yorkshire moors in the north of England, freezing in winter, cold in summer. She saw him as an almost saintly figure. Senior Constable Terry Clarke was a sweet-talking man who sang baritone in the local choir on a Sunday. Whenever he saw someone, he would stop and greet them. For the children – he knew them all by name – there would always be a sweet.

She soon realised, after joining the police force and being assigned to a police station in Sheffield and then London, that there were villains to be dealt with, and not all the children looked forward to an encounter with the local policeman, or in her case, the local policewoman. Some of the children were plainly disruptive, some plainly criminal, some plainly abusive.

It had been just after her fifteenth birthday that her hormones had kicked in. Brian Hardcastle, a headmaster's son and a tall, skinny rake of a boy, had not been the most suitable introduction to the joy of sex.

The barn where there consummated their lust, each taking the other's virginity, was hot and smelly. It was a five-minute affair: with him being disappointed in his performance – he had read books on the subject – and her being ecstatic. For a while, her father had tried to confine her to her room, but her mother had eventually intervened. 'It's a phase she's going through. Exploring her sexuality,' she had said. She had learnt the phrase from a book in the local library. Her father, increasingly annoyed at the ribbing he received at the pub over his wayward daughter, kept away for a few months, but in the end the ribbing ceased and he went back to his five pints a night. He was glad when Wendy joined the police force and went to Sheffield. Once out of the village, she found the need for a multitude of men had subsided.

Her husband came along when she was nineteen, an old man – at least, in her mother's eyes – of twenty-nine.

***

'One room, please,' Wendy said as she stood at the reception desk at the Abbey Hotel in Malvern. It was five-star, the sort of hotel where Marjorie Frobisher would stay. She also knew that it was beyond her salary, and if it had not been official business and a police-issue credit card, she would have found a room above a pub.

Her room, second floor with a view overlooking the Priory, was splendid. Smoke-free, which she did not like, but the window opened wide. She had a warm bath. Too many cigarettes and too many big meals had left her body worn and sagging. She had promised many times to change her ways; she always failed within a day.

Refreshed, she headed downstairs. The worst approach with the receptionist who had identified the missing woman would be to flash her badge. She knew it would put her on the defensive. It seemed best to identify her first. She was not in view, and Wendy did not want to go asking questions and raising suspicion. A good meal, a couple of glasses of wine, and an early night seemed the best approach. The next day she would find the receptionist; indulge in idle conversation about the local tourist highlights, television programmes – especially the one she was interested in.

***

Farhan met Samantha again. She was pleased when he rang. They met in the same prearranged spot as before. She brought two curries: one for him, one for her, from an Indian restaurant not far from her office. He appreciated the gesture.

'Samantha.'

'Please call me Aisha. I prefer Aisha.'

'Aisha, there was an incident the first night at the hotel. The woman you met, did you speak to her?'

'Not really. She arranged for us to come in. I think she disapproved.'

'That's probably correct.'

'Aisha, it's best if you think before you speak. I should really ask you to come down to the station and make a statement...'

'You're trying to protect me?'

'You and Olivia.'

'You've met her? What was she like?'

'I'm not sure it would be appropriate for me to tell you.'

'Did you like her? At least, you can tell me that.'

'I did not like her as much as you.'

'I would have been upset if you had,' she replied.

'She has her reasons, the same as you. Let's go back to the first night. What happened?'

'Sutherland was high on alcohol and drugs.'

'Were you?'

'Not at all. I don't even drink. I play along with the client, same as Olivia. You need to be a good actor sometimes.'

'Please continue.'

'As I told you before, we were on the floor with him.'

'And then?'

'The woman walks in unexpectedly. She must have assumed we had gone, as we were not making much noise. She was checking that all was okay, I suppose.'

'What did Sutherland do?'

'He jumped up and exposed himself to her. She looked as though she had never seen a naked man before. With her standing there and it getting late, I went into the bedroom with Olivia. We dressed in our going home clothes and left soon after.'

'Going home clothes?'

'Yes, of course. I can hardly walk in the door at my parent's house looking like a painted tart. I change into my regular work clothes, take off the perfume.'

'And the woman?'

'We were out of there in five minutes. Sutherland had sobered up by then, and she was serving him coffee. We weren't looking, but it appeared relatively calm. It wasn't for us to nursemaid them. I assumed her job was to take care of him. She may have been available as well. I don't think she was, but I never asked or cared.'

'Is there any more?'

'No, that's it. You can ask Olivia if you like, but she will confirm my statement.'

'I will take your statement, Olivia's too, if it's necessary.'

'I finish my degree in a couple of months. I'm not sure if I want to sell myself again.'

'I would have thought after one of your clients was murdered, it would not be a good option.'

'You're right of course. I've seen things, met people, been places. I'm not as naïve as you think.'

'It is the same for me,' Farhan said.

'If I stop, can we meet again?' she asked. 'Socially, that is. Or is what I have done too much for you to forget?'

'I think I can handle the situation. This is a murder investigation, and you are a material witness. It would not be advisable for us to meet socially at this time.'

'A confidential witness.'

'I don't intend to reveal your name unless it is absolutely necessary.'

'You don't want anyone to know your girlfriend is a former prostitute.' She smiled. Farhan realised she was teasing him.

'We need to keep this professional.'

'Sorry, I've embarrassed you, Detective Inspector Ahmed. We will meet again, hopefully soon. For myself, I will remain pure and chaste until you call.'

'It may be some time.'

'Time is not the issue. When is more important.'

They parted, unaware that they had yet again walked a significant distance. He knew he had made an error in letting his personal feelings interfere with his professional responsibilities. He would talk to Isaac when it was opportune, for advice.

***

Isaac instinctively did not like Fiona Avers from the first moment he met her at Robert Avers and Marjorie Frobisher's home. 'I would like to ask you about your mother.'

'Before you carry on,' she said, attempting to take control of the discussion, 'I despised my mother.'

'Why do you feel the need to tell me that before I've asked you any questions?' Isaac had seen it before. The desperate need of a witness to explain their intense dislike of a person, as if somehow it exonerated them from the crime. Often it did, but not always.

'I just want to make it clear, that's all.'

Isaac could see why Fiona Avers had never become a major star, as her mother had. He had watched her mother on the television a few times, even downloaded some episodes of her current programme off YouTube. He also found a movie she had made twenty years previously.

He did not find the characters she portrayed particularly endearing, but Marjorie Frobisher was, had been, a beautiful woman. The daughter was not. For once he felt calm. Too often a potential witness – attractive and easy to the eye – had caused him to soften his interrogational style. It was not going to happen this time.

'Are you saying that you do not miss your mother?'

'I told you in the first sentence. Don't you listen?' Fiona Avers had the manners of an alley cat.

'The disappearance of your mother and the murder of Charles Sutherland may be related. Your confrontational style is not conducive to this discussion.'

'What do I care about Charles Sutherland? The only time I met him, he wanted to put his grubby paws all over me.'

'And where was that?'

'Here, in this house. My mother was having one of her celebrity get-togethers. I didn't receive an invite – too embarrassing, having her ugly daughter around.'

'Why do you say that?'

'You've got two eyes. You tell me.'

'I'm not sure I understand.'

'I'm not beautiful, that's the problem. I may not be totally ugly, and it doesn't concern me, at least not too much, but to my precious mother, beauty and poise and grace were all-important. I'm clumsy, more likely to break the best china teapot than pour a cup of tea from it. That's how she saw it. It was always the same, even from childhood.'

'So why did you come to the party?'

'It's my home. I've a right to come, and besides my mother owed me. If she didn't make the introductions, ensured I got a part on some programme, I would have made a scene.'

Isaac saw clearly that if Fiona Avers decided to make a scene, no one would have been able to stop her.

'Did she help you?'

'She pretended to. Introduced me to a couple of producers: "drop around anytime, and we'll give you an audition".'

'Did they work out?'

'Hell, no. The first one was always too busy: come next week. The other one seemed to fancy tall, plain-looking women. He showed me the casting couch; I showed him a bunch of fives and a kick in the shin. He showed me the door.'

'What are you doing now?'

'The word got around that I'm difficult to work with. Mother probably did little to discourage that. The only decent part on offer was the casting couch producer. I should have just let him fuck me, will next time.'

'Seems a tough way to get ahead in your line of business,' Isaac said.

'Ask Mother. She's been on more casting couches than there are casting couches. She's a terrible tart. I assume you've been told.'

'I am aware that the relationship between your father and mother was unusual.'

'It was no relationship. She told him, he accepted. He loved her, still does, and he's devoted to both Sam and I. Maybe not so much to Sam, but then he's a hopeless case: drink and drugs.'

'Your relationship with your father?'

'He's a wonderful man. I've told him enough times to give her the boot and find someone else.'

Isaac wanted to get back to the issue with Charles Sutherland. First, he needed a break. Fiona went and made two coffees. She returned and placed them on the table; best china, he noticed.

'Let us get back to the incident with Charles Sutherland.'

'It was late in the evening. I was drunk, too many vodkas and whiskies, maybe a couple of beers as well. Sutherland was equally drunk. Father was upstairs asleep. He doesn't have a lot of time for entertainment people. He finds most of them vacuous and self-obsessed, which they are – my mother being the prime example.'

'Your father came to the party?'

'He played the perfect host. He ensured everyone had a drink and was fed. He spent about three hours at the party, and by then a few had left, a few were drunk and asleep in a chair, and some others were sniffing cocaine.'

'Which were you?'

'I was drunk, but not drugged. I've tried drugs, the less harmful variety, and they make me psychotic. Alcohol suffices for me.'

'Charles Sutherland.'

'I'm at the back of the house. It's a big house, as you've seen. I'm sitting there drinking steadily. He comes in on his own. He's clearly high on drugs, and I'm definitely drunk. He sees beauty in me, and I see a handsome man in him.'

'It's just the two of you?'

'The beautiful woman. The handsome man. That's what alcohol and recreational drugs do to you – make you see something that is not there.'

'I think you are playing down your appearance,' Isaac said. He had to admit that beautiful was not a description he would use, but she had some character in her face. Her manner with people was her main disadvantage.

'You don't need to be kind. Let me continue.'

'Okay.'

'We start fooling around, groping each other.'

'I thought you said his advances were unwelcome.'

'I was not entirely truthful. Anyway, soon after, I've got my skirt up around my arse, and he's on top of me going for dear life.'

'Sexual intercourse?'

'That's sounds clinical. It was just a drunken fuck.'

'So why the hatred?'

'As I'm climaxing and he's struggling to come, in walks my mother. It appears that the party has come to a conclusion and she, and one other, are the only ones left. Except for Charles Sutherland and yours truly.'

'What did you mother say?'

'Nothing. She wasn't interested in me, only the man she had brought in to fuck.'

'Sutherland's reaction?'

'He jumped up, left me dangling without concluding his part.'

'What do you mean?'

'He failed to ejaculate, shoot his load. Clear enough?'

'Clear enough.'

'And what did you think of your mother with another man?'

'Not much. She was always playing around with one man or another, but in my father's house, with him upstairs asleep... I was angry.'

'There's a scene with your mother, but what's this got to do with Sutherland.'

'He takes her side. Calls me an old tart, and said if he hadn't been drunk, he wouldn't have touched me with a barge pole. It's not the first time a man has said that to me. I was livid, making a scene, a lot of noise as well, I suppose. Anyway, my father comes down, sees what's going on, and takes me out of the room and puts me to bed with a cup of cocoa and a hot water bottle.'

'Charles Sutherland?'

'He left soon after.'

'And your mother?'

'Ten minutes later, the front door slammed shut, and she came upstairs as if nothing had happened.'

'Why ten minutes later, if Sutherland had already left?'

'She still needed fucking.'

'Who was the man?'

'Richard Williams.'

Isaac realised that here, in this one embittered woman, was the motive for two murders: the murder of Marjorie Frobisher, if she was indeed dead, and the murder of Charles Sutherland.

Chapter 21

Wendy had not announced the previous day when checking in at the hotel that she was a police officer. Experience had taught her that people become secretive and guarded once an ID badge is flashed in front of them. Even the innocent start to clam up, check what they say and how they say it. She needed the receptionist free and willing to talk. She was not a difficult woman to recognise as all the staff appeared to be young – in their twenties and thirties – except for her.

Felicity Pearson, in her late forties, maybe early fifties; her photo courtesy of a board in the hotel foyer showing 'Employee of the month'. She had already been interviewed by the police; she would not necessarily welcome a second time.

Wendy decided the best approach was to engage in idle chatter when the reception was quiet. She waited her time. It came around eleven o'clock in the morning, when those who were checking out had, and those checking in were waiting until two in the afternoon.

'I was thinking of taking a walk in the hills,' Wendy said.

'That's a good idea. It's best to take a coat. It can get cold up there at times, even snow in the winter, but not today,' the receptionist replied.

'I don't want to be gone for too long.'

'Why's that?'

'They're repeating the episode where Billy Blythe dies.' Wendy thought it a good enough way to direct the questioning towards the missing woman.

'She was in here, you know.'

'Who was?' Wendy, sounding suitably vague, replied.

'His sister.'

'You watch the programme?' Wendy said. *A fellow devotee, ideal*, she thought.

'I never miss it.'

'Nor do I. It's a shame about his sister,' Wendy said.

'I just said before. She was in here.'

'Edith Blythe?'

'Yes, his sister.'

'That must have been exciting. What was she like?'

'She didn't say much. She didn't like it when I recognised her.'

'Why's that?'

'I've no idea. She left soon after. I think it was because of me.'

Wendy noticed that Felicity Pearson was ignoring other people standing at the reception. 'You'd better deal with them first.' She did not want the receptionist getting in trouble, and then walking out of the door in a huff.

'Give me five minutes, and then we can chat some more.' Wendy could tell that the woman liked nothing more than a good conversation.

Five minutes later she returned. 'Marjorie Frobisher, that's who it was. Mind you, I wouldn't have recognised her.'

'Why do you say that?'

'Her hair was a different colour, and she wore large sunglasses.'

'How did you know it was her?'

'I only knew it was her when she came to the counter and asked for the linen on her bed to be changed. We only do it every third day, but she was adamant.'

'What did you do?'

'I phoned up housekeeping. They sorted it out.'

'You've not explained how you knew it was her.'

'You remember how she used to look when she was sad. One side of her mouth appeared to droop slightly lower than the other.'

'Yes, of course.'

'That's what she did with me. I was so excited, I asked her for her autograph.'

'Her reaction?'

'I could see she wasn't happy, but she remained polite and signed a piece of paper for me. I framed it, put it next to the television at home.'

'What happened after she had signed it?'

'She went upstairs and packed her case.'

'When she left, where did she go?'

'I organised a taxi for her.'

'Do you know the taxi she took?'

'Bert picked her up. We always try to use him for the guests. He's been driving for us for years.'

'Where can I find him?'

'Up the road, blue Toyota. You can't miss him.'

'Thanks.'

'Why are you so interested in where she's gone.'

'Her husband has asked me to find her, bring her home.'

'You've been engaging in idle conversation, making me neglect the guests, pretending to be a fan of the programme…'

'I am a fan. I also need to find her.'

'I hope nothing has happened to her.'

'We're not sure. We think she may have come to some harm.' Wendy felt she owed the woman some gossip in return.

'Is it anything to do with Billy Blythe? I never liked him. The actor who played him, his death.'

'Yes,' Wendy replied.

'Well I never,' Felicity Pearson said. The last words Wendy heard from the receptionist as she went out to find Bert, the taxi driver, was her telling some guests the latest gossip on Marjorie Frobisher. She could only smile.

***

Isaac had made two appointments that day at Marjorie Frobisher's house: the first in the morning with the daughter, Fiona Avers. The second in the afternoon with Sam Avers, the son.

Sam Avers, the elder of the two children, arrived drunk. He was unapologetic. He had a five-day beard and his breath smelt, so much so that Isaac was obliged to move chairs to one side to avoid a frontal assault of stale beer.

'Mr Avers.'

'Call me Sam, everyone does.'

'Okay, Sam. We are conducting investigations into the disappearance of your mother and the death of Charles Sutherland.'

'What's his death got to do with her?' Sam Avers responded. He coughed violently as he spoke. He lit another cigarette.

'We are not sure. I had hoped that you would have some further information that would assist us.'

'Why me? I hardly knew the man, and as for her…'

'Your relationship with your mother?'

'Hardly ever saw her, and when I did, she was off out somewhere with her rich friends.'

'Were they all rich?'

'Most were, but she hardly wanted them for their money. She had plenty, not that she gave me much.'

'I am told by your father that they give you a generous allowance and a credit card. Is that correct?'

'They only give it for me to go away. I'm an embarrassment to them. Did he tell you that?'

'I understand you live here.'

'I come and go, mostly go. I don't want to be around here any more than necessary.'

'You come here, ensure your money is available and leave.'

'That's about it,' the drunken man said. He had gone to the drinks cabinet and was pouring himself a large whisky. 'You want one?' he said. Isaac declined.

'On duty, is that it?'

'Too early for me,' Isaac replied. It wasn't true but he certainly did not want a large whisky, and he did not want to drink with the man. He did not like him; was being careful not to offend or rile.

'Suit yourself. I have to give the old man credit, he certainly keeps a good drop of whisky here, only the best.'

'Before we discuss your mother, let us consider Charles Sutherland.'

'I only met him once or twice. He could drink – more than me.'

'Where did you meet him?'

'Here once, in town another time.'

'What happened here?'

'We got drunk.'

'Nothing else?'

'Are you insinuating that I'm gay, that I fancy men?'

'Not at all. This is a murder investigation. It is important that I am thorough.'

'And besides, he liked women. The more he could get hold of, the better.'

'How do you know that?'

'I ran into him at a club in town once. He had a couple of women with him, real classy.'

'Can you please elaborate?'

'I go over to him. He's drunk. Wants to tell me what a bitch my mother is. He expects me to argue with him. I'm harmless when I've been drinking, which is most of the time, but he's angry drunk.'

'He insults your mother. What do you do?'

'I agree with him, of course.'

'And then?'

'He invites me to sit down with him. It appears he had paid plenty for these women, and he doesn't mind sharing.'

'How long did you stay in the club?'

'About two hours, and then we went to his place in Mayfair.'

'With the women?'

'Of course, what else would I go there for?'

'Continue.'

'He took one, I took the other, and then we swapped. Eventually, I fell asleep, and the next I knew it was early morning, and a bird was sitting outside on the balcony railing making a noise.'

'The women, where were they?'

'They had gone, so had Sutherland. I left soon after, nothing for me to do there.'

'Why leave? I understand from your father that you do not work.'

'Not much.'

'I spoke to your sister before. She is very fond of her father.'

'She would be. He always spoilt her, buying her presents.'

'You were not spoilt?'

'By him? No way. The most he would give me was a lecture about how to stand up straight, be a man. He was a fine one to give lectures.'

'Why do you say that?'

'He couldn't even control his wife. What sort of man allows his wife to fuck anyone she wants to, even in his house?'

'Did that happen often?'

'Not often, I suppose.'

How often?'

'There was that time with Richard Williams. He's been screwing her for years. Did he tell you that?'

'I'm aware they were involved in the past, before your parents were married.'

'They're still involved. If you want to find out where she is, you'd better talk to him.'

'Your dislike for your mother, is it a strong enough motive to wish her harm?'

'Are you accusing me of murdering my own mother?'

'I need to ascertain the intensity of your dislike towards your mother.'

'I hated her. Not enough to kill her and she's the one with the money, not my father.'

'I thought your father was successful in his own right.'

'He made some money, but nothing like her. She was the earner in this house. No doubt why he allowed her to screw around.'

'Are you an earner?'

'I'm just a drunken layabout. My father must have told you that.'

'He mentioned you had some issues. Just one more question before we conclude.'

'Let me get a top up.' Isaac counted three whiskies consumed by Sam Avers since he arrived. It was apparent that he did not intend to stop until the bottle was drained.

'Your father. Capable of murder?'

'Him? I don't think so.'

***

Wendy Gladstone, armed with the new information, set off to find Bert, the taxi driver. He was not difficult to find. The taxi rank, a five-minute walk up the road, only had places for three vehicles. Bert's was the second. The one in front was a grey Vauxhall – looked as though it could do with a wash. Bert's blue Toyota was fresh and clean, and she could see why the hotel used his in preference to the other taxis in the small town.

'Felicity recommended me,' she said.

'From the Abbey?' he replied. She could see that he was closer to seventy years of age than sixty. He still had a luxuriant growth of hair on his head, a small bald patch just starting to show. He was dressed in a suit with a white shirt and tie. She was impressed.

'The Abbey, yes.'

'She should have phoned. I would have come down and picked you up, saved you the walk.'

'I enjoy walking,' she said, which had been true enough before arthritis set in. Now she had to take care, not walk too fast. It annoyed her that she was not as agile as she had been as a child, and then as a young woman. She complained little, and certainly to no one except her husband.

'Where can I take you?'

'I'll be honest, Bert. I've been asked to find one of your clients.'

'Are you police?'

'I was not entirely honest with Felicity down at the hotel. I told her it was her husband who had asked me. My name is Wendy Gladstone.'

'What's the truth?' the taxi driver asked. Wendy could see that he was an active man, quick of mind.

'We're treating the woman's disappearance as suspicious.'

'You're from London?'

'How did you know?'

'The accent mainly. Some others were asking about her.'

'I grew up in Yorkshire.'

'Maybe you did, but it's a London accent now. Pure cockney, although now you mention it, there's a bit of Yorkshire in there.'

'You mentioned some others looking for her?'

'You never confirmed that you were police.'

'Police Constable.'

'I didn't like them.'

'Who?'

'The two who were looking for her.'

'Did they say who they were? And I haven't mentioned who the woman is yet.'

'Felicity was desperate to tell me. My wife was excited when I told her.'

'And you?'

'I've never taken much notice of her before. I don't watch the television apart from the sport's channel.'

'Are you free to talk?' she asked.

'The taxi meter is running. I assume that's fine by you?'

'Fine, expense account. You may as well have the benefit of it as well.'

'Can it stand a decent meal?' he asked.

162

'Yes, why not.'

'Hop in, we'll treat ourselves to a good meal up the road.'

Bert, or Bert Collins, his full name for the report she would have to write up later, apparently enjoyed the little luxuries in life. He ordered the best, including the best wine. She knew she should not, and had been promising to go on a diet, but in the end she matched him course for course.

'She didn't say much, just mumbled a few words and paid the fare,' Bert said between gulps of wine.

'Is there anything you can tell me that will help me find her?'

'I dropped her off at the railway station in Worcester, which made little sense. We have a perfectly good railway station here which connects into Worcester.'

'Did she give you a reason?'

'I saw no reason to ask. She was paying, and Worcester is farther than the local station.'

'When you dropped her off, did she say where she was heading?'

'She saw the time and a train coming into the station. She made some comment under her breath and dashed off. I assumed she wanted to catch the train.'

'Where was it heading?'

'Paddington. Two and a half hours. I take it myself when Arsenal is playing at home.'

'She never arrived.'

'I wouldn't know about that. She paid my money, and as I said, she dashed off. There wasn't another train for some time after, so I can't see where else she could have gone.'

'The other two men. What can you tell me about them?'

'They sat in the back of the taxi and asked me to drive them around the area. They said they were up for a business conference and were taking the opportunity of a couple of hours to do some sightseeing.'

'Did you believe them?'

'No way.'

'Why do you say that?'

'It was raining heavily, could barely see where I was going, and there were no business conferences that I knew of.'

'Would you know if there was?'

'I'm confident I would.'

'As you're driving around, what did they ask?'

'They made small talk, and then they started asking about this woman.'

'Which one?'

'This Marjorie Frobisher.'

'Did that cause you some concern?'

'It did. How did they know about her? They weren't staying at the Abbey. I know that Felicity Pearson is a bit of a gossip, but why should two men, business men, be interested in the whereabouts of a woman off a programme on the television.'

'Did they say why they were interested?'

'I asked. They made up some lame reason that their wives watched the programme. Then they started offering me money, wanting to take me to the pub for a few drinks.'

'Did you tell them what you told me?'

'No. I just said that my shift was coming to a close, which wasn't true, and dropped them back at the taxi rank. That's the last I saw of them.'

'Why didn't you tell them anything?'

'You were honest. Bought me a nice meal.'

'Is that the only reason?'

'It's a good enough reason for me,' he said. There was still half a bottle of a good wine to drink. Wendy thought they might be able to drink another bottle after that. She was sure Bert would not object.

Chapter 22

Richard Williams did not appreciate the official request to present himself at the police station. He was a man used to giving orders, not receiving them. 'What right have you to demand my presence here? I'm a busy man.'

'Some new information has come to light. Information in relation to you,' Isaac said. Farhan, as usual, at his left. Richard Williams, dressed formally in a suit, sat opposite Isaac. He had brought legal representation: Quinton Scott, Queen's Counsel, of Scott, Scott and Fairlight. To Isaac, he looked landed gentry. To Farhan, he looked like a man who did not appreciate anyone who had not been born with a silver spoon in their mouth, or a white complexion with blue eyes. He had reluctantly shaken Isaac's hand, made a clear attempt to avoid repeating the same mistake with him.

Isaac commenced the interview, following the official procedure, noting the time of the interview, informing the client of his rights and asking those present to state their names and details.

'My client is here at the express request of the police. He is willing to answer any reasonable questions that are put to him,' Williams' QC said.

'Mr Williams, we are in possession of information that clearly indicates you lied to us on previous occasions,' Isaac said.

'I reject that accusation. I have upheld my responsibility and always given the truth when asked.'

'I hope that these accusations can be validated. It will be seen as police harassment if they are fabrications. The Commissioner of Police, Charles Shaw, will take a dim view of this if I am obliged to inform him,' Scott said. Isaac, a usually patient man, was enraged at the QC's attempt at intimidation.

'Let me remind you that this is a murder investigation,' Isaac said. 'I am sure that Commissioner Shaw will fully endorse my position.'

'Very well, continue.' Quinton Scott appeared subdued for the moment.

'Mr Williams, you mentioned on a previous occasion in your office that your relationship, your intimate relationship with Marjorie Frobisher, occurred many years ago, and that you have remained as friends since then.'

'That is correct.'

'Recent information indicates that your relationship has continued.'

'Our friendship has.'

'There was a party at Marjorie Frobisher's house when it became more than a friendship.'

'Who told you this?' Williams said. His legal adviser maintained a thoughtful pose, arms folded, listening to the conversation.

'Is this true?'

'No.'

'Mr Williams, I am led to believe you are lying. We are not here to pass moral judgement, we are here to ascertain the truth. Whether you are or are not sleeping with her only concerns us in relation to our enquiries.'

Quinton Scott felt the need to speak. 'My client has clearly indicated the current and past statuses. He is not required to say anymore.'

'That is his right,' Isaac continued. 'However, Mr Williams is the last person to have seen Marjorie Frobisher alive, and that is by his own admission.'

'Is that correct?' Quinton Scott turned towards his client to ask.

'I knew she was in Malvern, at least for some of the time. I went there and met her.'

Quinton Scott turned to Isaac, 'DCI Cook, I would request fifteen minutes with my client.'

'Interview halted at 11.30 a.m.'

'Thank you,' the QC said.

'I'll send in two coffees,' Farhan said.

A begrudging grunt from the QC; thanks from Williams.

***

Forty minutes later the interview recommenced. In the interval, Farhan and Isaac had managed to grab a bite to eat. Richard Williams and Quinton Scott had asked for a pizza each. A young female police officer had delivered them to the interview room.

'Interview resumed at 12.10.'

'My client would like to make a statement,' the QC said.

Richard Williams commenced. 'I have maintained a relationship with Marjorie Frobisher over the years. This has been infrequent in its nature, but as I had indicated before, we have a history of when we were both struggling to make our way in the world. There have been years when we have just been friends, others where we have been intimate.

'Marjorie phoned me from Malvern. I went there to meet her. The programme was in need of her, and I did not want her to be absent. There are a number of reasons as to why I did not tell you, not the least that I am genuinely fond of the woman. Also, the ratings and the advertising revenue were sure to be enhanced by her being on the screen, grieving elder sister, vengeful and determined slayer of those who had killed her brother.

'She was frightened. I reasoned with her, and she agreed to return to London within a few days. I offered to provide her with security, although the reason it was needed remained obscure. That is the end of my statement.'

'Do you have any knowledge of why she was frightened?' Isaac asked.

'She has skeletons in the cupboard, the same as most people.'

'Hers were substantial?'

'Yes.'

'Are you aware of a child?'

'I am.'

'Is there any more you can tell us about this child?'

'It was before we met.'

'Was the child yours?'

The QC intervened. 'My client will not answer that question.'

'It's okay, Quinton,' Williams said.

'The child was not mine.' He addressed Isaac.

'Do you know who the father is?'

'She would never tell me.'

'Did she know?'

'Are you insinuating that she may have been sleeping with more than one man?'

'Yes.'

'It's possible, of course. She was promiscuous in a casual manner. Most people were then. It was a time before HIV and Aids.'

Does Robert Avers know about this child?'

'How would I know? You'd better ask him.'

'Do you think he knows?'

'No idea.'

Isaac could see that he had exhausted one line of questioning. He could not fault Richard Williams in his responses. 'Did you at a party at her house have sexual relations with Marjorie Frobisher?'

'Are you trying to imply that because of Charles Sutherland and his daughter, I am somehow responsible for his death?'

'I am purely attempting to ascertain whether you deny the incident.'

'I'd prefer to forget it.'

'Why is that?'

'Her daughter, plain Jane, legs up in the air with Charles Sutherland's bare arse bobbing up and down. Not one of the prettiest sights.'

'How did Marjorie Frobisher react?'

'Badly.'

'Out of shame?'

'No. She had just had the sofa reupholstered. Her daughter and Sutherland were hardly the cleanest of people. She didn't want him spraying his mongrel sperm over it.'

'She didn't care about the daughter?'

'She never had. Why should she start then?'

'Fiona Avers has a reason to dislike her mother,' Isaac commented.

'I didn't like the way Marjorie treated her children, but it wasn't for me to complain. That was Robert Avers' responsibility.'

'Is there any more?' Quinton Scott asked. 'It appears that we have lapsed into innuendo and questions on morality.'

Isaac followed official police procedures and then hit the stop button.

Williams and Scott left soon after. Isaac spoke to Farhan. 'What do you reckon?'

'He answered the questions. I can't see that he has a motive for murder.'

***

Isaac and Farhan had been tailed in their cars again. They contacted Richard Goddard. Usually, they would have just contacted the vehicle identification department, but they knew the car registrations would be classified.

Wendy, back in the office, had rearranged the furniture, to Farhan's chagrin. She reckoned the two cars tailing them might be tied in with the two men that Bert, the taxi driver, had mentioned in Malvern. Isaac was not pleased with her presence in the office, as not only did they have to contend with the smell of stale cigarette smoke, now they had the smell of wine too. Farhan was certain that she was slightly hungover.

As soon as she had debriefed them, she decided to focus her investigations at Paddington Station. On the way through Worcester, she had spoken to the ticket seller on duty at the railway station. It had been busy the day that Bert had dropped off Marjorie Frobisher, the ticket seller had said. And besides, he added, most tickets are sold from a machine. She had managed to get tapes from the security cameras at the station. They were typically kept for a period of time and then erased. One day more, he had told her, and the video would have been gone forever. The tapes she passed over to Constable Bridget Halloran, the CCTV viewing officer, on arriving at Challis Street. She would scan through using facial recognition technology and a trained eye.

Her time in the office with Isaac and Farhan was brief, and she soon left. Farhan moved his desk to where it had been at the first opportunity.

'What did the two women he paid for say? Did they see anything?' Isaac asked.

'I've already told you.'

'I know that, but we need to be sure about this. We are aware of a child. We know of Charles Sutherland, who said he knew something. We have Richard Williams, who says he doesn't know who the child is. If Williams doesn't know, how would Sutherland?'

'He must have overheard something,' Farhan said.

'If he heard Marjorie Frobisher talking on a mobile phone, that would be a one-sided conversation, and she's hardly likely to say the child's name.'

'She could have told him.'

'If she wouldn't tell Richard Williams, she's hardly likely to tell Sutherland.'

'What if she told Williams?' Farhan asked.

'If she did, then it means two things.'

'One, he lied to us, and two, he's a potential target.'

'Are we conclusively stating that Charles Sutherland was murdered because he knew something?'

'Who else could have done it?' Farhan asked.

'Christy Nichols, Jess O'Neill, Fiona Avers.'

'They each had a strong enough motive: one he had forced to indulge in oral sex, another he attempted to rape, and the other was indulging in sexual intercourse with the man until her mother walked in.'

170

'He was poisoned. Whoever it was needed to get hold of the poison and know the dosage.'

'Fiona Avers is callous enough. I just don't see Jess O'Neill and Christy Nichols doing that, do you?'

'Jess O'Neill could if she was vengeful enough,' Isaac replied. 'What do you reckon to Christy Nichols?'

'She seems too timid.'

'And what is it with these escorts? Why are you protecting them?'

'I gave my word that I would keep their identities confidential for as long as I can.'

'You know you will have to reveal them at some time.'

'I hope that will not be necessary.'

'You'd better hope for a confession from someone. That's their only chance. I hope you explained that you can't give a guarantee.'

'I did.'

***

With the pressure of work, Isaac just hadn't had any time to devote to Sophie. He thought she was starting to become clingy, talking about moving in with him, or him moving in with her. Neither option appealed, and besides, there was still Jess.

After the interview session at the police station, their conversations by phone had been few and far between, and whereas the attraction remained from both parties, the easy banter, the repartee, the teasing, more from her than him, were conspicuous by their absence.

He had not dwelled too much on Farhan and his desire to keep the two escorts' identities concealed, although it was out of character for his offsider. He had always been a stickler for following investigations by the book, but he assumed he had his reasons.

Isaac was aware that he was not faultless either. There were times when he had gone easy on a female witness if he thought they were not involved.

Chapter 23

'DI Larry Hill, Islington Police Station. We've got a body. Police records show that you know the name.' Isaac looked at the clock by his bedside. It said 2 a.m. Fully awake now after missing the original message, Isaac asked the caller to repeat.

'What's the name?'

'Sally Jenkins, do you know her?'

'Yes.' One of the people he had been planning to interview, but never got around to it as he was too busy elsewhere. Isaac quickly dialled in Farhan.

'It looks as if someone climbed in a window at the back of the building, forced entry, grabbed the woman and held her face down in the sink. Clear signs of a struggle,' Larry Hill said.

'What's the address?'

'14 Crane Grove.'

It took Isaac three minutes to exit his apartment, another twenty minutes to get to Islington. It was early morning; the traffic was light. The road had been blocked off – tape had been put across to keep out the neighbours, the gawkers, and the plain nosey.

Most were still in their pyjamas, even though it was a cold morning. Farhan had beaten Isaac to the murder scene. Farhan waited for him to park his car. Then they proceeded to the house, showing their identity badges to the uniformed constable standing outside. It was clear that Sally Jenkins lived well. The upstairs flat in a typical terraced house had been tastefully renovated – in the last year, Isaac thought. The decorations were fresh, the television and stereo equipment good quality. There seemed to be little in the way of food in the house, which Isaac did not see as suspicious. He rarely ate at home. The bed, queen size, showed only one occupant; one side was neat, the other ruffled. It appeared she preferred to sleep close to the open window. It was apparent on examining the body that she slept in the nude.

'Any signs of a sexual attack?' Isaac asked.

'Forensics can tell you that,' Larry Hill said. 'From what I can see, I would say not. Apart from the bruising on her legs where she kicked out, it just seems to be death by drowning.' He was a good-looking man, late forties, with the slightest sign of middle-aged spread and appeared competent. He had a healthy tan, clear skin and white teeth. Isaac had developed a knack of summing up people at the first meeting. It sometimes annoyed Sophie, the few times he had taken her out. It seemed too clinical for her.

'One person or two?' Farhan asked.

'I would say one,' Hill responded. 'It's not that big in here. Two, they would have held her legs firm, stop her making a noise. Professional, I'd say.'

'Why do you say that?' Isaac asked.

'Have you seen the body?'

'Yes. I met her when she was alive.'

'If Charles Sutherland was a professional assassination, and Sally Jenkins is too, then Marjorie Frobisher is almost certainly dead,' Farhan said.

'You mean the woman off the television?' Larry Hill had heard them talking.

'You weren't meant to hear that,' Isaac said.

'You think she's dead?'

'Larry, forget what you just heard. People are dying as a result of her.'

'Policemen included?'

'Nobody is safe. Certainly not Farhan and myself.'

'They said she used to play around.'

'Larry, I don't think we should discuss this anymore. We'll be taking the case over from here.'

'This is my case.' Larry Hill saw his authority being usurped.

'You're getting yourself involved in something that could get messy.'

'That sounds like a threat.'

Isaac attempted to appease the man's anger. 'This is not the first body, almost certainly not the last.'

'That's my decision. I will conduct the investigation into Sally Jenkins' death and keep you advised. The others you can deal with.'

'We'll accept your assistance. Find out what you can about suspicious people, how the window was opened.'

'DCI Cook, I've been around a while. I know how to conduct a murder investigation.'

'Apologies. We're all a bit on edge. Your assistance is appreciated.'

With no more to do, Isaac and Farhan exited the building. The weather had taken a turn for the worse. The previously eager onlookers had – bar a few – retreated inside and back to bed or to watch news reports on the television. All the major channels were in the street with their cameras focussed on the house.

'What next?' Farhan asked.

'No point going home,' Isaac said.

'I need to have a shower and change. I'll be there in an hour.'

'Give me ninety minutes.' Isaac realised he may as well return home and take a shower too. A murder scene gave him an uncomfortable feeling. A shower always seemed to help, as if he was washing the horror and the sight of the dead body away.

'Any ideas?' Farhan asked as he was getting into his car.

'We need to find this damn woman. She's the key to this.'

***

Cecil Broughton, the station manager at Paddington Station, had seen the transition of the railways for fifty years. He was still an upright man, close to retirement at sixty-five, hopeful of a reprieve due to the government considering pushing the retirement age up closer to seventy. Wendy Gladstone liked him immediately.

'Pleased to meet you,' he said as she entered his office. It had a warm feeling to it, almost a relic of an earlier age, the walls adorned with pictures of trains through the years, mainly steam. The paint on the walls was flaking in places and the carpet threadbare – how he liked it.

'Some people are taken aback when they enter.'

'Why's that?' Wendy asked.

'They expect the office to be modern and smelling of air freshener.'

'More like old leather in here.'

'27th November 1965,' Broughton proudly said.

'I was just starting school,' she replied, not fully understanding the significance of the date.

'My first week here, pushing a trolley.'

'Fifty years in the one place?'

'I moved around over the years, but I always intended to finish my time at Paddington. I remember that day well.'

'Why?'

'The last day a steam train exited this station, *Clun Castle*, heading through Slough, Swindon, Bristol, before terminating in Gloucester.'

'Do you remember them all?'

'Most, I suppose. Trains have been a passion all my life.'

What the last train had to do with the smell in the office still eluded her.

'It's the seats,' he said.

'Pardon.'

'That's the smell. I retrieved them from *Clun Castle*.'

'You sound resentful of the trains today.'

'Not at all,' he reflected. 'Brilliant technical achievements, just lacking in character. Anyway, you didn't come here to reminisce about trains from the past, did you?'

'Interesting subject, no doubt,' she said, although the modern trains suited her fine. She had been on the occasional steam train, school excursions mainly, and she only remembered them as slow and exceedingly smelly.

'You're trying to find a missing person.' Wendy could only reflect as she sat there how different he was to her husband. Broughton, alert and in his sixties; her husband, a few years younger, yet older in mind and body, and bitter about his life.

'We believe the woman boarded the Paddington train in Worcester.'

'Are you certain?' he asked.

'She probably bought the ticket from a machine at the station.'

'That makes it difficult.'

'Why's that?'

'How to identify her. Do you know what she was wearing?'

'I've already passed on details to your people. We're reviewing the tapes from Worcester Station. You have more cameras at Paddington, and people trained to watch the monitors.'

'Major issue these days. No idea where the next idiot is going to let off a bomb.'

'Any problems in the past?'

'Not since 1991.'

'February 1991. IRA, two bombs; one here and another at Victoria. No fatalities here, one dead at Victoria,' Wendy said.

'You've got a good memory.'

'Probably not as good as yours. I was assigned to Victoria to assist in the investigation.'

'It's best if I take you up to our video surveillance department. You've time for a cup of tea?' he asked. 'British Rail has an excellent reputation for making tea.'

'A tradition worth upholding,' she replied. 'I don't remember the sandwiches with the same fondness.'

'These days they come in a cellophane bag. At least they won't be stale. Not all traditions are worth preserving.'

The tea arrived, hot and milky, just the way she liked it, two spoons of sugar as well. She noticed that the station manager had Earl Grey with no sugar.

***

The walk from the office, through the heart of the station with its milling passengers, to the surveillance department took less than five minutes. Broughton's office had been nostalgic; the area she entered was not. It was modern and efficient, with numerous monitors displaying all areas of the station.

Brian Gee, a young man in his early thirties, was in charge. He introduced himself and gave the police constable a guided tour of his domain. 'State of the art, best there is,' he said.

'I'm not really into computers.' She noticed that Brian Gee was a remarkably active man, almost hyperactive. Her youngest son, Brad, had been the same as a child but had grown out of it; Brian Gee had not. He was fidgeting, moving from one foot to the other, fiddling with a pen, or picking up a piece of paper only to put it down again.

'It's not everyone's cup of tea, I suppose. I'll admit to being a computer nerd.'

'Any luck finding the missing woman?' She had supplied a description earlier before arriving at the station, although it had been necessarily vague: green dress, just below the knees, sensible black shoes, a dark overcoat, and a blue hat with a brim. She had also mentioned the sunglasses and the name of Marjorie Frobisher.

'With your description?'

'How many people were on the train that day?' she asked.

The station manager responded, 'Probably no more than one hundred and fifty.'

'Can't you isolate it to them?'

'It's not that simple,' Brian Gee replied. 'We're not looking at the trains per se. We mainly focus on the platforms, the restrooms, the main concourse. There were two trains on the platform at the time of interest. The train we are interested in, and another from the west of the country. In total that's about five hundred people. We're looking, could be a few hours yet, and then she could have changed her clothes. Even with all this technology, it's still a needle in a haystack.'

Wendy could see that it was going to take a while. She determined she would wait it out. At least at the railway station she could find somewhere outside to smoke.

***

Isaac and Farhan had not spent much time in the office since the death of Sally Jenkins. Isaac decided that his best approach was to call Richard Williams to the station. There was a great unknown to be resolved. If Sally Jenkins was killed because she knew something, then how did she get that information? And if she had that information, did that place the source in danger as well?

The situation with the media was also starting to become a nuisance. The disappearance of Marjorie Frobisher had caused speculative interest from them, with their probing cameras and microphones. The death of Charles Sutherland, now officially confirmed as murder, had taken their interest level up to serious. The death of Sally Jenkins, not a celebrity but known as the personal assistant to the executive producer, created further interest.

Isaac rethought his plan to bring Williams into Challis Street as his arrival would be seen by the media. He did not want to create added speculation on the television and in the press.

Detective Superintendent Goddard, on advice from Charles Shaw, the Met Commissioner, saw that the only option was to make a formal statement. He realised he should have done this earlier, after the death of Charles Sutherland, but he had been hesitant. Angus MacTavish had been against it, even threatened his career.

It was evident the commissioner had used his contacts and had cleared the press conference.

The press conference, hastily set up for two in the afternoon, had not allowed Isaac time to meet Williams. He had phoned him, found him to be uncommonly subdued, and sorry about the death of his former personal assistant. 'I had a lot of time for her. We had some fun together,' he said. Isaac wasn't sure if it was a genuine heartfelt emotion or whether it was for his benefit. He chose to believe the former.

He would force Williams to reveal his real emotions at a later date and to detail every bit of hidden information he possessed. Isaac and Farhan remained convinced that the deaths would continue. People were dying for a reason still unknown, and until they knew that reason, the case was going nowhere.

Charles Sutherland had known something, or had he? Sally Jenkins had died for a similar reason, but she'd had no way of finding out the information unless it was by eavesdropping, or someone had told her. If it wasn't Charles Sutherland, then who, and why?' Both Isaac and Farhan were nervous when they explained their fears to their boss, Detective Superintendent Goddard.

'We're stuck with this,' he said, 'whether we like it or not.'

Chapter 24

'Ladies and gentlemen, members of the press. Good morning.' The assembled audience for the hastily arranged press conference waited impatiently for their opportunity to put questions. They knew they would have to listen to the official police statement first: Detective Superintendent Richard Goddard to give the initial address, Detective Chief Inspector Isaac Cook to follow on. Neither man was excited at the prospect, although Isaac knew his parents would be proudly watching on the television.

Richard Goddard read from a prepared statement. 'Charles Sutherland, it is confirmed, died as the result of poisoning. We are treating his death as murder. You are now aware that a subsequent death, confirmed as the murder of a young female, is possibly related. Both were involved in a television programme, one as an actor, the other as the personal assistant to the executive producer.

'I should state that the assumption that both murders are related must remain just that, an assumption. In both cases, there appears to be no motive.

'What I can tell you is that the disappearance of Marjorie Frobisher still causes us concern. We are anxious to ascertain her whereabouts at the earliest opportunity. It is clear that when the floor is thrown open to questions, her name will be mentioned. Let me emphasise that we believe her to be missing.

'I will invite those present to ask questions. Please announce your name, the organisation you represent, and to whom you are directing the question. Please do not expect us to indulge in idle speculation.'

A quick flurry of hands in the air, a flashing of cameras as the individuals in the throng attempted to be first with their question.

'Barbara Halsall, Sky News. Detective Chief Inspector Cook, is it not a fact that you are looking for Marjorie Frobisher's body, and that the police believe her to be dead?'

Isaac's reply, predictable. 'Unless we receive information to the contrary, we continue to believe that she is alive and well.'

'Is it not clear that she is dead?' Barbara Halsall was entitled to one question; she had taken two. It was not unexpected. She had been on the television almost as long as Isaac had been alive. Few would stand in her way when she was asking questions. Richard Goddard attempted to remind her that she was only entitled to one question. She ignored him totally.

'There is nothing to indicate that Marjorie Frobisher's disappearance is related to the current murder enquiries.' Isaac knew it was a weak response.

'Stuart Vaughan, BBC. It must be obvious to anyone, even the man in the street, that her disappearance is related.'

'It is a consideration,' Isaac conceded.

'Are you able to confirm that Sally Jenkins was naked when found?'

'Please announce your name and organisation first.' Richard Goddard attempted to wrest control of the proceedings from the media flock. He knew he would not be successful.

'Claude Dunn, News Corporation. Is it true she was found with no clothes on?' The media had become sensationalist.

'That is not the focus of this press conference,' Isaac said. He assumed Dunn must have paid someone at the crime scene for the information.

'Geoffrey Agnew, ITV. Charles Sutherland had intended to reveal details about Marjorie Frobisher. Can you let us know what those details were?'

Richard Goddard answered. 'No details were revealed.'

'A hoax on his part?' Agnew ignored the other questioners in the room, his raised voiced drowning them out.

'I did not say that.' Richard Goddard felt cornered. Angus MacTavish was watching, as was Commissioner Shaw on the television in Downing Street. The detective superintendent did not want his career to go down the drain due to an ill-chosen rebuttal. 'Both murders are ongoing investigations. All avenues of enquiry will be investigated in detail. It would be inappropriate for either myself or Detective Chief Inspector Cook to speculate.'

'And the prostitutes?' Agnew interrupted. Again, Isaac realised that someone had paid money for that information. Farhan, watching from the rear of the room, hoped it wasn't Christy Nichols or Aisha, and if it was Olivia, why? It seemed more likely to have been one of the staff in the hotel. He knew he had to find out.

'Ladies and gentlemen, I believe we have informed you as to the current situation. Regular press statements will be posted as new information becomes available. I thank you for your time.' Richard Goddard wrapped up the press conference and exited the room, followed by Isaac.

'How do you think it went, sir?' Isaac asked.

'Hopefully, well enough to save our careers.' It seemed a pessimistic reply to Isaac. He chose not to comment.

***

With the press conference concluded, Isaac was free to meet Richard Williams. It was after six in the evening when he arrived at his office in the city. Williams opened the door, the new personal assistant nowhere to be seen.

'DCI Cook, tragic business.'

'I may need to bring you into the station at some stage.'

'I thought it would have been today. Why didn't you?'

'Media scrum down there, too many people sticking their noses in. Did you have a similar problem?'

'I don't follow you,' Williams replied.

'Sally Jenkins had a tendency to listen in.'

'I believe I told you that the other week.'

'You did. Now the question is, did she hear or know of something that people would kill for?'

'Not from me.' Richard Williams seemed a little too nonchalant for Isaac.

'I'll level with you,' Isaac said. 'We have two bodies, a missing woman, and no motive, other than several women who were pleased when Sutherland was murdered. One was even delighted.'

'Sally wasn't one of them. She didn't like him and his leering remarks, but she only met him once to my knowledge.'

'And when was that?'

'Some months back. We were wrapping up production for the year. We all met at a hotel near the production lot and had a decent meal and a few too many drinks. Sutherland was drunk, making suggestive remarks, but I don't remember him going near Sally.'

'Are you sure?'

'Not totally. It was after all a party. Left the Ferrari here, took a taxi.'

'Sally left the party with you?'

'Not that she would have known about leaving.'

'Why's that?'

'Mixing her drinks, totally out of it.'

'And she said nothing?'

'About Sutherland?'

'Yes.'

'She didn't say anything that night; the next day, she could barely remember the previous evening.'

'You were with her?'

'At the place where she was found dead. I paid for it, the renovations as well.'

'The night she died?'

'I told you before that I had sacked her.'

'And you let her stay in the place?'

'Why not? I'm not a total bastard.'

'The night she died?' Isaac returned to the standard question. The question that invariably invoked a reply of 'I didn't murder her' or 'My alibi's watertight.'

'I was with my personal assistant, the new one. In her bed, if you must know.'

'She will testify to that?'

'I don't think she'll be euphoric about it, but I'm sure she will.'

'Sally Jenkins knew something. If it didn't come from Sutherland, it must have come from you.'

'I don't know of anything that would warrant murder.'

'You argued with Marjorie Frobisher before she disappeared. Was anything said in the heat of the moment, anything unexpected?'

'How many times have we discussed this?'

'How many times have you evaded the answer?' Isaac responded, his voice raised.

'Marjorie may have mentioned about the child she had when she was a lot younger, but she never mentioned the name, even if she knew it. That may be good enough for a gossip magazine, but it hardly seems sufficient to justify murder. If you wish to discuss this matter again, I will make sure my legal adviser is present.'

Isaac left soon after. The briefest of handshakes as they parted.

***

Angus MacTavish and Richard Goddard met at a pub some distance from Downing Street. The detective superintendent was anxious to be updated about the current situation, and to ascertain how his career was progressing. He was not naïve, he knew that the years of loyal service, the innumerable courses and qualifications, and unblemished service record counted for nothing if people at the top, often nameless, disapproved of the nominee. His future revolved around a missing woman, not the two murders. He also knew that he may be forced to make decisions that would affect the ongoing investigations. A major celebrity in the country was impacting his career; he did not like it.

There was no point in discussing the matter with Commissioner Shaw as he was no doubt feeling the pressure as well. His appointment was due for renewal, and questions were already being raised about his suitability. The detective superintendent, a political animal, knew why the questions were being asked. They were political in nature, lacking in substance, and were there to apply pressure on Commissioner Shaw to rein in his people. He also knew that Commissioner Shaw was not a man easily swayed. Neither was he. It was a dilemma he would face if the pressure came. It was clear that Angus MacTavish would have no trouble applying the pressure.

'Goddard, it's good to see you.' The meeting started well. The Red Lion, a short distance from MacTavish's office, hardly seemed the ideal place, as it was well frequented by politicians from both sides of the house, but MacTavish had arranged a private room on the first floor.

'Change of location?'

'Somewhere private.'

'I saw some from the other side of the house downstairs.'

'Don't worry about them. They're as thick as two short planks.'

'You saw the press conference?'

'You handled it well. You had to make a statement of some sort. Otherwise the media would have started sticking their noses in more than they already are.'

'They're a damn nuisance.' Both had ordered a pint of Fuller's London Pride, on tap, and a meat pie, a speciality of the house.

'What do you have?' MacTavish asked. He had already downed the first pint, ordered another.

'Two murders and a missing woman.'

'Apart from that.'

'There are a few suspects for the murder of Charles Sutherland; none apparent for Sally Jenkins.'

'Who would want to kill Sutherland? I'm told he was not the most pleasant person, but murder?'

'Three had a strong enough reason for Sutherland.'

'How do these people make so many enemies?'

'A male chauvinist pig is an apt description for Sutherland.'

'Not really relevant, is it?'

'It will be if one of the women killed him.'

'You know what I'm referring to.'

'Marjorie Frobisher.'

'Precisely. Where is this woman? Is she dead? Is she likely to be dead soon?'

'Are you stating that if she's not dead, she may be soon?'

'Detective Superintendent, I don't know.'

'You have some updated information?'

'I am aware that there is an assassination order out on her. Don't ask me who or where or when.'

'Why?'

'I don't know. That's the truth.'

'What do you want to do about this?'

'If you find her, protect her,' MacTavish said as he finished his third pint. Richard Goddard had just drunk one. He was prepared to order a half, but with MacTavish downing them so fast, he ordered another pint instead.

'Assuming we find her, where do we protect her? If someone's serious about killing her, are we being given the all clear to use violence?'

'Don't look for official permission from me or anyone else. If it goes wrong, everyone will deny responsibility.'

'The risk seems too high.

'That's negative.' MacTavish slammed his beer down on the table, the froth spilling out over the rim of the glass.

'It seems realistic to me.'

'With great risk comes great reward. Do you get my drift?'

'I'm an ambitious man. I don't deny that.'

'And there's an assistant commissioner's position coming up shortly.'

'Are you saying it's mine if this is handled correctly?'

'That's up to Commissioner Shaw. He's looking for a peerage. You look after us; we look after him. You know how it works, don't you?'

'Yes, of course. We'll do what is necessary, but I'm not willing to put my men's lives at risk.'

'The black inspector looks to be a smart man. Ambitious, is he?'

'Also very competent.'

'He'll be looked after as well.'

***

The question from Agnew at the press conference had interested Farhan. How did he know about the two women Christy Nichols had signed for?

The young detective inspector knew that it wasn't necessarily the most secret piece of information. But failing a motive, it was one of their few possible lines of enquiry. Isaac was following up on Sally Jenkins' murder, with Larry Hill providing assistance where he could. Wendy was trying to find the missing woman, and Richard Goddard's last visit to the office had revealed that if Marjorie Frobisher was alive, it was up to the department to protect her at all costs.

Isaac had asked why, until their boss had taken him out of the room for a five-minute chat. On his return, Isaac ceased asking and acquiesced to his senior's request. Farhan thought he should have been more persistent.

Too many unknowns Farhan thought, but kept his own counsel. Isaac believed that following up on how Agnew knew about the prostitutes was shooting in the dark. As he had reasoned, someone let them into the hotel, Christy Nichols had shown them into Sutherland's suite, and numerous people had seen them leave.

As Farhan had explained to Isaac, they did not leave the hotel as women of the night. They would have changed, and to those moving around in the foyer of the hotel, they would have looked no different from the majority of the people there.

Farhan found himself at a variance with his DCI, who now seemed more focussed on Marjorie Frobisher than Charles Sutherland and Sally Jenkins.

Farhan was still living on his own, although the children were fine. His wife had instigated legal proceedings against him for the division of the assets – meagre as they were – and maintenance of the children.

Ironic, he had thought when he received the notification, that his wife, traditional and conservative, had no issues with embracing English law when it suited her. In her own country, she would not have found such a favourable response from the courts, where the man held predominance, but he had spent a long time in England and he saw no issues with his wife's legal demands. He just hoped that it could be dealt with without the bitterness and acrimony that so many seemed to go through when a marriage failed.

But it was not the failed marriage or the assets that concerned him the most, it was the children. Would they receive a moderate education and upbringing? Would his daughter be allowed to integrate into British society as an equal, free to choose her direction in life, free to choose who she married when the time came? He saw England for all its beauty and its benefits. It was a country he had come to love, a country that was allowing him to fast-track his career.

Chapter 25

Farhan acknowledged several minutes after leaving the office that his personal issues were just that, personal. There were two bodies, possibly more if he and Isaac did not come up with a solution soon. He laid out his plan of action. First, he first wanted to meet Aisha, although he felt sure she had not spoken to the reporter.

Christy Nichols seemed the most likely to have told the media. He realised he had not spoken to the hotel employee who had smuggled them into the hotel. He had deemed it not necessary in the initial investigations; realised now that it may have been an error of judgement on his part. Maybe that person had seen something, knew something. Christy Nichols would know who that person was.

Geoffrey Agnew proved to be of little use to Farhan. 'I only spoke to the person on the phone.'

Pressed further, Agnew claimed that the voice was muffled and that he was not sure if it was male or female. Farhan did not believe him, told him that it was a murder investigation and that withholding information was a criminal offence. Agnew, a pugnacious little man, continued to state that he was not withholding information, and any future conversations would be with his company's full legal team in attendance. Farhan knew he was wasting his time.

Christy Nichols would be easier to deal with, and she would not be threatening in her manner or evasive in her answers. At least, he hoped she would not be. He liked her. She was an ambitious woman in an industry that rewarded ambitious people, as long as that came with aggression and a complete lack of feeling or emotion. He thought that she did not have the aggression; she had even admitted it. Victoria Webster certainly did, and Christy Nichols admired her for it, but would never emulate her.

He felt fortunate that he worked within an organisation that rewarded people for their ability, not their gender or their religion or their colour, but then he was not so sure of that. The Met prided itself that it was equal opportunity, but who were the most senior people in the organisation? He knew the answer. They were male, white, Anglo-Saxon, and Christian. Sure, there were signs of change: Isaac was one example. There was every indication that he was in line to move up in the police force, but how far would he go? How far could he go? Farhan dismissed his pessimism and focussed on doing his job. He was not leaving the police force, period. It was where he belonged, he knew that.

He found Christy Nichols at the apartment where she lived on her own, a two-bedroom, first-floor conversion of a terraced house. The location, close to Hampstead Heath, was fine, the condition of the building, mediocre. She was apologetic when he knocked on the door, although she had agreed to their meeting at her apartment, instead of a local coffee shop or at the local police station as Farhan had suggested.

'Apologies for the mess.' She had made some attempt at tidying up. She was dressed in a pair of shorts and a tee-shirt.

'That's fine. You should see my place,' he replied, although he had to admit his housekeeping, woeful as it was, did not look as bad as hers. The bathroom door was ajar, and he could see the washing hanging from the shower rail.

'Take a seat, not the one in the corner though.' He could see why. It was occupied by what appeared to be an old rolled up woollen jumper, but turned out to be an old cat. 'That's Cuddles,' she said. It did not seem cuddly to Farhan. He had no great affinity for animals, no great dislike. His wife had abhorred pets in the house; he would not have been overly concerned. A family pet was good for the children, gave them a sense of responsibility.

Farhan sat on one of the two remaining chairs. Christy Nichols sat on the other, the tee-shirt tightening as she adjusted her position. He did not feel comfortable in her presence. 'Did you watch the press conference?' he asked.

'I saw some of it and then switched it off,' she replied.

'Why was that?'

'It reminded me of the events at the hotel.'

It seemed a fair response to Farhan. After all, she had been in the room next door when a murder had been committed, and Sutherland had forced her into giving him oral sex.

'One of the reporters knew about the two escorts at the hotel.'

'That seems possible,' she replied.

'Why do you say that?'

'I don't think it's the first time prostitutes have been in the hotel, do you?'

'It probably happens all the time. What interests me is who told the reporter.'

'I certainly didn't.' She went on the defensive and stood up.

'Please, the issue is not whether you did or did not. I'm not here about whether it was illegal.'

'Then why are you here?'

'Four people knew of the two women in the hotel.'

'The escorts, myself and the person who let them in.' She had resumed her seat.

'Do you know the fourth person?'

'I paid him.'

'How did you arrange it?'

'I spoke to the person who showed us to the rooms.'

'Is that the same individual you paid later?'

'No, so that makes it five, doesn't it?'

'It may be more,' Farhan said. 'I need to meet these people at the hotel.'

'It could still be the escorts. The information would have been worth several hundred pounds to someone like Geoffrey.'

'Geoffrey?'

'Geoffrey Agnew. I know him personally.'

'How?'

'Degree in Journalism. Part of the course required us to spend time as trainee journalists. I spent three weeks at the

192

television company. Work experience, they called it; supposedly assisting in typing up the copy for that day's broadcasts.'

'And?' Farhan knew the answer.

'I learnt how to make a mean cup of coffee, and how to balance everyone's lunch order on one arm, while I struggled to press the lift button.'

'I can sympathise.'

'Similar experience for you?' she asked.

'The first couple of weeks after leaving the police college. First Pakistani, first Muslim, the first person with a university degree in the station.'

'What happened?' she asked.

'They found out soon enough that I did not bring any hang-ups with me, that I was moderate in my faith, and I was potentially a good policeman.'

'And a good person as well.'

Farhan left soon after. She had given him a name at the hotel, and an impression that she liked him not only as a policeman but as a friend. He found himself to be in a dilemma. There were Aisha and Christy and family issues to deal with. There were also two murders, possibly more. He felt that life was becoming too complicated.

***

Isaac could only reflect on the differences between Linda Harris and Sally Jenkins. One was still very much alive and sitting opposite him; the other, very much dead, and lying on a slab in a morgue. He acknowledged that Richard Williams had great taste in women.

Sally Jenkins had been young and beautiful and clearly a rich man's floozy. Linda Harris, Sally's replacement, in bed and out, according to Williams, somehow did not ring true. To Isaac, she did not seem the sort of person who would be swayed by the executive producer's charm. He thought she would have been more than capable of finding a man more her age with the wealth and the vitality she needed. He knew it was not for him to make moral judgements, only to observe and question, and to solve the murders.

A missing woman was the least of their worries, but now they were to protect her if she ever reappeared. Richard Goddard had explained the situation to him. He still didn't understand fully, although he was confident that his boss didn't either.

As the detective superintendent had said, 'It's our futures on the line here. If we get this right, influential people will look after us.'

'And if we don't?'

'We're stuffed.' Not the answer an ambitious policeman wanted to hear. Isaac saw his progression to the top as a result of competent, even exceptional policing, but he was a realist. He knew how it worked. Commissioner Charles Shaw sat in the chair that he wanted to occupy one day, although he would let his senior keep it warm in the interim. He knew that as a decent, hard-working member of the force he could climb the promotion ladder, although it was easy to slide down it if he did not play the game, flatter the inflated egos of important people, and let others take credit for results he had achieved.

Charles Shaw sat in his chair not because he had been the only contender, but because he had played the game, made the right connections. Isaac had to admit he had done a good job. His reorganisation of the bureaucratic structure of the Metropolitan Police had been good, and apart from the threat of terrorist-related activities, crime levels were down in the city. The other contenders when the previous commissioner had stepped down did not have the political savvy, had not gone to school with the prime minister, or sat on the PM's Anti-Terrorism Committee.

Isaac did not have the contacts, but he did have Richard Goddard, who had the ear of Commissioner Shaw. He was certain there was more than a mutual respect involved, although he had never asked.

***

Linda Harris had suggested the restaurant; Isaac had agreed. He hoped it would not be too expensive, as he felt obliged to pay, and getting expenses paid took forever. The mortgage on his apartment was placing him under a lot of pressure, and now he had been landed with a bill to replace the oven. He needed a promotion, not a demotion, although he realised that he was placing himself in the category of expendable, knowing too much.

Isaac ordered fish, lightly grilled, with a salad – in line with his new regime of looking after his health. He was aware that tomorrow it could be a late night and another pizza. Linda ordered a Greek salad. Both chose orange juice. The seats they occupied were close to the corner window with a limited view of the street. Camden Town, where they met, was trendy, with many of its streets of run-down terraces being renovated. Isaac appreciated the colourful atmosphere; she loved it.

'I come from Devon. Too quiet down there for me,' she said. He had dismissed her at Williams' office as another rent-a-lay. As he spoke to her, he was not so sure. Sally Jenkins had been obvious, not especially articulate, and dressed in the office in a tarty manner. He remembered Linda in the office wearing a long-sleeved blouse, but apart from that, couldn't remember much else. At the restaurant she wore jeans with a white top.

'What brought you to London?'

'Secretarial college, and then I found work here.'

'You realise why we're meeting today?' he asked. He had finished his meal; she had barely started.

'I suppose it's to do with my predecessor's death. I'm not sure how I can help. I never met her.'

'Is there anything you can tell me about her? Any reason why someone would want her dead?'

'Apart from her lousy administration skills? I wouldn't have thought that was a reason for murder, although if she had been around, I would have felt like throttling her.'

'No good at her job?' Isaac asked. He had ordered a second glass of orange juice. He was in no hurry to leave.

'Virtually incompetent, but she wasn't employed for her office skills, was she?' Isaac thought it was a refreshingly open statement.

'What do you know of her relationship with Richard Williams?'

'Apart from him being the boss, and her the employee?'

'Yes.'

'He was sleeping with her.'

'Yes, I know.'

'He has a history of relationships with his staff,' she said.

'I am aware that Sally Jenkins enjoyed the good life he provided.' Isaac looked for a response. He could see none.

'Are you trying diplomatically to ask whether I was sleeping with him?'

'It may be relevant to the investigation.'

'The answer to your question is yes.'

'Thank you for your honesty.'

'He's used me as an alibi, hasn't he?'

'Do you corroborate his statement?'

'He was with me all night.'

Isaac felt the need to probe. 'Sally Jenkins was obviously with Williams for her own personal reasons.'

'And you want to know if my reasons are the same?'

'It may be relevant.'

'I'm not sure how. For the record, Sally Jenkins was incompetent, attractive, and easily swayed by a rich man with a fancy car.'

'Are you?'

'Not at all. For one thing, I'm competent; the car and the wealth are not important.'

'Then why?'

'He's a charming man, treats me well. Neither of us is under any illusion. It's purely fun for a while. I'll leave soon enough. Does that satisfy?'

Isaac chose not to comment. He had a casual relationship with Sophie, and it suited both of them fine. It was not for him to form an opinion on Linda Harris or Richard Williams.

The relationship between Jess O'Neill and Williams had concerned him a lot, but he had discounted it, given her the benefit of the doubt. He realised as he sat across from a beautiful woman that he had not seen Jess for a while. Their last meeting had left both of them more than a little upset.

'Sally Jenkins was murdered for a reason,' Isaac said.

'Are you concerned that I may be targeted as well?' She seemed unconcerned.

'If, as we believe, she died for something she knew or overheard, then the situation remains that you may know or have heard something.'

'I'm not sure what. You believe that Richard may know something?'

'It seems a logical conclusion. We are assuming Charles Sutherland died because he was going to talk to the magazine about what he knew.'

'And you believe Sally Jenkins knew as well.'

'It's possible.'

'Either she was involved with Sutherland or she heard something. Is that what you are saying?'

'We've discounted any involvement with Sutherland. The only information she could have would have come from Richard Williams. There seems to be no other explanation.'

'I certainly haven't heard anything in the office, although I'm not an eavesdropper. Apparently, she was.'

'If you haven't heard anything at work, maybe you have elsewhere.'

'How?'

'Does he talk in his sleep?'

'He doesn't sleep much.'

'Why do you say that?'

'Not because of me. It's the man's metabolism. He sleeps for three or four hours, and then he's prowling about, making a cup of tea, snacking from the fridge, writing emails. Mildly annoying. I need eight hours at least, or I'm cranky the next day.'

'In his limited sleep time, does he talk?' Isaac returned to the original question.

'Sometimes, but I take little notice. I'm a heavy sleeper, take a sleeping pill occasionally. Do you think Sally heard something?'

'It's a possibility.'

'If someone thinks I heard something as well?'

'You need to take care, maybe distance yourself a little from him.'

'That's not an issue. I'm not sleeping with Richard anymore. It was only a short-term fling for both of us. He likes his women a little more common than me, and I do not need a man attempting to prove his virility. I've more pride than that.'

'You'll continue to work with him?'

'I said I would until I've fixed up the administration, or until he finds a Sally Jenkins replacement.'

Isaac felt satisfied with her responses, not certain about her safety, but there was an unknown assailant, and the police could not protect everyone in potential danger. And if the murders were professional, would the police even be capable of waylaying a determined assassin?

Chapter 26

Wendy, frustrated with the slow progress on checking the security videos at Paddington Station, decided to leave early and return the next day, but not before calling in at Challis Street. She needed to check if there had been any success at finding the missing woman from the video she had obtained in Worcester.

Bridget Halloran greeted Wendy as she entered the office on the lower floor of the building. She was a good-looking woman, with a strong Irish accent. She and Wendy had hit it off when Bridget first arrived in the building a few years earlier. Both had a story to tell and an easy-going sense of humour. Wendy enjoyed being out in the field, Bridget preferred the office, even the reports that needed preparing. She had helped Wendy a few times with her spelling, which was atrocious. It can be rectified, Bridget had assured her, but Wendy never took her advice, and as long as Bridget remained in the building, she never would.

Wendy was almost fifteen years older than Bridget, yet they were firm friends, inside and outside the police force. Both were partial to a good drink, too many sometimes, and Wendy's husband had complained on more than one occasion when the taxi driver had had to assist her into the house. Bridget's long time, live-in lover had tried complaining, but as she told Wendy, 'If he starts complaining, he'll get the back of my hand and a quick push out the front door.' It was a fair statement, as a small inheritance from a favourite aunt had allowed Bridget to put the deposit down on the house, and she had no intention of allowing her lover to have any financial stake in it. Not unless he made an honest woman of her, and he didn't look like doing that anytime soon. Besides, she wasn't sure she wanted to be an honest woman. She felt the need to play up on occasions, and doing so with a ring on her finger would have offended her strict Roman Catholic upbringing. Wendy had covered for her a few times.

Bridget knew the lover would not be checking too hard on her. He was not ambitious, maintained a mundane job working for the council, but he provided company. He had his part to play in the agreement, and as long as he abided by the conditions, he was free to live with her rent-free.

'Any luck with the video?' Wendy asked after they had spent more than a few minutes nattering, making plans for another night out.

'She boarded the train. Let me show you.'

All Wendy could see was a grainy screen with what looked like a dead fly in one camera, out of focus and blurry.

'It's not very clear,' she confessed, not sure if it was her eyesight.

'They never are. No one cleans the cameras. The pollution slowly builds up. Just squint your eyes a little, may help.'

Wendy squinted; it helped a little. All she could see was a woman vaguely matching the description getting into the third carriage of the Paddington bound train. Another five people appeared to get on as well, and they were clearly not middle-aged. One was male and old, the way he walked attesting to that fact. Another two apparently newlyweds, or newly enchanted with each other. The other two, children from what she could see. It had to be Marjorie Frobisher, although the face was concealed and the resolution on the camera did not help.

By the time they had finished looking at the video, it was too late in the day to return to Paddington Station. She had phoned Brian Gee, the self-confessed computer nerd, and sent him an email attachment with the three best stills taken from the Worcester Station video. She then called the station manager, a matter of courtesy, to thank him for his help and to suggest that perhaps they could catch up for a cup of tea tomorrow, her treat, which seemed a lame remark. He was British Rail – the tea was his, and he didn't have to pay for it.

***

Christy Nichols had passed on to Farhan the details of who was involved in smuggling the two escorts into the hotel. He should have met with them first, and then Aisha.

He decided against meeting Olivia if he could. He saw
her as a decent woman indulging in an unusual occupation to
provide for her family, who would not have understood.

There had been pressure to reveal his contacts, a
procedural requirement. He knew if there were an audit of the
department, he would receive a severe reprimand. Not revealing
the women's identities would hamper his promotion prospects;
giving their names would cause him a moral dilemma, as they had
spoken to him in confidence.

Farhan understood that Detective Superintendent
Goddard was not willing to rock the boat if it affected his
ambition, but would turn a blind eye if it did not. Farhan had
decided come what may that Samantha's and Olivia's true
identities would remain concealed, but Christy Nichols knew the
agency.

Marion Robertson, the principal of the agency, may not
have felt such reluctance, especially if pressure was applied: legal
pressure, running a house of ill-repute, profiting from the
proceeds of prostitution, employing illegal immigrants. He was
certain she was not guilty of any crime, certainly none that was
too serious, but if pressured, those doing the questioning would
almost certainly bring up the possible avenues of enquiry, and she
would have other women on her books. Farhan knew the
possibility of the two women being identified was strong. He had
to let them know.

He phoned Olivia. She was not pleased to hear from him.
He explained the situation and asked whether she had told
Agnew. She said her identity was more important than a few
hundred pounds, and besides, her husband's financial situation
had improved, and the need to prostitute herself was not as
important, although they were looking at a bigger house to buy.
Farhan saw that selling herself caused her no personal issues.

He explained the possibility of her identity being
revealed. It caused her great alarm. He said that he would never
reveal it, but others might. He advised her to consider her
position, and if he thought her identity was soon to be revealed,

he would attempt to contact her in advance. She thanked him. She sounded genuine.

Aisha was also disturbed when he phoned her, although initially she had been delighted. He had been honest with Olivia; he would be with her. Olivia meant nothing to him, Aisha did. They agreed to meet.

***

Farhan, personally involved, wishing he could be detached but knowing he could not, thought a better location than Hyde Park would be more appropriate. Aisha had taken a half-day off from work. She had something to tell him. He hoped it was not a confession.

A riverside hotel, overlooking the Thames with a clear view of Tower Bridge, was chosen by both. She arrived in her workday clothes, a smart business suit, sombre in colour, as befitted her chosen profession of lawyer. Farhan arrived, suit and tie, although he loosened his tie once they were sitting down. Both were a little excited; both showed it.

'I've got some good news,' she said. Farhan breathed a sigh of relief – it was not to be a confession. A waiter hovered, anxious to take their order. They ignored him.

'Aisha, this is official,' he said. He knew that what he needed to ask her should have been done in a more formal setting. Smiles and touching of hands across the table did not constitute official police proceedings. He knew he could not stop.

'Let me tell you my news first.' She seemed oblivious of what he wanted to ask, uninterested in her other life. She knew she was acting like a love-struck teenager out on a first date. The teenager she was not, but love-struck and the first date were certainly correct. She would not say it openly, but if asked, she would have admitted that she felt more than a fondness for Farhan Ahmed, the upright and serious detective inspector. He knew her story, her ambition, her screwing men for money. She hoped he would understand, not as a policeman but as someone she could spend the rest of her life with.

The waiter, increasingly annoyed at being ignored, eventually succeeded in taking their order. Both ordered fruit juices and salads. Business was brisk, and it was evident the establishment had the policy of quickly sit the patrons down, feed them, and get them out of the door as fast as possible, credit cards suitably debited. The punters, as the hotel landlord, a foul-mouthed Irishman, referred to the patrons. He only cared about the money in his bank account. The service the hotel provided was only there to ensure the maximum return on investment. He was not wrong about his concern for profit, for the situation in the city was challenging for any business. Rents were high, labour costs through the roof, and a riverside hotel overlooking the Thames could not easily relocate down past Canary Wharf to somewhere cheaper. The owner, a Russian businessman, based in Moscow, mansion in Kensington, knew that only too well.

Farhan also flashed his police badge and directed his glance towards a couple of young girls, obviously under age, sitting with a group of men, two tables away. The waiter understood. Farhan and Aisha would not be rushed out of the premises if the hotel did not want trouble.

'Tell me your news,' he said.

'I've passed my exams.'

'Congratulations.'

'They've offered me a more senior position. There will be some delay before I start representing clients on my own, but it's a great start.'

'Did you see the press conference with Detective Superintendent Goddard and DCI Cook?'

'I couldn't watch it. It was on the television at my home. My parents were watching it, making comments. I was too ashamed. I left the room. They wanted to speak about it later; how disgraceful it was that women behave in that manner. I changed the subject, left the house, and went for a walk. I don't want to think about that life. It's almost as if it's a dream.'

'Unfortunately, it's not a dream, and it's still a murder investigation.'

'I've not been back to Marion Robertson since. I can't imagine giving myself to another man purely for money now. I should be embarrassed to say that to you.'

'Why aren't you?' he asked.

'Maybe you can't forgive, not totally, but you are able to put it to one side, not judge me too harshly.'

'It depends on the woman.'

'Am I that woman?' she asked coyly.

'There's still the fact of two dead bodies to be dealt with.' Farhan tried to bring the conversation back to official. He knew he was losing the battle: the weather was too good, Aisha too cheerful, and her beauty distracted him totally.

'I only know about one,' she said.

'Someone told a reporter that you and Olivia were in the hotel with Sutherland.'

'It wasn't me. How can you ask? You know me well enough to know that I wouldn't do that.'

'I know. Still, I had to ask.'

'Why me? Why not Olivia? Why not the staff at the hotel? It was hardly a great secret; it's not the first time I've been there.'

'I phoned Olivia. I've yet to speak to the staff. I've also talked to Christy Nichols.'

'Why didn't you meet with Olivia?'

'I wanted to protect her identity, and besides, I don't believe she would do it. Her secret is too important.'

'And you think I might. Don't you think my secrecy is important?'

'Of course I do. That's why we haven't met recently.'

'I don't understand.' The mood had become chilly. 'You are risking my secrecy now.'

'We've met here. It would be construed by the casual observer that we are two people enjoying each other's company. Here, in this crowded place, is the most secret place. We are here because I want to protect you. Because I had a legitimate reason to meet with you.' The mood warmed.

'You've used someone at the hotel talking out of turn as an excuse to meet up with me again.'

'In part, I admit. But there still remains someone we don't know about. Someone that was able to get him naked and to take a drink voluntarily.'

'With the drugs he was on, that could be anyone.'

'Are you indicating that it could have been a man?'

'No, although it could have been his minder.'

'We've discounted her at the present time.'

'I certainly saw no one else. Olivia probably didn't either. I've stayed chaste since we last met. I said I would.'

They both ordered a glass of wine, not because they were drinkers, but because the situation required a relaxant. One hour later, they were upstairs in a room alone together. Not because of the alcohol, not because of her former profession, not because he had not been with a woman for a long time, although that had been an unsatisfactory coupling with a cold and unloving woman. It was because they wanted to be together; because they both felt a strong emotional tie.

It was early evening when they left the hotel. He, feeling guilty that he had acted unprofessionally; she, elated in that she had experienced sex without money and had not needed to pretend. He knew his house that night was not going to feel so lonely; she, satisfied that she had found a man that she could love, a man her parents would approve of, a man who knew her secret.

Chapter 27

Early morning rush hour was not the best time to find a parking spot anywhere near Paddington Station. In the end, Wendy found a loading zone and put a police parking permit in the car window.

She knew a few delivery vehicle drivers would be cursing her – the bad language a certainty – but she had no option. Brian Gee's information seemed important. She did not like using police privilege unless necessary.

'I've found her.' She had barely entered the room when Brian Gee came up to her, shook her warmly by the hand and announced his success.

'Where?'

'The photos you sent. We were able to correlate them against the people on the station around the time the train arrived.'

'Was she wearing the same clothes?'

'That's what made it easy. We also managed to get a facial. It's not crystal clear, but it's okay. A new camera had just been installed, so it wasn't yet choked with pollution.'

Wendy phoned Isaac with the news.

After the quick phone call, she turned her attention back to Brian Gee. 'Positive ID?'

'Ninety-five percent. That's good enough for me.' He offered her a cup of coffee, tepid, out of a machine in the corner. She realised that if she wanted a British Rail cup of tea she would have to go and see the station manager, which she intended to do before she left.

'What else do you have?'

'She was met by someone.'

'Any idea who?'

'What we can see is one person, slightly taller than her and wearing a thick coat and a baseball cap.'

'Male or female?'

'Judging by the way the person walked, I'd say it was a man.'

'Any idea as to age, colour?'

'I'll give you copies of the video. Apart from male, thick coat, baseball cap, there's not a lot more I can give you. We know they exited the station and headed in an easterly direction.'

'Was she pleased to see the person?'

'Yet again, you can make your own decision. She seemed to greet the man. After that, she can be seen walking at his side with his right hand holding onto her left arm. It's difficult to tell if it was a friendly gesture. The station was very busy. Maybe he was just ensuring he did not lose her.'

She realised that she should pick up the video and head back to Challis Street at top speed and give the tape to Bridget, but she still had a cup of tea on her mind. Station Manager Broughton had the tea ready when she arrived, as well as a cheese and tomato sandwich. It was not stale. His office still had the unique smell she remembered from the previous day. It was homely and comfy, not like her home with her increasingly vague and complaining husband. She knew that one day she would need to consider placing him in a nursing home, maybe before she retired. What would she do then? Maybe travel, maybe take a course, maybe find someone else to keep her company, purely platonic? She could not see herself being on her own.

By the time she arrived back at the car, it had been four hours. The delivery driver trying to park, not intimidated by the official police sign, and not showing any respect for a woman, gave her a verbal dressing down.

'You think just because you're the police, you can fuckin' park wherever you like.' He was an uncouth man, heavily tattooed, and had the appearance of someone who belonged to a motorbike gang. The tee-shirt emblazoned with Harley Davidson – a testament to the fact.

'You watch your mouth, or I'll slap a ticket on your truck for a failed brake light.'

'There ain't no problem with my lights. I checked 'em this morning.'

'There will be once I kick one of them out.'

'That's police harassment. I could have you nicked for that if I make an official complaint.'

Wendy, suitably angry, had seen it too many times. She knew that if she had been police and male, the irate truck driver would not have engaged in a slanging match, and he would have moderated his language. Female, police, middle-aged, and it was a different situation.

'Okay, I'll tell you what we do,' she said. 'I'll kick out your brake light, maybe hit it with a jack handle for good measure.'

'You do that!'

'You can call over a policeman, or I can call one for you on my police radio.'

'You do that.'

'Once he arrives, I'll show him my police ID, nice and shiny, and you can show him your truck's registration.'

'You're threatening me.' He did not seem as confident as before, and there were the parking fines to consider. He hadn't paid them, and his driving licence had expired.

'Threat? I don't think so.' She knew she had him on the defensive, realised that she should not have indulged in a verbal exchange on a busy street. After a congenial few hours at Paddington, this unpleasant foul-mouthed man had made her see red. Her temper had been a problem a couple of times over the years, even prevented her promotion.

'Okay, I'm leaving,' the driver said and drove off, cursing under his breath. Wendy left soon after, laughed to herself as she saw the driver five minutes later arguing with a policeman over an apparently bald tyre at the front of his vehicle.

***

Isaac was keeping his distance from Jess O'Neill, even though she had phoned a couple of times. He realised that if he met her, he might have weakened, and of the three women with a motive to kill Charles Sutherland, hers was very strong.

He had noticed the change in Farhan. It concerned him that he may be falling into the same trap that he had in the past. He decided to talk to him at some stage.

The information that Wendy had passed on from Paddington Station about Marjorie Frobisher, apparently still alive and now in London, concerned him. Charles Sutherland had probably died as a result of information he possessed about her. That would indicate a professional assassination, but none of the three women appeared to have any background that would suggest they were trained killers.

Could there be another woman? Isaac thought. It seemed plausible, but if it wasn't one of the three females they knew about, could it be someone else known or someone hidden in plain sight? The delays in identifying suspects and charges against persons, innocent until proven guilty, still occupied the media. His infrequent watching of television in the past had changed; TV had now become a necessity, so much so that he had installed one in his apartment, one in the office.

Sophie did not like the one at his home. Even complained when he had interrupted his undivided attention for her to watch the news. Isaac wasn't sure where the relationship was heading. Casual sex, no obligation, no guilt, sounded great to the average hot-blooded male, but he had realised in recent weeks that he was getting older, it was maybe time to settle down. He wasn't sure why he felt this. In the past, it had been a thought in passing and no more. Maybe it was Jess O'Neill. He felt the need to see her. He knew he could not unless there was some new information.

***

The next day Isaac's momentary lapse to think about Jess O'Neill was abruptly halted. A news flash on the television in the office. One of the two prostitutes known to have visited Charles

Sutherland on the day of his demise had been identified. He was aware that Farhan would be upset by the news. He phoned him.

'What are they saying?' Farhan asked.

'They said her name was Olivia. Is that one of the women?'

'She did it for her family. I said I would never reveal her identity.'

'You never did. It's not your problem,' Isaac said.

Farhan realised that it was his problem, and he felt the need to elaborate why. Here he was in a relationship with the other woman. If one was identified, it would not be long before the other one was found. He had to focus on protecting Aisha, helping Olivia if he could, although she would not be receptive to hearing from him. He knew he had to contact Aisha and quickly.

On ending the phone conversation with Isaac, he called Aisha – she was occupied with a client at the legal firm where she worked. He left a message, hoped she would get back to him before she heard the news from a third party. He realised he was in love. It was a complication he would not have chosen.

Still married, a divorce settlement that would almost certainly cost him the house, but that was not an issue as long as the children were fine. And then, how many police regulations had he broken? Fraternising with a witness who may be a murderer, behaviour unbecoming, concealing evidence. He could see his career dashed on the rocks of public opinion and police regulations. If it became known, would he be suspended?

Phoning Olivia was not necessary. She phoned him soon after the news broke. He reflected that she sounded calmer than he expected. 'I told my husband.'

'I maintained your confidentiality.'

'It was that Marion Robertson,' she said.

'Are you certain?'

'I phoned her. I thought she was a decent person, but prostitution always was a dirty business.'

'Why would she do that?' Farhan asked.

'There have been some reporters fishing for information, ever since that reporter on the television. If they ask enough questions, knock on enough doors...'

'Have they found out where you live?'

'Marion Robertson doesn't know my home address. Besides, she only ever contacted me on an anonymous phone number that I gave to her.'

'But she knows where we met and the school run. She set up our meeting.'

'Oh, my God, she does. They are bound to find me. I should never have met you.'

'I understand that, but it is a murder. I would have found you anyway, the same way as the reporters. I've done the best I can.'

'I know that. How am I going to protect my family?'

'It may be best to go away for a while until it blows over. Why did you tell your husband?'

'I had to. Too much guilt; he didn't deserve to find out from someone else.'

'How did he take it?'

'What do you think?'

'Badly?'

'He's in shock, not talking. I did the right thing telling him. I can only hope in time that he gets over it. Could you forgive someone you cared for?'

'In time.' He did not intend to elaborate that he already had.

The call ended; the phone rang again. 'I've just come out of a long meeting. I'm pleased to hear from you,' Aisha said.

'I don't think you'll be happy when I tell you what has happened.'

'Tell me?'

'They've found Olivia.' Farhan could hear an audible sigh on the other end of the phone. He wished he could have told her face to face, but it had not been possible.

'But how?'

'Marion Robertson. She's admitted it to Olivia.'

'Has she given my name?'

'I've no idea. I'm heading over to see her right now. Olivia obviously had a contactable phone number. How about you?'

'I changed it. You know that. I gave you the new number.'

'Marion Robertson doesn't have your contact number. How about an address?'

'No, although she knows I work in the city. I suppose they could find me.'

'Let's hope not. It's best for you not to worry. I'll see what I can do to protect the two of you.'

***

Bridget was in a talkative mood when Wendy entered her office, clutching the hard disk with the footage of Marjorie Frobisher at Paddington Station. Wendy was still a little miffed after her argument with the van-driving lout. A cup of tea, not as good as British Rail, soon calmed her down. Wendy assumed that Bridget's computer set up was not as good as Brian Gee's, but then she knew little about such matters, could barely write an email, and her typing skills were definitely one finger at a time. She had asked Bridget how she managed to type so quickly, barely looking at the keyboard, her eyes focussed on a monitor to the right of the laptop. Bridget said it was easy. Ten lessons to learn how to break the bad typing habits, and then learn the basics, centre line on the keyboard, first finger of each hand on the raised bumps on the F and the J, left hand F, right hand J.

The teacher at the local college had explained that the two letters formed the reference point. Wendy had repeatedly tried, even drove her husband crazy as she laboured away at night trying to get the hang of it, but the habit was too firmly entrenched. She gave up after six weeks and went back to banging the keyboard. Besides, if it became difficult, there was always Bridget.

'It's not very clear,' Bridget said. She had ordered in some cakes, Wendy's favourite. *There goes the diet,* Wendy thought. Not that she would ever have dieted, but it was always good to believe it was possible.

'The man she met?' Wendy asked.

'His complexion looks on the dark side, but I'm not sure if that is the camera or the lighting.'

'Can't you reference it off Marjorie Frobisher?'

'Are you certain it's her? With those sunglasses on, it's hard to tell.'

'Almost one hundred per cent.'

'It's not going to be easy to follow her down the street.'

'With all those cameras?'

'That's not the problem. It's the software and the time delays in accessing the film. There'll be a backup server somewhere; it will have been recorded. May take some time.'

'We don't have the luxury of time.'

Bridget phoned for some more food to be brought in. 'It's going to be a long day, maybe night. Are you up to it?' she asked Wendy.

'Not a problem. I'll keep you fed.'

'Slave driver,' Bridget joked. Wendy knew her husband would be complaining. *Tough*, she thought. This was more interesting.

Chapter 28

Isaac told Farhan that he was a bloody fool and should have known better. 'She is a witness, maybe more involved than we believe.'

'I met both of them, separate occasions,' Farhan said.

'I know that.'

'I kept clear of Olivia, as I knew some of her family history. I made a promise.'

'I don't think we have the luxury of giving promises.'

'I know that, but I needed her cooperation.'

'You're too kind-hearted. You know that?'

Farhan had not seen Isaac so angry before. 'What would you have done?' he asked.

'I'm not the one who has been sleeping with a witness, am I?'

'It wasn't intended, but what would you have done with the two witnesses?'

'Probably the same as you, but sleeping with one of them…'

'You make it sound sordid.'

'What was it, an easy lay? I realise that life must be difficult for you at the present moment with your wife and children not around, but sleeping with this woman. Next you'll be telling me she lives at home with her parents, contributes to the rent money.'

'She does.'

'Good God, Farhan, how do I protect you!' Isaac exclaimed. His anger was not levelled at Farhan for what he had done. Most men would have acted in the same manner, but he was a policeman, an upholder of the law, and here he was, sleeping with a prostitute who may have seen a murderer. It was indefensible. Isaac knew he should report it officially, but Farhan was too good a policeman, too good a person, to allow his career to be thrown away.

Richard Goddard had got him out of a couple of tricky situations in the past; maybe he could help. Farhan had hoped it could be kept between him and Isaac. Isaac explained it could not, and if the women were to be protected then Detective Superintendent Goddard was the best man.

Farhan relented, in part because he knew Isaac was right, but mainly because he wanted to protect the women, especially the one he loved. Her selling herself to help her get through her studies should have automatically condemned her. However, his years in the police service had made him realise that some people were good, while others were bad. Aisha, he knew, was good, as was Olivia. He hoped Detective Superintendent Goddard was good as well. He was not so sure about Marion Robertson. He would reserve judgement on her until she had been given the opportunity to mount a defence. He realised it was conditional on his being a serving policeman, and that was clearly in the balance.

***

Richard Goddard sat quietly while Farhan explained the situation about one of the escorts being identified. He explained his reason for confidentiality. Richard Goddard stated that he was not correct, but Farhan countered that, for a moderate Muslim, it was not open to discussion. He had seen the injustices against women. He was not willing to allow their lives to be prejudiced because of mistakes they may have made.

Farhan went on to explain that both women had their reasons for indulging in prostitution, and they should be protected from a scurrilous press. They were potentially material witnesses, and it was up to the police department to protect their identities. Detective Superintendent Goddard saw this as illogical.

Farhan counter-argued that legally in the United Kingdom they had not broken any law except the law of morality, and that was not a punishable offence, except by a higher power.

Isaac, amazed at the fluidity of Farhan's argument and the fluency of delivery, in the end could only sit back and declare him the winner. Goddard, suitably impressed, thanked him for his honesty and his reasons but failed to give him his unanimous support.

'Detective Inspector Ahmed, this is all very well, and given I want to give you a kick up the arse as well as a severe dressing down, which I do, how can I protect them and you?'

'Official Secrets Act?' Isaac asked.

'What has the Official Secrets Act got to do with this?'

'It's there to restrict information. Why not for these women?'

'I'll need to meet with my contact; see what we can do.'

'Angus MacTavish?' Isaac asked.

'I suppose it was pointless trying to keep that confidential,' Goddard admitted.

'What about the women?' Farhan asked.

'They need to keep a low profile. Explain that you need to know where they are.'

'Thank you, sir.'

'Don't thank me. We're not out of trouble yet, and you've still to receive my reprimand. Isaac will tell you that I don't mince words. You've been a bloody fool. Whatever you do, don't go sleeping with the witnesses until this is over. That applies to you as well, Isaac.'

***

Farhan, suitably humbled after his admission and thankful that there was a potential solution, focussed his attention on the two women. As much as he wanted to phone Aisha first, he decided that Olivia was the person most under threat. As a precaution, he had called Marion Robertson, indicated that she had committed a criminal offence by revealing the name of a witness. He was confident that she would say no more until he got to her office, which he intended to do within the hour.

Olivia was pleased to hear Farhan on the end of the phone. 'What can you tell me? What's going to happen?' she asked. Her husband was on the phone line as well. Farhan could hear him breathing.

'You're not alone?' Farhan asked.

'My husband is here with me. We're going to be alright.'

'I'd like to thank you, Detective Inspector Ahmed,' Olivia's husband said.

'This must be a difficult time for you both.'

'We love each other,' Olivia said. 'My husband will forgive me in time, I hope.'

'In time, as my wife says. I knew what she was before I married her and I know she only did it for the family. It will be hard, but we will survive.'

'Do you want to come to the house?' she asked.

'I don't think that's necessary, and besides, I already know where you live. I believe it would be best if we don't meet. Someone might be following me.'

'How do you know my address?'

'I'm a policeman. Your car registration plates. Caroline, am I correct?'

'Caroline, yes.'

'This matter is more involved than you realise. I'm not at liberty to say more. This goes beyond the death of one person.'

'What can we do?' Olivia's husband asked.

'Are you able to leave the country?'

'We've discussed it, for the sake of the children,' the husband responded.

'Any possibility?'

'My father was South African. I've citizenship there.'

'When can you go?'

'We had thought in two months. I need to give notice at work, and there's the children's schooling.'

'It would be best if you leave now.'

'I understand,' the husband said.

'Are you suggesting we hide, have fictitious names?' Olivia asked.

'Nothing so melodramatic. The press is fickle, short-term memory. You'll be forgotten in time, and there is still the other woman.'

'Is she leaving as well?' the husband asked.

'Possibly. I don't believe Marion Robertson knew how to contact her.'

'She told me she didn't, but you'd better check. She hasn't come out too well in this.'

'Maybe there are extenuating circumstances. I'll reserve my opinion until I've met with her.'

'We can leave within the week, maybe two days,' the husband said.

'Keep in contact. I'll do what I can to protect you.'

'Thank you, Farhan,' Olivia said. Her husband thanked him as well.

With one woman's situation hopefully resolved, Farhan turned to the one woman he hoped he could protect. Her phone, barely the first ring before she answered.

'Aisha, where are you?'

'Close to the office. Can we meet?' she asked.

'It's not possible. We need to maintain a distance until this blows over.'

'Why?'

'They know me. I don't want them following.'

'You would know if you were being followed, wouldn't you?'

'Most of the time, but some of them are good. The risk's too great.'

'Then it's good that we spent time together yesterday,' she said.

'I wish we could repeat it today, but your safety is more important than my lust.'

'Don't you mean love?'

'Of course, but I need to protect you now.'

'That's what people who love each other do, isn't it?'

He had to agree. 'Yes, that's what they do.'

'What do you want me to do?'

'Maintain your normal routine. Go to work, go home, act normal.'

'I'll try. It won't be easy.'

'It will not be easy for either of us, but your protection is all that matters now.'

'It will kill my father if the truth comes out. He has a weak heart.'

'Then follow my advice. Is that clear?'

'It's clear, but this is a time we should be together, not apart,' she said.

'That may be, but it's not possible. Believe me, I will be thinking of you. I can only hope that this is concluded soon.'

'Will it be?'

'I've no idea. We're floundering at the moment, not sure what the significance of the missing woman is.'

'You've never mentioned that before.'

'I'm talking out loud, that's all.'

'Are you saying Marjorie Frobisher is the key to this?'

'She worked with Sutherland, knew Sally Jenkins, and she disappeared before the murders started. It's suspicious.'

'Maybe she knew she was being targeted?' Aisha said.

'Until we speak with her, assuming she's still able to speak, we'll not know.'

'There's something about her early history,' Farhan said.

'Maybe I can help?'

'Maybe you could.'

'Give me some details,' she said. Farhan realised that he was in error, but Aisha was a smart woman, legally qualified, and she may find something the experts had missed.

'Until we know what this information is, I don't think we are any closer to solving it.'

'Send me what information you have that is relevant, some dates, and I'll scurry around. That way we can keep in touch, even if only by phone.'

***

Two minutes after ending his conversation with Aisha, Farhan arrived at Marion Robertson's office. 'I need to put my case forward before you judge me out of hand,' she said.

'I'm here with an open mind. If you help me, then maybe I am able to help you. Are we agreed?' he said.

'I had no option but to give one of the names.'

'Olivia?'

'Yes.' Farhan could see the woman was not as relaxed as at their previous meeting. She was moving around the office, unable to sit down. Farhan had chosen to sit on a chair close to her desk. He needed her to be calm.

'Please sit down.' He took the initiative and made two cups of tea using the machine in the corner. For several minutes, nothing was said.

'They threatened to expose me.'

'Who did?'

'The two men who came here.'

Farhan realised that if the woman had been threatened, then maybe she had no alternative. She certainly seemed less sure of herself, almost demure as she sat behind her desk. The assuredness, the inner calm, no longer apparent. He suggested they sat in more comfortable chairs.

'It may be best if you tell me the full story,' Farhan said calmly.

'I am ashamed of what I did.'

'You had no problem with supplying women for sex.'

'I've never had any qualms about this business. There has never been any serious trouble. I always reasoned that it was a necessary service, and no one was hurt.'

'Were you an escort once?'

'For many years. It's a long story, but I never sold myself on a street corner, and there were never drugs involved.'

'And now?'

'The mobile phone, the one with the gold case that you observed last time. That was given to me for services rendered, not some other woman. He is a wonderful man, very decent, very generous.'

'Why did you give Olivia's details?' Farhan realised that he had not been shocked by Marion Robertson's revelation.

'Is she alright?' She seemed genuinely concerned. Farhan was certain it was not a pretence. Some of her self-assuredness had returned. She sat easily in the chair. Farhan, in charge of the situation, made another cup of tea for the two of them.

'Hopefully, she will be all right.' He was unsure if he should elaborate just yet. He was aware that Olivia and her husband were buying airline tickets and were planning to leave within two days. If Marion Robertson had been pressured, then maybe she could be pressured again. What she didn't know, she couldn't tell.

'I can only hope she accepts my apologies.'

'Maybe, in time.' Farhan said. Olivia did not seem a vengeful woman; a little contrite about what she had put her husband through, but it was clear that she had no great issues with selling herself if it looked after her family. Farhan was certain she would do it again, but it was not for him to offer an opinion.

It made him reflect on Aisha. *I hope she does not think of prostitution in the same way as Olivia,* he thought. He determined to ask her the next time he saw her. He felt he could forgive her for past sins, but future sins? That seemed too much to consider.

'Will they find out where she lives?' Farhan decided not to answer the question. He had found Olivia's home address and he knew that anyone else determined would find it with little trouble.

'I said to both women that I would protect their identities to the best of my ability. I intend to do that if it is indeed possible.'

'And is it?' she asked.

'I'm not certain yet.'

'Are you able to protect me?' Marion Robertson looked unsure of herself again.

'Do you need protection?'

'The two men.'

'What can you tell me?'

'They threatened me.'

'It's best if you describe their visit here. It was here, I assume?'

'Yes, in this office.'

'I'll record this conversation. Is that okay with you?'

'Yes, that's fine.'

Farhan placed his mobile phone on the table, on record. He knew he would have to write a report afterwards – easier to record now and play back later.

'Marion, please commence. Take your time and take a break if you need.'

'I could do with a glass of water.' Farhan poured one for her.

'Last week, Thursday, mid-morning, I was in the office. I had just arranged for one of my girls to meet up with an overseas client. He's a regular when he is in the country. He always treats the girls well, so I had no problem fixing him up. It was close to eleven o'clock when two men walked into the office.'

'Just one question before you continue,' Farhan interrupted. 'Why the office? Surely you could run this business from home.'

'At home, I'm the dutiful wife; here, I'm the Madam.'

Farhan could see no reason to judge. At least the husband did not have a cold bed and a cold wife in it.

'The two men came in,' she continued. 'Normally, I keep the door locked, but for some reason I had failed to do so.'

'You assumed they were looking for you to arrange some women for them?'

'Not at all. There is no sign on the door. That's all strictly done online or by phone.'

'Understood.'

'They came in, polite and well-mannered. One sat where you are sitting now, the other one stood. It seemed as if he was there to intimidate me. He succeeded. I felt very insecure, but I maintained my composure. They said that the reason for their

222

visit was a matter of the gravest seriousness. I was unsure what to think. There have been a few well-known clients over the years, including the son of a dictator in the Middle East, although he was a gentleman.'

'Did they introduce themselves?'

'The one sitting said his name was Howard Stone. He even showed me a business card.'

'Do you still have the card?'

'He said it was his last one and would I mind if he kept it. The other one did not offer his name, and apart from a few words, said little.'

'How long were they here?'

'About twenty minutes in total. They were both well-dressed, spoke well.'

'Not heavies, then?'

'Heavies? If by that you mean gangsters, then no.'

'So, what did they say or do that scared you?'

'The one sitting spoke calmly. He told me that they represented some clients in town, important clients, who were disturbed that a senior member of society had been potentially embarrassed, personally compromised, due to his involvement with one of my girls.'

'Did they say who this senior member of society was?'

'No, they were cagey when I asked.'

'Who do you think they were talking about?'

'I assumed it was a politician. The rich don't care unless the wife is likely to take half the assets if their dalliances became public knowledge. The politicians always worry about their reputations.'

'Has that happened in the past?' Farhan asked.

'It's happened, although I was able to keep the woman I supplied out of the newspapers. Luckily, the wife came to a confidential agreement with her husband, so no more was said, at least to us.'

'Let's assume it is a politician. What happened next?'

'The one sitting down told me that it was imperative that this person remained free of any indiscretions.'

'Did he say why?'

'He would not elaborate. I told him that my girls were specially chosen for their discretion and that they would not speak to anyone, or cause trouble.'

'And then?'

'His manner changed. He became surly, accused me of running a house of ill-repute, and that his client would ensure that firstly I would be out on the street where I belonged, letting any derelict fuck me for the price of a decent meal. My apologies for the bad language. I'm just repeating verbatim.'

'No need to apologise.'

'And secondly, he would ensure that my husband would be publicly disgraced as the consort of a whore. I could not allow that.'

'You care that much about your husband?' Farhan could not see his wife making such a statement. Marion Robertson, an escort, a supplier of women for sex, and in his society a person to be condemned, was more honourable than all those that professed piety. He admired the woman immeasurably.

'Yes. He's a good and kind man who accepts my peccadilloes with a forbearance that many would not.'

She had moved closer and touched Farhan on the knee. 'The silent one came close and leant over. He spoke quietly into my ear.'

'What did he say?'

'He told me that they had total authority, and if I did not give him some names with contacts immediately, they would personally see that I was revealed as the Madam of a brothel, and my husband would have an unfortunate accident.'

'Who did you think they were?'

'I thought they were connected with the government.'

'Why do you say that?'

'Their training. It was psychological intimidation. A gangster would have felt the need to be physical.'

'Why Olivia?'

'They were clear as to whom they wanted contact details for.'

'Samantha and Olivia?'

'They never mentioned Charles Sutherland.'

'You assume it was related?' Farhan asked.

'I don't know what I thought. I was shaking like a leaf, almost wet myself. It took me hours to calm down afterwards, and I couldn't tell my husband.'

'Why not?'

'I didn't want to upset him.'

'Why didn't you give them Samantha's phone number as well as Olivia's?'

'I wasn't sure that I had it. She tends to change the number regularly. Olivia is easier to contact. I knew her number worked.'

'How?'

'I had phoned her up earlier in the day, another client.'

'She was agreeable?'

'As always. I believe she likes the thrill of it. Is she a different person outside of the business?'

Farhan wasn't sure how much to say. What if the two men returned? Would she give up any more secrets if pressured? He assumed she would.

'A decent person.' He did not intend to elaborate.

'What if they come back?' she asked.

'Difficult question. Do you know any more about Samantha?'

'Not really.'

'Are you surprised that she changes her phone number regularly?'

'Not really. I don't know what her secret is, but she's very careful. Besides, she told me that she didn't want any more clients for a while. I sensed she had met someone and didn't want to confuse a normal relationship with selling herself on the side.'

Farhan relaxed back in his chair, almost certainly blushing.

'If they ask for Olivia again?' she asked.

'Her phone number will not work.'

'Is she safe?'

'I'm not sure. You've been threatened. Olivia is hiding, and Samantha is keeping a low profile. Our investigations have placed not only you three at risk, but indirectly brought about the deaths of two people.'

'You're a policeman; you can't stop doing your job because it may have unfortunate outcomes.'

'That is true, but it's a hornet's nest we've stirred up. We've no idea how it's going to end.'

'You said you were separated from your wife.'

'That's correct.'

'If you need company, let me know. I'll see that you are treated well. No cost, of course, but a man needs an outlet. No point bottling up the tension.'

Chapter 29

Isaac decided to visit the production lot. He wasn't sure why, apart from the fact that all three persons, two dead and one missing, had a close involvement with the place.

Until Wendy came up with some fresh information or Detective Superintendent Goddard was more forthcoming about why Marjorie Frobisher was so important, then the cast and production crew were his best bet. Maybe a snippet of information, a remark made in passing, and then a new avenue of enquiry would open up. Isaac hoped he would not make a fool of himself if he ran into Jess, but assumed he probably would.

Larry Hill had taken over the investigation into Sally Jenkins' death, at least as far as ascertaining who could have murdered her, and how that person had got into her apartment. Was the person known to her? Was Sally Jenkins relaxed when the person mysteriously appeared in her apartment after breaking in? And now Larry Hill was intimating that maybe the murderer did not come in through the window, only made it look as though he or she did. The person who had held the hapless former PA under water could have been male or female. There seemed to be no way to clarify this.

It was remarkable when Isaac arrived at the production lot how busy it was. Everywhere he looked, he saw activity.

He saw why soon enough – Ian Stanley. The series producer with the Napoleon complex was out on the war path, shouting at whoever. He saw Isaac soon enough.

'I hope you're not going to hold us up today,' Stanley said brusquely.

'Not at all. Under the circumstances, I thought it would have been quiet out here for a few weeks.'

'Are you joking? We're here to produce thirty minutes' worth of entertainment, five days a week, and then it's syndicated to two dozen television stations around the world. If we don't supply, they sue for lost advertising revenue.'

'But you've had two people murdered?'

'At the end of the day, you'll find me sympathising.' Isaac could not see Ian Stanley sympathising about anybody.

'How was the news of Sally Jenkins received out here?'

'Look, I don't wish to be impolite, but I'm busy. Can this discussion wait?'

'Sure,' Isaac replied, 'just interested to know what everyone thought.'

'A few sad faces, but everyone knew she was only working with Richard Williams because she was an easy lay for someone with money. I made an inappropriate comment once about her screwing the boss, while everyone else was being screwed by him. She was so dumb, she didn't respond, just laughed. I only hope she was better in the sack than in the office. She was damn useless, always stuffing up everyone's pay and expenses.

'That new one, Linda Harris, she's good. No idea what she sees in Richard, money or no money. I reckon she could find any guy she wanted. She seems too smart for the job, and if she's screwing Richard Williams, it must be for a reason.' Isaac noted the comment.

'Mind you,' Ian Stanley went on, his voice raised after bawling out a couple of men hastily erecting a backdrop, 'I don't know what Jess O'Neill saw in him either, and she was screwing him.'

'Is she here?' Isaac asked, upset by Ian Stanley's aspersion about Jess and Richard Williams. He hoped it did not show: it did.

'You fancy her as well?' the little man smirked. 'Can't say I blame you – if you like Richard's seconds, that is. You didn't give Sally Jenkins one as well, did you?'

It was evident to Isaac that the respect accorded him initially by Ian Stanley, due to being a ranking police officer, had dissipated. Stanley only saw him now as a black man in a suit.

Stanley's voice had carried. Soon Jess appeared. She gave Stanley a nasty look but said nothing. He only smiled and continued pushing everyone around.

'Foul-mouthed little man. I can't stand him.'

'Jess, it's good to see you. I'm sorry you heard that.'

'Give me ten minutes, and I'll be alright. He's been trying to get me off the set for a few weeks now. Any chance to make a comment or weaken my position, he takes it.'

'Will he succeed?'

'It's hard to say.'

'Why's that?

'He's good at what he does. Someone mild-mannered, politically correct, wouldn't have a chance to put this together. You don't know how much work is involved out here. Most nights I don't leave before ten at night, and he's often still working.'

'You're looking good, by the way. How are you?'

'I'm fine. It took me some time to get over that grilling you gave me down at station.'

'I was just doing my job.'

'I'm okay. My brother-in-law said you were going easy on me. It didn't feel like it at the time.'

'What about Sally Jenkins?' he asked, hopeful that it would be a more sympathetic response than Ian Stanley had offered.

'I was sad for a day or so, but she only came here a few times. Excited the men whenever she appeared, gave the women something to gossip about.'

'No other concerns about her death?'

'Of course there are! We're all worried who's next. Charles Sutherland has been murdered, so has Sally Jenkins. What about Marjorie Frobisher? Do you believe her to be dead?'

'Jess, I've no idea.' He did not elaborate that the missing woman had been seen a few days earlier.

'These deaths and Marjorie Frobisher are all related, aren't they?' she asked. Isaac noticed that as lovely as she looked she was obviously feeling the strain. *Was it Ian Stanley's innuendoes? Was it a concern that maybe she could be targeted next? Did she know something she wasn't telling him?* he asked himself. He hoped it was not the latter.

'It seems likely, but so far we've drawn a blank. We have ideas as to what the link may be, but it's vague.' Isaac felt he had spent long enough with her. Excusing himself – this time he managed to avoid the kiss – he left the production lot and headed back to his office.

***

Wendy could see that Bridget had raised more questions than answers. How would she be able to follow up on the mysterious person who had met Marjorie Frobisher at the railway station? It seemed an impossible situation. The cameras close to the station had given some clues, but cameras weren't everywhere in the city. The best she could do was to retrace the steps of the missing soap opera star as she had exited the station. Maybe someone had seen something, remembered something. She realised her chances of success were slim, but sometimes something came out of it.

She had been good at tracking missing children in her early years with the police force by trying to think as they would. Maybe it could work this time. She wasn't the sort of person to rush to Isaac Cook – understanding as he may be – and announce that she hadn't a clue. No, she was determined that she was going to find this woman, dead or alive, and at the present moment, alive seemed to be a distinct possibility. Whether safe and comfortable in a hotel or a decent house, or in a situation of despair, she had no idea.

Isaac and Farhan continued to follow up on the events that had occurred since they had been assigned the case. Then it had been a missing woman, but now! Both were struggling with how to proceed.

Also, what about the child that had been adopted? Who knew the answer? And then there was the complication of Farhan sleeping with the prostitute, still in contact with her. Isaac had noticed the secretive messages and Skype on video. He knew she was a good-looking woman, but the young detective inspector was playing a dangerous game. If their boss found out, officially he may be required to pull him off the case.

Both had come in for criticism over the handling of the case: sometimes valid, at other times racially biased. Isaac knew full well that there were people within the confines of the building who would quite happily see them fail, even at the cost of a few unsolved murders. Isaac resolved he would protect Farhan, whatever the cost. And then he had his own problems. There he was sleeping with Sophie, wishing it was Jess O'Neill. Once, in a moment of passion, he had whispered her name into Sophie's ear; not that she minded – at least, that was what she had said. Isaac hadn't been so sure, though.

Sophie had always proclaimed that it was casual sex, no strings attached, no exclusivity, but he knew enough of the world to know that women are not wired that way. They see love when there is none, reject exclusivity and profess free choice, but only say it for the man's benefit, hoping the man is wise enough to realise that what the woman really wants is exclusivity and no free choice.

The situation, both professional and personal, was becoming untenable for both men. There were just too many loose ends, and the mysterious offspring of a promiscuous woman and someone of great influence in the country seemed to be the loosest end. It was crucial to find out who the person was, but there was no obvious candidate. And Richard Goddard was keeping his distance. Isaac assumed it was to do with the upcoming promotions within senior management. He realised that his boss was desperate for an elevation, and unsolved murders didn't help.

Isaac did not like it one bit. Both he and Farhan were now carrying guns. In all his years with the Metropolitan Police, he had never once felt the need to arm himself. Of course, like all policemen he had the benefit of training and was always aware that a situation may arise when a weapon was required.

***

Isaac was sure of another long night when he met up again with Farhan in the office. Farhan had been out at the hotel checking on who had told the journalist about the prostitutes. Isaac suspected that he had also been meeting with the Indian woman; the other escort had apparently disappeared. Farhan knew where she was, he had told Isaac that much. Isaac had let the matter rest there and decided not to pursue it further. He realised that if it were important, Farhan would tell him.

The British press had finally descended on Olivia's house, to find the doors locked tight, and the neighbours bemused by the microphones thrust in their faces and the questions relating to their neighbour, Caroline Danvers. Most had said she was well-respected in the community.

Mrs Edgecombe, seventies, a little hard of hearing, and pleased at the attention, stated categorically that she had always thought something was not quite right. The press had latched on to her for a couple of days, but realised soon enough that she was an embittered lonely woman whose husband had run off with a younger woman twenty-five years previously – a woman who looked remarkably similar to Caroline Danvers/ Olivia.

The media left after a few days, finding that there was no story at Olivia's house. They turned their focus to the other woman.

It was the reason Farhan was in communication with Aisha on such a regular basis. She was worried, and there was only one person she could turn to, only one person she trusted. Farhan was not sure what he could do to help; the press was voracious, and if they wanted to find someone, they would.

'What do we do now?' Farhan asked Isaac once they were both settled back in the office after a meal at a local Asian restaurant. They had eaten there before on several occasions, and it had been fine, but tonight… Isaac wasn't so sure; his stomach was feeling queasy.

'What do you mean?' Isaac understood his colleague's concerns. It had been dragging on for too long, and there was no clarity about where they were going with the case. The leads were drying up – had dried up, if they were truthful.

'What do we have?' Farhan asked. 'We've two murders, virtually no ideas, and no clear direction as to where this is heading.'

'You're right, of course.'

'We're no nearer to finding Marjorie Frobisher, and although Wendy's done a great job, she's just coming up with blanks.'

'Wendy still seems to be our best bet.' Isaac was not too comfortable with Farhan's comment. He had known her longer than Farhan, and to his recollection, she had never failed to deliver the goods. He remained confident that she would find the woman.

'Okay, we'll give her time,' Farhan said. Isaac could tell the pressure was building up on his colleague. He felt it necessary to comment.

'You seem to be under too much pressure, becoming emotionally involved.'

'I suppose I am.'

'The woman at the hotel with Sutherland?'

'Yes,' Farhan replied emphatically.

'You're trying to protect her. An admirable sentiment, but you know it's not going to succeed. The press will find her soon enough.'

'That's the problem. It looks as if they have.'

'We'd better talk this through. You can't protect her on your own. She's a material witness, maybe not in the murder, but certainly due to her association with Sutherland. Did you expect to protect her indefinitely?' Isaac felt that a love-sick colleague was counter-productive, even though he felt empathy with him.

'I had hoped to protect her. But now it's complicated.'

'You've slept with her?' Isaac knew the answer but felt the need to ask again.

'You know I have.'

'Since you were given a warning to keep your distance?'

'Not since then, but it's been difficult. I've wanted to.'

'You know what she is, has been?'

'An escort, sure. I'm beyond making a judgement.' Farhan squirmed in his seat. He was pleased that he and Isaac were having the conversation – embarrassed that they were.

'Are you emotionally involved?' Isaac sat upright in his chair and leant across his desk for emphasis.

'I know it's illogical. I've a wife and children, and there I am falling in love with a woman who has been selling her body for money.'

'Love is blind, or so the saying goes,' Isaac said. It seemed a throw-away phrase, clichéd, but it appeared to sum up Farhan's predicament.

'As you say, love is blind. What do you reckon I should do?'

'Protect her.'

'But how?'

'What about the other woman?'

'I know where she is, but unless there's an official request, I'll keep it to myself.' Farhan did indeed know where Olivia had gone, even had a phone number. The woman was grateful and trusted him enough to tell him that the children were in school, that her husband and she were trying to work through it, and unless she received a legal request to return to the United Kingdom, they were staying in South Africa.

'You'll still have trouble keeping her out of this. If we ever find a murderer, there will no doubt be a summons issued to all witnesses to come forward, including your girlfriend. You realise that?'

'I know. What do you advise?' Farhan sat sheepishly in his chair.

'She needs to disappear.'

'But she has a career, a good career.'

'What will happen to her career when they find out?'

'It's a prestigious law firm,' Farhan said. 'I imagine that a former prostitute, high-class or otherwise, will not last long there.'

'You're right. They'll have her out of the door within five minutes. She won't have the benefit of being innocent until proven guilty. The first hint of scandal and she will be condemned.'

'She knows that. She's putting on a brave face but she's worried about the shame it will bring on her family.'

Isaac sympathised, but he could see little hope.

Questions were being asked by the media on the television and in the newspapers about what was going on. Were there going to be other murders and what were the police doing? Not very much seemed to be the consensus view.

'She can't be protected, you know that,' Isaac affirmed.

'So, what are you going to do? What are we going to do?'

'It's not your problem, Isaac. You've got your career to think about.'

'To hell with that. If we don't solve these murders, neither of us has a career. And besides, I need you with me helping, not moping around, staring at the camera on your laptop.'

'We have to get her out of the country. Is that what you think?' Farhan asked, grateful that Isaac was willing to go out on a limb for him.

'The sooner, the better. You'd better give her the facts straight, face to face.'

'I will.'

'And don't go sleeping with her.'

'I won't,' Farhan replied, although he wasn't sure that his answer had been entirely truthful.

Chapter 30

It was clear that Marjorie Frobisher had walked away from Paddington Station in the company of a man; it was not known if she had been reluctant or willingly. Wendy felt that willingly was the more likely of the two scenarios. She was applying her experience to the problem. Wayward children, when they reappeared, invariably made for someone they knew, someone they trusted.

Isaac had suggested Richard Williams as the most likely person to protect her, but he had denied seeing her when Isaac had phoned him. In fact, he had been quite annoyed over the accusation that he was possibly obstructing a murder enquiry, threatened legal action if such a statement was made again. Isaac felt convinced that he was in the clear, although angry that he could not tell the man what he thought of his pompous manner.

Besides, he had heard Linda Harris's voice in the background, and the clinking of glasses indicated they were not in the office. Isaac resented him for his good choice in women, when he was feeling the early signs of rejection from Sophie.

As much as she had alluded to not being concerned when he had inadvertently mentioned Jess O'Neill's name in a moment of passion, she had not been available to come over the last couple of times he had phoned. He couldn't feel any undue sadness, only a little frustrated that the relationship was over.

He was determined to speed up the case. After that, he would be free to call Jess. He knew she would be available.

Wendy, convinced that the only solution was to get out on the street and to commit herself to good old-fashioned legwork, was outside Paddington Station early the next morning.

The morning was bleak. Wendy had dressed accordingly, although it was not a flattering ensemble: a jacket with a scarf, trousers, and solid walking shoes. She completed it all with a red woollen hat her husband had given her.

The clearest images that Brian Gee, the nerdish computer man at Paddington Station, and Bridget Halloran had managed to come up with showed that Marjorie Frobisher and the unknown man had walked down Praed Street, in the direction of St Mary's Hospital. The rain had started; Wendy was not in a good mood. The dampness in the air was starting to play havoc with her arthritis, and she knew at the end of the day she would be in severe pain.

She soon reached St Mary's Hospital, a maroon plaque commemorating the discovery of penicillin by Sir Alexander Fleming proudly displayed underneath his laboratory window. Marjorie Frobisher had been seen this far down the street, but after this the trail had gone cold.

The weather worsened and she decided that a warm place and a quiet coffee would be a good idea. She found a little café. It didn't look very enticing, but as she opened the door, she felt the heat. Taking a seat close to the window, she ordered a latte and a cake and pondered the situation. Was she wasting her time walking the street? What could she do? Should she go home, admit to Isaac and Farhan that she had no further ideas?

Desperate to do something, she indulged in idle conversation with the waitress, a pleasant looking woman in her late forties, the tattoos on her arm not to Wendy's taste.

'I'm looking for someone,' Wendy said after the waitress asked what she was doing out on such a miserable day.

'Anyone important?'

'Someone you'd know.'

'Not Marjorie Frobisher?' The waitress's answer surprised Wendy.

'You know her?'

'Doesn't everyone?'

'I suppose they do, but why assume it's her?'

'I told everyone in the shop that I had seen her. They all thought I was a bit crazy, and without my glasses my eyesight is a bit dodgy.'

'You didn't report seeing her.'

'I was going to, but everyone convinced me otherwise, and then it became busy. I suppose I forgot.'

'You've reported it now.'

'You're the police?'

'Yes. Is that okay by you?'

'As long as I'm not in trouble.'

'Of course you're not. We need to talk. Are you free to sit down and have a coffee with me?'

'Yes. Sure.'

Wendy noticed that the waitress, Sheila, was a nervous woman, unsure of herself. She also noticed that she took a piece of cake with her coffee. Wendy knew she would be paying for it.

'Did you speak to Marjorie Frobisher?'

'She didn't speak. The man with her did the ordering.'

'Tell me about him?'

'He spoke quietly, well-mannered. He didn't leave a tip; I remember that well enough.'

'Did he seem friendly with Marjorie Frobisher?'

'I kept staring, couldn't help myself.'

'I understand. It's not often you see celebrities walking into your café.'

'We see the occasional one when they're visiting the hospital across the road, but she was my favourite. I always watched her on the television, and here she was, sitting in my café, drinking my coffee. It'll be something to tell my family when I get home tonight.'

'This is serious. You can't tell anyone yet. Can I trust you to keep this quiet?'

'I won't say a word.' Wendy knew that as soon as the waitress got home, she would be telling everyone. There was hardly any way they could silence her, and she was the team's first concrete lead for several weeks.

'Did she look happy?'

'She seemed pleased to be with the man.'

'Is there any more you can tell me about him?'

'As I said, he was polite. In his late fifties, I suppose.'

'Fat or thin?'

'He certainly wasn't fat. He seemed a nice man.'

'How long did they stay?'

They stayed for about twenty minutes. As to where they went, I don't know. They just walked down the street. Apart from that, I've no idea.'

'Thanks, you've been a great help.'

'Is there a reward?'

'No reward. How would a fifty pound tip sound?'

'Great. They don't pay much here.'

Wendy realised on leaving the café that her pains had subsided, and there was no need to continue plodding the streets.

***

Isaac felt the need to follow up on a matter that had been giving him some concern. It had only been a casual remark by Ian Stanley, the irritating series producer and nemesis of Jess O'Neill, but it had raised some questions.

Linda Harris's earlier comment that her relationship with Richard Williams was just a bit of fun had seemed too frivolous at the time. Ian Stanley's statement about her competency had reaffirmed his suspicions. After his senior's indication that MI5 was interested in Marjorie Frobisher, Isaac's suspicions about Williams' PA seemed all the more relevant.

He bit the bullet and invited her out for dinner, socially this time. She accepted readily, too readily for Isaac, as Sophie was clearly out of the picture, not even returning his phone calls, and Jess was still off-limits.

The next day, close to seven in the evening, he met Linda Harris at a discreet restaurant close to the city centre. She ate chicken; he ordered beef. Two bottles of a particularly good wine were drunk with gusto by the two, though Isaac wasn't usually a drinker.

'Why are you working for Williams?' he asked.

'I needed a job.' She had dressed for the occasion: a short yellow skirt with a white top. Isaac had come from work and was still wearing a suit.

'You look too smart for the job.' Isaac realised he was heading into dangerous waters.

'Why do you say that?' she asked. Isaac could read the signals: the alluring smile, the closeness of her chair to his, the holding of his hand across the table.

'Sally Jenkins.'

'You're using her as the standard as to what is competent?'

'I suppose so,' Isaac replied.

'I'm competent, suitable for the job. She wasn't. But as we've agreed, she was not there for her administrative skills.'

'She was there because she was an easy lay, you said that yourself.'

'Are you insinuating that I'm an easy lay as well?'

'You told me that you were sleeping with him.'

'I told you that he was with me, in my bed.' She reminded him of their previous conversation when she had provided her boss with an alibi.

Isaac sensed some pulling back from her – she was no longer holding his hand. He excused himself to go to the toilet. He took the opportunity to splash some water on his face, hoping to revive himself a little.

Returning to his seat, he decided to stop sounding like a policeman and to enjoy the evening. The woman was attractive, too attractive, and she was great company.

Why not just enjoy the moment? he thought.

'I'm sorry. I'm acting as a policeman.'

'That's okay. I understand the pressure you're under.'

'Tell me about yourself. You said you came from Devon, but what are your plans for the future?'

'Find a better job,' She was holding his hand across the table again. Both had ordered dessert. 'I'm capable of a better job, but I'm not in a hurry.'

'Why?'

'I'd rather find myself a decent man, settle down, have a few kids.'

'Williams?'

'Not at all. I don't need a sugar daddy.'

Isaac, slightly more sober after easing up on the wine, took stock of the situation. On the one hand, he was here in the company of a beautiful, desirable woman, available if he was reading the signals right. On the other, as a policeman he knew there were questions that needed asking.

'The disappearance of Marjorie Frobisher concerns a lot of people,' he said.

'Newspapers, fans, you mean?'

'In higher quarters.' Isaac still had his suspicions about the woman sitting opposite. She seemed too smart; as if she was directing the conversation, ensuring he didn't probe too much.

'Political, is that what you mean?'

'Yes.'

'I wouldn't know,' she said. 'I'm just a humble personal assistant who's screwing the boss.' Her remark was a little too curt for Isaac.

'Linda, who are you?'

'Linda Harris, humble personal assistant. That's all.'

'We're aware that Marjorie Frobisher is somehow significant, although we don't know any details. Do you?'

'Why should I?' Her manner was frosty.

'You may have overheard something in the office.'

'You realise that you've spoilt a lovely evening by your suspicions.'

'I realise that, but it's my job.'

'I thought we were meeting outside of working hours, both off duty.'

'Off duty, that is not a term I would have expected a PA to use.'

She stood up, put on her coat, the weather outside not as frosty as the atmosphere inside the restaurant. 'DCI Cook, I'll bid you goodnight. In future, our meetings will be at your police station or my lawyer's office.'

Standing outside, as she walked briskly down the road, he could see her in an animated conversation on her phone. Whatever she was, he remained convinced she was more than Williams' bedtime companion and office administrator.

***

As Farhan was preparing for an early night, at his cold and lonely house, his phone rang. It was Olivia calling him from South Africa. She was not in a good mood; her cover had been blown.

Still thankful that he had tried to help, she had been forced to take the children out of school as the playground teasing was becoming objectionable, and it was not their problem, only hers. Also, her husband was having trouble accepting that she only sold herself for the family. Farhan was truly sorry, but Olivia still had the advantage of distance, and one or two inquisitive reporters in South Africa would soon be distracted by another, more important story.

Farhan knew he had to help Aisha. He knew he couldn't protect her if the news organisations picked up any clue as to who she was and where she was. She had told him earlier in the day about someone suspicious in her office and a couple of late-night phone calls to her house, no voice at the other end.

Farhan could only see one solution. 'You've got to leave,' he said.

She protested. 'My career, it's so important to me.'

'And your family, what about them?'

They had met at a small café in Regent Street, not far from her office. They had been pleased to see each other, although neither had made a move to embrace the other. Farhan could see she was upset.

'If they find out, it will kill them.'

'I suppose you should have thought about that before you started selling yourself.' He wasn't sure if his comment had been overcritical.

242

'You're right of course, but I needed to survive, ensure I passed my studies with honours. It all costs money, and my parents don't have that sort of money.'

'It's history now. Anyway, we would not have met if you had been working in a café.'

'At least there has been one good thing to come out of it.'

Farhan felt like leaning over the table and giving her a kiss. He decided that it was best if he did not. The future for them as a couple looked bleak. It was up to him to think clearly for both of them. She was obviously the better educated, but she was about to be outed as a prostitute. All that she had strived for, lost in an instance.

They had ordered coffees. Farhan drank his; Aisha barely sipped at hers. He could see in her face the sign of worry. She said it was due to the pressure of work, a particularly challenging case, involving a man accused of insider trading on the stock market.

She had tried to explain the intricacies of the case, as a diversion from the reason they were meeting. Something to do with the man's position as the financial officer for a major insurance company in the city, subject to a takeover from a larger, more aggressive company.

It was Aisha's first major case, although she was acting as a junior. It was a great compliment for her to be entrusted with the responsibility, but now it looked as if it was falling apart.

Farhan had ordered two more coffees. 'Aisha, the only chance is if you disappear. Caroline's being hassled now.'

'Is that Olivia's real name?'

'Yes, but it's best if you forget it.'

'I will.'

'We should be meeting at the police station.' Farhan had run it past Isaac first, told him the approach he was going to take. Isaac had advised him to take great care, and not to go rushing off to a hotel room with her. Farhan had said that he would be careful, but sitting with Aisha now, he wanted to forget his promise. He had to keep reminding himself that he was a serving policeman on duty, and she was a witness.

'Is there no hope?' she asked.

'If they can find Olivia, they can find you.'

'But how? You said that Marion Robertson had given Olivia's phone number to the two men who had visited her, but she didn't have mine.'

'That's true. Are you certain they are looking for you?'

'I'm pretty certain, but how?'

'Who would know where you work, where you live?'

'Only you.'

'I've kept it to myself. I received a severe dressing down from my boss for keeping you and Olivia secret.'

'If there's a court case, will I be required to be a witness?'

'You're the lawyer, what do you reckon?'

'It will depend on whether he pleads guilty or not.'

'Or she,' Farhan reminded her.

'Could it be a she?' she asked.

'Why not? The man was found naked. From what we know, he was certainly heterosexual.'

'Perversely so,' she replied. On a personal basis, Farhan did not want to know the details. On a professional basis, he had to ask.

'I must ask what you mean by that comment. Officially, unfortunately.'

'Can't you forget what I just said. I don't want to think back to that night.'

'Give me a generalisation, then.' He realised that maybe it was not relevant. If it became so, he would persevere with the question at a later time.

'He wanted us to put on a show first, toys, that sort of thing.' She kept her head low, avoided eye contact.

'We'll leave it at that.' He didn't want to hear more.

'What must I do?' she asked.

'Ideally, you should leave immediately.'

'The country?'

'Yes.'

'I can't do that.'

'You'd better let me know who's on to you. Every time you're contacted, every time there's a silent voice on the end of a phone line, let me know. We'll decide as it occurs. If I tell you the situation is impossible, then you must leave immediately. Is that clear?'

Aisha finally drank her coffee and left. She could not resist the opportunity to kiss him before she walked out the door. Farhan hoped she would be safe.

Chapter 31

Late afternoon the next day, and all three were in the office. Wendy had finally got the message not to keep moving Farhan's desk; not the other one about exhaling the smell of stale cigarettes over the other two.

She should have taken the hint with the window behind Isaac being open, even though it was cold outside. She preferred a room to be warm and cosy, just like Station Manager Broughton's office at Paddington Station.

A good-looking man, plenty of women, she thought. *Twenty years ago, I would have made a play for him myself.*

Isaac brought their meeting to order. 'Wendy, can you update us, please.'

Before she replied, Isaac leant over and closed the window.

'The person she met is almost certainly a friend.'

'You've had some luck?' Farhan said. Wendy noticed the look of the man had taken a turn for the worse since she had last seen him. He looked worried, and his clothes looked as though they could do with a good iron.

The look of a recently separated man, she thought. She thought back to ten years previously, to a rough patch in her marriage when she had moved out of the marital home. It had only been for three weeks before he apologised and she had forgiven him. She nearly left again on entering the front door of the house. The dirty dishes in the kitchen sink were disgusting, the waste paper bin was overflowing, the washing machine refused to work due to severe overloading and the place stank.

It had taken her two days to clean up the mess, two days when she could have easily have walked out of the door again. She finally calmed down, but the anger remained for months, tense months, where they barely spoke to each other.

'Luck! Good old-fashioned police work. Out on the street, talking to people.' She could sometimes be acerbic. How many times, when she had found a missing person, had she heard the word 'luck' mentioned.

It wasn't luck that had found the café; it was a case of placing herself in the right environment. The rain had helped and directed her towards the café, but if it had not, she would have kept walking the area, asking questions. Eventually, she would have stumbled upon the waitress, although it could have been days, maybe weeks. She was pleased it had been sooner rather than later, as her arthritis was giving her trouble, even though she had not walked far the previous day.

'Wendy, please continue,' Isaac said. He had worked with her before, knew she could be a bit touchy – the reason why he had not broached the subject of the stale cigarette smell.

He was aware that it would lead to a lecture about civil liberties, freedom for a person to decide whether they were damaging their health or not.

'She knew the person she met,' Wendy said. 'The waitress confirmed it was Richard Williams from a photo that I showed her the next day.'

'He knows that obstructing the course of justice, especially in a murder investigation, is a serious offence. His fancy Queen's Counsel will not be able to protect him.'

'I've not met Richard Williams. Is he the sort of person to risk imprisonment?' Wendy asked.

'Not at all,' Isaac replied. 'He's a sharp operator. If he is protecting Marjorie Frobisher, there must be a reason.'

'But meeting in London? Surely they realised the possibility of being seen. We're not the only ones looking for her,' Farhan speculated.

'Maybe they're not thinking straight. Maybe the woman is irrational. The waitress said she didn't say much. Williams may have been compromised into helping.'

'I agree with Wendy,' Isaac said. 'We're aware of the special relationship between the two of them.'

'It's up to you, Isaac,' Farhan said.

'I need to go and see him. It would help if Wendy keeps checking, tries to find out where she is.'

'I'll start on it tomorrow,' Wendy said, glad to be out of the office again. She only hoped a long soak in a warm bath and some medicine would reduce the pain in her legs.

***

Isaac felt his time the following morning would be best spent with Richard Goddard. He had set up a meeting for nine o'clock. He sensed that his superior officer was not looking forward to a visit, but it was important.

At 9 a.m. Isaac was outside his senior's office. Ten minutes later, Goddard appeared. As he was a man who was a stickler for punctuality, it seemed odd to Isaac. He chose to make no comment.

'What is it, Isaac?' There had been none of the customary 'sit down for a chat' welcome. Isaac was disturbed. He had not seen his boss like this before, and they had worked together for some years.

'Marjorie Frobisher.'

'Have you found her?'

'We think she's alive.'

'But have you found her?'

'Not yet. Soon, I imagine.'

'It would have been best if she had stayed missing. Isaac. It's become complicated.'

Isaac chose another line of questioning. 'Is there anyone else looking for her currently?'

'Why do you ask? You and DI Ahmed had people following you at one time. Is that still occurring?'

'We've not seen them for some time, but I still feel they're watching us.'

'Why do you say that?'

'I suspect someone's been planted.'

'What do you mean?'

'A woman working with Richard Williams may be more than she seems.'

'Why do you say that?'

'She's smarter than she pretends to be; definitely not the sort of woman Williams would typically employ.'

'Attractive?'

'Very.'

'There's your answer. He chooses them attractive, easy to lay. That's what your reports have indicated.'

'She doesn't seem the type that would be an easy lay, certainly not for Williams.'

'Is he sleeping with her?'

'Apparently. She gave him a cast-iron alibi when Sally Jenkins was murdered.'

'And you think she's a plant? Do you fancy her?'

'A plant, it's possible. Fancy her? I suppose I do, but I've kept my distance.'

'Are you still protecting that other woman?'

'If you mean Jess O'Neill, I've kept my distance, at least until this case is resolved.'

'Make sure it stays that way. This is becoming too complicated, and no one knows why.'

Isaac still felt that his boss knew more than he did. It seemed critical for him and Farhan to know as much, but how? If their boss did not want to tell them, there wasn't much that he could do to prise it out of him. He decided to try again.

'Sir, I need to know. We're chasing around after a woman who is directly or indirectly related to the deaths of two people. What if there is another murder? A murder we could have prevented with additional knowledge.'

'I understand what you're saying.'

'We need to meet Angus MacTavish,' Isaac said.

The detective superintendent quickly exited the office and made a phone call.

'Midday at his office,' he said on his return. 'If he tries to talk you down, stand your ground.'

'I believe I can handle him,' Isaac replied.

***

Wendy, before she continued the search for the Marjorie Frobisher in London, went into the office at Challis Street. It was empty. Isaac, she knew, was meeting Detective Superintendent Goddard. Farhan, she had no idea where he had gone. She made a strong cup of tea, extra sugar, and raided the biscuit jar. As no one was around, she opened the window and lit a cigarette, careful to ensure the smoke and ash went out of the window. She vowed to cut down.

The cigarette dispensed with, she phoned Bridget Halloran. She knew she would be able to assist. 'I need to find Marjorie Frobisher,' Wendy said.

'What did you find out?'

'She met a friend. Someone we know. We need to find out possible locations where he may have taken her.'

'Couldn't you just ask him?'

'DCI Cook will deal with that, but the situation is complicated.'

'What do you mean?' Bridget asked. It wasn't necessary for her to know, but Wendy reasoned that she had gone out of her way to assist, and besides she was a friend who she trusted.

'We need to find her before other people do.'

'What if they find her?'

'We're not sure. She could disappear again.'

'And not come back this time?'

'That's a possibility.'

'Then, for all our sakes, we'd better find her first.'

'Strictest confidence.'

'You can trust me, you know that,' Bridget replied.

'I know. I just had to say it, though.'

***

It came as a complete surprise to Isaac how agreeable Angus MacTavish was when he met him. Richard Goddard had expected him to be gruff, unpleasant, but here was the firm handshake, the pat on the shoulder, and 'pleased to meet you'.

Mrs Gregory had dealt with the tea and cakes. She took a shine to Isaac as well.

With all three men seated comfortably and Mrs Gregory in the other room, Angus MacTavish spoke. 'DCI Cook, you want to know about Marjorie Frobisher.'

'Yes, sir.'

'You realise that Detective Superintendent Goddard and I have met several times to discuss this matter.'

'Yes.'

'DCI Cook, are you aware of a child?' MacTavish asked.

'Yes.'

'And how important it is that the child does not find out who the mother is?'

'As well as the father?' Richard Goddard said.

'Detective Superintendent Goddard is right,' MacTavish said. 'In fact, the father is more important than the mother.'

'Who is the father?' Isaac asked.

'That's the problem. I just don't know.'

'You have a shrewd idea.'

'That's all I have. I know that Detective Superintendent Goddard thinks it's the prime minister.'

'Could it be someone else?'

'It's possible.'

'It may help if I have some names,' Isaac said. 'We're chasing shadows, coming up with blanks at the present moment.'

'Tell me what you've got. How about the two murders? Any leads there?' MacTavish asked.

'We know how they died, but why is unclear.'

'Tied in with this damn woman's disappearance?'

'Circumstantial,' Isaac said, 'but failing any other motives, it seems more than likely. Charles Sutherland was threatening to say something, and Sally Jenkins had a tendency to eavesdrop.'

'They may have been eliminated because someone thought they did know something,' MacTavish said.

'Someone killed them purely on the off-chance?' Richard Goddard asked, anxious to remain vital to the meeting. He had seen it before. Take DCI Isaac Cook, the tall, attractive and very black policeman along to meet someone important, and they would be immediately charmed by him, while he, the more senior of the two, a dour white man, would be left floundering. Still, he was pleased that Angus MacTavish was opening up, something he had not done with him.

'Detective Superintendent Goddard mentioned on the phone that there may be someone who is a plant,' MacTavish said.

'A woman,' Isaac said. 'She's close to the action, not involved in the murders.'

'You feel she may be keeping her ear to the ground. Can you find out if that is the case?'

'I can try. Do you want her to know we're on to her?'

'No, I don't think so. It may only precipitate another action.'

'Such as another murder?' Richard Goddard asked.

'It's possible,' Isaac said.

'Marjorie Frobisher? Dead or alive?' MacTavish asked. Isaac wasn't sure what to say. He saw no reason to trust the man; no reason not to.

'We believe she is alive.'

'Then keep her that way. I don't believe this government or any other government deserves to be in power when they condone murder as a solution.'

'Is that what's happened?' Isaac asked.

'A can of worms. Anything's possible,' Angus MacTavish said.

'What about the plant?'

'I'll check her out for you. May take a few days.'

'Thank you,' Isaac replied.

'What do you reckon?' Detective Superintendent Goddard asked as he and Isaac drove away.

'He's a politician. How would we know if he was telling us the truth?'

'He could have just been spinning us a line.'

'Exactly. We keep the news relating to Marjorie Frobisher to ourselves. I'd say she is as good as dead if we don't find her first.'

'And if we do?'

'I've no idea. It's not our function to protect people; our function is to catch murderers, prevent further murders.'

'With Marjorie Frobisher, that amounts to the same thing.'

'You're right, but protect her from whom? Who can we trust?'

'Nobody, Isaac. Nobody.' Detective Superintendent Goddard summed up the situation succinctly.

Chapter 32

Farhan was not handling the situation well. On the one hand, he had a wife he did not love, but still the mother of his children. He realised he had not been giving them the attention that they deserved recently. Not because he didn't want to, but because of the pressure of work, and now the situation was intense. There had been two murders so far, and the number could rise. And then there was Aisha, whom he did love but could not meet, although he had made an exception when it looked as though her cover was about to be blown. He knew it was wrong, but he couldn't help himself.

He knew the right thing to do, but how? He had been married off in a loveless marriage to a cold and passionless woman. Apart from Elaine Downton, a casual fling before he had married, he had slept with no other woman. That was until he had met Aisha. One night in a hotel room with her, and he knew he wanted to spend his life with her, but was it possible?

Isaac's penchant for bedding attractive women never ceased to draw admiration from the men in the police force, but the head of such a fine Service needed to be stable, with a stable family life.

Farhan knew that in time Isaac would settle down and that he was equally at ease with the man on the street or someone in high office. Isaac had told him how the Government Chief Whip, Angus MacTavish, had acted towards him: magnanimous, friendly. Farhan had not been surprised; it happened all the time.

Farhan knew that he did not possess Isaac's innate charm. He was aware that he was not an unattractive man, but his features were not as easy on the eye. Sure, Elaine Downton had told him he had a good heart, and Aisha told him he was attractive, and that beauty is more than skin deep.

No doubt they were correct. He did have a good heart, a need to help. Isaac did as well, but he had both the exterior beauty and the inner goodness. No, Farhan admitted openly to himself, *I'll be happy to make detective superintendent.*

He also knew that while the unresolved issue of his wife remained, and his involvement with a prostitute, whether or not he married her in due course, his career was going nowhere.

He phoned Aisha. The case she had been working on had turned out successfully.

Farhan and Aisha arranged to meet later that day. Important issues to discuss, she said. They met at the same hotel down by the river, ended up in the same bed. The important matter was that she wanted to be with him. Farhan had suspected as much when he had agreed to the meeting. His protestations at the folly of it were feebly attempted.

After their lovemaking, she explained the situation. Her career was looking good, her parents were pleased, always telling their extended family back in India about how well their Aisha was doing. Also mentioning that she had a boyfriend, a senior man in the police force, a man going places.

'I'm sorry. I had to tell them something. They are still steeped in the traditions of the home country. They still believe in their making a choice as to who I'll spend my life with.'

'Have you made that choice?' he asked.

'Yes.'

'I'm not sure about the senior policeman.'

'You will be; I'm sure of it.'

'I won't be anything if this crime is not solved.'

'Maybe I can help.'

'I know we discussed this before, but how?'

'A different perspective. I'm a criminal lawyer.'

'A successful criminal lawyer now,' he joked.

'As you say, successful.'

They were glad of the opportunity to spend time together. He knew the trouble he would be in if anyone found out that he had slept with her again. Murder enquiry or no murder enquiry, he would almost certainly be suspended, pending a disciplinary hearing. The only hope of redemption would be if he came up with a new take on the murders.

'Can we come back to Sutherland?' He was aware of her wish not to discuss the matter.

'If you must.'

'Someone was able to induce him to take a drink while he was naked.'

'It can only be a woman.'

'If it wasn't either you or Olivia, then that leaves the woman who let you in.'

'Christy?'

'I wasn't aware you knew her name.'

'She introduced herself when we first met. Timid sort of woman. Just good manners, I assume.'

'I've ruled her out,' Farhan said.

'Any reason?'

'No apparent connection that would tie her in with Sally Jenkins.'

'Are the two murders related?'

'That is the assumption. The disappearance of Marjorie Frobisher seems related as well.'

'All three could be unrelated. Have you considered that?'

'Initially, but it seemed to be going nowhere.'

'And now?'

'About the same. Sally Jenkins, we're not sure. Probably someone she knew, but who? Her previous lover doesn't seem to have a reason to kill her, and his alibi is cast iron.'

'Cast iron, why do you say that?'

'He was in bed with another woman.'

'Proven?' Aisha asked.

'According to the woman.'

'Do you believe her? Maybe she's protecting him out of some misguided loyalty, maybe love. The same as you're protecting me.'

Farhan could see the reasoning. He would discuss it with Isaac, not mentioning where the discussion was held. Maybe they should just focus on one murder at a time, treat it in isolation, and not try to tie it in with the other.

It was eight in the evening when they left the hotel. Farhan back to a cold and miserable house, Aisha back to her proud parents. How she wished she had met such a good man before she had become a prostitute, but then she would not have met him. How he wished he was free to make the choice he wanted to, but there were the children to consider. He knew the road ahead was far from clear. At least, for tonight, he was pleased they had met, had made love, had discussed the case.

***

Isaac intended to meet Richard Williams at the earliest opportunity, but he did not want to barge in and then find the man's QC submitting a writ for police intimidation. It was best to wait until Wendy had found the missing woman.

Possibly then he could knock on the door. Hopefully, talk to her, calm her fears, and gain her confidence.

Bridget, as always, was pleased to see Wendy when she popped her head around the door. 'What can I do for you?' Some quick gossip and then down to work, a cup of tea in one hand, a biscuit in the other. Wendy knew the cost of assistance would be a pub lunch washed down with a couple of strong drinks.

'The woman's somewhere. We need to find her and soon.'

'She could be in a hotel. Almost impossible to find,' Bridget replied.

'Let's assume it's not a hotel. Let's work on the assumption it's a property somewhere. We know where Williams lives; it's not going to be there.'

'Why?' Bridget asked.

'Too obvious. Besides, he needs somewhere to bring his women.'

'Romancer, is he?' Bridget, always eager for some salacious gossip.

'Sugar daddy, more like.'

'Flashes his money around?'

'Ferrari. Gives them a good time. Mid-life crisis, although he should be past that by now.'

'Sounds my kind of guy,' Bridget joked.

'Unfortunately, you're not his kind of woman.' They knew each other well enough for Wendy to tease her.

'Mature and experienced?'

'Your skirt's not short enough for one thing.'

'And my breasts are not pert and upright, just dangling.'

'We both suffer from that complaint. Let's get back to Williams.'

The joking over, both women focussed on the task. Wendy felt sure the woman was ensconced in a comfortable and secure property somewhere.

'If she's not at his house, then maybe he has other properties, flats he rents out. Can you find them?' Wendy suggested.

'I can search the records.'

The results of two hours' searching and a pub lunch identified three properties: a house in Twickenham, a flat down near Canary Wharf, and another flat not far from Hackney. Wendy relayed the news to Isaac. She would check them the next day.

***

Isaac, severely angry with Farhan, did not mince his words. 'How many times have you been told to keep away from this woman? If you're seen, it's the end of your career, mine as well. And what about our boss?'

'You're not going to tell him, are you?'

'Not unless I have to,' Isaac replied. It was good that their office was insulated so his voice didn't travel. He was not a man given to anger, rarely a raised voice, but Farhan's admission that he had met with Aisha again had upset him greatly.

He had gone out on a limb to protect Farhan. Even asked their boss the last time to keep it to a severe verbal reprimand,

258

not to put anything in writing. What if it turned out that the woman was involved in the murder? Isaac shuddered at the thought of the repercussions.

He knew that Farhan had led a sheltered life; no seducing the willing females in his later years at school and then sowing his oats after a night down the pub. Farhan, he realised, was easy prey to an experienced woman with no inhibitions about initiating sexual congress.

'How am I going to protect you?' Isaac continued. 'Look, you're a good policeman, and we work well as a team, but meeting with this woman again? I thought we agreed that you were going to talk to her, ask her to leave the country.'

'I did meet with her, but she wants to stay.'

'They'll find her eventually; you know that?'

'We both know that.'

'Both, do you mean you and her?'

'Yes.'

'This is going to end badly. She has to disappear if you want to protect her.'

'She has just been involved in a prominent legal case. Only as the junior, but the man got off. She's elated, she wants to stay.'

'She may be the most brilliant legal mind in the country, but she's also a prostitute – sold herself for sex. Do you think there is any chance for her? Her past history will surface. If not now, at some stage in the future. These things can't stay hidden forever. She must know that.'

'We both know that.'

'Have you been sleeping with her again?' Isaac asked, quickly adding, 'Don't tell me. It's better if you don't answer that question.'

'She's a smart woman; she had some ideas.'

'You've been discussing the case with her?'

'More like questioning.'

'At least that's acceptable. What did she have to say, your girlfriend?' Isaac ventured some humour. Farhan chose not to respond.

'We're assuming that the murders and the disappearance of Marjorie Frobisher are related.'

'What else do we have?' Isaac asked.

'According to Aisha, what if we are wrong? What if they are unrelated?'

'It's a possibility, but how do we ascertain that?'

'Instead of trying to make the connection, we isolate them totally from each other.'

'Sutherland's death could be unrelated, but Sally Jenkins? Why would anyone kill her?'

'Other than she knew something about the missing woman?'

'I suppose so,' Isaac replied.

'What if there is no missing woman? How would we approach the case of Sally Jenkins?' Farhan asked.

'We would look for a motive; for someone who had a reason to want her dead.'

'She wasn't raped.'

'And not a break-in that went wrong, judging by the condition of where she lived.'

'So it must have been someone she knew,' Isaac said.

'DI Hill, the crime scene officer, is intimating that someone came in the front door; the break-in may have been a subterfuge.'

'Only Richard Williams had a key.'

'But why would he want to murder her? And, anyway, he was in bed with Linda Harris.'

'She's an unknown,' Isaac admitted.

'What do you mean? I know you have your suspicions, even took her out for a meal. What was your intent there, professional or personal?'

'Both, I suppose, but she's not involved. At least, I assume she's not. She was not around when Marjorie Frobisher disappeared, nor when Sutherland was murdered.'

'So that means she's innocent of all crimes?'

'I'm not sure,' Isaac admitted.

'Why do you say that?'

'What do we know about her?'

'We are aware she's working for Williams, sleeping with him.'

'I asked MacTavish to check her out.'

'And…'

'I'm still waiting for his reply.'

'Did you fancy her?' Farhan asked.

'At first.'

'And after?'

'She became upset when I started probing. The evening ended badly.'

'What about the other woman? Are you still in contact?'

'Not for some time. It may be a good idea to maintain contact, seeing that she's a witness.'

'And potential plaything?' Farhan jested.

'So far, I've managed to keep it under control. I'm not the lothario that you are, obviously.'

'You know we'd both be in trouble if Goddard found out.'

'I've not done anything wrong yet,' Isaac announced with regret.

'Would you have slept with Linda Harris if your night had turned out differently?'

'Probably.'

'What do we really know about her?' Farhan asked.

'I think she's a fellow government employee.'

'And if she is?'

'Then she's clear of any involvement in the murders.'

'I'm not certain she is.'

'What do you mean?'

'If she's willing to indulge in sexual relations with a man purely because it's her job, what else is she capable of?'

Isaac had to agree, disturbed that a woman he almost slept with, probably would if the opportunity presented itself again, was no better than the two women who had sold themselves to Charles Sutherland.

It seemed ironic to Isaac that Farhan was getting more action than him. He knew full well that he had been sleeping with his woman again; the look on his face evidence of the fact.

Chapter 33

Wendy, pleased that the weather was more agreeable, had staked out the first place of interest, a small two-storey terrace in Twickenham. She could see that Richard Williams liked his investments well-maintained: the small garden at the front was neat and tidy, the paintwork on the exterior façade in remarkably good condition, in contrast to the other houses in the street. She assumed it had been freshly painted. Compared to her home, a dreary run-down property close to the docks, it was beautiful. Her husband had never been into home repairs, and she did not have the skills to do the work. Williams' terraced house was the sort of place she would love to own, knew she never would.

She parked her car across the street. For three, close to four hours she watched the house from inside the car. The only people she saw, a young couple pushing a child's buggy. They were clearly the tenants. Bridget had already ascertained it was rented out to a couple with one child. Wendy realised the missing woman was not at this location.

After a quick lunch she drove out to the next location, a flat close to Hackney. She would have gone to the apartment down by Canary Wharf as her second choice, more upmarket than Hackney, but it was early afternoon, and the traffic was building up. Even so, it still took her the best part of ninety minutes.

It was clear that the second property was not as salubrious as the first. It appeared to be on the third floor, in a drab, red-brick, ex-council property. There were two problems on arriving: one, she could not see the entrance to the flat, only the front window, and two, parking restrictions on account of the late afternoon rush hour were about to apply. She could only stay for thirty minutes.

She phoned Isaac. She found his manner a little distant – as if he had something on his mind. Disregarding his curtness with her, she told him about the house in Twickenham, and the flat in Hackney. She also let him know that she regarded Canary Wharf as a better possibility, and that tomorrow she would drive out there.

Farhan, meanwhile, had phoned Robert Avers to ask if he had heard from his wife.

The man's response surprised Farhan. 'I'm not going to sit at home waiting for her to knock on the door. She screwed around enough, now it's my turn.'

Farhan understood where he was coming from, careful not to let on that they believed his wife was alive and somewhere in London.

***

The next day, Wendy drove out to Canary Wharf, a massive redevelopment of the former West India Docks. Now a major financial centre, comprising major banks, financial services, and media organisations, it was also the home of some very impressive upmarket properties, primarily high-rise executive apartments.

She was convinced that it was the most likely location to find the woman: comfortable, secluded, an ideal place to hide out if you could afford it. No need to trudge down to the local supermarket to buy some food, just phone, and one of the expensive restaurants would deliver to your door, along with a good bottle of wine. And, from what Wendy had heard, Marjorie Frobisher enjoyed the good life, despised the poverty of her childhood.

It was clear that the flat, on the thirteenth floor, was too high to see anyone at ground level, unless the occupant stood right against the window.

The concierge at the front door, she felt, would not offer much help. Besides, she did not want to alert the missing woman to the fact that someone was looking for her. The easiest way was to enter the building unseen.

Observing the concierge, a smartly dressed man in his late twenties, she waited until he was distracted by a car pulling up at the front. A woman got out of the driver's seat. Wendy assumed her to be in her early fifties, obviously well-heeled judging by the shopping in the back seat of the vehicle. As the concierge went out to help, Wendy slipped past and into the building.

The lift was on the twentieth floor and descending. She hoped it would arrive at the ground floor before the concierge saw her: it did. Quickly, she pressed thirteen on the row of buttons, the speed of the lift surprising her.

Exiting the lift, she moved swiftly to flat number 1304. She pressed the bell, a woman came to the door. Wendy apologised, said she had mistaken the numbers, and it must be 1340.

The concierge barely noticed her, as she brazenly exited the lift on the ground floor and walked out of the building. He did not see the broad smile on her face.

***

Isaac knew that the situation had changed. Marjorie Frobisher was alive and well; the evidence, indisputable. Wendy had been sure, and she did not make mistakes. As she had stated, when she phoned him from Canary Wharf, 'I know that woman as well as my own mother.'

How to proceed concerned him. If he confronted her, what could he say? She had been missing for a long time, but she had not committed any crime. What would he ask her? Who was this mysterious child? Who killed Sutherland and Sally Jenkins? Why did she choose to stay missing?

If the woman decided to remain mute, there was not a lot he could do. And then, if she was scared again, she could disappear without a trace. She had done it once successfully; she could do it again.

And if he was being watched, those interested in the woman could follow him out to Canary Wharf. Could she end up dead if he acted inappropriately? Farhan, as good as he was, was not sufficiently experienced to advise on the matter. Sure, he could offer valuable advice, but what if it went wrong. Who would take the blame? He knew the answer without asking – it would be him. Richard Goddard, his detective superintendent, was the ideal choice for advice, but he was looking for a promotion, apparently very friendly with Angus MacTavish. Could either of them be trusted?

The questions outweighed the answers, and now there was the disturbing information about Linda Harris, apparently sleeping with Richard Williams for Queen and Country on official orders.

Angus MacTavish had phoned some hours earlier; said that he had been advised that Linda Harris was involved and that she was a very smart woman – devious, the word he used.

But who was MacTavish? Did he genuinely believe that no political party, even his, deserved to be elected if it sanctioned government approved murder?

Isaac felt that he had to make decisions based on his own sense of decency and to see how they turned out.

Richard Williams, the executive producer, somehow seemed integral to solving the murders. Isaac reasoned the best approach would be to meet him again. He still felt that of all the people involved, he was probably the most innocent, but then there were doubts there, Sally Jenkins being the most obvious.

What if Linda Harris was giving an alibi for Williams purely to ensure that when Marjorie Frobisher reappeared, she would be able to report to her superiors? Was she sleeping with Williams, and if she wasn't, why did she go along with his statement that she had?

Isaac could see that he had to confront Linda Harris, hope that Marjorie Frobisher was safe, at least for a couple of days. He had already asked Wendy to stake out Canary Wharf, and see if she could keep the missing, now found, woman safe.

***

Farhan and Isaac met again in the office later that day: Farhan to further discuss what Aisha had suggested; Isaac to assess how to handle the situation with Richard Williams, and whether he could be involved or not in his former PA's death.

Farhan was in a good mood; his regular conversations with Aisha continued, and his wife was no longer talking about a reconciliation. Apparently, her parents, despairing of her 'no good' husband, had suggested a divorce from Farhan and marriage to a cousin of hers, someone she genuinely liked: a devout Muslim and a good provider, as he owned a number of shops close to the family home.

He should have been distraught at his children being taken from him, but he was a practical man, moderated by his years in the police force. Life, he had come to see, was not black and white, right or wrong, good or bad. Life was about compromises, not absolutes, and his children being with a good man and a good woman, even if the man was not the biological father, was better than being in the conflict zone of a liberated man and a pious woman. He would accept the decision and wish them well.

He felt relief – as if a weight had been lifted off his shoulders. Aisha still remained a problem – an irresolvable problem.

Isaac wanted to sound out Farhan about what they had. It was evident to both of them that the situation was coming to a head. Too much was going on not to have a breakthrough in the near future. Richard Goddard had been pleased when Isaac had phoned him earlier, and let him know that he felt confident it was all coming to fruition. He failed to mention that Marjorie Frobisher had been discovered.

The detective superintendent had always been a mentor to Isaac, and it upset him that he could not be entirely honest with his boss, but there remained some uncertainties. The detective superintendent was in line for a significant promotion. Angus MacTavish could have some bearing on that promotion, and he was a definite uncertainty. Isaac could not be sure about his boss at the present moment, although nothing in his history had indicated a subversive, dishonest nature.

'Farhan, let's come back to what your friend said before.'
There was to be no jesting from Isaac this time about the
girlfriend.

'Sally Jenkins?'

'Richard Williams appears to be an obvious candidate, but
why? Isaac asked.

'We're clutching at straws again,' Farhan said. 'It's possible
if it was somehow related to Marjorie Frobisher, but murder?
Would Williams be capable of committing such an act?'

'I can't see it.'

'Neither can I?'

'Who else then?'

'Linda Harris? She was around at the time.'

'She's providing an alibi for Williams. If she left him and
went over to Sally Jenkins' place, would he have known?'

'Almost certainly.'

'How far from Williams' place to Sally Jenkins'?'

'Twenty minutes, no more.'

'So it's possible,' Isaac said.

'What do you intend to do? Who do you talk to first?'

'Linda Harris. If she's the murderer, she may have acted
under orders.'

'And if she did?'

'Then she's a very dangerous woman. If Sally Jenkins'
murder was premeditated because of what she may have known,
what about Marjorie Frobisher?'

'She's dead, or soon will be, and neither you nor I will be
able to protect her.'

'A disturbing reality.'

'An accurate picture, though. If her death is sanctioned
officially, then she is a dead woman.'

***

Isaac phoned Linda Harris. Offered his apology, asked to see her
again.

'What was the response?' Farhan asked on Isaac's return from the corridor outside their office. He had heard Isaac ingratiating himself with the woman.

'Tonight, same restaurant as before.'

'Any idea how you will bring the matter up?'

'Whether she killed Sally Jenkins or not? I don't think the evening will go too well if I do.'

'If she can sleep with Williams, and murder another woman, what chance do you have of finding out the truth?' Farhan saw a danger in Isaac's approach.

'We can't do nothing.'

'Devil or the deep blue sea. There's no other option for us, although it looks as if you, at least, will be having some fun.'

'As you did with a witness.' Isaac could not resist a little jest.

'A witness on our side. Yours could as easily kill you as make love. It's not an exciting prospect.'

'Don't worry, I'll be fine,' Isaac said.

Farhan was not so sure. His boss was possibly becoming involved with dangerous people, government-sanctioned people. He only hoped he knew what he was doing.

***

Linda Harris was undeniably friendly when she met up with Isaac. 'How are you? Good to see you,' she had gushed. Isaac, forewarned, was not convinced.

'I'm fine. Sorry about last time,' he said. He had to admit she was stunning, dressed in a floral dress, short as she preferred, and a pair of red high-heels.

'I dressed especially.'

'You look beautiful.'

'Good enough for dessert?' Her comment seemed a little too forward for Isaac, but he had to admit that she was.

'Main course, even.'

'I think we should have something to eat first, don't you?' To Isaac, it all seemed a little too orchestrated, a little too teasing. He knew some details about the woman, which caused him to be wary. Sure, he wanted her for dessert, although he would have preferred Jess O'Neill. Apart from a couple of occasions, in a pub out near where she worked, he had not seen her for some time.

He had lambasted Farhan for his indiscretions, although he had not been blameless. However, with Jess, it had remained platonic. He knew he wanted her, knew she wanted him, but so far it had not progressed beyond a passionate kiss on a couple of occasions.

Regardless of Jess, Isaac knew that Linda Harris would be dessert if the evening progressed well enough.

First, there were some questions about Richard Williams' alibi. Not answers veiled by confusion or outright denial; answers openly given, once he had broached the subject of her true employer. And even then, would she be open and truthful?

They chose a table near the back of the restaurant. Isaac ordered pork, Linda chose the veal. A good Chardonnay complemented the meal. Isaac drank sparingly; Linda with more enthusiasm.

'Linda.' Isaac knew he had to speak.

'Don't ruin the evening.' She sounded genuine.

'I hope I'm not.' He knew how he wanted the evening to end. Personal assistant or not, lover of Richard Williams or not, secretive government employee or not, he intended to bed her if the opportunity arose.

'I'm aware that you have received some information about me,' she said.

'I have.'

'And you want to know more?'

'There's been two murders, probably more if we don't find the killer, or killers?'

'Killers? Could there be more than one?'

'It's possible. We still don't have a clear motive for either murder.'

270

'Isaac, I honestly don't know about the murders.'

'So, why are you sleeping with Williams?'

'You sound jealous.'

'Should I be?' Isaac obliquely failed to answer her question.

'You know I work for the government, MI5.'

'That's what I've been told.'

'My superiors have given me authority to reveal certain facts if the situation came up.'

'Has it?'

'I believe it has. You are the lead policeman on the investigation into the two murders, although initially you were looking for a missing woman.'

'Marjorie Frobisher.'

'Precisely. That's who I'm looking for,' she said.

'But why? Why is she so important?'

'I'm assigned to find the woman, spy where I need to, do whatever is necessary to find her.'

'And sleep with Williams?'

'Yes, sleep with Williams if it helped with the investigation.'

'Has it?'

'Not really, but he's a decent man, a little older than normal for me. I'm still a healthy liberated female. I need to be laid on a regular basis.'

'That's a stunningly frank admission.'

'And you're a modern virile man who needs to get laid on a regular basis, as well. Am I correct?'

'That's correct.'

'And you're not getting much action lately. Jess O'Neill is definitely off the menu.'

'You know about her?'

'It's my job to know. Besides, the two of you are not the most discreet. I saw you both in a pub the other week, very cosy from what I could see.'

'Why is Marjorie Frobisher so important?' Isaac asked the most important question.

'I'm assigned to find her. As to why? I've no idea. That's the truth. Obviously, it's something important, but I don't know what.'

'I don't know either.'

You probably know more than me. Can we change the subject?'

'Are we having dessert?' Isaac asked.

'I hope so, but not here. We'll only frighten the other diners. Your place or mine?'

'My place,' Isaac replied. 'It's closer.'

Chapter 34

In the two days at Canary Wharf, conveniently based near the restaurant and a café she frequented, Wendy had seen little. She believed she had seen the woman at the window a couple of times, but it was high up, and it had been no more than a blurry silhouette. The only visitor that she recognised, almost certainly Richard Williams, judging by the way he walked. It was not possible to see the face, due to a heavy coat, a cloth cap, and a voluminous scarf. He arrived in a small car, not a Ferrari.

Isaac had phoned a couple of times, purely for an update, and Farhan had phoned once. Apart from that, she had been left alone. It suited her fine. The warmth of the sun out next to the water, or in the café, had helped her arthritis, the best it had been for some time.

She knew that her house, once her husband was established in a retirement home, would need to be sold, the rising damp too costly to repair; at least, on her meagre income and her husband's pension. The constantly moist atmosphere in the house kept chilling her bones and her body. She couldn't wait to leave.

It was on the third day when she saw the commotion. An ambulance pulled up outside the building where the missing woman was hiding. Wendy was quickly on the phone to Isaac, who was soon in his car and on the way over to meet her. Wendy, not wasting any time, was in the building, flashing her police badge at the concierge as she dashed through. Not needing to check which floor, uninterested if it was any other than the thirteenth.

Marjorie Frobisher was prostrate on the floor, the ambulance paramedic hovering over her.

'Is she dead?' Wendy shouted.

'She's still breathing.' The reply.

The paramedic was a young woman in her early thirties.

'Do you know her?' the paramedic asked. Wendy could see the name tag attached to the front of the woman's uniform: Patricia Edwards.

'It's Marjorie Frobisher.'

'The actor?'

'Yes, her.'

'I thought it was.'

'Will she live?' Wendy asked anxiously. It was her responsibility, and now the woman was dead, dying. She was not handling the situation as well as she should have.

'Touch and go, I'd say.'

'When will you know?'

'Not for me to say. I need to stabilise her, deal with the immediate situation, and get her to the hospital.'

'Any idea what happened to her?'

'Not sure. Maybe a heart attack.'

'Does it look intentional, murder?'

'I'm not the police. I'm only here to deal with the medical condition. You'll need to ask a policeman whether it's murder or not.'

'I'm a police officer, Constable Wendy Gladstone.'

'Then you can tell me.' Wendy could see the paramedic was busy. Isaac was five minutes away, and he would want answers. The key person was incapacitated, and she was responsible. Why hadn't Isaac confronted Marjorie Frobisher before? Whether the woman lived or died, there was trouble coming; she could sense it.

***

Five minutes later, and Isaac entered the room. He saw the woman being taken out on a stretcher.

'DCI Isaac Cook.' He introduced himself to the paramedic.

'She's stable. It looks as though she'll live.' She had correctly anticipated what he was going to ask.

With that, the woman left with her patient. Isaac needed to spend time with Wendy and to check out the flat. He phoned Farhan and asked him to get over to the hospital.

'What's happened?' Isaac turned his attention back to Wendy.

'I don't know. She hasn't left the building in two days.'

'Anyone else been in the building?'

'Plenty in and out.'

'And did any of those contact the woman?'

'I wouldn't know. She's up on the thirteenth floor. I could hardly stand outside her door for all that time.'

'I suppose not. We should have contacted her when she first appeared.' Isaac regretted his lapse, regretted he hadn't told Richard Goddard.

And where did Linda Harris fit into the puzzle? he thought. She had confirmed she was MI5, although she had been adamant that she was only looking for the woman.

The previous night she had been anything murderous. He felt remorse afterwards, hoped that Jess would never find out, vowed not to sleep with the woman again.

Marjorie Frobisher's current condition represented trouble – trouble with a capital T.

A close investigation of the apartment revealed nothing unusual. The clothes in the wardrobe were the same as on the CCTV at Worcester and Paddington Stations. A half-eaten meal was on the dining table. Isaac noted it for checking. He phoned the medical examiner, asked him to come over. It was not a murder scene, at least, not yet, but the apartment would need to be sealed off and thoroughly checked.

It was evident that Wendy had done no wrong, but Isaac knew how the police force worked. Whenever there was a disciplinary action, there was always a scapegoat. He was the guilty party, not her, but he was young and a future detective superintendent, even head of the establishment. They would protect him, but he was not going to let a woman approaching retirement take the blame for his actions. He realised that if he took the blame then the pressure would be placed on Detective Superintendent Goddard to explain why his DCI had not followed procedure.

***

Farhan arrived at the Royal London Hospital in Whitechapel within five minutes of the ambulance transporting the unconscious woman. He left the car in a no-parking area and flashed his badge at the surprised security guard. Farhan gave him the keys and told him to move it if it was in the way. It was not his usual way of dealing with the general public, but this was an emergency. The pieces were coming together, or they would if the woman lived.

Her cover was broken; she was vulnerable. He hoped she would realise that the only protection for her was in coming clean about all she knew.

Farhan had phoned Robert Avers on the way, his number on speed dial. He sensed the man was not overly pleased. Apparently, he had been cutting quite a dashing figure around town with a woman young enough to be his daughter, although the one he had been squiring was attractive, whereas the daughter, by her own admission, was not.

Once in the hospital, Farhan flashed his badge again. Soon, he was outside the emergency room. He noticed the media starting to arrive; someone had tipped them off. He could see the hospital being deluged with cameras and microphones. Her reappearance was big news. The radio and television stations would be blasting it to the world incessantly for the next few days, until it became old news, replaced by something else.

Farhan chose to ignore the media presence. He phoned the local police station to send over some uniformed men to hold the press and any fans at bay.

Doctor Sangram Singh came out to speak to Farhan. He was a distinguished man, and as Farhan found out later on, highly respected. Due to the importance of the patient, he had been brought in to take charge. 'She'll be fine,' he said.

'What was the problem?' Farhan asked.

'Anaphylactic shock.'

He quickly phoned Isaac to update him. His reply, 'What from?' Isaac knew what it meant.

'Nuts, probably. We'll check it out.'

'Robert Avers is there?' Isaac asked.

'Along with half of the London press, or soon will be.'

'Local police?'

'They're here. I phoned them to take control.'

'Detective Superintendent Goddard wants to see all three of us.'

'We're for the high jump?' Farhan knew it meant trouble.

'Someone is, or maybe he just wants an update.'

'We can't talk to her, not for four or five hours at least. She's sedated.'

'Make sure there's a police guard on her door. It's important.' Isaac hung up. He had a defence to prepare.

***

It was unusual for Detective Superintendent Goddard to summon the team to his office. In fact, it was the first time for Farhan and Wendy.

'Isaac, what's going on here?' The detective superintendent did not seem to be in a good mood. He was not one of nature's most affable men at the best of times, but Isaac had great respect for him. Always saw him as a man he could trust, although recent events had shaken that trust.

'Marjorie Frobisher is alive,' Isaac said.

'I only have to turn the television on to know that.' It was a curt reply.

'We can question her now. Find out this great secret.'

'And when you find out, what then?'

'Hopefully, it will clarify why Sutherland and Sally Jenkins were killed.'

'Hell, Isaac, this is getting dangerous. What if certain parties don't want this solving? What if the woman's rising from the dead is putting people on edge? I've already had Angus MacTavish on the phone.'

'What does he want?' Isaac asked. He had noted that the customary cup of coffee and harmless chat had been dispensed with.

'What do you think? He wants to know what the woman is saying.'

'And you've told him what?'

'Nothing. You told me she's sedated.'

'She'll be speaking later today.'

'I hope so, for your sakes.'

'Constable Gladstone, pleased to see you,' the detective superintendent, showing a momentary friendliness, addressed her.

'Nice office you have here, sir.' Compared to Wendy's, it was palatial. Large window, panoramic view, a full bookcase and some comfortable chairs. Not for them, though. The three were sat on one side of the desk, the chairs not very comfortable. Their interrogator on the other side sat on a high-backed leather chair.

'Constable.' The previous civility gone. 'I've seen your expenses. Extravagant in Malvern, but I let it pass, as you did find some additional information about Marjorie Frobisher.'

'Sorry, sir. I'll be more careful in future.'

'Okay, but now there is an expense claim for a restaurant down at Canary Wharf, directly opposite where this woman was found.'

'I'll retract it if it's a problem, sir,' Wendy said timidly.

'That's not the problem. The problem is with DCI Cook.'

Isaac, now sitting upright and rigid in his chair, prepared himself for the worst.

'Isaac, how long have you been aware of the whereabouts of this woman?'

'Two days, going on three.'

'And you chose not to tell me.'

'We were unsure of the situation. She seemed safe enough, and we were staking out the building.'

'What did you expect me to do? Rush off to Angus MacTavish, cap in hand. Is that how you see me?'

'No, sir.' Isaac wasn't sure he could say much to excuse his actions.

'You don't trust MacTavish, do you?'

'I thought him a decent man, but he's a politician with a fearsome reputation for always being on the right side.'

'Isaac, you should have come to me. Now I have MacTavish baying for my blood and the head of the Metropolitan Police asking questions. What can I say? My people chose not to place their confidence in me. It hardly sounds like a ringing endorsement for a promotion.'

'Sir, do you trust MacTavish?' Isaac asked.

'Not totally, but if you had told me soon enough, we could have discussed this. I was not about to rush out the door and over to his office. Someone is after the woman, someone who would prefer her dead, instead of recovering in a hospital bed.'

'That's why we kept it secret.'

'Then who found out?'

'I've no idea,' Isaac admitted.

'DI Ahmed, Constable Gladstone, any ideas?'

'No one that I'm aware of,' Farhan said.

'Not from me,' Wendy added.

'Isaac, let's go through this in detail. Who visited her in Canary Wharf?'

'Only Richard Williams.'

'And what's he got to say?'

'I've not spoken to him yet.'

'Don't you think you should?'

'After we leave here.'

'Do it officially. He's got a lot of answering to do.'

'I will, sir.'

'DC Gladstone, DI Ahmed, you can both leave. Thanks for your time. And DI Ahmed, get to the hospital and make sure the woman is safe and still breathing. Constable Gladstone, submit your remaining claims today while I'm in a generous mood.'

'Thank you, sir.' They spoke in unison.

With the door closed and Isaac alone with his boss, the detective superintendent talked more openly.

'Isaac, I expected better from you. Why are you letting your hormones get in the way of your policing?'

'It's not that, sir.'

'Then what are you doing sleeping with Linda Harris?'

'How do you know, sir?'

'MacTavish told me.'

'How did he know?'

'What does it matter. He's somehow involved, but Linda Harris?'

'She admitted she was MI5.'

'Licensed to sleep with whoever?' Isaac thought his superior's remark inappropriate.

'With Williams, yes.'

'Did you not stop to think? She may have checked the messages on your phone while you were asleep.'

'If she found out, then she's not as innocent as she looks.'

'Isaac, why are you assuming that because she's beautiful, seductive, and available, she's not a highly-skilled operative. If she had been plain and ugly, you would have suspected her.'

'If she had been plain and ugly, she wouldn't have ended up in my bed.'

'That may be, but you can see where I'm coming from. It could have been you who gave her the lead she was trying to get from Richard Williams. Can you imagine the trouble that would cause?'

'End of my career, I would assume.'

'And mine. I'm not ready to retire yet, neither are you, but you've got to control the overriding need to bed every attractive woman that comes along. No doubt it's great fun, and obviously

280

finding these women comes easy to you, but they're impacting on your ability.'

'There's one I would not mind making a longer-term commitment with.'

'I hope you haven't slept with her as well.'

'No, sir.'

'And what's she going to say when she finds out about Linda Harris?'

'I don't know, sir. She's been trying to contact me. Urgent, supposedly. I assume she knows by now.'

'Wrap this case up. It's been going on for too long.'

'I will, sir.'

'And don't go sleeping with Linda Harris. Or Jess O'Neill.'

'I won't, sir.'

***

Isaac, suitably chastised, returned to his office. Wendy was there filling out her expense form. Farhan was almost back at the hospital.

Isaac idly surfed the internet for a few minutes, noting that all the news websites in England were headlining the reappearance of Marjorie Frobisher and her narrow brush with death. Isaac felt he needed to act, and decisively, if he had any hope of reclaiming some credibility. Isaac knew his boss was correct, and that he shouldn't have bedded Linda Harris, but she had been available. He pondered Jess for a while, almost certain that the romance was over before it had started. He was saddened at the prospect. Maybe she would understand that it was in the line of duty, but he knew she wouldn't. She was a woman who would regard fidelity in a relationship as paramount.

He wasn't sure what he was going to say to her. He needed a few days before he contacted her. Jess O'Neill was personal; Richard Williams was not.

He phoned the man, informed him that his presence was required in the building the next morning, 9 a.m. prompt. Williams acquiesced and told Isaac that his legal representative would be present as well.

Wendy, meanwhile, had obtained a signature from Isaac and had rushed off to Richard Goddard for his countersignature. The man had been polite to her, so she felt comfortable this one time to knock. Some medical bills were coming up for her husband, and she needed the money back as soon as possible.

Isaac mulled over the situation, realised that he wanted to speak with Jess O'Neill, clear the air if that was indeed possible. He knew it was the right action at the wrong time. He expected the worst.

'Jess, how are you?'

'Fine. What's going on?'

'What do you mean?'

'You don't phone for a few days, and then you're out with Richard Williams' latest bit of skirt.'

'Jess, that sounds like jealousy.'

'Of course it is. Do you mind explaining?'

'I needed someone to bring a new perspective to the case.'

'What a load of hogwash and you know it. You fancy her, admit it.'

Isaac, momentarily stunned, did not know how to respond. Should he tell her the truth? That the woman was MI5 and potentially very dangerous.

No, he decided. His boss had summed up the situation succinctly.

'She's a beautiful woman, Jess. I'll agree to that. This case is going nowhere, and until it does, we cannot be together.'

'You're just spinning me a line.'

'It's the truth. I had to see if she had overheard something. I'll explain later, but Williams is central to all this.'

'Because of his friendship with Marjorie Frobisher?'

'Exactly!'

'But you have her now. You can ask her.'

'Whether she will tell us anything is hard to say.'

'If I find out that you slept with Linda Harris, this romance is over before it started.' She hung up the phone. Isaac realised that he would need to address the deception another time. He knew he would need to tell her the truth. He did not look forward to that day.

Wendy, having returned with her signed expense sheet, bid farewell to Isaac and left the office early. It was the promised night out with Bridget. Next day, she would have a pounding headache and a rasping voice. A friend was coming over to her house to look after her husband that night, as she did not expect to be home until late.

Later that day, Farhan phoned to say that Marjorie Frobisher was awake and talking, but still mildly sedated. The doctor's advice, another two days before she would be fully coherent. He also said that Robert Avers was there as the dutiful husband, while his young lover had left the waiting room at the hospital in disgust. Neither of the two children had been seen, and the media was a damn nuisance and interfering with the normal business of the hospital.

Chapter 35

Quinton Scott arrived at nine in the morning as agreed. His client did not. As a Queen's Counsel, Scott was extremely expensive. He was a busy man, but as Isaac noticed, he did not seem to be in a rush to move on. Quinton Scott, if asked, would have said the meter's running, it all goes on the bill.

Farhan had made himself available, substituting another detective to keep a watch on Marjorie Frobisher. Wendy had not shown up, phoning in to say she wasn't feeling well and would be in late. Isaac knew, from the voice at the end of the phone, the nature of the illness.

It didn't matter as she had little to do – all missing persons accounted for.

Approaching 10.30 a.m. and with no sign of Williams, even his QC was starting to look agitated. Isaac felt it was time to find the missing man.

A phone call to his office, no answer. Strange, Isaac thought. The production lot yielded no results either. Williams' home phone and mobile, no answer as well.

Isaac felt there was cause for concern. Williams may have hidden a witness, may have committed an indictable offence, but he had one of the best Queen's Counsels in his corner. His unavailability made no sense.

It was clear the man was not coming; the QC left soon after. The interview was rescheduled to the next day, same time.

Wendy came into the office shortly after. She did not look well. Isaac could have expressed some sympathy, told her to take the rest of the day off, but there was a job for her. A job for both her and Farhan – find Richard Williams.

His house, a three-storey terrace in Holland Park, was the best possibility. They drove out to the house. After two minutes knocking on the door, the last twenty seconds vigorously, they realised that no one was at home, or, at least, no one who was willing to answer the door. Unable to break the door lock with a swift and hefty shove, they relocated to the back of the house, down a narrow alley to one side. The door into the kitchen at the rear was unlocked.

Entering, they moved slowly around the ground floor, up to the first floor and, finally, the second floor. There on the floor in the main bedroom lay the body of Richard Williams, a gunshot wound clearly visible. It looked like suicide, but why? Farhan phoned Isaac, who phoned Forensics and a medical team. This time, Isaac made sure to call Richard Goddard.

***

Richard Williams was dead. Whether suicide or other was immaterial at the present moment. The case into the murders had taken an unexpected turn. Isaac knew that Marjorie Frobisher was the key, but she was still not fully conscious.

If he insisted, the medical team at the hospital would have been obliged to bring her around for him to ask a few questions. What were the questions, though? Isaac wasn't sure, and Richard Goddard wasn't much help, constantly on the phone for an update: Who murdered Williams? Is it suicide or murder? What do I tell MacTavish?

Isaac had few answers, although some suppositions. He could not see Williams as the type to commit suicide, although the weapon that had delivered the fatal shot was next to the body. And if it was suicide, why? Hiding Marjorie Frobisher away at a secret location, protecting her, was at best a minor crime. There had been questions, but with a smart legal mind such as Quinton Scott's and a solid reason in that the woman's life was at risk, he would have probably got off with a suspended sentence, even credit from the admiring public for protecting the life of a much-admired celebrity. A true friend, a man worthy of admiration, would be how the public would see it; Isaac too.

If Williams had not committed suicide, then that meant murder or assassination. Was it a murder intended to look like a suicide? Was it part of a well-orchestrated plan? And where was

Linda Harris? Isaac had sent someone to check out her accommodation, but it had been vacated; hurriedly, according to the landlady.

'Paid me before she left,' the landlady had said. 'No, I don't know where she's gone, but such a lovely woman. Plenty of boyfriends, no doubt, but I never saw any here.'

Isaac failed to understand why Linda Harris was taking a room in a pleasant house when she dressed as if she could afford a place of her own, but then he did not know much about her. Sure, she was good company, obviously competent and certainly agile in his bed, but who was she? A minor functionary at MI5, or was she capable of more?

He had to find her, but who knew where she would be? Angus MacTavish, but could he be trusted? Richard Goddard? Isaac ruled him out. He would know little, maybe ask MacTavish, but suspected he would not tell him. The only way he could think of making any headway was to go to the production lot. Williams' office in town was empty, maybe there was a clue there. He changed his decision about the production lot and headed to Williams' office.

***

Richard Williams' office was locked when Isaac arrived. It wasn't far from the police station, and the traffic was remarkably light for the time of day. The concierge on the ground floor let him in after he had shown his badge. Nothing seemed out of order. Williams' desk was neat and tidy, a few papers to one side. He reasoned there would be nothing of much interest there.

Linda Harris's desk seemed the most obvious. Sitting down on the chair that she and Sally Jenkins had occupied, he opened the desk drawers one by one, starting at the top left. He wore gloves, should have obtained official permission, but time was of the essence.

Richard Williams was dead, Marjorie Frobisher was under guard, but Isaac knew he was dealing with professionals. If they were determined to tie up loose ends, himself included, they would. No amount of protection would save anyone.

He thought that if Linda Harris had managed to find out the address at Canary Wharf, she hadn't used it. Or maybe she had? The doctor at the hospital had said anaphylactic shock. Something she had eaten, but Marjorie Frobisher would have been particular with what she ate, and the restaurant her meals were coming from was first-class. Surely they wouldn't have made an error.

If Linda Harris, MI5, and probably Angus MacTavish had wanted Marjorie Frobisher dead, Isaac reasoned, wouldn't it have been easier to have killed her down at Canary Wharf? Wendy had been watching, but she had been some distance away. Entry into the building was not too difficult, people were going in and out all the time, residents, tradesmen, people delivering furniture, people taking it away.

The questions continued to build, yet Isaac could not supply answers. Someone had to know, or maybe there were puzzles within puzzles, questions within questions.

The contents of the desk offered no help, but Isaac had assumed they would not. If Linda Harris, if that was her name, were a trained professional, she would hardly have left any clues behind. Everything was neat and tidy, and the computer was password locked. Isaac phoned for his people to send down a team, to secure the office and to take the computer and break its password. He thought there would be nothing on it, but it was possible – more of a long shot.

He realised that Linda Harris was long gone; vanished without a trace, probably out of the country by now.

***

Farhan stayed at Richard Williams' house until the investigations were concluded and the body removed to the morgue. The initial report from Forensics showed that the gun found at the scene, a Glock 17, did deliver the fatal shot. Farhan had noted the serial number, passed it on to the relevant people to trace the ownership – he had little hope of a result.

Farhan had been pleased when Gordon Windsor had walked into the house earlier to take charge of the examination of the body. The man had done a good job with Charles Sutherland.

'DI Ahmed,' Gordon Windsor said later, pulling down the mask covering his face and standing away from the body. He prepared to remove his coveralls, a clear sign that he had completed his work. 'Clear shot to the head, professional.'

'Murder?'

'There appears to be some attempt at making out it was suicide, but I'd say whoever shot him was disturbed.'

'The back door was open,' Farhan replied.

'Is that where he exited?'

'He?' Farhan asked.

'Could be a she, I suppose. Why do you ask? Anyone in mind?'

Farhan felt no need to elucidate.

As Williams' body left the premises in a body bag, Farhan left too. There seemed no reason to stay longer. The gun was off to ballistics to confirm that bullet and gun were related – Farhan saw it as a formality. Fingerprints looked to be unlikely. Initial investigation at the crime scene showed the signs of a professional, which raised the question why the murderer had fled if he or she had been disturbed. Why not just take out the person disturbing them, two for the price of one? More questions, few answers.

Isaac was drawing a blank as well. He saw no option but to head out to the production lot. The landlady at Linda Harris's accommodation provided little information, just said that Linda kept to herself, had no men over, and two or three nights a week she never came home at all.

First, he planned to meet up with Farhan and Wendy in the office; or was he just delaying the inevitable of meeting Jess again. He wasn't sure. He updated their boss as to what was happening. He said he would be at the meeting as well. Isaac would have preferred that he wasn't.

***

The weather had turned miserable as Isaac drove back to the office; it matched his mood. He had committed an error of judgement in sleeping with Linda Harris, had possibly given her vital information, and he was bound to be confronted out at the production lot by the one person he wouldn't be able to lie to.

Farhan, meanwhile, was in a more upbeat mood. His wife had submitted the papers for divorce, the conditions acceptable. After dividing the assets, more to her as she would take responsibility for the children, he would still be left with enough to put a down payment on a small apartment. Maybe, with Aisha, somewhere better, but that was idle folly.

She was still a former prostitute, even though now a promising lawyer. How would he explain it to his parents, his extended family? Could it be kept a secret? And his career, so important to him – would it be jeopardised? He knew it would. Even if his family never knew, the police would, and their records were impeccable.

The police force was egalitarian, accepting of all religions, all colours, all sexual persuasions. A former prostitute married to a detective inspector should not have counted against him, officially that is; unofficially, he knew it would.

He was aware that eventually he would need to make a decision, but not yet. The inquiry into the two, now three, murders was coming to a climax, he was sure of it. Soon, he would be able to spend time with Aisha. Then he would be able to ascertain if the love between the two of them was real, or whether it was infatuation from him for a liberated, passionate woman, or from her for a reliable, decent man.

And besides, Farhan had to be honest. He was heading up to detective superintendent at most; she had the possibility of becoming a QC. Would a QC be comfortable with a mid-ranking policeman? He wasn't sure – time would tell.

Wendy, feeling better after a few hours in the office on her own, welcomed both Isaac and Farhan on their return to the office. She had prepared some coffee for them, as well as a plate of biscuits. Chocolate, apparently her favourite, as half of them had already been consumed before Isaac and Farhan had a chance to take one.

Richard Goddard entered soon after, the frown on his forehead all too apparent – the pressure was getting to him. Wendy offered him a coffee; he accepted.

He felt no need to be discreet. Farhan and Wendy were there, and he wasn't about to send them out of the room this time. 'DCI Cook, it looks as if you've been sleeping with a murderer again.'

Wendy looked over at Farhan with raised eyebrows. Farhan just shook his head imperceptibly in return, a clear sign that he didn't know either what the detective superintendent was referring to. Farhan had known about Linda Harris, but the 'again' he did not.

'We're assuming she's the murderer,' Isaac replied. *No time for embarrassment*, he thought.

'And where is she?'

'No idea, sir.'

'What are the chances of finding her?'

'She appears to have vanished. I was about to ask Constable Gladstone if she can find her.'

'No problems, I can do that,' Wendy said.

'But where do we look?' Farhan asked.

'No idea,' Isaac replied.

'What do you mean, no idea?' Normally a man who kept his emotions in check, Richard Goddard was clearly showing the early stages of anger. His impending promotion depended on the solving of the murders, yet he didn't know which solution his superiors wanted. Did they want the culprit, any culprit? What if the killings were sanctioned assassinations? Was he expected to sweep them under the table?

'Marjorie Frobisher seems to be the key,' Farhan said.

'Farhan's right,' Isaac added.

'Then you'd better get over there and talk to her. That's if she hasn't been killed in the interim. As a team, your ability to get your key witnesses killed is outstanding. If you were as good at keeping them alive as you are at bedding them, then we would have wrapped this up weeks ago.' Isaac and Farhan sat sheepishly. Wendy enjoyed the moment. She liked to gossip, although this was not the sort of gossip she could tell Bridget after a few too many drinks.

With little more to say, Detective Superintendent Goddard left the office.

For twenty seconds, no one said anything. It was up to Wendy to break the silence.

'Do you want me to look for Linda Harris?'

'She may be difficult to find,' Isaac said.

'I'll do my best. Where do I start?'

'Her accommodation, although the landlady won't be much help.'

'Leave her to me. They always know more than they admit to; busybodies, all of them.'

As soon as Isaac had passed over the details, Wendy left the office.

Farhan and Isaac continued to discuss the case.

'What was Detective Superintendent Goddard referring to when he first came into the office?' Farhan asked, not expecting an answer.

'I made an error of judgement once before.' Isaac did not feel the need to elaborate.

'Another Linda Harris?'

'Change the subject.' An unusually curt reply from Isaac.

'Apologies. If Williams was murdered by Linda Harris, and she bolted out the back door, then who came through the front?' Farhan asked.

'Good question, and why didn't they phone the police?'

'They had something to hide?' Farhan answered rhetorically.

'The only person who would have come in the front door would be Linda Harris.'

'Or the cleaner.'

'We've discounted her,' Farhan said. 'The one day of the week she doesn't come. Besides, she would have phoned us.'

'Nobody else to our knowledge had a front door key, apart from Williams, the cleaner, and possibly Linda Harris.'

'Another woman?'

'It's possible. Williams may have had someone else.'

'Let's stand back and analyse this,' Farhan said. 'Linda Harris we know is MI5.'

'Correct.'

'Is she capable of murder?'

'Unknown, but let's assume she is.'

'Did she give any indication of that in the time you were with her?'

'No. But what does that mean? We're not even sure of her name.'

'Let's assume she is, but not the murderer of Richard Williams.'

'Then she disturbed the assassin.'

'Assassin?'

'Let's call it that. Who else would feel the need to murder him?'

'Nobody. This means he knew the identity of the mysterious child.'

'Maybe. Maybe not. We're assuming Charles Sutherland and Sally Jenkins did, but it's pure assumption.'

'But they died.'

'As did Richard Williams.'

'Can we stop this continuing if these people are determined.'

'I don't see how.'

'Marjorie Frobisher?'

'She's a dead woman. We can't protect her.'

'We need to tread carefully here. Can we trust Richard Goddard?'

'We must.'

The day had passed by the time the two men had concluded their discussion. Wendy had phoned in; the landlady was chatting happily about this and that. Wendy said she was just lonely, glad of a bit of company. And yes, she loved gossip and keeping her nose close to the front window. Wendy said she was in for a couple more hours before she had found out all she could.

Isaac told her to take her time. He, meanwhile, had to talk to his boss.

Farhan, unwisely, considering the escalating momentum in their investigation, planned to meet Aisha – he could not keep away.

Chapter 36

Richard Goddard was preparing to leave when Isaac knocked on the door to his office. The man was anxious to leave; Isaac eager to discuss Marjorie Frobisher.

'Can this wait, Isaac?'

'I'm afraid not, sir.'

'I've only got five minutes. I'm meeting with Angus MacTavish, and then I've a function to attend.'

'Five minutes it is. We believe Marjorie Frobisher is targeted for assassination.'

'Is she still safe in the hospital?'

'We're protecting her the best we can.'

'What do you want from me? We're walking into a minefield here.'

'A minefield and we don't know the way out. What do you suggest?' Isaac asked.

'We need to protect the woman.'

'Once she leaves the hospital?'

'I'll need permission.'

'From whom? And can you trust them?'

'I'm not sure who I can trust. Believe me, it would have been better for all of us if she had stayed hidden, even dead.'

'I can't believe you're saying that, sir.'

'Neither can I, but there you are. There's a mystery surrounding this woman, but nobody knows or isn't talking. Does the woman know?'

'I assume so.'

'Then get over to the hospital and stay with her. Sleep there if you must, but protect her, get her to talk. Frighten her if you have to. She'll need to be told about Richard Williams.'

'I'll deal with it.'

'The husband. Is he still there?'

'I believe so,' Isaac replied.

'Can you trust him?'

'I don't think he's involved in any of the murders.'

'He had reason to wish Williams dead. Playing around with his wife.'

'A suspect in his murder. Is that what you think?'

'It's possible.'

'Not likely. The crime scene examiner believes it's a professional hit. The shot was too precise for an amateur, and Robert Avers has no history with weapons.'

'Okay, but find out what she knows. Now is not the time for her to hold back. Whatever the truth is, it must be serious. Three murders now, maybe four if we don't act.'

'Angus MacTavish?' Isaac asked.

'What about him?'

'What are you going to tell him?'

'I'll be careful. I've no idea where he stands. He may be fine, but as you say, he's a devious politician. He'll bend with the wind, and if that means the whitewashing of a few murders, then he may turn a blind eye. I know the man is looking for a knighthood in the next New Year's Honours list.'

***

Farhan was pleased to see Aisha again. She was looking forward to him meeting her parents, but it was still premature. Until the murder of Charles Sutherland was solved, she was still a material witness.

They had chosen a secluded restaurant not far from where they had first met.

'Aisha, we need to be careful.' She was demonstrative, wanted to sit near him and give him a hug and a kiss. He was still wary of his detective superintendent's statement and the berating from Isaac.

'I've got another important case coming up. I want you to come and see me in action,' she said excitedly.

'A junior, do you get to do much?'

'Not really, but I would like you there.'

'I'll try.'

'You're busy, I know that. It's in the news. Marjorie Frobisher is in the hospital. Richard Williams dead.'

'It's coming to an end soon. I hope it is, anyway,' Farhan said. He, like Isaac, was tiring of the case. It had gone on for too long, with too many murders, and too many questions. No matter how hard they tried, they couldn't decide if it was one murderer, or two, or three.

Aisha said she couldn't stay long; she had to get home. Farhan would have preferred her to stay, maybe spend the night in a hotel. She said it wasn't possible, as she had to travel up north early the next day to meet the client.

'Will my secret be safe?' she asked.

'I'm trying. Nothing is certain. It could still come out.'

'It depends on who murdered Sutherland, I suppose.'

'If they plead guilty, then maybe there'll be no witnesses called.'

'If they don't?'

'You're the lawyer. You can answer that.'

'The defence will call every witness they can, looking for discrepancies in the evidence, contradictions in statements given.'

'That's what you would do?'

'Yes, of course. I just hope they don't find out.'

'So, do I,' Farhan said. Personally, he hoped they wouldn't. Professionally, he realised there was a strong possibility. The renewed interest in the case after the murder of Richard Williams and the reappearance of Marjorie Frobisher had caused a frenzy among the vulture press. They were still in attendance at the hospital, although their numbers were diminishing. How long before they disappeared: not known.

The plan to protect the woman that Isaac had briefly relayed earlier depended on creating a smokescreen, and then whisking the woman away unseen. It would be two days maximum before she was ready to move, and still Isaac had not interviewed her.

Farhan and Aisha parted company two blocks from her house. He had driven her home for the first time. They parted with a lingering embrace and kiss.

She would not be back for a couple of days. She promised they would find a room when she returned. Farhan knew he was breaking all the rules.

***

Wendy came into the office the next morning, updated Isaac and left. The landlady, ever-vigilant, had seen her now-departed lodger with a man outside the house on a few occasions, a big, burly man.

Not that she was nosey, the landlady had said. It was just that she liked to make sure all was in order on her street. Wendy had nodded in agreement, but quietly thought she was a busybody. She had one in her street, two doors away, who was always complaining about something or other. One day, the noise from the people who had just moved in; the next, someone's dog defecating in the street. Wendy took little notice of either, and while the noise could sometimes be irritating, it only lasted for an hour or so, and as for the dog, the owners always cleaned up.

The only good thing from the landlady was a car registration number. Wendy intended to trace it; Isaac told her not to be disappointed if it turned out to be a red herring. The security services were known for using the addresses of nondescript buildings on registrations and official forms. She said she wouldn't be, and besides, she didn't give in that easily. Isaac wished her well.

The day had started well. Marjorie Frobisher was awake and able to talk. Robert Avers was there with her, and even the two children, Sam and Fiona, had been in, although neither stayed long. Apparently, Sam Avers had left in a huff, and the plain-looking daughter, Fiona, had walked out swearing.

Jess had phoned, wanted to meet him to discuss things. Isaac had told her he was busy, and that he would get back to her later in the day. He wasn't sure if he would, as he knew what she wanted to talk about, and he had no excuses. He thought it unusual for him to feel unfaithful to her when he had never actually been faithful to her in the first place, never slept with her, never kissed her apart from two or three times.

With Wendy out looking for Linda, and Farhan dealing with some long overdue reports, Isaac visited Marjorie Frobisher. Farhan had checked with her husband and the doctor in charge. The doctor's advice – one person, keep it low-key, friendly. Robert Avers' advice – similar. He also mentioned that he had told her of the death of Richard Williams, and she was taking it as well as could be expected.

***

As Isaac arrived at the hospital, he noticed that the media contingent had mostly moved on. The police guards outside her room were still diligent, although he knew that if a professional hit were planned, they would not be much use.

Her room had more flowers than the florist's shop he visited every Mother's Day, as well as cards from well-wishers. Her room, more like a five-star hotel suite than a private room in a hospital.

He moved to the bed, introduced himself, and put out his hand. She shook it limply. Robert Avers acknowledged him with a slight wave of his hand and a weak smile.

'Miss Frobisher.'

'Call me Marjorie.'

'Marjorie, you are aware why I am here?'

'Yes.'

'I understand that you are not fully recovered. I don't want to tax you any more than necessary.'

'That's fine.'

'Is there anything you want to tell me?'

'I'm not sure what you want from me.'

'You were missing for a long time.'

'I was frightened.'

'Are you still frightened?'

'Yes.'

'Frightened of whom?' Isaac realised that too much pressure would make her retreat into her shell.

'Important people.'

'We can protect you.'

'Not against the people who are after me.'

'And do you know why they are after you?'

'Yes. I know something.'

'Are you able to tell me?'

'I don't know who you are.'

'Detective Chief Inspector Isaac Cook. I showed you my badge.'

'That means nothing.'

'What can be done to remove your fear?'

'Nothing. These people are determined. If you are one of them, or not, makes little difference. Once I leave here, my life will be forfeit.'

'You know that sounds a little melodramatic.' Isaac realised the conversation was going nowhere as the woman was clearly frightened, and she wasn't willing to trust him.

'This is not a script from a soap opera, you know. This is real life,' she said.

Isaac found the woman to be more intelligent, more astute than he had imagined. She turned away from him and spoke to her husband. 'Do you know this man?'

'Yes, he came to the house to interview Sam and Fiona.'

'Is he from the police?'

'I'm certain he is. I've no reason to doubt him.'

Returning her gaze to Isaac. 'I need protection.'

'There's protection here.'

'How safe am I here?'

'I cannot guarantee total protection. We can find a safe house for you. Will that do?'

'If I tell you the facts?'

'We can take into custody those responsible.'

'You cannot touch them. They killed poor Richard, and all because of me.'

'I'm sorry about that,' Isaac said. 'What about Charles Sutherland?'

'He knew nothing – thought he did.'

'And Sally Jenkins?'

'Her ears were as big as her breasts. Always snooping. She may have heard too much, but Sutherland…'

'Are you saying that he was lying to the magazine?'

'Of course he was. Some innuendo, salacious gossip, nothing more. Mind you, he could make anything up and sell it to the magazine. He may have discovered the partial truth, but he didn't know the facts. Got himself killed over it, though.'

'Why do you say that?' Isaac asked.

'He had some dirt on my earlier life. I was a bit of a tart, screwing around before it became fashionable. It's hardly newsworthy, and the magazine would have kicked him out on his ear soon enough. Those who frighten me know that. I'm surprised they bothered with him.'

Isaac saw that Sutherland may be a murder, Sally Jenkins – an assassination. As for Richard Williams, it was clear that he had known what Marjorie Frobisher did.

Appearing to be tired, Isaac left her with her husband holding her hand. He did not look a happy man.

***

Richard Goddard was anxious to know what Marjorie Frobisher was saying. Isaac had promised to give him an update. He had decided that Goddard had done him right in the past, and there was no reason to believe he would do him wrong now.

'She says that Sutherland knew nothing of consequence.'

'Professional hit?'

'According to Marjorie Frobisher, he knew very little.'

'Could his death be unrelated?'

'It's possible.'

'The woman. What have you promised her?'

'Protected witness status. Can you organise a safe house for her?'

'I need something in return.'

'Name it.'

'Give me a murderer, any murderer, within the next few days.'

'Charles Sutherland's our best bet,' Isaac said.

'Any luck with Linda Harris?'

'Not yet. Constable Gladstone's following up on a lead.'

'What do you reckon?'

'If she's MI5, she won't be found.'

'I hope you weren't fond of her.'

'No fondness there,' Isaac replied.

'Let Constable Gladstone get on with it. Can you and DI Ahmed focus on who killed Charles Sutherland? What did Marjorie Frobisher say about Sally Jenkins and Richard Williams?'

'She's reluctant to say too much. I interpreted her comments to mean that Williams knew what the great secret was, and Sally Jenkins had a tendency to eavesdrop. We should regard their deaths as suspicious.'

'Professional assassinations?'

'It looks to be that way.'

'Okay. I'll organise the safe house. And I want one murderer under lock and key within two days.'

***

Farhan and Isaac met in the office two hours later. Isaac was concerned that one murder, Charles Sutherland's, was coming to a resolution but was not certain what it would be. Farhan knew Aisha wasn't involved, and if there was a murderer under lock and key, as well as a signed confession, then he may be able to protect her.

'We need to go through the possible suspects again,' Isaac said. It was just the two of them in the office. Wendy had phoned in – she was drawing a blank on the car outside Linda Harris's accommodation. She made it clear that she was not giving up.

'We can eliminate the two women,' Farhan said.

'Which two women?'

'The two escorts.'

'The two prostitutes,' Isaac reaffirmed. Farhan did not like the terminology.

'As you say,' Farhan agreed.

'Just because you're involved with one, and the other one you shipped out of the country, doesn't abrogate them from responsibility.'

'I realise that, but neither knew they were meeting with him in advance. He was just an address to them.'

'Who else then? Christy Nichols?' Isaac asked.

'You've omitted one person,' Farhan reminded Isaac.

'Jess O'Neill. I've not forgotten. Although her motive is not as strong.'

'Why do you say that?'

'Sutherland forced Christy Nichols to perform oral sex on him. With Jess O'Neill, he had attempted to force himself on her, but she managed to get away.'

'That's true, but he may have reawakened painful memories – memories that wouldn't go away.'

'We need to call them both into the station,' Isaac said. He imagined Jess's reaction would be hostile.

***

It was nine o'clock the next day when the first of the two women arrived. It had been several weeks since Farhan had seen Christy Nichols. Then, she had been a disappointed woman, consigned to being an 'agony aunt' for a local newspaper.

He remembered leaving in a hurry when it had become clear that he was welcome to stay the night. He had to admit when she walked into the police station that she looked exceedingly attractive; he wondered wistfully why he had not seized the opportunity. No longer despondent, she was full of vitality and dressed exceptionally well.

'I found a decent job. Copy editor for a quality magazine. Not that scurrilous publication that Victoria Webster puts out.'

'Good to hear,' Farhan said, but little more. She was in the police station due to a formal request, and he did not want to appear too friendly. She had brought along a lawyer, Eileen Kerr. The woman, severely dressed in a dark suit with a white shirt and thin tie; her voice, rasping and deep, the sign of a heavy smoker. Isaac had encountered her in the past, and he did not like her. He made a point of telling Farhan that the woman was aggressive, competent, and would not take any nonsense.

They used the same interview room as when Jess O'Neill and Richard Williams had come in. The formalities completed, Isaac led off. 'Miss Nichols. We have reason to believe that Charles Sutherland's death was murder.'

'I thought that was clear.' Eileen Kerr interjected.

'As you say, clear.'

'Miss Nichols, can you please recount the events of that night.'

'I'd rather not.'

'I understand your reticence, but we need to ensure that nothing was missed, no matter how minor.'

'Miss Nichols,' her legal adviser felt obliged to comment, 'has complied with the police. The matters which you are now asking her to repeat are deeply embarrassing. Is this necessary?'

'Yes, we believe it is,' Isaac replied.

'He asked me to perform an act on him. I told DI Ahmed?' Christy Nichols asked.

'Very well. I let the women in. Later I went to the apartment, and Charles Sutherland was on the ground with the women. He was offensive, naked, flashing his genitals at me.'

'And what did you do?'

'Nothing. The women left quickly, and I was there alone with him.'

'And that is when the incident occurred?' Isaac asked.

'Yes.'

'He made you perform fellatio on him.'

'Yes.'

'Is this necessary?' Christy Nichols' lawyer asked again.

'It's fine, Eileen.' Christy Nichols leant over and spoke to her lawyer.

'Was he violent with you?' Isaac asked. He needed to push some more.

'He grabbed my arm, forced me down on my knees. Threatened to harm me.' Farhan noticed the quiver in her voice as she spoke. He felt sorry for her; Isaac showed no emotion.

'I cannot allow this to continue,' Eileen Kerr said.

'I'm nearly finished,' Isaac said. 'Miss Nichols, did you at any time threaten him?'

'I may have. I was angry, frightened. I don't want to remember.'

'This must stop. This is police brutality,' the lawyer said.

'Meeting concluded at 11 a.m.' Isaac pressed the stop on the timer and switched off the recording equipment.

***

'What did you think?' Farhan asked Isaac after Christy Nichols and her lawyer, possibly lover, had left. Feeling hungry, both had walked down the street to a small Italian restaurant.

'The motive is strong enough,' Isaac replied.

'Is she capable of murder?'

'What do we know about her?'

'Not a lot. Apart from what she's told us.'

'We need to find out more,' Isaac said. 'Let's be clear here. It's either Christy Nichols or Jess O'Neill. Both had the motive. One had the opportunity. Is there anyone else we're missing?'

'If it's not a professional hit, then it's either of the two women.'

'I'd prefer it was neither, but we can't let them off. From what I can see, decent women placed in difficult circumstances with an unpleasant and odious man. He's no great loss to society, yet someone has got to pay for liquidating him.'

'Isaac, we're here to uphold the law, not discuss the relative merits of the murderer and the murdered.'

'You're right. We'd better bring in Jess O'Neill.'

'We're forgetting Fiona Avers. She had a motive,' Farhan said.

'If it remains unresolved after speaking to Jess O'Neill, we'll call her in. In the meantime, how's Wendy going?'

Farhan phoned her. Apparently, the trail for Linda Harris had gone cold.

'Call her into the office. There's something more important for her to do.'

Wendy took forty minutes to arrive. 'Christy Nichols. Have you read her file?' Isaac asked.

'I've had no need to.'

'You do now. We need to know more about her,' Isaac said. 'Where she came from. What her life was like before London. Also, would she be capable of murder?'

Chapter 37

Jess O'Neill's facial expression clearly revealed her mood as she entered the interview room. Isaac had seen her walk in, but she had purposely looked the other way. He sensed it was going to be a difficult interview. Her brother-in-law, Michael Wrightson, accompanied her.

'Let it be put on record that my client is here under duress,' Wrightson said after the opening formalities had concluded. 'She answered all questions submitted last time in an open and frank manner. And, as we know, at some embarrassment. Reopening old wounds and painful memories is neither appreciated nor required. Let me further add that if as a result of today's interview it is clear there is no viable reason for her presence, it will be necessary to register a complaint.'

'Please note that certain information has come into our possession,' Isaac said after the threat from Wrightson. 'It has necessitated the presence of Miss O'Neill, as well as others, here today.' Isaac looked over at Jess. She failed to make eye contact.

'Then please submit your questions,' Wrightson responded. 'My client is a busy person.'

'Very well,' Isaac replied. 'Miss O'Neill, thank you for coming.'

'I am here under the advice of Mr Wrightson.' Still no eye contact.

'We have reason to believe that the murder of Charles Sutherland is not related to the killings of the other two people. As such, it is necessary for us to re-evaluate the evidence.'

'My client gave a full account of her relationship to Charles Sutherland, and her dislike for the man, last time. Do we need to go over that again?'

Isaac chose to ignore Wrightson's comment. 'Miss O'Neill, did you at any time threaten the man with physical harm?'

'When he was trying to rape me?'

'Yes.'

'I probably did. What woman wouldn't?'

'I am sorry. I am just trying to ascertain the facts.'

Farhan chose to remain silent. He knew the relationship between the interviewer and the interviewee. He had to admit that she was a fine-looking woman.

Wrightson continued to interject. 'This line of questioning is unacceptable.'

Isaac ignored him. He addressed Jess again. 'Can you tell me about your knowledge of poisons?'

'Is this an accusation?' Wrightson asked. 'My client does not need to answer.'

'No, you are right. She does not need to answer. I, however, need to ask.'

'Michael, it's alright,' she said to her lawyer.

Addressing Isaac, this time making eye contact. 'If you are asking whether I poisoned Charles Sutherland, the answer is no. The accusation that I would be considered is abhorrent. I did not like the man, but murder…'

'I am sorry for asking. There are others with a motive who have been asked the same question. It would be remiss if I did not ask you the question.'

He whispered in her ear, 'He's giving you a lead. Take it.'

Looking back at Isaac, this time a little friendlier. 'I have no knowledge of poison, other than tear gas while on assignment in the Middle East. Is that poison?'

'Thank you for your answer.' Farhan sensed the desperation of his boss to eliminate her from the inquiry, although none of her answers proved her innocent.

The interview concluded within sixty minutes. As Jess and her brother-in-law left the room, she leant over to Isaac and quietly said, 'You bastard!'

Farhan, not far away, heard what she said. He knew what it meant. He wondered how Isaac would explain away the actions that had generated such a venomous comment.

***

Wendy was delighted: the expense card reinstated, or, at least, the opportunity to use it without criticism.

Christy Nichols, the records had shown, came from a small village in the Lake District, close to the Scottish border. Wendy was heading up there, her husband in the hands of a live-in nurse for three days. Isaac had approved the cost, no option but to. He knew their boss would query it, but he wanted a result, and there were only two suspects. One he felt was innocent, not because he wanted her to be, but because her story had checked out. Jess O'Neill had grown up in in north London. She had left school with good marks and gone straight to university, majoring in English Literature. It hardly seemed to be suitable training for administering drugs, poisonous or otherwise.

The Lake District, two hundred and fifty miles to the north of London, seemed too far to drive. Wendy chose to take the train, three and a half hours to Oxenholme. She departed at eleven in the morning from Euston station, arriving just after two in the afternoon. A short taxi ride took her into Kendal, a small town of about twenty-eight thousand inhabitants. She rented a car and checked into the Castle Green Hotel. The brochures said it was the finest hotel in the town; Wendy could not disagree. The wine list looked suitably impressive. She decided to exercise the credit card that night.

The address of Christy Nichols' family was to the west. She decided the following morning would be more suitable. Light rain was falling, and she had been told that the mist could come down at any time. It appeared that the family home was isolated and down some winding roads. Wendy, although a competent driver, felt more familiar with the bumper to bumper traffic in London than an isolated country lane.

Isaac phoned as she was seated at the bar; reminded her to go easy on the credit card. *Too late*, she thought.

He updated her on his and Farhan's activities that day. And how Jess O'Neill appeared to be in the clear. Wendy thought to herself, *he needs to be careful there*. And also on how Christy

Nichols seemed to be the more likely of the two, although Isaac failed to elucidate on his reasoning. She decided not to press for an answer.

Isaac was a DCI; she a lowly constable. He had the brains, the training, the instincts. He had learnt to read body language, the furtive eye movements, the change in voice tone of a defensive person, or someone just telling a plain lie. She hoped he wasn't allowing his overactive libido to get in the way.

She had known Isaac a long time. Almost from the first days when he joined the police force, then in uniform, right up until he changed over to plain clothes and his elevation up through the ranks. She had seen the women he had taken out, the women in the police force who had swooned over him. She knew he was partial to one of the women close to the murdered people, closer than she had seen him with others in the past. She reflected on Detective Superintendent Goddard's comment the other day when he had said 'Again'. She would ask her DCI when this was all over, not sure she would get an answer, maybe a knowing smile, but what use would that be? Perhaps some harmless titillating gossip for her and Bridget to speculate about, over a few drinks. She knew Bridget could keep a secret and would enjoy the story, even daydream that it was her on the receiving end of one of Isaac's amorous advances.

***

Farhan, with only loose ends to deal with, busied himself with the preparations for moving Marjorie Frobisher to the safe house. A suitable location, fifteen miles to the west, seemed ideal. Richard Goddard had approved the cost for a one-month rental on a country cottage. The woman had been precise in the quality required: no one-room apartment, no doss-house, no third-rate accommodation. Farhan had checked it out. It looked suitable for the demanding woman. To him, it looked fantastic. His wife, realising that he was close to her favourite actor, was phoning him, asking for an introduction. He felt he did not need her communication as the divorce was progressing. A solicitor from his side, another from hers, and it was proceeding amicably. He had even managed to see the children a couple of times in the last week.

Aisha was back from her trip out of the capital, hoping to catch up that night if possible, the following if not. Farhan, desperate as he was, realised there was another priority. He had to ensure Marjorie Frobisher was safe and secure. Her husband had taken a shine to him before. Apparently, she had as well. A condition of her transfer was that he was to take responsibility for her safety. He had no option but to agree.

The plan was simple; the execution, not so. The media presence had virtually evaporated, apart from a couple of junior reporters stationed out by the main entrance looking bored: armed only with a camera and a microphone, namely an iPhone. Farhan hoped they would disappear.

First, Marjorie Frobisher would put on a surgical gown. Then she would lie on a stretcher, suitably bandaged, and be taken out to a waiting ambulance. It was to look as if the patient was transferring to another hospital for specialist treatment. Once clear of the hospital and confident of no prying eyes, she would exit the ambulance and get into a car driven by a policeman, the windows tinted. The vehicle would then proceed to the cottage.

Robert Avers was aware of the plan, but he would not be going to the cottage. It was too risky.

Farhan would stay at the cottage with her until she was calm. She had agreed that she would tell Isaac all he needed to know once she was comfortable. Isaac was frustrated by her hesitancy. He could only see permanent protection for her if she revealed what she knew.

If the media was made aware of the facts, then what point would there be in liquidating her. She had told Isaac that the situation was complicated. There were other issues to consider, and Richard Williams had died because of her. She did not want others to die as well. Isaac had noted that she failed to mention Sally Jenkins.

Richard Williams, more crucial to the investigation, remained on a slab at the morgue. His body was not to be released for a few more days.

***

Wendy, a little the worse for wear, left her hotel at eight in the morning. She had slept well but woken with a throbbing headache, although not throbbing enough to deter her from a good English breakfast of two eggs, three bacon rashers and a couple of sausages, washed down with two cups of tea.

Christy Nichols' home address – Farm Cottage, Underbarrow, Cumbria. It lay five miles to the west of where she was staying. It took Wendy twenty-five minutes to drive there. A small village, it consisted of no more than fifty cottages, most of them of a stone construction. A public house stood at the main crossroads.

Wendy had to admit it was a pretty place, somewhere she could live, although she realised the climate in winter would be savage – not conducive to someone with arthritis. She had felt the pain more since venturing north, and while it was only a couple of degrees colder, it made a difference. South, a long way south where the sun shone every day, was where she was heading if the opportunity arose.

Farm Cottage, she found out from a local woman standing on a corner waiting for the bus, was up a narrow, winding lane heading away from the village. 'Don't go up there,' the woman had said.

Wendy had asked why – the answer confusing, unintelligible. She would have pursued the matter, but the bus appeared, and the woman was gone. As she climbed the slight incline towards Farm Cottage, she could see an old farm house and no perceivable activity. She did not want to go in, just to observe. Ten minutes later, a woman with an old dog at her side appeared at the front of the house.

Wendy stayed for a few hours walking around the area. It was a walker's paradise, and she did not look out of place, apart from her stopping every few minutes for a rest. As lunchtime was approaching, she decided to return to the public house she had seen on her way up. An open fire was blazing inside, even though it was not bitterly cold outside.

'Gives it a cosy feeling,' the landlord said when she asked.

'What do you have to eat?'

'Typical pub lunches. My wife's steak and kidney, or maybe mushroom, if you prefer.'

'Steak and kidney for me. A pint of your best local bitter, as well.'

'These days, it's not local.'

'Your best, anyway.'

'Ten minutes for the pie, the beer straight away.'

Wendy noticed the pub was virtually empty, like pubs up and down the country. The local point of personal interaction supplanted by the world of instant communications and streaming movies on the internet. She missed the old days in many ways. A computer baffled her, a smartphone seemed only useful for making phone calls, the occasional SMS, and as for email, it was fine, but she could see little point in it. The police report she would usually write in long hand, and then ask Bridget to type up, the only cost a little bit of gossip. A small price to pay for such a valued service.

'What brings you up here?' the landlord asked. He was a red-faced man with an extended belly. She instinctively liked him.

'I was on business in Carlisle. I just thought I'd take the opportunity to check out the Lake District.'

'What do you reckon?' he asked. He had joined her with a pint of beer as well. Wendy could see from his appearance that he often had his beefy hand clasped around a pint of beer.

'Very pretty. The winters must be tough up here?'

'Can be. Last year was not so bad. Something to do with global warming, I assume.'

'Probably,' Wendy said.

'Are you a hiker?'

'I used to be.'

'Not now?' he asked. Wendy noticed that he had poured himself another beer, bought another for her. 'On the house,' he said as he put the two beers down on the bar.

'Thanks. Arthritis, unfortunately.'

'I've got a bit myself. It's a nuisance, but that's how it is.'

'I had a stroll up near Farm Cottage.'

'It's grim up there.'

'It seemed pretty enough.'

'Did you see anyone?'

'Just a woman and an old dog.'

'Sad story.' Wendy put her glass of beer down and took off her jacket. The fire in the corner too warm for her.

'What do you mean?'

'Bill Nichols, a strange character, used to come in here occasionally.'

'What about him.'

'Believed in corporal punishment, taking a strap to the kids if they played up.'

'Is that allowed?'

'No, of course not. But it could never be proved. His kids always supported him. Attractive children they were.'

'Where are they now?'

'I've no idea. They disappeared a few years back. The son sometimes comes back to see the mother. The daughter, not seen her since. Pretty young thing, she was.'

'What were the children's names?' Wendy asked.

'Terry, the son. The daughter, Christine, Christy. No, it was Christy. They never said much; fear of a leathering from their father, I suppose.'

'Where's the father now?'

'Dead. Accident, they said.'

'How?' She had resumed her drinking.

'He was more a subsistence farmer. Always believed the old-fashioned ways were the best. He would have used a horse and plough if he could have.'

'Did he?'

'No, but he would have. No profit margin if you don't rely on mechanised farm equipment. He had to use a tractor occasionally. Mind you, he kept a lot of cattle up there, as well.'

'So how did he die?'

'Strange story. He believed in preparing his own fertilisers, pesticides. He would come in here and complain about the prices the companies were charging when he could make them for a fraction.'

Wendy realised the landlord was talking about a subject which interested her greatly.

The first customers since she had entered the pub came in. The landlord left to speak to them, sell them some beer, and ask if they wanted to sample his wife's steak and kidney. They did. Five minutes later, he returned.

'He made a mistake, or at least, that's how it's recorded.'

'Mistake with what?'

'He used to mess around with some nasty poisons, arsenic in particular. It used to be in rat poison, not today, though. Anyway, it appears he's brewing up some rodent killer – accidentally pours some into a glass of water that was sat on his bench in the barn. Dead within minutes, they said.'

'Do you believe it?'

'No reason not to, but this is a small community – people gossip.'

'What did they say, the gossips?'

'That the wife poisoned him, or one of the children.'

'What do you believe?'

'I'm not one for gossip.'

Wendy could see no reason to stay longer in the Lake District. There would be no trouble with her expenses this time. The first thing the next day, she planned to fill out the forms and to get Detective Superintendent Goddard to sign them.

***

It was the first arrest in a case that had gone on for too long. With a clear motive and the knowledge to carry out the murder, Isaac felt he had enough for an arrest.

Farhan knew the address, so he drove. Isaac was the first to enter the small apartment. She was alarmed to see the detective chief inspector, fractionally calmer when she saw Farhan come in behind him. A uniformed policewoman accompanied them.

'Christy Marigold Nichols, I am arresting you on suspicion of the murder of Charles Sutherland.'

The woman, stunned, collapsed to the floor. Farhan lifted her up and sat her on a chair.

'I've done nothing wrong.'

'Would you please accompany us to the station,' Isaac said. It was a time for formality and following the official procedure by the book.

A police car that had followed Farhan and Isaac to Christy's apartment transported her back to the station, where she was officially charged. Her one phone call Farhan made on her behalf to Eileen Kerr, her lawyer.

She arrived soon after, fuming, desperate for reasons for the arrest.

Isaac explained the situation and informed her that a formal interview would be conducted later in the day. If she wished to have additional legal representation, then there was time to arrange it.

The lawyer, realising the situation was serious, hurried down to the holding cell to meet her client. Christy Nichols sat in a foetal position at one end of the rudimentary bed provided. She was incapable of speech. Eileen Kerr requested a doctor. One was supplied.

A strong sedative, and the accused woman subsided into a prolonged sleep.

'Tomorrow,' Eileen Kerr advised. 'I need to take advice from my client and to consider my position. This may require someone more experienced than me.'

Farhan felt a deep sadness for the woman in the cell.

Chapter 38

Isaac did not feel the sadness that Farhan felt – he felt relief. Christy Nichols who, according to Wendy, had had a turbulent childhood; mitigating circumstances would obviously be put forward in a trial. At least, the defence would put them forward, but murder was murder. The guilty had to pay for their crime, whether the murdered person was despicable or the childhood of the accused atrocious.

Wendy had been jubilant on her return from the north. Christy Nichols was in the cells before she had caught the train back to London. Now came the hard part, at least for her, the writing up of her report. She knew Bridget would not refuse to help.

According to Farhan, Christy Nichols was not handling the situation well, protesting her innocence. He had been to visit her; check she was okay. Apart from needing a shower and a change of clothes, she appeared confused. Farhan arranged for a policewoman to visit her home and obtain what she required.

Isaac felt confident that Jess O'Neill was innocent of one murder.

He had decided to tell Jess if she asked about Linda Harris, tell her if she didn't. He could always say it was in the course of duty, but he thought it a lame excuse. When would sleeping with someone be an acceptable part of a criminal investigation? He knew why he had slept with her – because he wanted to and because she was available.

As he picked up the phone to make the call, it rang. 'Isaac, MacTavish wants to see us,' Richard Goddard said.

'When?' Isaac asked.

'Now,' the reply.

Five minutes later, both were downstairs waiting for a car. Twenty minutes later, they were in Angus MacTavish's office. The man was in a jubilant mood. Isaac did not like it; he saw trouble. A possible attempt to interfere with the normal process of law.

Mrs Gregory had entered on their arrival, given Isaac a friendly smile and the choice piece of home-made cake with his cup of tea. He thanked her for her kindness.

'Great work,' MacTavish said. Richard Goddard accepted the compliment on his department's behalf.

'This wraps up the murders?' MacTavish continued.

Isaac replied, 'Only Sutherland's.'

'What about the others?'

'We do not believe they were committed by the person in custody.'

'Why not?' MacTavish asked.

'No motive.'

'But she's a murderer? Does she need any more motive?'

Isaac realised that MacTavish knew his statement was illogical; knew that MacTavish wanted the loose ends tying up, and the truth was dispensable.

'She'll never be convicted of the other two murders,' Detective Superintendent Goddard said.

'Why not?' MacTavish persisted.

'She had a clear motive for Sutherland. She never met Richard Williams and Sally Jenkins.'

Angus MacTavish stood up, turned his back on the two policemen. He faced the window. 'Officially, we need to wrap it up here.'

'The reason?' Richard Goddard asked. His promotion was due to be confirmed in a couple of days. A wrong word and he knew what would happen.

'Too many questions being asked.'

'Are you asking us to break the law? Conceal a crime?' Isaac asked.

'It's not up to me. It comes under the Official Secrets Act.'

'It's a whitewash,' Isaac said in an unchecked outburst.

'You've heard of the Civil Contingencies Act?' MacTavish, now facing them, said.

'Our version of the American's Patriot Act,' Richard Goddard replied.

'We're invoking it.'

'We!' Isaac said.

'The elected government of this country. The people charged with the responsibility of knowing what's best for the people – that "WE".'

'We're condoning murder here. You realise that?' Isaac was angry and on his feet. All this time: three deaths, one solved, two to be pushed aside.

'I understand your concern, but the national interest is more important.'

Isaac resumed his seat. 'Are you confirming that two of the murders were committed by people employed in Her Majesty's service?'

'Not at all,' MacTavish replied. 'All I'm saying is that there are to be no further attempts to find a culprit for those two murders.'

'We admit we failed – case closed. Is that it?'

'Either you charge the woman you have in custody with the three murders, and make it stick, or else you state… State whatever you like: Suicide, lover's pact, whatever, but drop it.'

'This is contrary to what people expect of their government and their police.'

'For Christ's sake, Goddard.' MacTavish looked away from Isaac and directed his gaze at Isaac's boss. 'Your promotion is on the line, my career as well. Sometimes it's necessary to make decisions for the people regardless of what they expect.'

'Understood, sir,' Isaac said, although he felt uncomfortable with MacTavish's outburst.

As they drove back to Challis Street, both saying little, both still stunned by the meeting, Detective Superintendent Goddard leant in Isaac's direction. 'Are you going to follow MacTavish's directive?'

'Do you expect me to, sir?'

'I expect you to act as a policeman.'

'Your promotion?'

'Does MacTavish talk for the government or his own vested interests?'

'I don't know, sir.'

'Neither do I. I've not received any instructions from my superiors at New Scotland Yard. Until then, we continue. If my career is down the drain, so be it. We can't give up, just because a blustering Scotsman tells us to.'

'This could get dangerous.'

'I know that. What about Marjorie Frobisher?'

'We're moving her soon.'

'Make it happen today. And make sure she is safe. Her best defence, ours as well, is if she talks.'

***

Farhan, updated on the situation in a quick phone call from Isaac, moved the date for the transfer forward. The two remaining reporters stationed at the hospital had fortunately left. Robert Avers, tired of waiting for something to happen, and in need of solace, had apparently left for his young lover.

That was what he had told Farhan, although it was more likely he had tired of his wife's constant need for attention, the celebrity variety, of which she had been starved for so many weeks.

Doesn't the woman get it? Farhan had thought the last time he spoke to her. *Her life is under threat, and she still wants to act the prima donna.*

As the planned evacuation from the hospital to the cottage commenced, one of the formerly bored and uninterested reporters reappeared at the critical moment.

He saw Farhan dressed as a male nurse. Quickly, he was on the phone to his superiors.

Exiting the rear of the hospital with the woman, Farhan, oblivious to the drama at the front, continued. The vehicle left as planned, unaware that a short distance behind them followed a motorbike, its rider helmeted.

'We're being followed,' the driver of the ambulance said.

Farhan looked out of the small rear window of the ambulance – the driver was correct.

Not sure what to do, he phoned Isaac, who assigned a police car to pull over the motorcycle, minor traffic infraction if required. It was five miles before the motorcycle was stopped. Changing the original changeover location presented no problem.

Marjorie Frobisher transferred to the police car and headed out to the cottage.

'I don't like it,' she said on arrival. To Farhan, it was charming and unique – a slice of heaven. Way out of his price bracket, way in hers.

'We need to keep you safe.'

'Here! I don't see how.'

'It's isolated. We have people in the area keeping a watch.'

'What is my life worth? I hide away for weeks, and then I'm brought to this.'

'Why were you hiding?'

'My life.'

'Then why complain? We're trying to protect you.'

'I know that. Very well, I'll talk to DCI Cook.'

***

Richard Goddard had received confirmation that his promotion was proceeding. He was soon to be a detective chief superintendent, not an assistant commissioner, as MacTavish had intimated. He realised it may take him away from homicide, possibly into more of an administrative role. It did not concern him unduly, but the current case did.

The promotion was verbal, not documented, and he knew why. It was conditional on a satisfactory outcome. He sensed the hand of MacTavish, although the police were meant to be independent. He was aware that the murders of Williams and Sally Jenkins may need to be covered up – it would not be the first time that national security had overridden the normal function of the police. The concern this time: that it wasn't national security, purely an indiscretion of someone in power.

He knew he needed to let Isaac run his race, hope that he made the right decisions. If Marjorie Frobisher's information was dynamite, what to do with it? What would Isaac do? Keep it under cover, release snippets of it to the press?

Soon-to-be Detective Chief Superintendent Goddard could see that it was not over yet, not by a long shot. He needed to talk to his DCI.

He phoned Isaac, who was on his way out to the cottage. He had taken a circuitous route, hopeful that he wasn't being followed. It would not have been an issue before, but now the press, alerted after the observant reporter had seen the events at the hospital, were speculating as to what was afoot.

'Isaac, we need to talk.'

'I'm on my way to meet with Marjorie Frobisher,' Isaac responded on hands-free.

'Let me know what she says.'

'Of course.'

'We need to consider how to progress.'

'What do you mean?'

'Is it national security? Do we comply with MacTavish or not?'

'I thought we had decided to press on,' Isaac said, a little perturbed at his boss's changed attitude.

'We have. We need to know the truth, but the national interest…'

'National interest? I would have thought that was best served by the truth.'

'Ordinarily, I would agree.'

'But now?'

'Find out what she says first. We'll discuss the implications afterwards. That's all I'm saying. I'm not asking you to hold back, just exercise caution.'

Isaac did not enjoy the conversation very much. It sounded as though his boss had gone soft.

***

Isaac found Marjorie Frobisher not in a good mood when he arrived at the cottage. He decided to ignore her complaints. The information she held was what he wanted. If it was as controversial as the events of the past few months indicated, then he was not sure what to do.

He was a policeman who was possibly about to be asked to commit an illegal act; namely, the covering up of two murders, purely because they were professional assassinations. Richard Williams did not concern him as much as Sally Jenkins. He had seen her distraught parents at the funeral, especially her mother. They deserved the truth. He could envisage their reaction to a verdict of murder by an ex-lover. That was what Isaac saw as the most likely wrap up to the case. He couldn't agree, couldn't see that he could do much about it.

Christy Nichols still needed to make an official statement, and they couldn't hold her for much longer. Once finished with Marjorie Frobisher, he intended to conduct the interview with Sutherland's alleged murderer. The evidence seemed too strong to believe otherwise.

'Miss Frobisher, are you ready to tell us the truth?' Isaac asked on his arrival at her hideaway.

'Yes.'

'You are aware that your reluctance to come forward has cost the life of several people?'

'Not Charles Sutherland.'

'No, that is clear. We believe his death is not related.'

'But Richard's is.'

'Yes, that appears to be the case, as well as Sally Jenkins. We've discussed this before.'

'I'm sorry about Richard. He was a good man, a good friend.'

'He was more than that, wasn't he?'

'We lived together in the past.'

'And recently?'

'We looked out for each other. If I had not become so close to Richard, if I had not told him what I'm about to tell you, he would still be alive.'

'That's hindsight. We can only deal with the future.'

'And what will happen to you? You're a policeman. Will they force you to keep quiet? Cover it up. Allow me to be killed.'

She had hit the nail on the head. How would he react? How would anyone react in the same situation? He had no answer that would suffice.

'I'm sworn to uphold the law.' Isaac knew it was a clichéd reply. He was surprised he had uttered it.

Farhan prepared some coffee. It was clear the woman could become emotional. A policewoman stood to one side.

'When I was younger, I formed a relationship with a man.'

'How young?'

'I was sixteen. He was eighteen.'

'Where did you meet?'

'At a school dance.'

'There seems to be nothing wrong in that.'

'There wasn't, although it was before the pill and loose morals.'

'You slept with him?'

'Up against a wall. I'd hardly call that sleep. It was just too people, children really, screwing. No point pretending it was anything more.'

'Then what?' Isaac asked.

'We used to meet up every few days. Don't attempt to imagine it was a typical romance. It was sex, whether in the park, or his school dormitory, or the back of a local cinema.'

'Did you like the man?'

'Yes. And he liked me, but we were different.'

'In what way?'

'I was middle class. He was upper, a member of the aristocracy. I was Mavis Sidebottom, daughter of a successful shopkeeper.'

'No meeting of each other's parents?'

'He wanted to meet mine, but I never introduced him.'

'Any reason why?'

'I could see the reality. I was fond of him, as he was of me, but there was no future.'

'What do you mean?'

'It was a long time ago. The class structure was much stronger then. The daughter of a shopkeeper and the son of a Lord would not have been considered a suitable match. That's for the movies, not real life. Maybe today, but not then.'

'The romance ended?'

'There was a complication.'

'A child?'

'People just didn't think about the risk of pregnancy. Assumed it wouldn't happen to them.'

'What did the father do?'

'Married me quickly in Gretna Green, and then told his father, the Lord.'

'What happened?'

'Paid my father to hush it up. I spent six months hidden from the world in a convent. Once it was born, it was taken from me.'

'And what became of the child?'

'For many years, I never knew.'

'When did you find out?'

'One year ago.'

'Did you contact the child?'

'No. It was such a long time ago; I didn't feel any connection.'

'Is the child the reason these murders have occurred? The reason you are frightened?'

'When I found out who the child was.'

'Who is this child?'

'If you know, you are at risk.'

'What about the father?'

'He doesn't want it known who the child is.'

'You've spoken to him?'

'I tried, but he hung the phone up on me.'

Isaac could see it was going to be a long day. He still had Christy Nichols to deal with, as well as Jess, who was anxious to see him.

The search for Linda Harris had been abandoned. Angus MacTavish had contacted him with the news that she had been assigned overseas. Isaac accepted the truth. There still remained the issue as to who had killed Richard Williams, the assumption that Linda Harris had come in the front door, while the assassin had gone out the back. If it had not been Linda, surely they would have reported the dead body rather than leave it to Farhan and Wendy to find.

Linda Harris, now clearly identified as MI5, would not have wanted to report the murder. That may well have warranted a closer inspection into her background.

Farhan phoned for some food to be delivered from a restaurant down the road. It was only pizzas – Marjorie Frobisher complained.

The interview resumed at two in the afternoon. Farhan asked the first question. 'Does your husband know about the child?'

'No. I never told him.'

'Is he safe?' Isaac asked.

'Those who want to silence me will not harm him.'

'Are you convinced that your life is in danger?'

'They killed Richard, didn't they?'

'Why would they do that? Why not you?'

'You couldn't find me, neither could they.'

'That's true, but now you're visible.'

'I couldn't disappear forever. I'd rather be dead than continue to live as a hermit.'

'Were you?'

'Was I what?'

'Living as a hermit.'

'Almost. Before I went to Malvern, a remote place up north.'

'Yours.'

'It belonged to my father. A fishing shack, nothing else. Nobody knew about it, not even Richard Williams.'

'Why?'

'His protection, not that it did him much good. He still ended up dead.'

'You're safe here,' Isaac said.

The woman made a disparaging gesture, shrugged her shoulders. 'I'm not safe here. If they want me dead, they'll find a way.'

'The police are protecting you now.'

'And the police could be called away, told to turn a blind eye.'

'Why would we do that?' Isaac asked.

'National security.'

'Who is this child? I need to know.'

'Ask Angus MacTavish. He'll tell you.'

The statement came as a surprise. MacTavish had always been suspect, but he was now directly implicated. Isaac needed to contact his boss.

Isaac wrapped up the interview, stating that he needed to take advice. She had not been willing to make any more comments, after revealing MacTavish as a key person.

'I'll be back tomorrow,' Isaac said as he put on his coat.

'If I'm still here.'

'Farhan will stay.'

It had been the night that Farhan had intended to meet up with Aisha. He had no alternative, but to comply. He hoped Aisha would understand.

***

Isaac's initial reaction to Marjorie Frobisher's comment was to ask to meet his boss, but he realised this was not the most important issue.

One murder investigation had to be wrapped up. Eileen Kerr, Christy Nichol's legal representative, was in the building and acting on advice from her client, she would be the sole person with the woman at the interview.

Farhan would normally have been with Isaac in the interview room, but he was out protecting Marjorie Frobisher. Wendy was delegated in his place.

Their boss chose to observe through a one-way window into the interview room – a room that was pleasant enough under normal circumstances, dreary under any other. The accused was led in, a policewoman accompanying her. Wendy felt sorry for her but did not let it show.

Christy Nichols was very pale, her head bent, avoiding eye contact. Her legal representative, Eileen Kerr, touched her on the arm in a gesture of reassurance and friendship.

'Could you please state your name.' Isaac had started the recording, both video and audio.

'Christy Marigold Nichols.'

'You are charged with the murder of Charles Sutherland.'

'I did not kill him. I hated him, but not enough to kill him.'

'Charles Sutherland died due to ingesting a lethal dose of arsenic.'

'I did not give it to him.'

'But you knew about the effects of arsenic. Is that correct?'

'Why would I know that?'

Wendy, on a prearranged cue from Isaac, spoke. 'Your father died of arsenic poisoning.'

'Yes.'

'Then you know of the effects of arsenic?' Isaac took over again.

'He used it for rat killer.'

'You were questioned at the time of his death?'

'We all were.'

Wendy spoke again. 'I visited the village where you lived. I saw a woman at the house.'

'My mother.'

'Your relationship with your mother?'

'There is no relationship.'

'Why is that?' Isaac asked. 'Because of the death of your father?'

'No.'

'Then why?'

'She never protected me from him.'

'Him?'

'My father.'

'What did he do?'

'He beat us and…'

'Did he abuse you?'

'Sometimes. When he was drunk.'

'And that was often?' Isaac asked. Eileen Kerr asked for an adjournment. Isaac refused.

'This abuse?' Wendy asked. 'We need to know.'

'He used to touch me.'

'Sexual intercourse?' Isaac had to ask.

'No. He wanted to touch me. He wanted me to touch him.'

'And you did?'

'If I didn't, he would beat me.'

'And your mother?'

'She let him.'

'She was there?'

'No, but she could have told someone, done something.'

'Why didn't you report it?'

'I was scared. If no one believed me, he would have beat me more.'

Wendy started to choke up. She had heard the story before when she had been looking for missing children. How many times, the father abusing the pretty daughter? How many times had the child been returned to the parents, their accusations dismissed? One child had been returned against her will. She had ended up dead, had hanged herself with a length of rope in her bathroom at home. Wendy, in her darkest moments, thought back to that girl.

328

Isaac had one question to ask, a crucial question, but it would have to wait. The accused was in no condition to continue. Her legal support argued for an adjournment. He had no option but to comply. The interview was to resume in sixty minutes.

Isaac met his boss in the adjoining room.

'What do you reckon?' Isaac asked.

'What are you trying to make her admit to? The murder of her father or Charles Sutherland?'

'Either, both.'

'Fine. Play it carefully. The father, she could get off on a technicality. It's an old case, recorded as death by misadventure. Proving that will not be so easy.'

'I realise that. I just need to break her denial.'

'Pretty woman. A shame, really.'

'Pretty, as you say, but we're here to solve a murder.'

'I understand that.'

Isaac was still anxious to discuss the other matter; his boss, not so keen.

'MacTavish?' Isaac asked.

'Wrap this up, and then we'll discuss it. Marjorie Frobisher's comment complicates the situation.'

'Why?'

'How did she know Angus MacTavish? He's not indicated this before.'

'Maybe he's not met her. Maybe someone else did.'

'Wrap Sutherland's murder up. We'll discuss MacTavish later.'

'Yes, sir.' Isaac knew it was the best he could expect.

***

Christy Nichols looked composed when she returned to the interview room. Isaac went through the formal restarting of the interview. Richard Goddard watched from outside. Wendy said little.

'It is evident,' Isaac stated calmly,' that you are aware of the effects of arsenic poisoning. Will you admit to that?'

'I knew my father used it to kill rats.'

'Did you hate your father?'

'What do you think?'

'Miss Nichols, please answer the question.'

'I hated him for what he did to me, what he made me do.'

'Enough to kill him?'

'I wished him dead.'

'You had the means and the knowledge.'

Eileen Kerr spoke, 'You are attempting to force my client to admit to a crime that the police have officially declared closed – death by misadventure.'

Isaac was careful how he proceeded. 'Charles Sutherland made Miss Nichols, by her own admission, commit an act that her father had made her do. My purpose is to establish whether the level of hate she felt for Sutherland was the same as she felt for her father.'

'I hated Sutherland. He brought back all those memories. Memories I had suppressed.'

'Memories so vivid that you saw your father standing there, not Charles Sutherland.'

'Yes. Of course I did.'

'And knowing this, you determined to kill him?'

'No.'

'I am putting it to you that you went back to his room, acted amorously, and ensured he drank the poison.'

'That's not true. You're trying to make me say it.'

Wendy felt that Isaac had overstepped the mark, but he had told her to keep quiet. Eileen Kerr wanted to speak, but could not, insistent as Isaac was on maintaining the pressure.

There was only one flaw that he could see. Where had she procured the arsenic? He decided to proceed. He was certain she was guilty. The issue of the arsenic would resolve itself later.

'Miss Nichols. You had the motive and the knowledge, and you are the only person with a sufficiently strong motive. You are guilty. Your continual denial will only worsen the case against you.'

'Are you saying I killed my father as well?'

'Did you? We can always reopen that case.'

'He was a bastard.'

'Who was?

'My father.'

'Is that why you killed him?'

Isaac had seen it before. The moment where the accused decides to ease their conscience.

'That was an accident. I saw him do it.'

'It gave you the idea.'

'The man was obnoxious. He made me swallow it.'

'Which man?' Isaac asked.

'Sutherland.' A one-word reply.

'Is that when you decided to kill him?'

'Not then. Later.'

'Why later?'

'I had to get some arsenic.'

'You had some?'

'At my apartment.'

'Why?'

'I'm not sure. It reminded me of what killed my father,' she said. Isaac could see a plea of diminished responsibility.

'Christy Marigold Nichols. Are you admitting to the murder of Charles Sutherland?'

'I'm glad I did it. Yes, I killed him, the horrible man.'

Eileen Kerr sat back on her chair, her arms folded. Wendy held a handkerchief to her eyes to conceal the tears welling up. Isaac, who should have been feeling a degree of smugness, satisfaction on a job well done, felt neither.

Richard Goddard was delighted, congratulated Isaac on his good police work. Isaac accepted the congratulations.

Sometime after, once the written statement had been dealt with, and Christy Nichols had been returned to her cell, Isaac came back to Marjorie Frobisher's comment.

Chapter 39

'What about Marjorie Frobisher?' Isaac asked in the comfort of Richard Goddard's office.

'What about her?'

'Her relationship to Angus MacTavish.'

'She mentioned his name. What does it mean?' The detective superintendent asked.

'I don't know what it means. She has dangled the carrot in front of us. Do we take it?'

'What do you want me to do?'

'Confront MacTavish.'

'And if he denies it?'

'We'll cross that hurdle when we come to it.'

'Is there anyone we can trust?'

'Nobody.' Isaac saw the truth in his senior's question. Who could be trusted? Marjorie Frobisher? Angus MacTavish? To Isaac, there was no clear road forward, only possibilities, lies, and more lies. He knew that he would need to make decisions that could solve the case or not – his career he saw as barely viable. Whatever happened, it appeared as if he would be on the wrong side of someone or something. If Angus MacTavish was hiding something, how to get him to open up? And what about Linda Harris? He had slept with her. Did she murder Williams, and then stage the open back door at his house?

Isaac remembered that there was one other issue to consider – Sally Jenkins. She had been murdered, and on the face of it by someone she knew. Someone who had not sexually violated her. If it was someone she knew, it could only be Richard Williams. If it was female, then Linda Harris.

Isaac could not see Williams as the murdering type, but then he didn't envisage Linda Harris in that role either. All his years of policing, training, and profiling and still he got it wrong. It concerned him that he still made mistakes. Mistakes that had resulted in deaths in the past. But what of the future? Would Marjorie Frobisher be another one if he acted inappropriately?

Only one man knew the answers. Isaac decided that he needed to see MacTavish, and if his boss was unwilling, he would go on his own.

***

Marjorie Frobisher anxiously paced around the cottage. Farhan kept to one side, letting her rant and rave. The situation was tense. She couldn't stay in the cottage; she couldn't leave.

Farhan realised that she was a difficult woman. His wife idolised her, or, at least, the character she portrayed. He wondered how his wife would react if she saw the reality. Would she be able to separate the actor from the person or would she be disillusioned? It was a moot point. He knew that he had to do something to calm their key witness down. If she left, how long would she remain alive? Both he and Isaac were convinced her life was at risk. If she stayed, would she keep hitting the bottle of vodka? *Either it's death by assassin or death by alcoholic poisoning*, he thought.

There was nothing in her records that indicated abuse of alcohol, but Farhan thought that it was another fact about the woman that had been carefully concealed.

'You need to stay. It's just too dangerous out there,' Farhan had said.

Sober, she had agreed. Now, he was not so certain. She was not there charged with any crime; she was free to come and go as she pleased.

He contacted Isaac for advice. 'She's difficult.'

'She must stay.' Isaac said, not entirely focussed on his DI's concerns. He had made the decision to phone MacTavish direct.

MacTavish's first action, after agreeing to Isaac's request, was to phone Richard Goddard. He was in Isaac's office within five minutes.

'What right have you to contact MacTavish?'

'What option did I have?'

'It was my call.'

'I agree, but your position is on the line. I'm expendable; you're not,' Isaac said.

'You're no more expendable than I am, but you don't know who or what you're dealing with. 'MacTavish is the government whip. He's got the dirt on everyone.'

'Everyone?'

'Everyone of importance. He's known all along.'

'You've known this?' Isaac asked, surprised at this revelation.

'I've always suspected it. Marjorie Frobisher's statement confirms it.'

'So what do we do?' Isaac asked.

'We go and see MacTavish.'

'Someone has to tell us something. Who do you suggest?'

'MacTavish, if he'll talk. The woman, if he doesn't.'

'I don't like this. I'm meant to be a policeman. This is out of my league.'

'And mine.'

'And what about Marjorie Frobisher?' Isaac asked.

'Tell DI Ahmed to restrain her by force if he has to.'

'She won't like it.'

'What do I care. Three people are dead as a direct result of her great secret. What she wants is of little concern. I'll not have her death on my conscience,' Detective Superintendent Goddard said.

***

Life out at the production lot had returned to a semblance of normality. The soap opera was to continue, murders or no murders – the ratings and the revenues decreed it.

It had been an awkward phone call. Isaac wasn't sure how to respond when Jess O'Neill called him. 'I'm running the show now. I've assumed Richard Williams' position as executive producer,' she said. Isaac heard no malice in her voice. 'You have someone charged with Charles Sutherland's murder. It's on the internet.'

'That's true.'

'They're also saying she murdered her father as well.'

'That's pure supposition. We're not pursuing that possibility.'

'If I didn't kill Sutherland, am I free now? Are you?'

'Probably, but I need another few days.'

'To come up with a suitable excuse as to why you slept with Linda Harris.'

'No...' He knew he stuttered the reply.

'Maybe there was a reason. I'll forgive you this time, but next...'

Isaac sensed a woman looking for a long-term relationship, a ring on the finger. He shuddered at the thought, smiled at the possibility. He also knew that every time they argued in the future, she would bring up Linda Harris.

'I need to tie up loose ends. We're not sure how to proceed.'

'Marjorie Frobisher?' she asked.

'Yes.'

'You're hiding her?'

'Everybody seems to know that.'

'Is she being difficult?'

'We're more difficult.'

'Best of luck. This weekend, can we meet?' she asked.

'It's a date,' he said.

'Not a police interview?' she joked.

'No, it's a date.'

'At last.'

'Ian Stanley. How is he? Now that you're in charge.'

'Sycophantic.'

'That bad?' Isaac replied.

'That bad!' she acknowledged.

***

The only friendly face was Mrs Gregory. Angus MacTavish was neither welcoming nor friendly. Isaac thought he was under pressure. His boss thought he was his usual self. The atmosphere in MacTavish's office matched the weather outside – cold and dark, threatening thunder.

'Detective Superintendent Goddard, why am I receiving phone calls from your junior? Don't you have your people under control?'

'DCI Cook is frustrated with the current situation.'

'Don't you have protocols where you are? If he has an issue, he should take it up with you.'

'He did, but he decided to act against my advice.'

'That sounds like a disciplinary matter.'

'It will be addressed at a later time.'

'DCI Cook, what do you want from me?' MacTavish, in his usual manner, had stood up and leant forward over the desk. It was meant to intimidate – it succeeded, at least with Isaac's boss. With Isaac, it had little effect.

Isaac knew his career was on the line, but no amount of blustering by the senior government official was going to dissuade him. He needed to know, and it was clear that MacTavish knew.

'Marjorie Frobisher mentioned your name.'

'I've never met the woman,' MacTavish replied.

'We know that's not true, sir.'

'Maybe at some function or other.'

'Do you know her, other than that?'

'No.'

'She said that you were the person to speak to regarding this secret.'

'Which secret?' MacTavish asked. Isaac could see his face reddening with anger.

'The child.'

'I told you I knew about a child. I've never given any indication that I know who it is.' MacTavish resumed his seat and sat back in a confident manner, assured that he had allayed their concerns, hidden the truth.

Isaac knew the situation; he knew the body language. He recognised a lie. Not sure how to proceed, he fumbled forward. MacTavish was a powerful man, and powerful men had people behind them, supporting them verbally and physically. Not that he was frightened of the man, but he wanted Marjorie Frobisher to remain alive, and the truth to be revealed. A politician may regard the truth as a luxury; he, as a policeman did not.

'If the truth was known,' Isaac asked, 'would it be catastrophic?'

'Yes,' MacTavish replied.

'To certain persons?'

'To this country.'

'Is the truth better revealed?' Richard Goddard asked.

'No.' A one-word answer.

'Mr MacTavish, this cannot continue,' Isaac said. 'Respectfully, you know what is going on. We need to know.'

'Why?'

'We have three murders. One has been solved, the other two still remain unsolved.'

'They are not to be solved.' MacTavish again, on his feet. Mrs Gregory put her head around the door to offer tea or coffee. He unexpectedly snapped at her. She retreated.

'We can't cover up murders,' Richard Goddard said. 'Police procedures won't allow it.'

'Then change the procedures.'

'But why?' Isaac asked. 'And what do we call them?'

'Call them whatever you like.'

'And the truth?' Isaac asked.

'Williams was ordered. The other woman, probably.'

'This is England. We can't do that.' Isaac protested.

'Not only will you, but you will also do it today; tomorrow at the latest.'

'Marjorie Frobisher?'

'She's a marked woman.'

'Why?'

'You're both subject to the Official Secrets Act. You're both serving members of the Metropolitan Police. You will both do as you are told.'

***

Farhan, updated soon after the meeting with MacTavish, had his own problems. Marjorie Frobisher was not going to stay where she was.

'She has phoned her husband.'

'Does she know she's a dead woman?' Isaac asked.

'She knows. She regards her current life as a living death. She says she would rather be out there with her people.'

'Where is she now?'

'Still here, but Robert Avers is coming. I can't stop her, not anymore.'

'You're right. Maybe she is better off in her own home.'

'What do you mean?'

'There's no resolution to this. If she's out there, it may help.'

'She may be killed.'

'What else can we do?' Isaac said.

***

Isaac realised the weekend with Jess was unlikely, and Farhan was none too pleased either. Both knew they had no other option but to comply, but unless something changed then Marjorie Frobisher would be dead, their careers, at least Isaac's, down the drain, and two murders would remain unsolved, three if Marjorie Frobisher died as well.

Robert Avers had picked her up and taken her to their house. Farhan followed at a discreet distance.

Isaac realised that Angus MacTavish was the problem. He wondered if he was the mysterious father, but discounted it. MacTavish had grown up in Scotland, and besides, he was several years younger than the woman. They needed to check out the schools that Marjorie Frobisher had attended. It was fair to assume a school dance would focus on schools within the area. It was an angle they had not pursued before, because that piece of information had only just come from the woman herself.

It was clear that Wendy was needed again. Isaac, in the meantime, would see if Marjorie Frobisher would give him the name of the father.

The next day, Wendy, in a remarkably jubilant mood, appeared in the office.

'We need to know who this man is,' Isaac said.

'You want me to check out some schools?'

'Yes.'

'If they're still there. It's forty years.'

'The records must still exist.'

It seemed difficult for Wendy to claim for an expensive hotel this time. Mavis Sidebottom, the childhood name of Marjorie Frobisher, had grown up in a village to the west of London, less than a forty-minute drive. The records clearly stated that she had attended St George's Boarding and Day School between the ages of 11 and 18, apart from a brief period of absence during her penultimate year. The dates aligned with her unexpected confinement.

It was also clear, as Wendy drove past Marjorie Frobisher's childhood home, that the middle-class childhood, the daughter of a humble shopkeeper, was a fabrication. The father had been a shopkeeper, but a shopkeeper of several hardware stores and the home had been a substantial two-storey house in a better part of the village. The school was for those financially able to pay. It had been a girls' school for over one hundred years, and before that a boys' school. The headmistress took delight in informing Wendy that for two years Winston Churchill had been a pupil.

The records, meticulously kept and preserved in a vault beneath the main building, were opened at Wendy's request. The vault was a treasure trove of history: full of artefacts and sporting cups, and among them, records of school dances.

Miss Home, an elderly and retiring woman, charged with recording the history of the school, opened up the relevant documents. They clearly showed that during the dates concerned, there were two school dances. Those attending from St George's and two boys' schools were recorded.

Wendy took copies of the documents to study. There seemed little purpose in visiting the other schools until the names had been checked out. She managed to treat herself to a nice lunch on expenses before she returned to London.

It was late afternoon when she walked into the office at Challis Street. Isaac was there. His day had been involved with going through all the aspects of the case, attempting to wrap it up, trying to figure out who killed who, and why?

'I need to check out these names,' Wendy said. Farhan not being there, she pushed her desk over into his area. Isaac could clearly smell stale cigarette smoke.

'Any names we know?' Isaac moved over towards her desk, sat on Farhan's chair.

'What are we looking for?'

'Member of the aristocracy; member of the government.'

'Aristocracy will have the family name, not the title,' Wendy said.

'True. I'll leave it to you.' He moved back to his chair.

***

Marjorie Frobisher, back at her home, apparently oblivious of the situation or choosing to ignore it, was making herself known to her adoring public. An impromptu interview on the steps of the house to the assembled media – according to Isaac, sheer stupidity.

Farhan had asked her to stay at home, but he had been overruled. She had breezed into her favourite restaurant as if she was the all-conquering heroine, back from doing battle, rather than the frightened woman who had run away and hidden. It seemed to be an act; an act she managed with great aplomb.

Isaac, regardless of her condition on returning from the restaurant, felt the need to confront her. Farhan had warned him that her condition was far from conducive to that. Isaac thought it might be opportune, as with a few drinks, she may be more willing to talk.

'Miss Frobisher, I need to know who the father is,' Isaac said as he sat in the front room of her house in Belgravia. She was clearly drunk, clearly in need of attention. Isaac was pleased that Farhan was with him, although judging by the lecherous look in the woman's eye, he was not sure it was safe even then.

'Forget about him.'

'Do you feel bitterness towards him?'

'Why should I?'

'You have spent a long time in hiding. Your life is at risk because of him.'

'It's not him.'

'Then who?'

'I told you before. Ask Angus MacTavish.' Isaac could see it was pointless. Robert Avers had taken himself off to the other room, apparently disgusted at her condition. It was evident she was not going to give Isaac a name. It was up to Wendy to find the father.

Once the father was identified, the son would soon be revealed. Isaac continued to deliberate as to who the son was, and why he was so important. Without a name, it was pointless speculation, and Marjorie Frobisher was of no use.

Wendy, meanwhile, excited at the prospect of success, had stayed late in the office. Normally, she would leave for home at six in the evening, but it was way past eleven, close to midnight, and still she laboured over the computer.

She admitted to no great computer skills, but she was proficient with Google. She was pleased that Isaac had agreed to come back to the office at her request.

'I've found him,' she said the moment he walked in.

'Congratulations. Who is he?'

'He's not a Lord.'

'What do you mean?'

'He inherited the title on the death of his father.'

'And?'

'The Peerage Act of 1963.'

'What does that mean?'

'Prior to it being enacted into law, no member of the House of Lords could take a seat as an elected Member of Parliament. He was able to renounce the title.'

'Marjorie Frobisher referred to him as a Lord.'

'That's what people call him. Technically, he's not.'

'Are you saying it's who I think it is?'

'Yes, there's only one person.'

Chapter 40

'I did not kill Richard.' It was not what Isaac expected to hear on picking up his phone at one o'clock in the morning.

'Where are you?' Hearing Linda Harris's voice again reminded Isaac of the guilt he felt over the night they spent together; the pleasure they had mutually enjoyed, but mainly the guilt.

'I am not in England.'

'Then why phone?'

'I just wanted you to know. Under different circumstances, we could have been something more.'

'I don't see how,' Isaac responded.

'We're very much alike.'

'Are we?'

'Yes. We are both ambitious.'

'I work for an organisation that tries to save lives,' Isaac said. 'Yours apparently condones death when it's in the national interest.'

'I was there to find out where Marjorie Frobisher was, nothing more.'

'Is her life in danger?'

'Probably.'

'Because of what she knows?' Isaac, regardless of his initial trepidation, was enjoying the conversation.

'Yes.'

'What does she know?'

'I never knew. I'm relatively junior. They never told me.'

'They?'

'My superiors.'

'Do they have a name?'

'I am not authorised to tell you.'

'Who is?'

'I don't know. I just wanted to phone and say I was sorry; to let you know that I did not kill Richard.'

'Sally Jenkins?' Isaac asked.

'She knew too much.'

'Are you saying you killed her?'

'Someone else did.'

'Who?'

'Richard.'

'Why?'

'She was blackmailing him, threatening to go to the newspapers.'

'About what?'

'Marjorie Frobisher. He did it to protect her.'

'You provided him with an alibi.'

'Yes.'

'Were you with him that night?'

'Some of it, but not in his bed.' With that, she hung up. Isaac, shocked by what he had been told, sat down for a couple of minutes to compose himself.

***

Richard Goddard, woken up from a deep slumber in the early hours of the morning, was initially angry. Upon hearing Isaac's voice, he moved to another room.

'Sally Jenkins was not assassinated,' Isaac said.

Isaac recounted the phone conversation with Linda Harris.

Goddard listened calmly. 'How do we handle this?' he asked.

'It's clear that Richard Williams knew, as did Sally Jenkins.'

'Can we prove that Sally Jenkins was murdered by Richard Williams?'

'The evidence is circumstantial. We'll never be able to prove it.'

'Are you sure?'

'Richard Williams had been in Sally Jenkins' place on many occasions. His DNA, fingerprints are everywhere. There's nothing conclusively tying him to the night of her death,' Isaac said.

'Apart from Linda Harris.' Richard Goddard realised, as did Isaac, that she was not going to come forward to point the blame at Williams. 'So how do we record it?'

'Crime unsolved, I suppose.'

'What about Richard Williams?'

'It appears to be a professional assassination. It doesn't make sense. Williams kills to keep the secret, and then he is shot because he knows it.'

'It's clear that he was not about to reveal it.'

'If Marjorie Frobisher had been liquidated, he may have.'

'Are we saying that she's safe now?'

'She still knows who this person is.'

'Will she tell?'

'Probably not.'

'She's still a target.' Richard Goddard stated the obvious.

***

An austere, wood-panelled office in the Houses of Parliament in Westminster; a meeting between two powerful men.

'Angus, have we dealt with all the loose ends?'

'Not yet. The woman remains alive.'

'And the child?'

'He continues to search for his parents.'

'What proof do we have that he does not know the truth?'

'If he knew, he would exercise his right to the peerage; his right to your title.'

'On my death?'

'He would have no issue with ensuring you had a convenient accident.'

'You know what to do.'

'I will ensure the instruction is carried out immediately.'

'She could still talk,' the father said.

'Her current behaviour indicates that possibility.'

'Angus, deal with this, and your elevation to the peerage is guaranteed.'

***

Two weeks had passed since Christy Nichols had been charged with the murder of Charles Sutherland. Sally Jenkins' death had been put on the back burner.

Richard Williams' death still occupied Farhan and Isaac's time, but only minimally. Apart from the occasional discussion, there had been no further developments.

Linda Harris's phone call, the only time she had contacted. Isaac was certain that he would not hear from her again.

Marjorie Frobisher, no longer in hiding, apparently no longer in fear of her life, was out and about, on the talk shows, in the magazines. Isaac found her a tiring woman, and he kept his conversations with her to a minimum. It was clear that the knowledge she had was not going to be revealed.

Farhan had met Aisha on several occasions, slept with her on some. The romance seemed solid, but without the constant pressure of a murder investigation that had dragged on for too long, he had begun to re-evaluate his life.

He loved her but was it a love that he could jeopardise his life and his career for? How much of it was genuine emotion? How much of it was the sexual awakening for him with a liberated woman? He realised that time would lessen the intensity for him and for her. With no further media scrutiny, her secret seemed to be safe.

Isaac had met up with Jess, although most times they planned to meet, she was too busy with her newly elevated position.

***

The accident occurred at exactly ten minutes past four in the afternoon. Widely reported, it marked another event in the turbulent life of Marjorie Frobisher.

As she left the restaurant in Sloane Street, Chelsea, apparently the worse for wear after a few too many drinks, she had inadvertently stepped in front of a taxi.

The verdict, after a short court case – the taxi driver had been charged with manslaughter – was recorded as accidental death. The defendant received a suspended sentence. It occupied the newspapers for a few weeks until the public tired of the accusation that the case was a whitewash.

Angus MacTavish duly reported to his superior. 'It has been resolved.'

Deputy Prime Minister James Alsworthy was delighted. Invariably referred to as 'His Lordship' due to his aristocratic manner, he had renounced his hereditary peerage so he could sit in the House of Commons. He would reclaim it when he tired of politics.

The former Benjamin Marshall, the adopted son of an influential family in the north of England, would never know. As Ibrahim Ali, an Islamic Jihadist convert, and the most vocal, most eloquent promoter of the movement for the introduction of Sharia in England, he had within his grasp the title of Lord Alsworthy, a seat in the House of Lords, and a fortune valued conservatively at fifty million pounds. An impassioned orator, the son of Marjorie Frobisher and James Alsworthy could not be given the prominence that the House of Lords would allow him, nor the opportunity to promote his cause.

The End

Phillip Strang

ALSO BY THE AUTHOR

Murder House – A DCI Cook Thriller

A corpse in the fireplace of an old house. It's been there for thirty years, but who is it?

It's clearly murder, but who is the murdered person and what connection does the body have to the previous owners of the house. And then why a fireplace? It was bound to be discovered eventually but was that what the murderer wanted? The main suspects are all old and dying, or already dead. Yet again, there's a motive, but what is it?

Isaac Cook and his team have their work cut out trying to put the pieces together. Those who know are not talking out of an old-fashioned belief in that a family's dirty laundry is not to be aired in public, and certainly not to a policeman - even if that means the murderer is never brought to justice!

Murder Without Reason – A DCI Cook Thriller

DCI Cook, now a Senior Member of London's Anti-Terrorism Command, faces his Greatest Challenge. The Islamic State is waging war in England, and they are winning.

Not only does Isaac Cook have to contend with finding the perpetrators, but he is being forced to commit to actions contrary to his mandate as a police officer.

And then, there is Anne Argento, the Prime Minister's Deputy. The man has proven himself to be a pacifist and is not up to the task. She needs to take his job if the country is to fight back against the Islamists.

349

Vane and Martin have provided the solution. Will DCI Cook and Anne Argento be willing to follow through? Are they able to act for the good of England, knowing that a criminal and murderous activity is about to take place? Do they have any option?

Hostage of Islam

Kate McDonald's fate hangs in the balance. The Slave Trader has the money for her, so does her father and he wants her back. Can Steve Case's team rescue her and her friend, Helen in time?

Three Americans are to die at the Baptist Mission in Nigeria - the Pastor and his wife in a blazing chapel. Another, gunned down while trying to defend them from the Islamists.

Kate is offered to a slave trader who intends to sell her virginity to an Arab Prince. Helen, to ensure their survival, gives herself to the leader of the raid at the mission and the murderer of her friends.

The Haberman Virus

A remote and isolated village in the Hindu Kush mountain range in North Eastern Afghanistan is wiped out by a virus unlike any seen before.

A mysterious visitor checks his handiwork clad in a space suit, and American female doctor succumbs to the disease, and the woman sent to trap the person responsible, falls in love with the man who would be responsible for the death of millions.

Malika's Revenge

Malika, a drug-addicted prostitute waits in a smugglers' village for the next Afghan tribesman or Tajik gangster to pay her price, a few scraps of heroin.

Yusup Baroyev, a drug lord enjoys a lifestyle many would envy. An Afghan warlord sees the resurgence of the Taliban. A Russian white-collar criminal portrays himself as a good and honest citizen in Moscow.

They are entwined in an audacious plan to raise the quantity of heroin shipped out of Afghanistan and into Russia and ultimately the West.

Some will succeed, some will die, some will be resurrected from their plight and others will rue the day they became involved.

ABOUT THE AUTHOR

Phillip Strang was born in the late forties, the post-war baby boom in England; his childhood years, a comfortable middle-class upbringing in a small town to the west of London.

His childhood and the formative years were a time of innocence. Relatively few rules, and as a teenager, complete mobility, due to a bicycle – a three-speed Raleigh – and a more trusting community. It was the days before mobile phones, the internet, terrorism and wanton violence. An avid reader of Science Fiction in his teenage years: Isaac Asimov, Frank Herbert, the masters of the genre. How many of what they and others mentioned have now become reality? Science Fiction has now become Science Fact. Still an avid reader, the author now mainly reads thrillers.

In his early twenties, the author, with a degree in electronics engineering, and an unabated wanderlust to see the world left the cold and damp climes of England for Sydney, Australia – the first semi-circulation of the globe, complete. Now, forty years later, he still resides in Australia, although many intervening years spent in a myriad of countries, some calm and safe – others, no more than war zones.

Printed in Great Britain
by Amazon